THE CONSORT OF RYL

A CORELLE OF DUR NOVEL

HAYLEY PRICE

A catalogue record for this book is available from the National Library of Australia.

National Library of Australia Cataloguing-in-Publication entry

Author: Hayley Price

Title: **The Consort Of Ryl**

ISBN: (Print) 978-1-7637998-8-2

ISBN: (ePub) 978-1-7637998-9-9

INTRODUCTION

I deliberately allowed you, my readers, to believe Corelle had died at the end of The Mariner Of Ryl, and I apologise for that if it distressed you.

I wanted to release The Consort Of Ryl without any fanfare, any cover or title reveal, any pre-orders. I wanted it to be a surprise. The seven books I have published about Corelle have demanded a great deal of my partner and me. Endless hours of writing, revising, editing, battling to get the stories seen amid a sea of millions upon millions of other books, all with no publishing house behind us. Every cent we have spent on art, software, bookmarks, stickers, banners, book signings, printing physical copies, we have paid ourselves. Sadly, the same cannot be said of every cent you have paid to read the books.

The monopoly of Amazon is unhealthy, but for independent authors, it cannot be avoided. It is the largest book selling platform in the world by an order of magnitude I cannot comprehend. Other entities also take their pound of flesh from the author's royalties, and at times, it feels like a labour of love even when a book is quite successful. I urge you to buy direct from your favourite authors whenever you can - ebook or physical book. That is the best way to give the author the maximum return on their efforts and ensure they can continue to write.

Corelle's tale ends here, and I hope you have enjoyed it. She was a complicated woman, and her fate was never clear, even in my mind. I wrote two more books beyond The Consort Of Ryl, but in the end, this felt like the perfect way to end her story.

Other projects await me, and I hope you'll stick with me as I produce my next books. I thank you from the bottom of my heart for your support over the last eighteen months. Without readers, I'm writing in a vacuum, and that's just not as much fun.

Corelle's journey has ended. That it has.

This book is dedicated to all the musicians whose music has uplifted me throughout my life.

At times, this book will change point-of-view. Please note that each new scene does not always follow the same timeline as the last.

A note for my American readers. This book is written in UK/Australian English. Many of the words will be spelled differently from what you're used to - realised, colour, centre etc. We pronounce the "h" at the start of "herb," so we preface it with "a" rather than "an."

In addition, we do not share your fondness for the letter 'Z.' I realise you may find this difficult and offer my humble apologies. We make up for this by using a plethora of "L's" where you would make do with one. Marvellous.

All the writing and artwork in this book was created by a real person. No AI was used at any time.

ALSO BY HAYLEY PRICE

The Vermilion Saga

The Vermilion Ribbon

The Vermilion Cross

The Vermilion Triangle

Corelle Of Dur

The Blade Of Ryl

The Fan Of Ryl

The Mariner Of Ryl

THE CORELLE OF DUR SERIES RECAP (SPOILERS)

In The Blade Of Ryl, Corelle sailed south to live out her banishment from Dur with Pettra, Raolos's wife, as her lover. A cruel fate lay in wait for Pettra, but Corelle managed to kill the former Bailiff of Dur, Glailam. Corelle became more and more dependent on wine as a salve for her shattered self-esteem.

A letter from Dur summoned her home to avenge the murder of Klordia, Wilash's wife. With Synna's aid, she learned elements of the Guild still lived and were holed up on a farm in the Eastlands. Despite their best intentions and efforts, Corelle and Synna could not take the Guild's new leader, Krage, captive, and he fled south.

In the Eastlands, Corelle met a woman named Vamma. Their relationship caught the attention of the Guild, who tried to kill her. Vamma left for safety in Ort, and Corelle followed her later when she accepted the Guild had escaped.

Synna told Corelle Arella had been with child when she had urged Corelle to kill her in Zhanghar, and Corelle wavered between leaving Dur or pressing Wilash, who knew the full story, to tell her the truth.

In The Fan Of Ryl, Corelle decided to visit Wilash, but what she learned almost destroyed her. She left Dur and became a mariner.

A year later, she returned to Alcmouth aboard the ship she worked on. There, she heard some devastating news. She spoke again to Wilash, and at a meeting with the Duke and Raolos, they promised to lift her banishment if she could find the Duke's son, who had been kidnapped.

Acting on information she learned from a member of the Duke's staff, Corelle set off for the Eastlands again, where she found the Duke's son hanged by the Guild.

She reunited with Vamma, and the two left for Alcmouth together, only to learn the land had been attacked by a southern race, the Qagrue, led by Krage, who named himself the new Duke.

Due to the lack of trained fighters, Corelle felt Durfolk could not resist the barbaric southerners, and she believed all her friends in Alcmouth must have been killed. She organised a defence in Ryl, then set off to Ort to learn all she could.

She discovered Raolos, Synna, and Wilash had survived, and in Ort she killed Gillar and Sisnop, former Guild leaders from Torric. The Qagrue had turned on Krage and claimed Dur as their own territory.

With the help of some former Guild members and the Ort citizens, the Qagrue in Ort were killed, but Corelle feared recriminations against the Ortfolk at some point.

As they wavered about the correct course of action, news arrived; Ryl had fallen, and Synna had been killed. Raolos, Wilash, and Vamma had fled to Malkartas.

Devastated, Corelle once more boarded a ship and resumed her life as a mariner.

In The Mariner Of Ryl, Corelle spent twelve months working on ships around the Torr Sea before she was recruited for a groundbreaking voyage to prove the theory that the Torr Sea region was one small part of a larger globe.

The theory was all but proved when the ship was destroyed, and Corelle, along with her friend Gaishkantah, was shipwrecked and washed ashore on another new land. She suffered terrible injuries and came to death's doorstep but recovered with the aid of the local inhabitants.

Keen to return home and see Vamma again, Corelle worked her way south. She reached Malkartas and struck up a relationship with Vamma once more. Vamma had married Raolos in the three years Corelle had been away, and in an argument with Corelle over Vamma, Raolos was killed.

Dejected, Corelle and Vamma returned to Dur, where they learned of the death of Corelle's father. Corelle took over her parents' shop and searched for happiness, but the intervention of a former Guild member, Denstal, brought Corelle into conflict both with him and the Qagrue.

Denstal's men killed Corelle's mother, and after Corelle formed an uneasy alliance with the Qagrue to bring Denstal to justice, she killed him.

Corelle's worsening mental health saw her prone to violent outbursts of temper, and with Vamma pregnant by Raolos, she felt concerned Corelle's violence might turn on her, so she left for Yerrsun, urging Corelle to seek help for her mental condition and rejoin her once she was calm.

Corelle went to a tavern, where she got into an argument with a patron and launched herself into a brawl.

Wilash and Derkhata, his wife, arrived in Ryl in search of Corelle after Vamma had scribed to them, but were told she had died in a brawl in a tavern. They travelled to the Eastlands to deliver the bad news to Vamma.

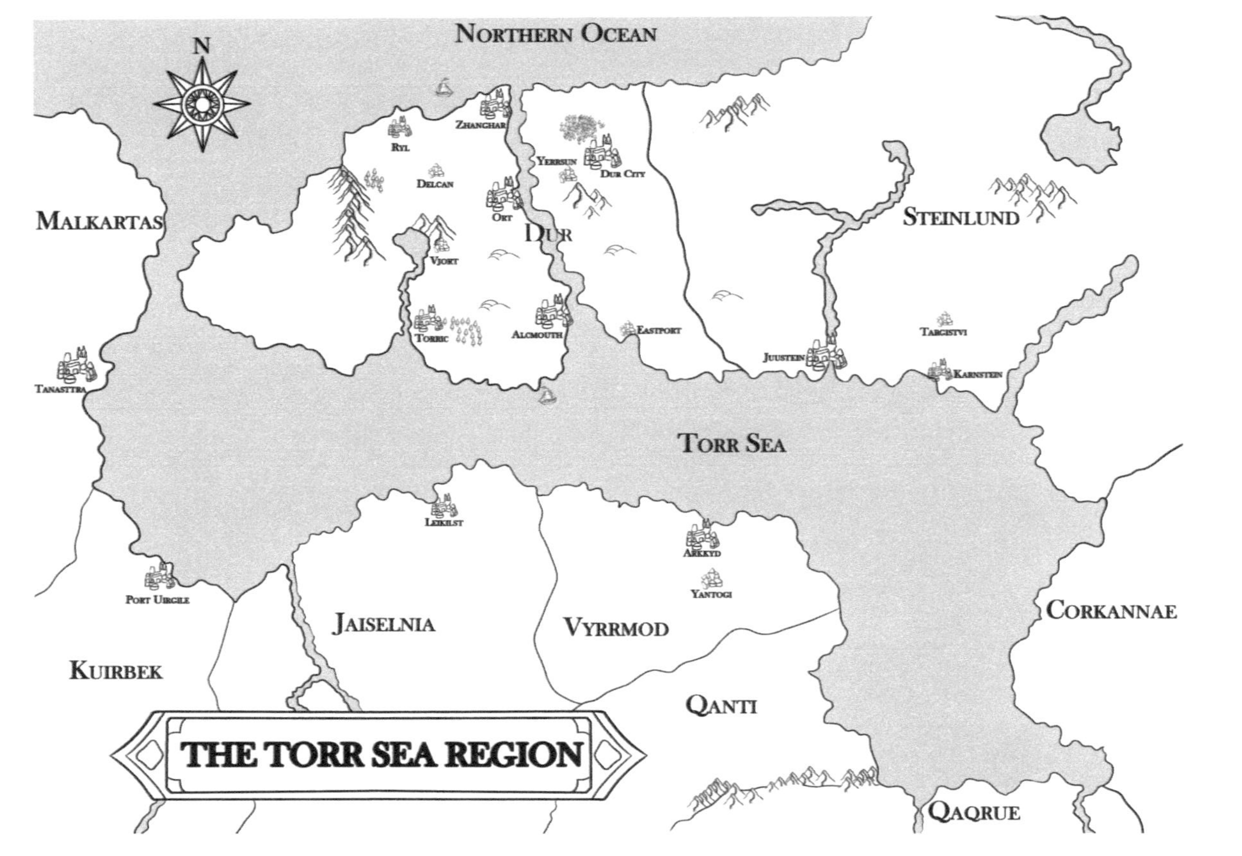

NORTHERN OCEAN
N
MALKARTAS
STEINLUND
ZHANCHARI
RYL
DELCAN
YERRSUN
DUR CITY
ORT
DUR
VJORT
TORREC
ALCMOUTH
EASTPORT
TARGISTVI
JUUSTEIN
KARNSTEIN
TANASTTRA
TORR SEA
LEIKILST
ARKKYD
YANTOGI
PORT UIRGLE
JAISELNIA
VYRRMOD
CORKANNAE
KUIRBEK
QANTI
THE TORR SEA REGION
QAQRUE

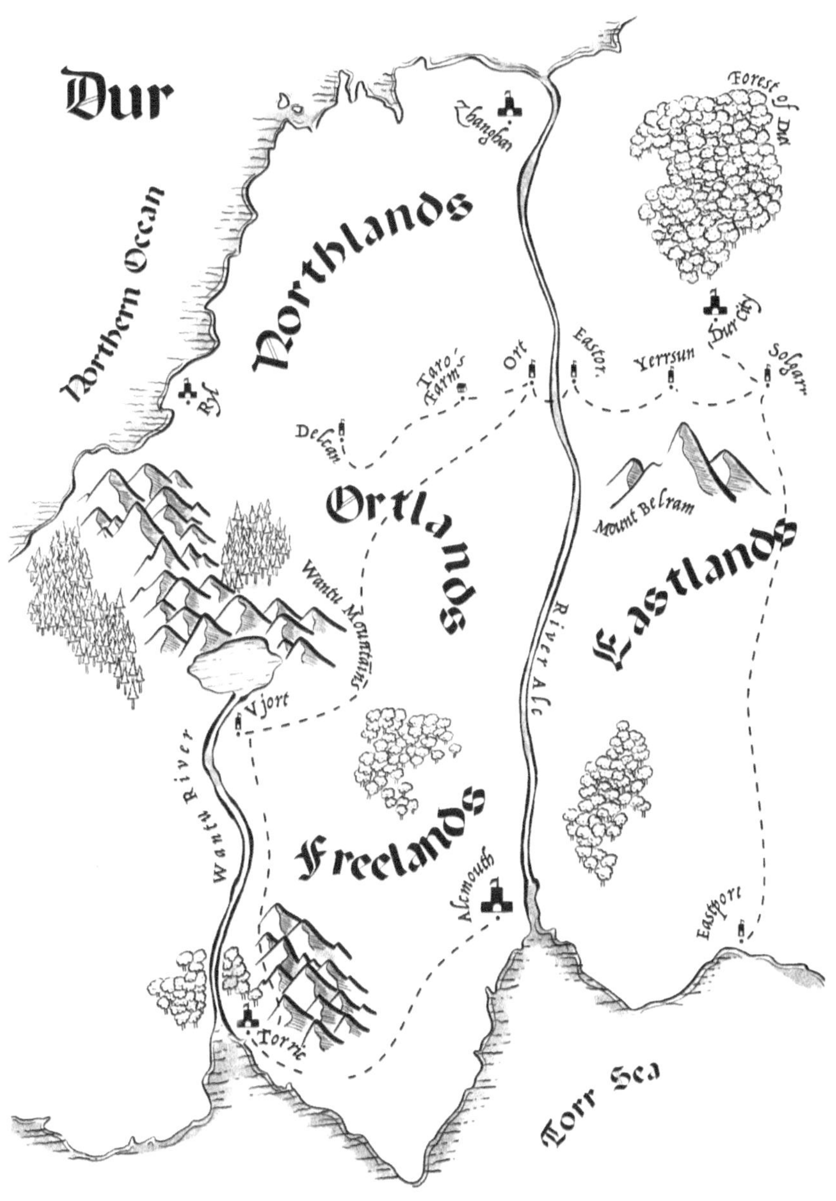
Dur
Northern Ocean
Northlands
Zhangban
Forest of Dur
Dur City
Taro's Farm
Ort
Eastor
Yerrsun
Solgarr
Delean
Ortlands
Mount Belram
Eastlands
Wantu Mountains
River Alc
Wantu River
Vjort
Freelands
Alcmouth
Eastport
Torric
Torr Sea

CHAPTER 1
CORELLE

Death felt like a cold, stone floor, and it smelled like stale, dried vomit. It brought agony to the inside of the head, as though somebody pounded it up and down on death's stone floor. It cleaved the tongue to the dry roof of the mouth and made it difficult to breathe. Nearby, stairs led upward to the next level of the deceased's journey.

If Corelle had only reached the first layer of death's domain, then she feared to continue. Her knuckles were scraped, raw and bloody. Her jaw hurt, and her legs sent waves of agony through her. She imagined the injuries sustained in the shameful incident in the inn had followed her wherever she had travelled to afterward.

It took considerable effort to raise her head. Sunlight streamed through a window nearby, and she squinted as she tried to understand why the sun shone in this place. At that, she realised she had not died, although her body suggested otherwise.

With horror, she remembered the details of the previous night. She had leapt at the innkeep with her fan in her hand but had tripped on a table leg and fallen to the floor. The man who had insulted her had laughed again, further heating her already boiled

blood, and she swung the fan at his legs. She had forgotten to spring the blade, and it struck his shin, harmless, then juddered out of her grip. He and his friends, however, took no mercy on her. They beat her, although she put up fierce resistance, as she had always done while she had served as a mariner. The innkeep threw her out into the street, and her fan after her. It skittered across the street.

In tears, she retrieved it and staggered home on aching legs the men had stomped on as she lay sprawled at their feet. Cowards, to attack a foe who lay on the ground. If she had her fan in her hand, she would have made them pay. When she reached the house, she found the key still in her pocket, a stroke of luck she did not deserve.

She lay on the floor and sobbed the morning away. Time to heed the words spoken to her by Vamma and the healer over the days before. She needed help for the problem in her head before it brought her ruin, left undone the things she had promised to do even as those promises drove Vamma out of the door.

Every healer she had ever spoken to had told her nobody knew anything about such matters, so how could she find that help? Neither Vamma nor the healer had given her any advice on how to find somebody who could provide the help they urged her to seek.

The Qagrue seemed more violent than Durfolk, so they might know more about such injuries. To go to them again would be more humiliation, but the alternative appeared to be death, and in short order. She would speak to the Commander in Ryl, Karaftasomething. She could not recall his full name. The Qagrue took ridiculous names, far too long to remember. He might reward her for her work yesterday. Together with his men, she had made Ryl a safer city, although guilt still whispered at her. She had accepted help from the Qagrue to kill Durfolk. She tried to convince herself Denstal had arranged for her mother to be killed and had deserved his ruin.

Her efforts failed. Corelle could not shake the ache in her heart. She had sided with the invaders against her own people. Another failure for her to throw onto the pile of lamentable things she had done. She might need to live for ever if she wished to find a way to forgive herself for all she had wrought, but if the healer had the right of it, she might not live much longer.

Weary and miserable, she rose and dragged her battered, bruised body up the stairs. She pulled her tunic over her head, too miserable to unbutton the garment, then forced her throbbing arms into the sleeves of another. She took another pair of trousers from her pack and kicked the ones she wore across the room.

Downstairs, she drank two cups of water in a futile fight against a thirst that refused to be defeated, then set out for the former Portreeve's Offices from which the Qagrue now ruled Ryl, determined to pursue her earlier idea and seek yet more help from her enemies.

The Commander could not meet with her until later in the morning, so she walked down to the docks to kill some time. The sea air might help her head, which pounded as though several smiths used it as an anvil. The dockworkers and mariners bustled around with cargoes and ropes. The tide must have changed not long ago, and everybody worked to unload two ships tied up at the dockside. Both ships had two masts, and she imagined they carried goods, cloths, and foodstuffs brought from Zhanghar. Three-masters never came direct to Ryl. The city did not have the population to attract their business.

The breeze, the familiar labour of the mariners, even the raucous cries of the birds as they flitted around the docks in search of some morsel of food, soothed her head and her temperament. At length, she returned to the Portreeve's Offices for her appointment with the Commander. An aide showed her into his office, which had once belonged to the Portreeve. He did not appear delighted to see her. "You did not follow our arrangement yesterday."

"Your enemies are dead, are they not?" Corelle could not understand why he would be so annoyed now his men would no longer lose their lives to Denstal's band of killers.

"They are indeed, but we did not bargain for them all to be killed. We wished to question them, learn their intent and how big their network is."

Impatient at his anger, Corelle tutted. "They were killers who would not have allowed your men to take them alive."

"It would appear not, but since you charged in ahead of my men, against my orders, we will never know. I lost four men, and I would rather not have done so."

"I am sorry for your men, but had they heeded my advice and left those clumsy swords at home, they might have fared better." Corelle's rage boiled inside her. He appeared determined to lay the blame for all the carnage at her door, which seemed both unfair and unkind.

He sighed. "We cannot change the past. You wished to see me. How may I help you?"

When Corelle opened her mouth to reply, she had forgotten why she wanted to see him. She frowned and mumbled a humiliated reply. "I cannot remember."

He looked at her with confusion on his face. "Are you in distress?"

The words sounded familiar. The healer had asked something similar last night, but why? If she could recall, she might remember why she had come here. With that, the memory returned to her. The healer had urged her to seek help for her head after he learned a mast had fallen on her. She gave one decisive nod of her head, certain she had returned to the right track, but regretted the impulse as waves of agony flooded her head and a bright light shone behind her eyes. She rubbed at her temples in search of some relief from the pain. "I have taken a blow to the head, and I need to find somebody with experience in such injuries."

He pursed his lips and exhaled. "I do not know whether my healers have such knowledge. Do none of your own healers know anything of the matter?"

"That they do not. I hoped yours might, since you are more violent than us."

"So speaks the woman who led the slaughter of nine men." His mumbled response sounded bitter, but Corelle could not unravel what reason he might have for such sourness, and he continued. "I will send one of our healers to you. Where do you live now?"

As she told him, he scribed the address on some parch, and she thanked him and took her leave. On the way home, she bought some bread. Without Vamma, Corelle must remember to feed herself. Back at the house, the clothes Vamma had placed in the basin days before seemed to float in blood. The bloodstains had not come off the tunic, and Corelle feared she would never get it clean. The trousers had fared better, and with some work tomorrow they might be cleaned sufficient to wear again. It went against all her instincts to throw clothes away, but the tunic looked beyond redemption.

She filled her pitcher, re-filled the basin with water, and dropped the tunic and trousers into the water again. An idea came to her, and she rubbed at the trousers with some of the white paste used to sweeten her breath. Foamy bubbles filled the basin as she rubbed, and although she did not know whether it would have any impact, she remained hopeful.

Corelle drained the pitcher, ate half the bread, then trudged up the stairs to bed. Life would be duller without Vamma, it seemed. Should she sail to Ort and head for Yerrsun? If Corelle pleaded with her and promised to change, Vamma might forgive her, and they could live together in her house in the town. Of course, Corelle could not take revenge on Krage from Yerrsun, and she had still not resolved the issue of Raopul. She sighed, then tossed and turned for some time before she fell into a troubled sleep.

CHAPTER 2
CORELLE

The next morning, Corelle lay in bed and wondered how she would occupy herself today. She needed to sail to Argoya to find Krage, if Denstal had told the truth. Raopul might be in Alcmouth, but he could be anywhere by now. He must be fifteen years by now, a small child no more.

A vicious headache had settled on her overnight, and it pained her even to sit upright in the bed. Some herbs might help with the pain, she reasoned, and since she could not tolerate the agony, she slunk down the stairs to refill her pitcher. Head in hands, she sat in the chair and cursed the ill fates that had brought this latest affliction to her.

A knock came at the door, a noise so loud and painful, it felt as though the person outside banged a stick on her head. Corelle shuffled to the door and pulled it open, if only to ensure the wretched visitor did not knock again. The Qagrue commander stood there alongside another Qagrue in a crisp, clean tunic, a satchel in his hand. He looked like a healer. Somebody nearby must have taken ill, and they needed directions from Corelle.

"Good day to you." The Commander had spoken, not the man at his side.

"And to you. What brings you here today?"

The Commander looked confused. "I have brought our healer to see you, as you requested yesterday."

Vague fragments of conversation returned to Corelle, fragments that suggested she had arranged for them to call today. "Of course. Please, come in." She held the door open wide so they could enter the house.

The Commander introduced the healer, but his name defied Corelle's ability to remember. It sounded like Lorrehark Sumbrid Akh Hark, but her mind lost its grip on the name as each syllable entered her ears. He asked her to sit and waved his finger around before her face while she tried to follow it with her eyes. He lit a candle, although the midday had not yet come, and he asked her to look up at the ceiling and down at the floor while he held the candle so close to her eyes, she could feel the warmth of its flame on her cheeks.

When he asked her if she had been affected by recent headaches, she mentioned the agony that coursed through her brain this morning. He peered into each of her ears, and she wondered if he could see her brain through them. She had never tried to look inside anybody's head through their ears before but resolved to try at the earliest opportunity.

His investigations bored her, and the Commander had not said a word throughout, doubtless as bored as Corelle. At last, the healer stood upright and sighed. "From what I understand, you have suffered blows to the head?"

"A mast fell on my head."

"A mast?"

"A mast." Why did everybody seem to question that a mast had struck her in the head?

"Is that the only blow to your head?"

"That it is not." Corelle thought back over her life and tried to recall other occasions she had been hit in the head. "Styrrach punched me." She held up a finger to indicate one occasion. There must be others, but none would come to mind. Intoxicated brawls while she had been a mariner, but she could not recall a specific incident. "I have been stabbed many times." The mention of the stab wounds might cover her embarrassment she could not remember any further blows to her head, and she folded the foolish finger away.

"You have been stabbed in the head?"

Corelle shook her head and winced in pain as flames shot across the inside of her forehead and scorched her eyeballs.

He sighed. "Something is wrong, that much is obvious. You do not have full control of your faculties. Your eyes struggle to follow my finger, and this headache seems more potent than I would expect. I am no expert on the brain, I fear."

"Nobody is, it seems." She had heard this story many times now.

"That is not true. There is a man. He understands injury to the head more than any I know of." He turned to the Commander, who had not spoken since he entered the house. "Romobreckh Sumbrid Akh Eckh." Another name Corelle would not remember.

"I know of him." The Commander nodded. "He serves in Ort-Bil-Torq, does he not?"

Corelle frowned. Ort-Bil-Torq? Had they renamed the city? Why?

"He does." The healer's reply cut off Corelle's attempt to question the strange name of the town. "He has studied head injuries in great depth since the Qanti war." Nothing they said made sense to Corelle. What did "war" mean? "Some of his techniques have been questioned." The healer gave a small cough, the kind people give when they attempt to disguise something they do not agree with but are too polite to say so.

Before she could ask what "war" meant, the Commander flicked his gaze to Corelle. "Would he treat a member of another tribe?" More confusion. Tribe? Corelle did not belong to a tribe. She came from Dur and belonged to nobody but herself and her closest friend, death.

"It could be argued she is a member of our tribe. She is a citizen of Qagrue and Dur." Corelle had heard this phrase before. A woman had used it in her shop. Corelle had killed the woman, although she did not think it had been because of the use of the phrase.

The Commander heaved a loud breath of… Resignation? Frustration? Corelle could not decide. "So be it. I will give her letters she can take to Romobreckh. He can see her or not, as he pleases. Beyond that, I can do nothing for her. She is an element of chaos, and I will be happy to see her sail away from Ryl-Bil-Nuiksea."

Corelle had sat in silence while they talked about her as if she had left the room. "I am here." Her patience with their rudeness had been exhausted. "I do hear you discuss me."

The healer spoke some words she could not understand, and the Commander turned to Corelle. "Our apologies. We did not intend to be rude. I will give you letters to take to Ort-Bil-Torq, where one of our healers might investigate your injury. Whether he will is at his discretion, you understand. He is"—he frowned—"how would you say, expert? I feel that is the word. He is an expert on head injuries. He may be able to help you."

Corelle could not let the town's new name pass without comment. "Do you mean Ort?" She tried to sound annoyed, to convey her anger at the Qagrue if they had renamed the town to something from their own guttural language.

The Commander's eyes narrowed. "I mean Ort-Bil-Torq. The river has been named Torq, the family name of our tribal leader. As the town lies on the river, it has been renamed. In your language, it would be Ort by the Torq."

She stared at him and fought an anger that threatened to erupt into violence. "The river is the Alc. The town is Ort." She emphasised each word as she strove to contain her fury. What right did these intruders have to rename Dur to their own fancy?

"Indeed, it is still named Ort. We have honoured your traditions but have added the river to the name, in our own custom."

"You have hon…" Corelle clenched her teeth and drew in a long, slow breath. The two men wore blank expressions. They felt neither anger nor sympathy for this decision, it seemed. *What is scribed, must be,* she thought. If she attacked them, she would die in the defence of the name of a town. She should leave and seek out this healer. Vamma would be proud of her if she sought the help this man might give her. At the least, he might help Corelle think with more clarity, and she could make a better choice about her next course of action. Each option pressed its own claim, and she had not yet come to a decision. She would seek out this man and see whether he would help her, then she would decide. "Very well." With some effort, she kept her voice level and calm. "I will sail to Ort on whatever you call the Alc and seek out this man. My thanks."

"When you are ready to depart, come to my office. My aides will have the letters ready for you. There is no more I can do for you, other than to wish you well." The Commander showed no emotion. Corelle, or a stone in the road; it seemed he would care no more for one than the other.

The headache pounded at Corelle's skull, as though myriad tiny animals battered at it from the inside. She might die on the journey, and doubtless the Qagrue would give her no Pyre or Sending. A determination came to her at that moment, a decision made in a rare moment of clarity. Although she would make some attempt to find Raopul, Krage would be her focus. So many wrongs must be avenged. "In truth, there is one more thing you can do for me, if it suits." The Commander raised his eyebrows but made no answer, so she continued. "Others may come in search of me. If any come to your office, please tell them I am dead. I care not what story you tell of my death. Please swear you will not reveal to any who seek me that I live. I have duties that seem fated to take me to my ruin, and if I die unsung far from Dur, the story will, at the least, give any who might care about me the chance to grieve."

He looked at her, his brow furrowed. "You are strange to me. So. It shall be as you ask. I will tell any who ask you have been killed in a brawl in a tavern."

The story he had created came too close to the truth of the incident two days previous, and shame threatened to engulf her. "My thanks. I will call for the letters tomorrow. I will arrange for my departure in what remains of today." Corelle turned to the healer. "My thanks for your help."

He smiled, but the smile bore a sadness Corelle could not understand. It seemed unlikely the Qagrue cared about the fates written for Durfolk. One day, she might right that wrong, but for now, Krage awaited, and the mere fact she had made the decision seemed to have lifted a load from her. Even her headache seemed subdued.

She rose from the chair to show the men out, then finished the water from her pitcher before she climbed the stairs to gather her belongings into her pack. The bloodied tunic's condition had not improved, so she abandoned it. She doubted she would have a chance to clean it again for some time. The trousers were cleaner, and she draped them across the stair rail to dry.

Corelle walked to her shop and unlocked the door. It lay much as it had when she had last been here, soon after they moved into the house, when she had returned to collect some last things they needed and locked the shop for what she had thought might be the last time. Today, she needed nothing other than to gaze around the shop once more before she left Ryl, a city she might never return to. Despite Vamma's best efforts to clean it, the bloodstain on the floor left by her mother still showed, a heart-wrenching reminder of the tragedy that befell her.

She went up the stairs and wandered the rooms as memories of her childhood ran rampant in her head. Gaish's letter lay on the table, and she picked it up. Some making lay unfinished in her old bedroom. Her mother's work, no doubt the making she had been engaged in before Denstal's men killed her. Corelle held it to her cheek, and a tear dripped from her eye onto the making. Angry, she threw it down onto the bed and turned. She locked the shop behind her, then took the key across the street to Saboti's shop and entrusted the old woman with it. Corelle invented the excuse she had to leave on a journey for a time. As the old woman embraced her, Corelle shed more tears, and she urged Saboti to take anything from within the shop or the accommodation if she had need of it.

Corelle's headache worsened as she walked back to the house. Tomorrow she would sail away from Ryl, and she did not believe she would ever return. Vengeance lay unfulfilled, but she would seek it in Argoya and try to finish off the last remnants of the Guild. Afterward, there would be nothing to live for, and in truth, she believed she would perish in the attempt to find and kill Krage. Darkness fell, but it brought no relief to a life lived in the shadow of death for many years, and her headache grew even worse.

CHAPTER 3
CORELLE

A cold wind blew along the River Alc, and a grey sky threatened rain. Corelle sat at the bow of the ship as it rose and fell in time with the music of the swell that crashed against the wooden hull. Tomorrow, they would reach Ort, where she would disembark and seek the healer the Commander had sent her to. She carried letters from him that asked the healer to help her if he could, and he had arranged passage on a ship that sailed from Ryl to Ort. The two-masted ship, crewed by Durfolk, had left Ryl five days earlier and had sailed straight past Zhanghar or whatever the Qagrue now called it.

In the common room, some of the mariners growled about the Qagrue while others urged their colleagues to use discretion. "Not all ears can be trusted to hear the words of Durfolk these days." They spoke in hushed whispers whenever a mariner became too vocal in his criticism of the invaders.

Corelle had talked with the master once for an hour or more, but the man could not be drawn on his opinion of the Qagrue. "I am a ship's master, and while somebody pays me coin, I will sail

this old keeler wherever they want me to take her." His face betrayed no emotion as he spoke.

She had offered to help with the work aboard, but the master had a full crew and did not need her assistance. Corelle spent some time each day at the bow, although it often pained her at times when she thought back to the times she had sat there with Deineike. Nonetheless, she enjoyed the feel of the wind as it whipped through her hair, or the songs it sang in the ropes and nets of the ship. Peace settled on her as she watched the riverbank slide past them, the occasional house or barn visible. At times, her memories seemed as clear as a spring stream, but at others she struggled to recall the name of the ship.

Ort lay one more dark night away, and tomorrow she would either persuade the healer to help her, or she would sail south to Alcmouth and search for Raopul. He had last been seen alive there, as far as she could calculate. How she would find any information, she had no idea, but she would not brood on the complications of the search at this stage. There would be time for that once she arrived in the former capital of Dur. Either she would find him, or she would abandon her search and seek passage to Argoya in pursuit of Krage, who owed her much and had not yet repaid any of that debt.

The next morning, Ort came into view ahead of them. Corelle stood on the deck with her pack over her shoulder as the ship manoeuvred into the dock. Another cold day had settled on the land, even as she thought spring should have arrived by now. The cloudy sky matched her mood, and her headache battered within her skull more than normal. Unless the Qagrue healer could help her, she feared she might not live long enough to kill Krage. Nothing but the vengeance that drove her gave her a reason to live, and she harboured such deep resentment for the Guild and all the misery it had brought to her life, she longed to complete its destruction with Krage's death.

The mariners threw ropes down to the deckhands in a light drizzle. The moment the crew secured the ramp in position, Corelle thanked them for their company and walked down onto the docks. She had not returned to Ort since the day she had left more than three years earlier on a journey that, in the end, took her around the globe of Ictharelian. The skyline looked familiar, and the docks had changed little enough, as far as she could recall. Raolos's tally house bore a new sign that announced it as the property of a Qagrue. They must have occupied it after Raolos did not return to run his business, and Gillar hanged Ibie. She felt a twinge of guilt for Raolos's death and a bitter sadness for Ibie's.

When she glanced at the sky, she saw no break in the clouds. She hunched her shoulders against the chill and thrust her hands into the pockets of her trousers. One of them closed over something metallic, and she pulled it out, curious. The key to Pettra's house. That would be useful and would save her coin, since she would not need a room at an inn. Then a memory pricked at her, and she realised the truth. She had lost the key to Pettra's house when The Ictharelian sank. The key in her pocket belonged to the house in Ryl. She had forgotten to return it when she left, and now it had travelled to Ort. Nothing could be done, so she turned and cast it into the Alc where it disappeared with a small splash. The river repaired itself of the damage the key had wrought, and small dimples from the drizzle returned to the surface of the water.

Corelle guessed the Qagrue would administer the town from the former Portreeve's Offices, so she headed up the familiar hill toward the square. There appeared to be more Qagrue in the streets of Ort than in Ryl. More of the businesses appeared to be run by Qagrue here too, and many signs announced Qagrue ownership. Whether the shops sold items only the Qagrue would value or nothing more than food, clothes, and so on that both Qagrue and Durfolk would buy, she could not determine.

The Portreeve's Offices had changed little. The Ortwood doors still gazed out with their customary stern authority across the square, but the woodwork had been repainted, and a Qagrue banner flew over the doors. Behind the counter in the lobby stood two people, one Qagrue, one Durfolk, and Corelle waited while the Dur woman dealt with the person she attended to. The Qagrue man offered to assist her, but she indicated she preferred to wait for the woman.

The woman's customer left, and Corelle handed her the letters. She broke the seal and opened them. To Corelle's irritation, the woman handed them to the Qagrue and told Corelle he would attend to her. Although he did not pour salt into her injury by any word he said, Corelle imagined he must have gloated within that she had, after all else, been obliged to deal with him.

He read the letters and asked Corelle to wait while he found the appropriate person to help her, then spoke to the woman. She left through the door behind her. Corelle's fury grew, and she struggled to contain it. She had been obliged to seek help from the Qagrue man, but he had done no more than send the Dur woman to obey his instruction.

She brooded in silence on a chair while she tapped her foot on the floor in an angry, rhythmical pattern. The man glanced up at her once, mayhap distracted by her foot, and he smiled at her. She tapped her foot louder, both to aggravate him more and to serve as an outlet for her anger. The fury that had driven Vamma away remained as strong as ever, and she hoped the healer could help her alleviate the onset of rages she could no longer trust herself to control.

After some time, the woman came back and spoke to the man. They talked in hushed tones, and Corelle could not hear what they said, but the man beckoned to her, so she approached the counter. "Where will you stay while you are in Ort-Bil-Torq?"

Corelle wondered what fate had befallen Raolos's and Pettra's houses. Doubtless, important Qagrue lived in each these days. The little coin she had would not last long if she stayed at a fancy inn like The Ort. The two Guild members Styrrach sent north to kill Raolos had stayed at an inn at the docks called The Dockside Inn at that time. Would it still be called the same? She rolled the dice. "The Dockside Inn."

He asked for the address, and he frowned when she told him. "I do not know it."

The woman did. "I know it. It is a rough and tumble place."

Corelle smiled at the memory of the night she had killed Adijon, the Guild member sent to kill Raolos. She had pretended Adijon had taken his own life, then she and Synna had run like the wind to escape before the Portreeve's men arrived. "That it is. I can afford nothing better."

"So." The man spoke to Corelle, as if to interrupt her conversation with the other woman. "We will send word to your inn if Romobreckh Sumbrid Akh Eckh will see you. Thank you, and good day."

He returned his attention to whatever had occupied him earlier. Corelle stood in silence at the counter for a moment, then turned and headed for the inn. She hoped they would have a spare room, or she might need to return to the officious man and update her address. On Southdock Street, she saw the inn ahead of her.

Her luck held. The inn had vacancies, and she took a cheap room for three nights. She reasoned the Qagrue would take their time to bear her letters to the healer, and he in turn would take his time to decide whether to see her. If he agreed to help her, she would need to be in Ort for some days, she guessed. Once she had dropped her pack on the bed, she returned to the street through the tavernroom. Neither the patrons nor the innkeep seemed familiar to her, and she hoped nobody would remember her either.

Corelle walked back up the hill and found Pettra's old house, where she had stayed the first time she had ever been to Ort. More painful memories existed within the house, none more than the time Raolos had caught her in bed with his wife. Somebody lived there now. It seemed in excellent condition, and somebody had planted a hedge along the front of the house adjacent to the street. She decided to call into Syme's tavern, where she had drunk wine both with and without Deineike down the years. A conversation with him and a goblet of whatever wine he stocked these days would brighten her mood today, but to her dismay the tavern had become a furniture shop that sold moderate grade items. An old man at a nearby shop who had known Syme told Corelle the innkeep had died two years earlier. His family had no interest in the tavern, and they had sold it to a Qagrue who had established the furniture shop.

The news saddened Corelle. She felt Syme's death severed some small connection to Deineike, so she set out to find the cake shop where they had bought pastries many times. It still served as a cake shop, although they no longer sold the pastry that had been Deineike's favourite. Corelle bought a sweet bun and found the same wall they had always sat on. She fought down tears. Her return to Ort had been less than successful so far, and she considered she might not even stay to see the healer.

When she returned to the inn, she had maligned the Qagrue. While she had been out, letters had been delivered that told her Romobreckh Sumbrid Akh Eckh had agreed to see her. An appointment had been scheduled in two days' time at his rooms in the wealthy quarter. Corelle wondered why a healer with such skills would base himself in Ort and why he worked from rooms she suspected were in his home rather than in some Qagrue administration building such as the old Portreeve's Offices. It mattered little, in truth. She would see him and find out what he might learn of her condition and what, if anything, he could do for her.

Corelle ate in the tavernroom, basic food but inexpensive, and she drank two goblets of wine before she retired to bed. The next day, she wandered the streets with no sense of purpose, surprised by how much the town had changed. The skyline seemed familiar, but the large number of Qagrue shops surprised her, and there appeared to be fewer Durfolk in the town than she could remember. She imagined the issue would be contentious, so she refrained from any question about the matter, but she stood opposite the Portreeve's Offices for an hour. Three Qagrue entered the building for every Durfolk. The southerners had settled now, and Dur would never be the same. She heard their language on every street, and she wondered where all the Ortfolk had gone. Had they left Dur? Had the Qagrue killed large numbers of them? Had they fled east and turned Bushy and Sparse's brother's inn into the most successful in Dur? She laughed aloud at the thought, then spun on her heels and headed for more aimless wandering.

CHAPTER 4
CORELLE

At the appointed time on the second morning, Corelle arrived at the address provided in the letters. Romobreckh's house stood one street away from Raolos's old home and looked as grand. A long path through the neat garden led to large double front doors. The two-storey house had many windows and would be large enough for a family with several children. She walked up the path, and a Dur woman answered the door. Corelle explained she had an appointment with Romobreckh Sumbrid Akh Eckh, whose name she had taken pains to memorise.

The woman led her into a small room with four chairs in it and invited her to take a seat. Corelle had become nervous, uncertain of what investigations the healer might perform, almost afraid he might declare her beyond any cure. To her surprise, as she faced possible death, a part of her did not wish to die, despite all that had turned in her life, and after she had been so certain for so long she craved an end to her torment.

A Qagrue woman came out of a door to check her name, then invited her to follow her into a large parlour set up to serve as the healer's room, as the chirurgeon in Torric had done. A small desk

stood in one corner, with three chairs arranged near it. A large table in the middle of the room held many unusual tools, and two Ortwood cabinets lined one wall. The healer sat in one of the chairs, and he beckoned to Corelle to sit in one of the others as the woman withdrew. The healer had long grey hair and bushy eyebrows on a round face. He might once have thought himself of a robust build, but in his later years he had become overweight. His eyes twinkled, bright and inquisitive, and he had long fingers. He held a scribing tool in one hand, and a piece of blank parch lay on the desk before him. The letters she had carried from Ryl also lay open before him.

"I see you have been sent to me by Karaftaraluq Sumbrid Akh Aluq in Ryl-Bil-Nuiksea. It is unusual for me to attend Durfolk, most unusual indeed, but Karaftaraluq's letters intrigued me. He says here…" He picked up the letters and read them. "Yes, he says a mast fell on your head. Is this true?"

The strange manner of saying "yes" or "no" still jarred in Corelle's ears, even though she had encountered it in multiple lands, and she doubted she would ever become accustomed to it. With a sigh, she told him an abbreviated version of the story of how The Ictharelian had been sunk. He nodded and scribed on the parch in what must have been his own language, since she could not read it.

"Have you suffered any other blows to the head?"

"That I have. I have been struck in the head in fights and so on."

He raised his bushy eyebrows and scribed some more notes. "Do you know anything of injuries to the brain?"

Tears threatened, but she would not let him see her grief. "I had a friend who died from one. I know very few healers understand much of the mystery of the brain."

He nodded. He resembled Vamma's grandfather in his resolute, humourless mannerisms. "Few indeed. None know the brain better than me, I feel." He did not appear conceited; rather, matter of fact.

"You are fortunate indeed I am in Ort-Bil-Torq. So. Let me take a look at you."

He half-rose from his chair, but Corelle spoke, and he sat again. "How can you know so much about an area others know so little about?" Corelle could not resist the urge to learn how he had come by his knowledge, given everything previous healers had told her; that so little could be known about an area that could not be accessed, after all else.

He smiled, a slight upturn of his lips, nothing more. "A good question, which is a good sign in itself. Not all agree with my methods. I have performed extensive experiments on animals. Many people are offended by this, but I have learned much from my studies of their brains. More than this, many of our fallen soldiers throughout the Qanti war manifested with brain injuries."

"Manifested?" The word puzzled her.

"Presented then. It is a medical term. It means they suffered brain injuries from blows to the head. The Qanti use a brutal weapon, a large metal ball on a short pole. They strike at the head with it, and large numbers of our soldiers came back from the war with hideous injuries as a result. Many died, and I petitioned Kandaltorq Sumbrid Akh Torq, our tribal leader, for permission to investigate the damage within their skulls."

"You cut into their heads?" The healer in Raolos's house had bemoaned the lack of this option, but it sickened her to think of it, nonetheless.

"Yes." So simple an answer for such a complex issue, to have violated the bodies of the fallen. "They could not object, for they had died, and their families all agreed to permit it, for our future benefit. It concerns you?"

"That it does."

The reply had been little more than a whisper, but Romobreckh heard it. "It bothers many, but you should be concerned the least of all, for everything I have learned brings me here today, where I hope to help you improve your outcome."

"What did you learn?" Her voice sounded deathly quiet even to her own ears, as though she feared to give breath to the words that might unleash descriptions of horrors best left unknown.

"I learned much. So. You have doubtless been struck on other parts of your body in these fights you speak of, and your skin has swollen." A nod of confirmation as Corelle recalled all she had done to aid Deineike's recovery, how hard she had worked to keep down her swelling. "This is the body's attempt to heal itself from a blow. It sends fluid to the damaged area to fight inflammation."

He looked at Corelle as though to check she had understood, and another nod prompted him to continue. "Our skin has plenty of give." He pinched some skin on her arm and pulled it upward. When he released it, it snapped back into shape and left nothing more than two white marks where his finger and thumb had been. "It copes with swelling well, although if inflammation takes hold, the swelling is not a good thing. The brain does much the same, but constrained by our skull, it lacks the space to swell. The fluid becomes trapped in our heads and presses on the brain. This leads to deterioration in brain function, and in many cases, it leads to death." How had he learned all this from a few animals and some dead men? It baffled her, and her head swam as she tried to comprehend. He stood. "May I look at you now?"

Corelle had come here for this purpose. It would be churlish to deny him, despite a cold dread that had crept over her as he had explained his studies. A wave of a hand invited him to proceed. He stared into each of her eyes, then reached for a candle. He lit it and held it close to her eyes before he moved it backward. He repeated the process twice against each eye. He instructed her to look around, and up and down. He inspected her ears. Much of what he did, the healer in Ryl had done. He kneaded her skull, and his fingers manipulated her head this way and that, heedless of the pain he inflicted on her as he pulled her hair. Then he sat and scribed notes for some time.

"So. You have many scars on your head, and your eyes tell me you have suffered a brain injury, such as some swelling or fluid on the brain itself. Your pupils do not react to the candlelight, you see. That is a reliable indication something is awry in the head. There is a large lump here." He touched her head. "Bumps on the head are common enough, but this lump has not reduced, and that is bad. It may suggest damage to the bone beneath. I suspect your brain bleeds. I found many cases where the brain had bled in my research, and almost always a large lump formed above the bleed."

Her ruin could not be far away, she believed. His words suggested she would die soon. These things could not be remedied because the skull impeded any effort to repair them, she seemed to recall. "Can nothing be done?"

He closed his eyes and tilted his head to one side. "We can do nothing if you prefer. I suspect you will die soon if we do not act, however."

Corelle frowned. Why would he do nothing? Had he misunderstood? His command of Dur, excellent though it might be, had led to confusion. "My apologies. I misspoke. I meant to ask if there is anything we can do."

"Oh." He paused, and a distant look came to his eyes as though he reconsidered her words. "Yes, there are things we can do. We must relieve the pressure on your brain first of all. There are two ways to approach this, although one of them is somewhat experimental at this stage." The word "experimental" did nothing to reassure Corelle, and she gulped. "In the past, I have cut a part of the skull away. This is the more traditional method. I call it "trappaneesh" in my language. I do not know how to translate it into yours." She gulped again. If he cut a hole in her head, she imagined it would kill her. "The other method is from more recent studies with animals. The fluid in our bodies contains salt, and high concentrations of it in any liquid lead the body to balance itself. If we introduce water with a high saline content into your body, it will find its way into your head, where it will draw off the excess fluid it finds there in order to redistribute the salt. As it pulls that liquid from your brain, the pressure is relieved. At the least, that is what I hope will happen."

"You have never tried this method?" Corelle understood some part of the explanation, which reminded her of the reason mariners did not drink salt water from the sea. Nonetheless, she did not wish to die from a cure intended to save her life.

"I have tried, yes. We cannot find a way to keep the liquid clean as we introduce it to your body. If I wish to cut your skin, I can heat my knife and kill all the bugs, then make a quick clean incision, and you are safe. As soon as water is poured from a container into a device to carry it into your body—a tube, in most cases—that water is exposed to the air. We cannot yet keep it free of the impurities that float around us, and they carry infection into the body. Worse, the impurities get into the blood. Nothing but death has resulted so far."

How, then, had the water not introduced infection into Deineike's leg when she had flushed it in Torric? She asked him, her curiosity too powerful to resist.

"This chirurgeon left the wound open, and you washed it with water?"

"That I did."

"Did you heat the water first?"

"That I did." Corelle cast her mind back and tried to remember everything that had turned.

He shook his head. "I would not have recommended this approach. Your friend must have been more than fortunate. Such a practice seems reckless, though in this case it appears to have been successful."

"The chirurgeon did say many would not have agreed with the

method." Corelle felt she needed to apologise for the man who had saved Deineike's leg, and at little cost.

"I have explained the risks. Any method that introduces water can also introduce these impurities. You were lucky."

Corelle's heart sank. Her options appeared to be certain death from some filth-infested water poured into her, or to have a hole cut in her head, which she believed would be every bit as fatal. She could not grasp why he seemed so confident in his work when it involved such deadly processes. More questions came to her. "If you cut a hole in my head, how will you heal it afterward?"

"I will not. If you live long enough, your body will attempt to heal itself. I have seen evidence of bone that has regrown over a trappaneesh hole. It is rare to see total regrowth, but it will attempt to heal itself." He answered questions in a blunt, direct manner, she felt.

Corelle pondered the answer. "In the meantime, I will have a hole in my head?"

"Yes. You will need to cover it and keep it cleansed. Your flesh will regrow over the hole, and if you grow your hair, none will know you have this hole."

What choice did she have? "Will it hurt?"

"Yes, but we will give you some herbs beforehand. I will only cut away bone from your skull. I will not touch the brain itself. To do so would be fatal. The brain is protected inside the skull. All I do is cut a hole, and the pressure is released. Excess fluid, along with any blood, will come out of the hole, and your condition should improve."

If Deineike could have accessed such treatment, she might be alive today, and Corelle's life would not have been so devastated. Too late for that now. She must suffer the hole in her head or die. "Very well. When will you cut my head open?"

"I can perform the trappaneesh in two days' time, if that suits."

"I do not plan to go anywhere. This is as good a time as any."

She shrugged as she replied. She had nothing to lose as far as she could see.

"Then be here in two days at the sunrise, and we will see whether we can right you. Before you leave, I must take some measurements and determine where I will cut." He again ran his hands over her head and pulled at her hair before he scribed more notes to himself. Then he bade her farewell, and the woman who had admitted her reappeared and took some details such as her name and where she could be contacted if they needed to delay the work. When Corelle stepped out into a cold, miserable day, the morning had not yet reached its midpoint.

Corelle had the better part of two days to occupy herself. She knew nobody in Ort, and she had little enough coin. Romobreckh had not mentioned payment, and she wondered whether some arrangement had been proposed in the letters she had carried to him. She considered a trip over to Eastort on the rowboat, if it still operated, but doubted she would find anything there to occupy her. Curiosity led her past Raolos's house. Like Pettra's house, somebody appeared to have taken it over as their residence. The gardens were well maintained, and the exterior of the house looked tidy. It had been repainted a bright red she did not think suited it. The colour reminded her of the blood spilled in the house, and she wondered what the new residents had done with the blood-soaked carpet from the large bedroom. She passed it by and hoped Durfolk lived there, not Qagrue. She felt certain Raolos would prefer his own kind had taken up residence.

Corelle had passed Raolos's and Pettra's house, both of whom had died thanks to her. The number of lives lost on her account could never be reckoned, and now she intended to kill again. Krage's death would bring her no remorse, but he would be another name on a long list, nonetheless. If anything lay afterward where Corelle might be judged, she would not be found worthy of Deineike's company.

She drifted back to the docks and found a bench where she could sit while she watched the bustle of work around her. The tide changed, and all the ships at the dock cast off, three more arrived, and the hubbub of activity began again.

In time, hunger drove her back to the inn. One goblet of wine turned into several, and she became light-headed. She sat alone in a quiet corner where she could see the door, two tables from where she had killed a man some years earlier. He had been a stranger, and her dagger had robbed him of all he had ever intended to be. He would have been happy to kill her if he could, and Raolos and his family also, a thought that did little to cheer her. She had never felt so alone. She missed Deineike and wondered whether that emptiness would ever disappear. She could attempt to find a courtesan who would be open to a dalliance with another woman, but she may not have enough coin for such an extravagance. Late into the night, she stumbled up the stairs to her room, collapsed onto the bed, and fell asleep as she wondered whether the man she had killed, Adijon, had stayed in this room.

CHAPTER 5

CORELLE

As with so many previous nights, nightmares plagued her. Corelle lay on top of Adijon's corpse as Arella and Deineike carved holes in her head and pulled pieces of her brain out through the holes. With each piece they pulled out, they cried, "I love you."

A courtesan with Pettra's face entered the room and asked where Vamma had gone. Corelle could form no reply as her brains were pulled out of her head by Arella and Deineike, and Pettra dissolved into a pool of blood before her eyes. The blood spread across the floor until it had spelled out 'I love you' in vermilion, and Corelle woke drenched with sweat despite the cool of the night. Her head ached and her stomach roiled, and she recalled all the mornings she had felt the same way after a night filled with too much wine.

Exhaustion brought more sleep, and when she woke again, she decided to seek some food. Another rainy morning awaited her outside. The rain disappointed her, and she could not understand why spring had not yet arrived. It must arrive later than before so it

could spend less time with the Qagrue. She smiled, amused by the gentle humour of her thoughts.

She decided to seek food somewhere other than The Dockside Inn and headed north toward the part of town where she had come ashore in the little rowboat and killed one of the Qagrue. It all seemed so long ago now. Ort had impacted her life more even than Ryl. She had met Taro in Ort, and had she not travelled to his farm, she might not have met Deineike. Raolos came from Ort, and because of him Corelle had sailed south with Deineike, and Styrrach had killed the love of her life. Later, she had taken part in a day that now seemed like a dream, right here in Ort, when they had killed all the Qagrue in the town. Denstal had been with her that day, and years later, he fled to Ryl where he had Corelle's mother killed.

Once again, she found herself back in Ort, and this time holes would be cut into her head to save her from the same death that had taken Deineike from her. Corelle wandered, morose, through the rain in no particular direction and found herself in a better quarter than the docks. She found a little shop that sold pastries. A few small tables with wooden boxes for seats served for furniture, but the shop sold a cake similar to Deineike's old favourite. Corelle bought two of the pastries, one for her and one for Deineike, and ate them both. The woman who sold the cakes looked over at her several times, and Corelle could not help but wonder whether the woman's sexual preferences ran to other women. When she had been younger, Corelle had told Arella she knew as soon as they met. If she had any such ability in those days, she had it no longer.

The woman smiled and asked if she wanted another cake. Corelle did not need any more food, but the desire to talk to another woman overwhelmed her, so she asked for a different pastry. The woman brought it over and placed it on the small dish the other two had been on.

"My thanks." Corelle smiled up at her. No other patrons

demanded the woman's time, and Corelle decided to strike up a conversation with her. "Would you like to join me?" She pointed to the wooden box opposite her, and the woman looked around as though to check no other customers waited on her service.

She sat on the box. "I am Ulmella."

"Corelle." Corelle favoured her with a smile.

"What brings you to my little shop?"

Corelle guessed her soaked clothes and hair might indicate she had walked some distance to reach the shop. Deep inside, she longed to say, "The fates brought me here to gaze into your eyes," or some other ridiculous thing, but her courage failed her. "Hunger." She felt disappointed in her lack of adventure.

Ulmella stood, removed her clothes, and breathed, "Take me now, on top of the pastries." Corelle blinked, and the vision faded. Ulmella sat across from her, a concerned look on her face. "Are you ill?"

"That I am." Honesty still found some favour in Corelle's life, it seemed. "I have suffered a blow to the head, and I lose my concentration and get dreadful headaches. Often, I cannot recall things."

"That must be awful." Ulmella's hazel eyes radiated compassion, and her short, blonde hair framed a pretty face. She had a high-pitched voice, like a young girl, but whenever Ulmella spoke, her voice soothed rather than irritated.

"That it is. Tomorrow I will have a hole cut in my head that may fix it. It may be my ruin, my guess." Ulmella swayed backward, and Corelle guessed she had gone too far with the description. "I apologise. So much detail..." What more could she say? Corelle had desired some conversation, and her mind had fumbled any chance of it.

"Think nothing of it. Doubtless your injury prompted you to share more than you intended." Ulmella smiled. Her teeth were pure white and straight, unlike most Durfolk. She must have used a lot of the white paste throughout her life.

"My thanks." Corelle looked down, embarrassed by the woman's graceful response. She tried a bite of the new cake. It tasted delicious, but she did not think she could manage to eat another.

"Is it good?"

"That it is. More than good."

Ulmella nodded. "Will you have a hole cut in your head, in truth?"

"That I will, it seems." Corelle laughed to lighten the idea of the treatment she would endure, as much for herself as for Ulmella.

"Will your..." Ulmella blushed and looked at the table. She looked even prettier in her embarrassment. "Will your brain not fall out of the hole?"

Corelle laughed, and for the first time in a great many days, she felt genuine amusement and even joy. "I hope not."

Ulmella laughed also, a high, clear laugh like a small bell with no imperfections. "As do I." She wiped at the tears of mirth that pooled in her eyes.

Corelle had no explanation for the odd reply, "I hope not." Another time, she would have responded, "That they will," or "That they will not." She must have spent too much time around people who spoke in different ways. "I should head back to my inn." The laughter had subsided, and the rain continued outside.

"A pity." A look of panic crossed Ulmella's face, and she rushed to elaborate. "A pity the rain still falls." Her cheeks turned bright red once more.

Corelle gazed at the woman, who might be five years younger than her. Nobody else had entered the shop as Corelle had sat at the small table, and she guessed the woman had enjoyed some company, nothing more. After all else, Corelle had nowhere to go and the entire day to travel there. "I could stay a while longer." She added a smile to the suggestion.

Ulmella reached out, touched the back of the hand that still held the third pastry, and spoke in a soft voice that carried hope, anxiety, uncertainty, and the suggestion that more lay in her words for any with the desire to delve deeper into them. "I would enjoy some company." The woman's touch thrilled Corelle and brought a tingle to her sex. She did not withdraw her hand, and Ulmella's fingers rested there for five heartbeats or more.

Corelle smiled and lowered the cake to the plate. Ulmella's fingers lingered, then she withdrew her hand. "Do you own this shop?"

"That I do." Corelle detected a note of pride in her voice. "I have owned it for almost a year now." Corelle smiled again. "Today is quiet." It sounded as though Ulmella felt she should justify the lack of patrons. "The rain, I think." She turned and gazed out at the incessant rain that fell beyond the glass of the door. "Would you like some ganlu?" The question seemed to come from nowhere, and Ulmella's voice became bright and hopeful.

"Ganlu?" Corelle had never heard of ganlu, whatever it might be.

"It is a leaf, crushed up. The Qagrue brought it to Dur. They crush the leaves, then infuse them in hot water. It is quite delicious. I love it."

Corelle had never heard anybody say they loved something other than another person. The idea one could "love" a drink seemed impossible to her. "You love it?"

Ulmella blushed. "That I do. I adore the taste. I drink it all day. I will make us some." She pushed her chair back and dashed behind her counter. Her simple green dress of rough material and simple making accentuated the flare of her hips below a slender waist.

Intrigued, Corelle followed her. It might be inappropriate to walk behind the woman's counter, but the concept of the ganlu fascinated her, and she yearned to watch Ulmella produce it. Some small displeasure that the Qagrue had introduced it whispered to her conscience, but she ignored it in the name of her curiosity.

Ulmella had a pot suspended over a fire, and she wrapped a cloth around the handle of the pot to lift it. Two cups stood on the counter, and she poured some hot water from the pot into each. She returned the pot to the fire and reached into a wooden box she took down from a shelf behind her. She came out with some black flecks in her hand—the leaves, Corelle guessed. She held out her hand toward Corelle, who bent down to smell the crushed leaves. They had a herby smell, pleasant, if a trifle stale. Ulmella tipped the leaves into the cups, a little in each, then used a spoon to stir them around.

She handed one of the cups to Corelle. "Be careful. The water will still be hot." The drink smelled the same as the leaves had, but the steam added a dampness to it. From the outside of the cup, she could tell the water would be too hot to drink, but to her surprise Ulmella sipped at it. "I like it hot." She sounded almost apologetic.

Corelle sipped at it. The water remained far too hot for her, and she felt she had not benefitted from the taste as she gasped and sucked air into her mouth to cool her throat. Ulmella giggled and pointed at her. "I warned you."

"That you did." Corelle joined in the laughter.

"Tell me. What turned that you need this hole cut in your head?"

Corelle hesitated to respond. Ulmella did not need to know everything that had turned in her life, and she wearied of the surprise and doubt the mast tale invoked in others. "I used to be a mariner." Ulmella raised her eyebrows as she sipped at her ganlu. "My ship sank, and some of the wreckage struck my head. The healer thinks some fluid is trapped beneath my skull, and he wishes to release it."

Ulmella nodded. "Can you not carry on despite this injury? Will the body not repair itself over time? You seem… normal." She smiled a shy smile, which Corelle returned.

Corelle placed the cup on the counter. "At times I am fine, and I understand everything, such as now. At other times, I find it difficult to recall my own name. The more stressed I become, the worse the effects, I think."

Ulmella nodded. "We must keep you free of stress, it seems." She sipped again at the ganlu, her free arm wrapped across her stomach as she leaned on the counter with one hip, one foot crossed in front of the other so only its toes touched the floor. Corelle studied her and saw an attractive young woman, thoughtful, it seemed, who ran her own business. Ulmella had defied the tradition and ventured out on her own to forge her own path in life. Corelle respected her commitment, and her sex tingled again as her gaze settled on the hazel eyes that watched her.

Corelle reached up to Ulmella's face and touched the warm, soft skin with the back of her hand. Ulmella tilted her head into the touch, and Corelle took half a step forward so they stood no more than a finger apart. She leaned forward and kissed Ulmella's lips. Still Ulmella did not move away, but Corelle remained hesitant. It would be enjoyable to explore the younger woman's body and drive tomorrow's fear away for a few hours. Ulmella had not asked her to stop, but neither had she shown any true encouragement. Corelle could find no answer in Ulmella's eyes, although they still gazed into her own, filled with warmth.

She pulled her hand away from Ulmella's face, but the younger woman caught it with the hand that had lain across her stomach, then put the cup on the counter and reached behind Corelle's head. As she pulled Corelle forward, her lips parted, and their mouths came together. Ulmella's tongue entered Corelle's mouth, tentative, flavoured by the taste of the ganlu. Her fingers intertwined with Corelle's next to their stomachs, and Corelle slid her other arm around Ulmella's slim waist to hold her against her body.

Corelle's tongue slid into Ulmella's mouth, across her perfect white teeth, and their tongues performed a gentle dance. With a soft, almost inaudible moan, Ulmella released Corelle's hand and raised both her hands to Corelle's face to hold it cupped between them.

Corelle pulled her head back and stared deep into Ulmella's eyes. "Have you lain with a woman before?"

Ulmella lowered her eyes and breathed her reply. "That I have not."

Corelle had suspected as much, but Ulmella seemed to desire some physical pleasure with her, and Corelle in turn ached to feel the woman's hands on her body. "Have you lain with a man?"

Ulmella nodded and raised her eyes again to Corelle's. "Once. I have never even thought about a woman this way before. Something about you…" She sighed. "As soon as you came into the shop, I desired you. Something." Ulmella seemed flustered, and her cheeks flamed red as she lowered her eyes again.

"Do not be embarrassed." Corelle stroked Ulmella's cheek. "You are beautiful."

Ulmella gave a short giggle. "My thanks." Her voice became so quiet, anybody on the other side of the counter might not have heard her.

"Where do you live?"

"I have accommodations here, in the rear of the building. I sleep here sometimes. Other times at my parents' house. They live on the river."

Corelle guessed the younger woman meant her parents' house stood next to the river and not that they lived on a ship or some such. She kissed Ulmella again, more fierce this time, and the younger woman responded in kind. Her tongue whipped around Corelle's mouth, she moaned again, and she pressed herself tight against Corelle.

From the corner of her eye, Corelle saw a figure flit past the shop, and Ulmella seemed to notice it also. She pulled back and turned her head toward the door. "I will close the shop. The bedroom is through there." Ulmella pointed to a door at the back of the shop, and she walked around the counter toward the shop door. Corelle did not move toward the door to Ulmella's accommodation, but she did pick up the cup and take a sip of the ganlu. The pleasant flavour reminded her of Orgel's drink. She wondered if the old woman still lived, but Ulmella returned and took one of her hands. "Come." The young woman pulled Corelle toward the rear of the shop.

Her accommodation consisted of a small parlour with two closed doors off it. A small fireplace stood in one corner of the parlour, an armed chair on either side of it. A small pantry with a basin and pump against the wall opposite the fire, and a round table with two wooden chairs completed the room.

Ulmella opened one of the doors and pulled Corelle through it. A small bed almost filled the tiny space, and she released Corelle's hand, then lay on the bed, her breaths rapid, her cheeks bright red, and her eyes still focused on Corelle's own. She raised her arms toward Corelle. "Show me what it is like to lie with a woman." Corelle knelt on the floor beside the bed.

CHAPTER 6
ULMELLA

Ulmella had told Corelle the truth. Something about the woman who had entered her shop captivated her as soon as she had walked through the door, soaked from head to foot. Her limp, untidy brown hair hung to her shoulders, and water dripped from her onto the shop floor. She wore a cloak, and when she took it off to drape it over a chair, her tunic clung to her body. The nipples of her full breasts stood proud against the saturated cloth of the tunic that clung to them.

She had ordered two cakes, both the same, then sat at a table and ate them. The woman wore an air of sadness, but her eyes never settled anywhere long. They flicked around the shop as if on an unending quest for some item she longed for. That worked to Ulmella's disadvantage as she could not help but stare at the woman, and several times those skittish eyes met her own. They would pause for a heartbeat, then off they would go on their journey around the shop.

Ulmella had offered the woman another cake out of courtesy, but they had struck up a conversation that both horrified and

intrigued her. The thought of a hole cut into the woman's head seemed barbaric, but without it, she might die, she had claimed.

Ulmella had offered her a cup of ganlu as a device to keep her at the shop for longer, since it would be hot and would take time to drink. As it turned, they had not drunk it at all, and now Corelle knelt beside her. She felt an ache between her legs she had never experienced before.

She had lain with a local man, a year before. The relationship had not lasted long, and when it ended, so did Ulmella's sexual encounters. At first, the sex had hurt, and although the pain lessened over time, she took little pleasure from it in the short time it took him to reach fulfilment and squirt his excitement inside her. Ulmella hoped she would enjoy her first time with a woman more than she had with the man, and it might last a little longer.

The experience did not disappoint on either count. They lay together for two hours at the least, and Corelle coaxed excitement from her she scarce believed a person could achieve. Ulmella moaned and screamed as waves of pleasure crashed over her helpless body, but Corelle would not accept that her body could take no more. She drove Ulmella ever higher until she lost all sense of her own existence. She felt clumsy in response but copied some of the things Corelle had done to her, and Corelle seemed to take pleasure from them, her back arched as she cried aloud in satisfaction.

Afterward, they lay in each other's arms, as wet with sweat as Corelle had been from the rain when she had first entered the shop. Ulmella's heart still beat as fast as the flutter of an insect's wings, and she questioned whether she could draw air into her body fast enough to sustain life, so frenetic had their lovemaking been. She stared into Corelle's green eyes; they seemed more at peace now, and could hold Ulmella's gaze for longer. Ulmella stroked Corelle's still damp brown hair and smiled. "My thanks." A warm glow of contentment sang throughout her body.

Corelle snorted and gave a short laugh. "I do not believe anybody has ever thanked me before when I have lain with them."

"My apologies, I..." Ulmella's embarrassment burned her cheeks, but Corelle kissed her forehead.

"It is sweet, in truth."

"Is it always like this? With women, I mean."

Corelle glanced at the ceiling. "It has been for me. I may have been fortunate. The women I have loved have all been..." She fell silent and closed her eyes.

"I am sorry. I did not mean to upset you." Corelle shook her head in silence, and Ulmella longed to change the mood back to the peaceful enjoyment of each other she had swept away with her casual question. "When will you have the hole cut in your head?"

"Tomorrow morning. I should head back to town, in truth. I must be there at the sunrise."

"Oh." The news disappointed Ulmella, who enjoyed the warmth of the other woman's body next to her, the satisfied glow still within her. "Must you leave? The rain still pours from the sky. You could stay here tonight and leave in the morning."

Corelle sucked in a large breath. "It is a long walk." Ulmella sensed reluctance.

"It is not so far." She kissed Corelle's shoulder. "It will not take much longer, I am certain. Where must you go?"

When Corelle explained where the healer's rooms were located, Ulmella felt certain Corelle could reach the man's house in less than half of an hour from the shop. Corelle did not reply, but as her fingers slid between Ulmella's legs again, Ulmella guessed she had won the debate.

They lay in the dark afterward, and Ulmella's thoughts turned again to the ordeal Corelle must face tomorrow. "Are you afraid?"

"That I am, a little. It surprises me, in truth. He tells me there will be pain, but he has some herb to dull it."

Ulmella frowned in the darkness. "Who will tend you afterward? You may be bed-ridden."

Corelle gave a short, almost bitter laugh. "I will tend to myself, my guess. There is nobody else."

Concern nipped at Ulmella's conscience. The woman would have a hole in her head and nobody to care for her. "Will you have some way to keep the hole clean and covered? My brother once broke his leg, and the bandages had to be replaced times without end."

"I know this. I tended somebody once who had broken a leg. No easy task." A sadness in her voice, unmistakeable.

Ulmella could no longer ignore her conscience. "You must stay here. I will tend you."

Corelle turned to face her and lay silent for long moments. "That I cannot. I appreciate the offer, but you have your shop to attend to. I will be fine."

What had she pondered in that silence? What fears ate at her? Ulmella's conscience would not allow her to accept the easy option Corelle had laid before her. "That you will not. I am no pushover, you know. I have an older brother, so do not try to fight me. You will stay here, where I can tend to you."

Corelle's gentle laugh tinkled in the air like a light rain on a window glass. "That you are. A pushover, I mean. This morning I did not know you, but tonight you lie next to me, sated."

"Then stay here while you recover, and you may sate me again, if you wish." She smiled, then realised Corelle could not see her face in the darkness of the room.

"You are kind, and generous, but—"

"I will hear no 'buts.'" Ulmella raised herself up on one elbow and spoke in a stern tone she reserved for sombre occasions. "You cannot care for yourself with a hole in your head. If the wound becomes..." The word she sought flitted from her mind like a young mutton as it plays in a field.

"Infected?"

"Shut up. I knew that." Ulmella had snapped in jest, and she kissed Corelle. "If it becomes infected, you might die. You promised to ravish me again. You cannot die with that promise unfulfilled."

"I made no such promise, but I know when I am defeated." Corelle's laughter filled the darkness.

"It is decided. What time will your hole be finished?"

"I know not. The midday, my guess."

Corelle may not be able to walk. In truth, she seemed not to have thought the thing through in the least. It all sounded chaotic, and Ulmella despised chaos and lack of organisation. "I will close the shop early and come for you. I will bring my father's carriage and bring you back here."

"Your father has a carriage?"

"That he does. He owns a tally house." Beside her, Corelle stiffened. "What is it?"

"Nothing. My apologies. Some time ago, tally houses in some of the cities created a… difficulty in my life that cost me a great deal. The ones in Ort played no part in it, but the memory came to me."

"I am sorry to hear of your problems, but you need not fear. My father is a fine man. When these wretched Qagrue came…." Ulmella hushed herself. She knew next to nothing about Corelle and must watch her tongue.

"I despise them." Corelle had a quiet menace in her voice, her words. "They cost Dur some fine men. I knew Ibie, and I still grieve him."

"You knew the Portreeve? My father celebrated when Raolos became the Bailiff, although they competed at the docks. My father said Raolos always operated with honour. He even refused to have his own name on the sign over his tally house from his sense of fair play."

"That he did. I knew him and his wife. I miss them both." Corelle sniffed as though she tried to hold back her tears.

"Let us talk no more of these sad events. Tomorrow you will walk to the healer, and I will collect you after the midday. Where are your belongings?"

"At The Dockside Inn."

Ulmella knew the inn. "That horrible place? Now I know I do the right thing. You would be certain to pick up an infection in that filthy inn."

"You are a bully. Do you know that?"

"I have an older brother." Ulmella laughed, comfortable with the decision they had taken. "You should sleep. You have a big day tomorrow." They fell silent, and the exertions of their lovemaking soon carried Ulmella away into a contented sleep.

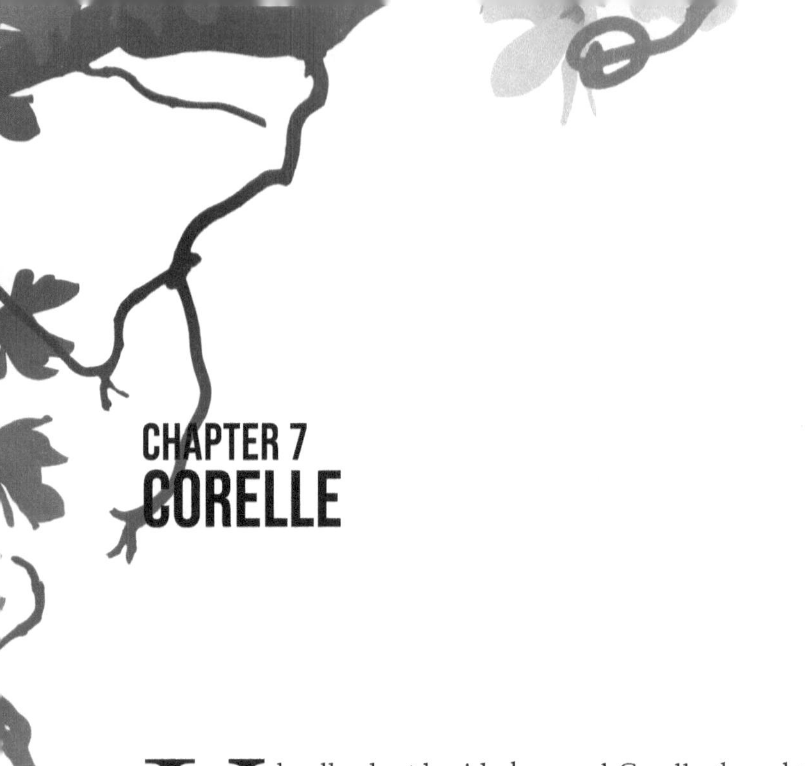

CHAPTER 7
CORELLE

Ulmella slept beside her, and Corelle thought back on the conversation that had resulted in her agreement to stay with the young woman after the Qagrue healer cut the hole in her head. Ulmella had the right of it; self-care in the inn would be less effective than the care of a virtual stranger. If Ulmella and her father's carriage appeared after the trappaneesh, Corelle would return to the shop with her.

Corelle drifted off to sleep, but the next day's events would not wait until morning. She dreamt she lay on a table while hands cut holes into her, her head at first, then her body when little remained of her head.

Ulmella woke before her in the morning and demanded further satisfaction before they rose, despite Corelle's tiredness from the nightmare-riven sleep. At last, Corelle set off for the healer's house, one of yesterday's cakes in her hands as breakfast. She left Ulmella in the shop, busy in preparation for the new day. The rain had stopped, and Corelle hoped the shop might be busier. Ulmella had sent Corelle off with the cake, a kiss, and a promise to be at the healer's house as soon after the midday as possible.

Corelle followed the directions Ulmella had given her. As the shop owner had said, she had walked for less than half of an hour when she reached the house. Her heart hammered in her breast, her nerves so stretched, she feared she might fetch up. She must have lost her mind, and she heaved in lengthy breaths as she wondered whether she should turn and walk back to the shop. Another day of Ulmella's firm body seemed a brighter prospect than the healer's house promised.

Corelle found the courage to knock on the door, and the same woman opened it. Corelle sat in the same chair as she waited, and when Romobreckh Sumbrid Akh Eckh came out for her, she followed him into the room. He asked her to lie on the table but did not ask her to remove any of her clothing. He asked how she felt, and she admitted her nerves shook her. He smiled and told her not to worry, which worried her the more.

He occupied himself with some tools and equipment for a time, and the woman came into the room. Romobreckh turned to Corelle. "We will strap you to the table, if you do not mind."

"Why?" It seemed unnecessary to Corelle.

"We have a herb drink for you that should numb much of the pain, but I cannot guarantee you will feel none, when I cut through the skin on the top of your head in particular. If you writhe in agony, or your courage fails you, and you move, the effects could be disastrous."

Corelle blinked as tears stung her eyes but gave her head a miserable nod. "If you think it best." The explanation worried her more than the straps themselves.

"So. We must cut off your hair, I fear. If a hair is introduced into the wound, there could be problems." The entire process seemed steeped in danger, but Corelle nodded again, and the woman cut at her hair. It had grown to her shoulders while she had been in Ryl, but a shaved head would be nothing new. She would hide it beneath a kerchief, as she had when she had been a mariner aboard the ships.

When the woman had finished, Romobreckh inspected Corelle's scalp and spoke quiet words to the woman, who carried out more work with the sharp knife she held. His standards had been more rigorous than hers, it seemed. The woman handed Corelle a cup, and she drank the liquid in it. "What is in the drink?" They helped her lie on the table as she asked the question.

"Some herbs from my land that do not grow here, mandrake and opium among them, and solanum, which can be found here. They should soon take effect." They covered Corelle with a bedsheet as the room swam before her eyes. Her stomach roiled, and she feared she might fetch up on the table as she closed her eyes and battled the nausea. When she opened them, she could not see the woman or Romobreckh, but she felt considerable pain on the top of her head despite the drink. The drink and the pain overwhelmed her, and the lanterns suspended above her merged into one brilliant light, agony to her eyes. She closed them against the brightness of the light, and when she opened them again, the lanterns had been blown out.

The room still swam, and the nausea had not lessened. Corelle had a headache and a ferocious pain at the top of her head she did not think she could bear. She squeezed her eyes shut and tried to move, but straps held her tight. The woman's face loomed above her when she opened her eyes again. She peered into Corelle's face and asked how she felt. Her voice sounded strange, as though she had spoken from a long distance away, and her voice echoed through a series of hills and valleys. Corelle tried to say she felt terrible, but the words would not form on her tongue.

The woman left, but Romobreckh appeared a few heartbeats later. He also peered down at her, and he turned and spoke to somebody she could not see. Hands fiddled with the straps that held her down, and the woman and Romobreckh helped her to sit up. The bedsheet fell away from her, and it seemed she had fetched up onto it. The woman pressed a cup to her mouth. Corelle's throat and mouth felt as dry as sand, and she gulped the drink down. It had not been water, but she did not care as it slaked her thirst.

They laid her down again but did not fasten the straps. She wanted to ask whether they had finished, but her throat had become so dry, she could force no words from it, so she closed her eyes and fell asleep. When she woke, she still lay on the table. She moved her head to look around, though white-hot streaks of agony shot through her at the movement. She saw nobody in the room, so she tried to call out. A feeble croak squeezed from her tortured throat, and the woman appeared a few moments later.

"How do you feel?"

"Dead." Corelle's voice sounded little more than a rasp, even to her.

The woman laughed. "You are not dead; you can believe me. Are you in pain?"

"That I am. Agony."

"Do you have somebody who will come for you and take you home?"

"That I do, I think." Corelle hoped… she could not remember the name of the woman from the shop. After all else, Corelle hoped she would come, whatever her name might be.

The woman smiled and left, and some moments later Romobreckh Sumbrid Akh Eckh came into the room. "You are awake. That is good. The procedure went well. Much fluid and blood came from the trappaneesh. There is a strong chance we may have eased your condition a great deal. I will give you some herbs to take away with you. Infuse them in water each morning and night and drink a cup. I have scribed the instructions in your language. You may forget otherwise. Keep your scalp covered as much as you can, and always keep it clean. It is possible some bone may re-grow, but the bones of the skull do not regenerate as much as in other parts of the body. I may have said this already to you, but it does not hurt to manage your expectations. You may have a hole in your skull for the remainder of your life."

"My thanks." His words only increased the furious agony in her head, and she could not concentrate. She hoped the woman would come and collect her soon.

"Do not attempt to move overmuch for some time. At least ten days. Do not bang your head, and keep the wound covered as it heals."

He had said ten days, not a tenday. Corelle wondered if the Qagrue used a different method to number the passage of the days. Why did Durfolk say a sevenday or a tenday, but not a twelveday? Why did she care, when to even think about it increased the severity of the agony in her head? She nodded once in response to his instructions.

"Do you have somebody to take care of you? There are dressings on your head, and they will need to be changed often for at least seven days before they can be removed."

"That I do. She comes for me at the midday."

He laughed. "It is well after the midday already. I will send a man to see if she is outside."

Corelle could not believe the day had progressed so far already. The drinks must have put her to sleep for longer than she had imagined. What if—she could still not recall the woman's name— had already given up and gone home? Corelle doubted she could walk back to the inn alone. The room swam, and Romobreckh Sumbrid Akh Eckh turned round and round before her as though he rode on the rim of a carriage wheel.

He left, and Corelle sighed as she wondered when she might know whether the hole in her head had achieved what he wished. One morning, she might wake up and realise everything had made sense for so long, the chirurgeon had achieved what he had set out to do. If it had done nothing, she imagined she would experience the confusion again the moment the effect of the herbs wore off.

Romobreckh returned to the room, the woman from the shop with him. The woman smiled at her, but it seemed a sad, rueful smile. "You look terrible." The woman gave a small laugh.

"Why did she laugh if I look so terrible?" Corelle found it a strange reaction.

Romobreckh spoke to the woman. "My man will help her out to your carriage. Thank you for your help, Ulmella." Corelle remembered her name at last. Ulmella.

"I could not leave such an old friend to suffer alone." They had known each other little more than a day, but the foolish woman described her as an old friend. Things made no sense, and Corelle gave up. She wanted to go to sleep again.

Romobreckh and Ulmella left the room, and another man entered. He helped Corelle to her feet, draped her arm across his broad shoulders, and helped her from the room and out of the house. Ulmella's carriage stood at the end of the path, a small, open-topped carriage with two benches that faced each other and a driver's bench at the front. The man helped Corelle into it, and she lay down on one of the benches, her feet on the carriage floor. She heard Romobreckh and Ulmella in conversation and pulled herself upright again.

"You have not mentioned payment." It cost her to voice the words as her head continued to throb in agony.

Romobreckh and Ulmella turned toward her, and he waved a hand. "Do not worry on it. A favour for Karaftaraluq Sumbrid Akh Aluq."

Corelle lay down again, too weak and confused to argue the point. She closed her eyes until the carriage jerked forward. Ulmella sat on the driver's bench and drove the single horse. Corelle's eyes closed again, and she slept.

CHAPTER 8
CORELLE

Corelle jerked awake again as the carriage stopped. "Here we are." Ulmella turned to look down on Corelle. "I will unlock the door, then return for you. You will have to walk a little here, I fear. I do not have the strength of the healer's man." Corelle closed her eyes and waited for Ulmella to return, and they struggled into the shop. Corelle had taken no more than two steps before she became exhausted, and Ulmella grunted and grappled with her to prevent a fall. At last, Corelle lay in Ulmella's bed as her breaths heaved from her. Ulmella gazed down on her, a smile on her lips but concern in her eyes. "Sleep a while if you can. I must return father's carriage." Ulmella leaned down and kissed Corelle's forehead.

When Corelle woke again, the room had turned dark, and Ulmella lay beside her. The younger woman's steady, rhythmic breaths suggested she slept, and Corelle marvelled she had not awoken when the young woman had come to bed. She battled a desperate thirst, and though it bothered her to wake Ulmella, she must. "Ulmella." She shook the woman and croaked at her. "Ulmella."

"What?" Ulmella sounded sleepy at first, then she snapped upright. "Is something wrong?"

"I am thirsty. I am sorry."

"I have water here. He said you might be thirsty. Wait a moment." Corelle heard noises that sounded familiar, but she had no strength to recall what they might be. Light sprang from a lantern, Ulmella slid from the bed for a few heartbeats, then she held a cup to Corelle's lips. With some effort, Corelle propped herself up on her elbows and guzzled the water as Ulmella tilted the cup for her.

"More please." Ulmella refilled the cup. Corelle quaffed most of the water in the cup, then lay down again. "My thanks." She believed she could drink the Alc dry, but the water had helped.

"Do you need anything else?"

"Sleep." Corelle took her own advice.

The next day went by in a blur. Corelle slept much of the day and could not contain her surprise each time she awoke. She had slept for the better part of two days, but her appetite for it appeared undiminished.

Ulmella popped into the bedroom from time to time and fussed at her. The first time she changed the bandage on Corelle's head, she gasped in horror at the sight of the wound. In the evening, Ulmella spooned some broth into her, and it warmed Corelle and seemed to return some strength to her. "Does it look bad?"

"That it does." Ulmella nodded in confirmation. "Your flesh has been closed, but there is blood and a vast bruise. It looks horrible."

"My thanks for this care. I can never repay you."

"You do not need to. I could not abandon you. Do not forget your promise." Ulmella winked, and Corelle managed a weak smile.

As Ulmella gazed on her, concerned, Corelle could scarce believe her luck. "I mean it. Few would have gone to the lengths you have for a stranger. In truth, had I the strength, I would be suspicious of your motives."

"You need not be. You are in need, and I can help. I am sure anybody would do the same."

Corelle knew from bitter experience most people would not, but she said nothing. "My thanks. May I have some water please?"

Ulmella poured a cup of water from her pitcher and helped Corelle drink it. "Can I ask you something?" The young woman's earnest gaze pierced Corelle.

"Of course." Corelle would not answer most questions with the truth—how could she? She would not deny Ulmella the chance to ask, nonetheless. Such a lack of gratitude would be disgraceful.

"I saw a fan in your boot. Why do you carry it there?"

Of all the questions Corelle could not give an honest answer to, this one must be the hardest. She could lie or fashion some half-truth, but she could not reveal the true reason, so she took Ulmella's slender wrist in her hand. "A dear friend gave it to me. I cannot bear to be parted from it."

Ulmella smiled. "I meant why do you carry it in your boot rather than in a vanity bag? You have lived a different life from me, I see that from your body, and do not seem the sort of woman to carry a fan." She glanced downward, and her cheeks flushed bright red. "I am sorry I asked."

Corelle did not see how her body would suggest anything about her life, then she realised. The scars. Her body bore many scars from the multiple times she had been stabbed by various Guild members. "That I have." Once more, her past had caught up with her and threatened these few moments of joy she had found at the rear of the cake shop. She tired of it, but how could she make it stop? There could be no rest until she killed Krage, but how could she explain that to this gentle, remarkable young woman who may never have left Ort in her life? "I have lost much and have had to fight to keep what I had. I have not always been successful."

"I have lived a sheltered life." Ulmella smiled and stood to close the shutter on the small window. "It grows late, and you look tired. I must rise early and bake in the morning. Let us sleep."

Ulmella took the bowl and pitcher from the room as Corelle lay in the bed and sighed. Would her past continue to plague her and forever require explanations she had no words for? Ulmella returned with the pitcher, pulled her dress over her head. She wore the same green dress she had worn on the day Corelle had first come to the shop. "Those small scars on your head." Ulmella slid into the bed as she spoke. "The healer said I must watch you. They suggest you have hurt yourself."

"That I have." Ulmella snuggled close to her, her arms about her. Her embrace comforted Corelle even as memories tortured her. "I lost somebody I loved, and it almost destroyed me. I harmed myself despite the efforts of good friends, Raolos among them, to prevent it. I became so bereft when she died, I no longer wished to live." Ulmella turned and blew out the lantern before she snuggled into Corelle again. "Ulmella, I will not harm you. I swear on the life of the woman I mentioned I will never hurt you. I would die to defend you, if needs must, but I will not harm you."

"I believe you." Ulmella's lips brushed Corelle's cheek. "You are tired. Sleep."

Over the next days, Corelle found she could sit up in the bed, and she slept less. From time to time, Ulmella came to spend a few moments with her and brighten her boredom. Corelle felt far stronger, and when Ulmella said one night she had closed the shop for the day and would heat some broth, Corelle asked to leave the bed and sit by the fire. Ulmella made her wait while she lit it, then helped her to a chair and wrapped a blanket around her. Once she had set a pot over the fire, she pulled a wooden chair next to Corelle, placed the cup and pitcher of water on it, then sat next to her and held her hand.

The flames danced before Corelle and soothed her. She reached up and rubbed the bandage on her head, the first time she had touched it. It gave a little in the middle, and she guessed that must be where the hole lay. They chatted for a time, and Ulmella told her how she came to own the shop. She had longed to operate her own shop where she sold cakes she baked herself. The idea had been a passion for most of her life, not unlike making had been for Corelle, it seemed.

Her parents had bought the shop when the previous occupant became too old to continue to work, and they had turned it into what she ran today. Success soon came, and Ulmella's reputation spread throughout the quarter. Even the local Qagrue called in most days to buy her cakes, and she had learned to speak their language well enough to make polite conversation. She sold them her cakes, but she had little time for them and wished they would return to their own land.

Corelle fascinated her with tales of her making and the journey aboard The Ictharelian. To her surprise and joy, Corelle found someone who found the tale of the mast plausible, but above all Ulmella wanted to hear of the giants. Like most people who had never seen them, she found it impossible to grasp their true size, and Corelle had to repeat many stories of their playful antics far out in the deep seas.

Corelle skirted the story of the Guild, and while she told her of Deineike, she blamed the head injury on her fall aboard The Friend-ship. Ulmella found the similarity between their injuries difficult to fathom. She wiped Corelle's tears from her face and also wished the Qagrue healer, with his hole in the head method, had been available to save Deineike.

The evening progressed until Ulmella would tolerate Corelle's protests no more and busied her back to bed despite Corelle's assurances she had not grown tired. They sat together in the bed while Ulmella told her how to make the cakes Deineike had been so passionate about and promised to bring her one the next day.

The lantern out, they lay together, and Corelle slid her hand down to Ulmella's bush. The young woman loosed a contented sigh as she parted her legs, and Corelle coaxed her to several peaks of excitement before they went to sleep. Pain spasmed through her head, but she ignored it as her fingers strove to repay Ulmella's kindness.

Corelle lost track of the days, but her strength returned with each day, and the pain diminished in equal measure. At times, she wandered out into the shop to watch Ulmella serve her customers. The young woman had an easy way with people, clearly suited to the life she had chosen, though few of those whose face Ulmella brought a smile to with her idle conversation would realise how kind she was. Few would have done what she had done for Corelle, and fewer would realise the generosity the woman had shown.

One day, soon after the midday, Ulmella came into the small parlour, handed Corelle a cake, and sat with her for a time. Nobody sat in the shop or stood at the counter, and she loosed a tired sigh as she took off her shoes and rubbed her feet. She said two of the Qagrue soldiers had been in the shop earlier, and she had overheard them talk about more ships that planned to sail from their land. Corelle sighed, miserable they sent even more of their people to her land, but Ulmella corrected her.

"They will not sail here. It is not the same tribe. I think that is the word they used. They are not a Duchy as Dur is, but a collection of different groups of people they call tribes. I have wandered from the story." She laughed and blushed. "This other tribe will sail for Steinlund, bent on the invasion of that land, it seems. Why they cannot stay in their own… Are you all right?"

The cake had fallen into Corelle's lap. The Qagrue intended to invade Steinlund? Unthinkable. *Gaish*. She must warn him. More, she must warn the Steinlund people. These invaders brought nothing good to Steinlund. "When do they sail? Did they say?"

"That they did not. What is wrong?"

"I have a friend in Steinlund. I cannot allow him to be placed in danger when they arrive. I must warn him."

"I see." Ulmella frowned. "I have parch. Do you have his address? We will scribe a letter to him, and I will take it to the couriers at once."

That would not suffice. His letter lay in her pack, still in her room in The Dockside Inn, but even if she had it here, she could not guarantee it would reach him in time, if at all. The entire land would be caught unawares, as Dur had been. Corelle could not stand by and allow their Duke and Portreeves, if they had such, to be slain as they had been in her own land. "I must sail there and warn them."

Raopul's face pushed into her mind. She had vowed to search for him and tell him of his father's death. Of course, she had no idea where he might be, and Gaish's situation seemed more important. She rubbed the fingers of one hand against her thumb in frustration as she pondered the dilemma.

Ulmella interrupted her thoughts. "Corelle, you cannot travel yet. You are—" With that, the bell above the shop door rang, and Ulmella tutted. She went into the shop, but Corelle could not hear what the customer had wanted. The bell rang again, and Ulmella returned to the parlour. "I have closed the shop for a time, so we are not interrupted again. You cannot sail to Steinlund. You are still far too ill."

"I must. I am stronger already, and I will grow stronger as I sail. I cannot abandon him. I cannot abandon them to the fate that befell us." Corelle's distress grew the more she considered the situation, and Ulmella dropped to her knees before her and threw her arms about her.

She turned her head to one side and laid it on Corelle's breasts. "You are too ill. You cannot do this. I know it burns you to accept it—"

"I do not accept it. I must leave and warn them. Who else will do so? You cannot. It must be me." Corelle felt the wetness of Ulmella's tears through her tunic. "I am sorry. I am forever grateful for all you have done for me, but I must go."

Ulmella's tearful eyes stared up into her face. "So be it. Before you leave, you must keep your promise."

"I made no such promise." Despite Corelle's protests, Ulmella led her into the bedroom.

CHAPTER 9
CORELLE

Ulmella walked to her parents' house and returned an hour later with the carriage. She drove Corelle to the inn. They exchanged few words, but Corelle saw the signs. Had she stayed much longer, Ulmella would say the words that would condemn her. Ulmella pulled the carriage up outside the inn and went inside with Corelle's key. When she returned with the pack, she had paid the innkeep for the rent of the room. She clicked her tongue and shook the reins, and the horse walked forward. Only two three-masters stood at the docks, and neither of them travelled to Steinlund. Corelle found a two-master headed to Alcmouth, where she believed more ships would depart for Gaish's land.

The master's charge for the voyage to Alcmouth would cost almost all her coin, and to her dismay Ulmella offered to pay for it. If anything, Corelle thought she should pay the young woman for the care and attention she had lavished on her, but she needed to reach Steinlund and could not work yet, so she had little option but to accept. She must hope she could obtain further passage once she reached Alcmouth.

The two women embraced on the dockside for some time. Ulmella urged Corelle to find some member of the crew to care for her bandages, gave her the herbs, and wished her luck. With one last tearful kiss, Ulmella climbed into the driver's seat and drove the carriage away. Corelle watched her disappear from sight, her emotions in tatters. They might have been content with one another in the little shop, and Corelle might even have helped Ulmella with it in time, but that dream now lay in pieces. The Qagrue had seen to that, but Krage remained accountable for their arrival in Dur in the first place. Raopul must also be sacrificed to Gaish's safety. The lad must be well into his teenyears by now and would have to learn of his father's death by some other means. More important tasks lay ahead of Corelle.

She wiped at her eyes with the back of a hand, certain she would never see Ulmella again, then trudged up the ramp and went to her cabin, where she lay on the bunk, too shattered to rise, and the ship slid out into the river and headed south. The master arranged for one of his officers to check on her and change her bandages, and she ventured out of the cabin only for food, water, and hygiene needs. Every day she drank a brew made from the herbs in accordance with the parch Romobreckh Sumbrid Akh Eckh had given to Ulmella.

When the ship docked in Alcmouth, Corelle faced two urgent problems. She needed a ship bound for Steinlund, and she needed a way to secure passage on that vessel. In the Master's Offices, the clerk told her only Steinlund and Dur ships sailed there for the most part, but at times a southern ship might combine the journeys if a cargo could be found.

Corelle trudged along the dock and checked the ships tied up there. To her delight, she saw a Steinlund sigil on a three-masted ship. Unbelievable fortune, but it only solved one of her problems. Thanks to Gaish, she spoke Steinlund well enough, and it did not differ much from Dur's own language, in truth. Her head aflame with agony, she walked up the ramp and sought out the master. She debated whether to explain the reason for her voyage and throw himself on her mercy but decided that might not be the best way to carry the news to Steinlund and opted instead for the use of her fame.

"My name is Yilmay." His face told her he recognised the name. "I sailed on the voyage that proved Ictharelian is a globe, with a good friend of mine, Gaishkantah. He comes from your land."

"I know both your names." He favoured her with a grand smile. "How may I help you?"

"I long to see my friend, but I find myself in unfortunate circumstances. As you can see, I am injured." She pointed to her head. "The cost of my recovery has drained me of my coin."

"Do not fear. You are welcome aboard my ship, and you need no coin to travel with us. You are famous, as is Gaishkantah. Will you entertain us with some stories of your voyage in the evenings?"

"That I will, with pleasure." She had rolled the dice and had avoided ones. Now she must hope she could reach Gaish in time.

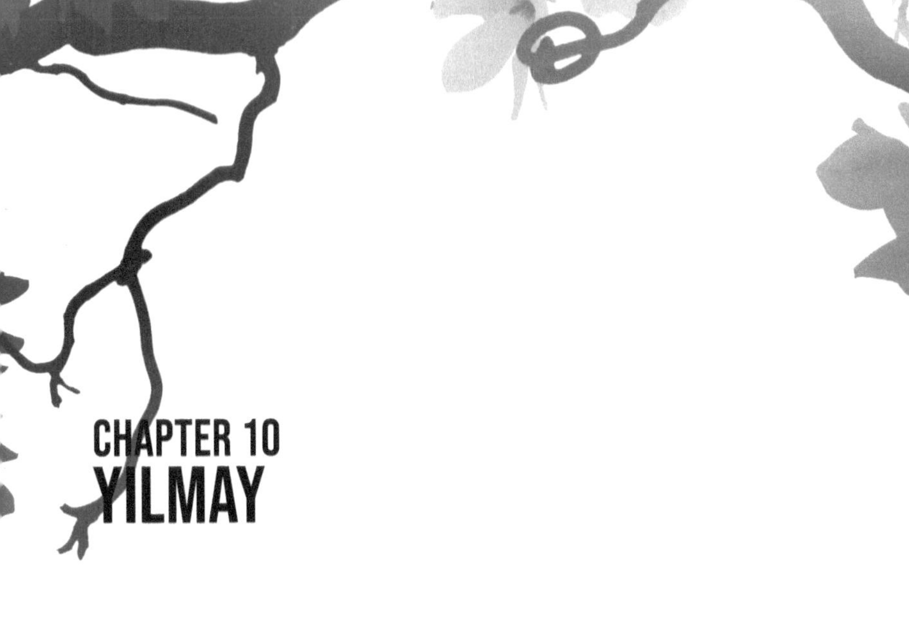

CHAPTER 10
YILMAY

The master told her the voyage would take eight to nine days. That would be adequate time for her to recover her strength, she believed, if she took things easy. She would miss Ulmella's care and her body, but Gaish and Steinlund depended on her. Whether Steinlund could fight off the Qagrue, she did not know, but she owed it to them to warn them, at the least.

Aided by the herbs and the help of a crew member, Yilmay found the journey tolerable, and her strength improved every day. Each night, the crew badgered her for a story about one of the lands she had visited. They had no interest in the giants, for they had all seen them, but tales of the size of Argoya, or the naked people of the village in Illfarlen captivated them. The tale of the injury from the animal in Tryngelk needed to be retold twice at the least, and she had all but run out of original tales when the crew told her they would arrive the next day.

The ship would dock in Juustein, the capital city of Steinlund. Yilmay's scalp itched without end, and she hoped it meant her flesh healed beneath the bandages. Her hair had already grown out a

little, and her scalp felt stubbly when she ran the palm of her hand across it. She had next to no coin and often wondered why she had set out on such a reckless plan while she had not yet recovered from the trappaneesh. Much of the time, her thoughts flitted to the bed behind the shop, where Ulmella's body writhed in ecstasy beneath her hands. Instead, she slept in a bunk in a cabin full of mariners and would wake up far from home and with little idea of how to find Gaish.

She wondered at the way Ulmella filled her thoughts rather than Vamma. She had been prepared to spend her life with Vamma, but whenever despondency or loneliness afflicted her now, Ulmella came to mind. Did she resent Vamma because she had left her in Ryl? She did not think so; she could not blame Vamma for her actions. Yilmay had been in a poor state of mind at that time. She shook her head; Ulmella or Vamma, it mattered little. She had turned her back on them both.

A few mariners sat around in the cabin. Two of them played a game she had not seen before in all her travels. It involved small tiles with two sets of dots painted on them, one in each half of the tile. The objective of the game seemed simple enough. Each player laid one of their tiles next to the other, but the number of painted dots in one half of the tile must match the number of dots painted on the tile the new one sat against. If a player had no tile with the correct number of dots, they rapped their knuckles on the table, and they forfeit their turn. As the player laid one tile on the table, they took another from a pool of tiles face down between the player. If a player played all their tiles before the other, and none were left in the spare pool, they were the winner.

The game ended, and the winner smiled as the other mariners praised his play. The praise for the winner amused Yilmay, since it seemed nothing more than luck as to whether a player picked up a tile that matched from the pool, but some skill might lie in the way the tiles were laid as the game progressed. She had not played, so she could not know what skill might be required.

Yilmay took Gaish's letter from her pack and sat on a bunk next to an older mariner. She asked if he knew how she could travel to the place it mentioned. He explained the city of Karnstein lay to the east of Juustein. It had a small port, though few ships sailed there other than the occasional supply ship that took food, clothing, letters and such once or twice each pass. Beyond that, he had little knowledge of the area and suggested the address might mean Gaish's home lay beyond the city in the agricultural lands to the north.

Once they arrived, she would check when the next supply ship might leave. If it sailed soon, she might try to obtain passage aboard it. If not… She had no plan for "if not." With little coin for a horse and no idea how far the ride would be, and in her still frail condition, she must roll the dice on the ship.

Her ship arrived in Juustein less than an hour before the midday, and she thanked the master for her passage. He wished her well and thanked her for the stories. He said some of the crew had enjoyed the stories so much, they had complained when they were on watch and might miss one. Some had even tried to slip away unnoticed to eavesdrop. Corelle and the master laughed together, and she wandered down to the deck as the mariners pulled the ramp into position. Many of them patted her on the back and thanked her for the tales, and a few of them gave her a small amount of coin as they wished her well in her search for her friend.

As Corelle walked from the ramp, she reflected on the bond between mariners. She doubted those who had not sailed could appreciate it. She had done no work aboard the ship, but the crew knew she had been a mariner, and one of much fame. They had welcomed her in a way she had not been welcomed in other groups or places; she was one of them and had felt comfortable among them even though she had no appetite to return to the mariner's life. The giant that had smashed The Ictharelian beneath her had changed her forever, and she could never again sail for a living. She had enjoyed the friendship of the crew, nonetheless, and she felt a twinge of sadness as she walked away from the ship.

Once she found the Master's Offices, she learned he named himself Dockmaster here in Juustein, and his Offices stood in a far corner of the docks. As she walked, she took in the strange skyline of the city and the docks before her, which bustled with activity. The city looked larger than Alcmouth, though not as big as Tanasttra, the largest city she had encountered on the Torr Sea.

The Dockmaster's Offices stood between two buildings that resembled tally houses, both with large double doors at the front and crates, barrels, and bales stacked in neat rows outside them. The Dockmaster worked from a one-storey wooden building with a bright red roof. Inside the door, Yilmay found a small area enclosed by a wooden counter. There were four desks beyond the counter, and a person sat at each, three men and a woman, busy with whatever work they performed. Given the unpredictable nature of dock work, it surprised Yilmay the Dockmaster would need four people to manage his Offices, but she knew nothing of Steinlund, so she kept her opinion to herself.

One of the four, a young woman with straw-yellow hair, stood and wished her a good morning as she came to the counter.

Yilmay brought a cheery smile to her face as she replied. "Good morning. I hope you can help me. When will the next supply ship leave for Karnstein please?"

"Please wait a heartbeat." Yilmay had never heard the expression before. It seemed unlikely the woman could find the information in a heartbeat unless she knew it already, and so it proved. Yilmay counted off her heartbeats as the woman returned to her desk and studied some papers. Although Yilmay prided herself on her ability to scribe and count, she lost track of her heartbeats after sixty-three. The woman's estimate had been well wide of the mark, as Yilmay had thought it would be.

At last, the woman returned. "It leaves in five days."

Neither bad nor good news, Yilmay decided. It might have been two tendays, which would have been too long to wait. On the other hand, she feared five days' wait in Juustein would be more than her meagre amount of coin could run to. What choice did she have? "Is there any other way to reach Karnstein before the supply ship leaves?"

The woman wrinkled her nose as she considered Yilmay's question. "I know of none. I am sorry."

"Fishboat." A man to Corelle's left had spoken, and the woman turned to him as he continued. "She could see if any fishboat heads that way. They sometimes go there for the makkrel."

The woman appeared confused. "Why do they not catch the makkrel closer to Juustein?" The man shrugged at her question. Yilmay doubted she could be more confused. She guessed the makkrel would be some kind of fish, but why would fishmen sail so far to catch fish?

Another man responded to the woman's question. "Too many boats. Less fishboats in Karnstein."

"Fewer." The first man again. Anger boiled inside Yilmay, and she reminded herself she must control it in this strange land. She knew nothing of their customs.

"Fewer. Less. All the same." The second man laughed.

"Why are there fewer in Karnstein?" The third man had decided to join the conversation. At this rate, Yilmay might need to ask when the next-but-one supply ship sailed, as she might still be in the Dockmaster's Offices in five days while the clerks debated the fishboat dilemma.

"Fewer people, of course." The blonde woman replied this time, and the third man tilted his chin upward and made a noise that sounded like, "Aaah."

"Pardon me." Yilmay saw an opportunity as they all drew breath to continue the debate. They all turned to look at her. "Where might I find a fishboat and make enquiries about Karnstein?"

"In Karnstein." At the second man's reply, all four of them collapsed into laughter that took a considerable time to subside. Yilmay clenched her teeth and thrust her hands deep into her pockets far from her fan.

"Come, I will point you in the right direction." The first man seemed ready to help, though tears of laughter still ran down his face. He rose, then appeared to recall the jest. "Karnstein." A fresh wave of boisterous laughter broke out.

At that, another man entered through a door in the rear of the building. He wore a bright blue tunic with some insignia on it. Yilmay hoped the Dockmaster had heard the laughter and intended to reprimand his wayward staff, and his first words appeared to confirm her suspicion.

"What goes on here?"

"She asked where she could find a fishboat to catch makkrel in Karnstein." Yilmay had forgotten which of the men played what part in the jest, but it did not matter; she despised them all. She tried to protest he had misspoken about her request, but he had not finished. "Larrishkantah said, 'Karnstein.'" The Dockmaster looked stunned for a heartbeat, then folded over and roared with laughter, which set the other four off again.

Yilmay fumed. The jest had not even been that funny in her opinion. She enjoyed a good jest as much as anybody, even if it came at her expense, but this one had not been as funny as these people made it appear. The man she thought had made the original jest had his head on his desk and pounded a fist on the desktop as he howled with laughter.

At that moment, to her relief, the door opened, and a man entered. Another customer, and this one not the object of the jest.

They must compose themselves and help her now. "What is so funny?" The newcomer's smile suggested that, unlike Yilmay, he might already have been affected by the mirth that rolled around the office. The Dockmaster explained the jest between bellows of laughter, though he had to pause several times. Yilmay could not have articulated her disappointment as the newcomer staggered back against the wall and joined in the laughter. If anything, he found it funnier than the other five, as he banged at the wall behind him with the flats of both hands.

Yilmay surrendered, pulled the door open, and stomped out of the office. She would find the fishboats herself, curse them. Screams of hilarity rang in her ears as she walked away, and a fresh, louder chorus broke out. She guessed they had found her departure even funnier than the jest. Buffoons. She almost hoped the Qagrue would hang them all once they arrived, although guilt consumed her as the thought entered her mind. She passed dockworkers who stood and stared at the building, laughter on their own lips even though they had no idea what they laughed at. Laughter spread like the most vicious disease, it seemed.

CHAPTER 11
YILMAY

O nce she had passed beyond earshot of the office, she stopped a man to ask where she might find the fishboats. If he replied, "Karnstein," she vowed to kill him, but he pointed down the dock and gave her directions that meant she would leave what he described as the "Commercial" area of the docks and take a street to the docks where the fishboats came and went.

Corelle thanked him and set off. His directions proved reliable, and before long she saw many fishboats as they bobbed at the dock, some of them tied to one another up to three deep out into the water. She pressed on and soon stood at the edge of the dock, but when she looked about for some sign of activity, she saw nothing. A small building stood off to one side of the dock area, wooden and in sore need of fresh paint, so she walked toward it.

When she pulled the door open, the smell of fish, already strong, almost overpowered her. She doubted she could abide to be inside the room with the door closed, but a voice called out from inside. "Hello?"

An old man walked into view, dressed in a blue tunic and outrageous, oversized trousers that appeared to be held up by straps across his shoulders. The trousers glistened, and Yilmay guessed they had been coated in some substance that caused the reflections that came from them. "Hello there. I hope you can help me."

"Come in my dear." She already felt nauseous from the smell and did not accept the invitation. Her ruin would be assured if she became trapped in the building with that smell.

"I am fine here, my thanks. I hope I can find a fishboat that sails to Karnstein in the next day or two. I need to obtain passage." She had one objective here, and it did not involve death at the hands of the stench of fish, so she saw no purpose in small talk.

He looked thoughtful for a number of moments. "Some do sail there, it is true. I know of none that leave soon though."

"Orlikksin." The word had come from somebody Corelle could not see inside the building.

"You say?" The man at the door turned to his left.

"I think I heard him say, know?" Yilmay wondered why the disembodied voice had said "no" at the end of the sentence. Some quaint local custom, she imagined, like endless laughter at the expense of polite strangers.

"Ask him, then." The old man turned back to Yilmay. "Orlikksin. He lives up aways. Blue door." He came out of the building and pointed toward a cluster of buildings in the distance at the top of a slight rise, four or five streets away.

Yilmay frowned. "There are no other blue doors but his?" The directions seemed too vague for her to have any chance to locate this man.

The man laughed, and Yilmay groaned inside and wondered what jest she had missed. "There are lots of blue doors, dear, but only one says 'Orlikksin' on it." He smiled. "He might go to Karnstein soon, know?"

"My thanks." Against her better instincts, she kept her voice cheery and ignored the peculiar habit that led them to add "no" to the ends of their sentences. She set off at once, desperate to be away from the fish smell, and made her way toward the houses the man had pointed to. To her surprise, she realised every door had a name painted on it. It must be a Steinlund tradition designed to make it easier to find everybody.

As she trudged up the rise, she wondered about the wisdom of the plan. The fish smell from the building had been so powerful, she had been certain she could not have survived it for more than a few heartbeats. It would be foolish to think the smell on a fishboat would be any less potent. The craft would have absorbed the smell into every part of its structure, those who worked on it would smell of fish, and worse, there might be actual fish on the boat that would also smell of fish.

It took her some time to find Orlikksin's house. The directions had been inadequate in truth, and she had been required to wander a large part of the area before she found the blue door with the fishman's name on it. She abandoned her Guild caution as she searched. Her head hurt, her temper had frayed to the limit, and she grew angrier at the poor quality of the directions as she hunted up and down the strange streets.

Orlikksin lived in a rundown wooden house, one storey tall, a battered blue door and two windows at the front. Most of the houses in the street had fared no better down the years, and she guessed this must be a poorer quarter of the city. Many of them had been painted at one time, but now the paint peeled from the wood, and they looked ready to collapse, in truth.

Yilmay knocked on the door and waited. The smell of fish surrounded the house, and she shook her head, certain she made an enormous mistake. From inside the house, she heard a cough and the shuffle of feet, and the door opened. The man who stood there did nothing to ease her dismay. If she had found Orlikksin, he could not be counted on to navigate a boat through the depths of the seven seas. He sported many days' growth of hair on his chin;

not a beard, rather the sign of a man too tired, busy, or lazy to shave. His red hair resembled a discarded, frayed rope, and he wore no tunic. Worse, his trousers were enormous, like those of the man in the building, but he had not thrown the straps over his shoulders. He held them up with a hand, though they slipped around his hips and all but exposed his manhood. He grunted something Yilmay did not catch but guessed had been some form of welcome.

"Are you Orlikksin?"

"Am." As soon as he spoke, he broke into a fit of coughs that reminded her of the time Taro had swallowed his tongue.

With a heavy sigh, she pressed on once his coughs abated. "Somebody down there"—she pointed in the rough direction of the docks—"said you might sail to Karnstein soon."

"Tomorrow." Another cough.

"I need to travel to Karnstein as soon as possible."

"Supply ship leaves in a few days. They can take you, know?" He pushed the door to close it, but she raised a hand to stop it.

"I cannot wait five days for the ship." She tried to sound forceful but polite. "Will you take me?"

He stared at her for a moment, then burst into laughter. She bent toward her boot, then controlled her annoyance before she could pull her fan.

"Never had a female on my boat. Do not think I ever will."

Female? What a horrible word, she decided. This might all have been a terrible idea, after all else. She vowed to make one last attempt. "Why?"

His eyes widened and his head jerked upward. "I know not." He might have spoken to himself. "Why can you not wait for the supply ship?"

"My friend is in peril, and I must reach him without delay. His name is Gaishkantah. I am Yilmay." She extended a hand toward him.

"Them that sailed around the land?"

"The globe. That we are. We are them. Those."

"Why is he in peril?" He lost his grip on his trousers. By the time he had tugged them up over his privates again, Yilmay all but died of shame and horror.

What should she tell him? She must be careful here, or she could spread a wild rumour that might spark panic, and the Qagrue might not even arrive. She withdrew the foolish hand he had not shaken. "He is ill." She would offer no more. Orlikksin had not earned her trust. She did not even like him, in truth.

"Can you work?"

Could she? She felt stronger than she had at Ulmella's house, but by no means had she recovered all her strength. "A little, my guess. I have also been injured."

"See that. Bandage. Bashed on the head, were you?"

"When The Ictharelian sank."

"Long time ago, that. Why are you still sore?"

"I only had a healer work on it a pass ago." She had lost her patience with him. "Will you take me or not?"

He scratched himself under one arm and stared at her. "We leave early. Before the sunrise."

"I can be there." The hour of departure did not concern her. "How long does it take?"

"You want to help us fish or go to Karnstein?"

She had no interest in the fish. She wanted to reach Gaish as soon as she could and nothing more. "I only want to go to Karnstein."

"Three days. It would be out of our way, know?"

"Why do you all add 'no' to the end of your sentences?" She had to understand the strange custom.

"It is short for 'you know.' It means... I do not know what it means. It is something we say."

They did not say "no," they said "know." That might be even

stranger, she thought. It made no sense to believe somebody already knew something when you told them. She could not recall Gaish had ever said it in all the time she had known him. It did not matter, and she lied. "I see. Will you take me?"

"I will take you. It takes us out of our way. You are famous though, know."

"My thanks." A sense of relief she could not put into words flooded her. "I will meet you by that building at the fish dock in the morning."

"Do not be late. I will leave without you. No skin from my nose."

She decided to give up on all the strange things these people said. She guessed Gaish must have lost the odd mannerisms as he sailed with mariners from other lands. "I—" He closed the door in her face. She thought it rude, but she would let it pass, since he would take her to Karnstein tomorrow and had not mentioned coin. She could not deny her relief. Once she reached Karnstein, she could find directions to Gaish's home and warn him. She would worry about how to reach Argoya once she had delivered her warning. With any luck, it would not prove as trying as the task of reaching him had been so far.

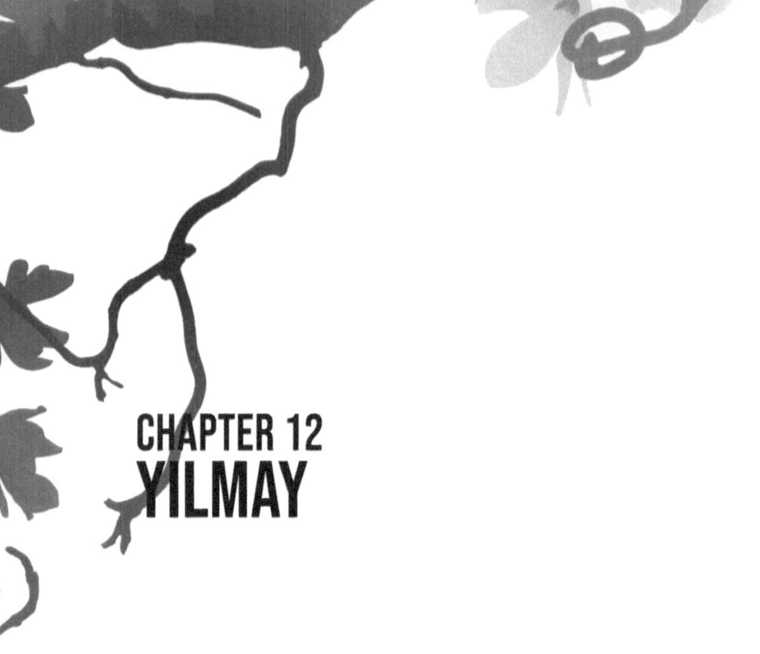

CHAPTER 12
YILMAY

Tiredness washed over Yilmay, and she thought it would be sensible to find an inn, take a room, and rest. She would need to rise early in the morning. No doubt Orlikksin would leave without her if she did not present herself at the dock on time. She would find an inn close to the docks so she would not have far to walk in the morning, and when she found one called Steinbedst Hotel, she guessed Deineike would have enjoyed the pun. The inn claimed to be the best but spelled it with a 'd' that added beds, as would be expected in an inn. The word "Hotel" intrigued her. She had not heard it before. The more she travelled, the more she learned. Her small room on the third storey had a grimy window that looked out onto the wall of an adjacent building. It had a small cot, a vanity stand, and a nightpot; nothing else. The nightpot, although empty, did not appear to have been cleaned for some time, and she hoped she would not have need of it through the night.

She lay on the cot and soon fell asleep. When she woke, she could not tell whether the day had turned greyer or twilight had arrived, but hunger drove her down the stairs in search of food.

The inn offered basic fare, most of which appeared to be fish, doubtless due to its close proximity to the docks. One of the meals featured makkrel, and she decided to try it out of curiosity. She found its taste unusual but not unpleasant. It had a sweetness she did not expect, and a fatty feel in her mouth. It came with tubers and some long, thin green vegetables, described as beans. She enjoyed the makkrel and felt pleased she had experimented with it, even though she could not recall eating fish prior to today.

After the meal and a goblet of wine, she went for a short walk before bed. Her bandage had not been changed for some days, and as she walked, she thought she might take it off. She found a clothing shop still open and bought two inexpensive kerchiefs, both bright blue. From now on she would wear a kerchief to protect her wound. Back in her room, she unwrapped the bandage from her head and tried to view the wound in the small reflecting glass above the vanity stand. Her bruises had turned yellowish-purple, and the closing looked neat, but she could not see it well, in truth. At some point, she must find somebody to take out the stitches from the closing. No redness could be seen, so she had avoided any infection or inflammation thanks to Ulmella and the mariners.

Corelle lay on the bed in the hopes she would fall asleep, and thus wake, early, but it took her some time to drift off to sleep. She had been free of the nightmares for a few nights, and they stayed away again tonight. There had been no danger she would sleep too late, since the noise from outside woke her long before any light of day appeared. The inn lay close to the docks, and bedlam broke out early here, it turned. Fishmen, in particular, arrived and yelled at one another, and dockworkers headed toward the commercial docks joined in as Corelle crossed the street. She stifled many yawns and found the small building in the darkness. Many men stood around, all dressed in the enormous trousers.

Corelle spotted Orlikksin and heaved a sigh of relief; he had the straps of his trousers across his shoulders today. She had seen all she wished to, and more, of his body yesterday. He grunted at her and led her to his boat, which involved a precarious scramble across a closer boat his had been tied to. Four other men had already boarded, and she sensed she had been later than they wished. "Cast off." Orlikksin yelled the order, and since she stood near the bow rope, she untied it from a cleat on the next boat and wound it into a neat coil as two of the crew watched her, faint smiles on their lips.

"Good enough." One of them laughed but nodded his head to her.

"You say?" The other seemed less convinced, and he clapped his friend on the back as they went about other work. The little boat flew a small sail as it nudged its way out into the Torr Sea. As they cleared the calmer waters of Juustein's docks, the crew piled on more sail, and the boat made decent progress through the dark.

Orlikksin showed her to the cabin below decks. The stench of fish almost made her fetch up, worse than she had expected, but she had little choice now. She must endure it or throw herself into the Torr Sea. Seven bunks hung in one communal room, and he pointed to a large crate and grunted she could store her pack in it. "Do you cook?"

"That I do, if it is simple food." Corelle had done little work in the scullery as a girl but had learned some simple recipes while at Taro's farm, as he refused to cook once she arrived. She could make a broth and fry meat and tubers. If they wanted makkrel, one of them would have to cook it.

"Take it in turns to cook aboard. You can start, make something to break our fast."

"I will try. What do you break your fast on?" Most mornings, Yilmay ate meat, bread, and cheese, so she hoped they would be satisfied with that.

"Makkrel." Her heart sank.

"I have never cooked makkrel." Her father had always told her honesty is the best policy.

"You will learn." He laughed. "Fry it up. Easy enough. You will find it there." He pointed to a large chest. "Make plenty. We get hungry." He smiled and disappeared up onto the deck.

She decided it could be no harder to fry fish than meat, so she hunted around the small scullery until she found a large round pan. Only one flat cooktop existed, and it seemed hot already. When she opened a door below, a small fire had already been lit inside. She glanced around and saw a small pile of wood nearby. The fish last night had felt so fatty in her mouth, she doubted any further fat would be needed to cook it.

The familiar sounds of mariners' shouts came from above her as she opened the chest. It had been lined with a metal inner, and when she lifted the lid of the inner, she saw the makkrel. They had been packed in with large blocks of frozen water, but that did not catch her attention and crush her spirit; the makkrel itself did so. It had not been prepared. Whole fish had been crammed into the chest. She had no idea how to prepare fish, or any food for that matter, other than tubers and the like. Taro had killed and cut up the meat on his farm, and at other times she had bought meat from shops that had prepared it before she bought it.

Yilmay pulled one of the fish from the chest and closed both lids. She dropped the large fish onto the small counter and stared at it in misery. She imagined she would need to cut off the head and what passed for a tail, since she believed those parts would be unfit for eating. She wondered if the fish had an actual tail but decided the finned thing at the opposite end from its head was its tragic excuse for one.

She hunted in the drawers and found a large knife, then ran a finger along its edge. "This would not cut water." She had muttered aloud because the blade had no sharpness at all. In truth, it would be more effective as a hammer. Her fan could not be allowed to perform the dirty, ugly work the fish would require, so she hunted for a whetstone. One of the other mariners came down while she searched, and she asked him if they had one aboard.

"What for?"

"This knife." She held it up. "If the fish still lived, I could bludgeon it to death, but it would not cut cheese."

He laughed and stepped over to the scullery, opened a cupboard, and produced a device that looked like a small axe. "Cut off the head and tail with this." He handed it to her, then opened the drawer and took out a smaller knife. Take the skin and bones out with this." She had to cut its skin off? Unexpected, in truth. And bones. This would be the only meal she would have to cook, she hoped. The complications seemed enormous. "We need two, not one." He laughed and wandered over to the crate that held the packs. He took something from inside it and went back to the deck.

Laughter suggested he had told his friends of the conversation, and Yilmay wondered how hard the little boat would be to sail alone. She could kill the five of them and sail herself to Karnstein. With a dejected sigh, she took a second fish out of the chest and set about both with a bloodthirsty vigour that would have shocked even Styrrach as she took revenge from the fish for the Dockmaster and his staff, the old man in the enormous trousers and his awful directions, the names attached to all the doors in Juustein, and Orlikksin and his crew.

When she believed she had the fish as ready as she could, she slapped both of them into the pan and placed it on the cooktop. It sizzled, and soon the smell masked the revolting smell of raw fish. Her mouth watered as the fish cooked, and she flipped them both over. The flesh had browned well enough, but the size of the fish concerned her, and she wanted to make sure they had cooked through. She did not want to kill them all with her cookery. That shame would be unbearable.

She hunted through the scullery and found some fruit in a

wooden box, but no tubers or vegetables. The fruit would not last a day if they all ate a healthy portion, and she reasoned they did not stay at sea long enough for illness to be a problem.

No other food appeared to be aboard. Did they eat nothing but makkrel morning, midday, and night? How strange. Either they must like it a great deal, or they would grow bored of it by journey's end. She checked the fish again and cut one in half to see how it cooked in the middle. It looked too pink to eat, so she cut the other in half also and used the small knife to slice along its body so the pieces became thinner.

She glanced toward the hatch, and the darkness had gone. The sky seemed blue as spring moved along, welcome after the cold winter in Ryl. It would be warmer here to the south, of course. She had wintered in Ryl, many days to the north.

She cut a piece of the fish from the centre and sampled it. It seemed cooked to her and tasted like the meal she had eaten last night. She would allow it to cook a little longer, she thought. Better safe than sorry out at sea, after all else.

One of the crew came down into the cabin. "Smells good." Corelle's cheeks heated with embarrassment. Two more came down the narrow stairs, and she guessed they had decided to eat. She rattled around in the cupboard for some plates, but found only two, and one of those had a large crack in its centre that suggested it might soon go wherever plates travel to afterward.

Orlikksin appeared and leaned over the fish. He sniffed at it. "Not bad for a first attempt." He let out a loud, hearty laugh and struck her in the back so hard, she flew forward into the counter. He picked up the pan and carried it to the table. As soon as he placed it down, the others tore chunks of makkrel from the fish and crammed them into their mouths. Aghast, Yilmay sat on the bench next to one of them and cut a piece of fish for herself with the small knife she had washed after she had used it to prepare the fish.

"Salt." As one of the men shouted, another stood and went to the cupboard. He returned with a round canister. He pulled the top of the canister away and poured salt onto the fish in the pan.

They ate in silence, and the six of them finished off both makkrel in short order. Yilmay ate hers from the knife, while the others watched and laughed at her. When all the fish had gone, Orlikksin broke the news to her that whoever cooked also washed the pan and knife.

One of the others leaned back against the hull. "Orlikksin says you sailed the ship all the way around the land."

She nodded. "That I did. All the way round the globe."

He waved a hand in the air. "You call it globe. Your ship sank, they say."

"That it did. A black and white giant crashed onto it and broke it in half."

One of the men leaned forward. "Black and white giant? Not blue?"

"Black and white. Not as big as the blue, but big enough to bring that ship its ruin."

"You say?"

"I say. I had been in the nest. It threw me into the water, and the mast hit me as the ship went down." She pointed to her head, then realised she had her kerchief on. She untied it and showed them the wound on top of her head.

"Cut you a bit then." One of the men gave a low whistle.

"This is the wound from the repairs. My brain swelled, and water and blood became trapped. Beneath this wound is a hole in my head. They cut my skull open to let it all out."

Some of the men groaned and cried in horror, and one yelled, "You say?"

"It is true. There is a hole in my head. Know."

Orlikksin pursed his lips and nodded. "We may give you light duties then, in case a wave comes over and the sea gets into your brain." The men laughed, and Yilmay joined in, defeated by the Steinlund folks' irrepressible appetite for unfunny jests.

The story had changed the relationship between them. Whatever they thought about a woman aboard, she had been a mariner, and her ship had sunk, which they seemed to respect even more. They no longer laughed behind her back for the next two days, and she learned life aboard became easier if she laughed at their jests, even the ones at her expense. The boat never ventured far from the coast, but they told her once they had dropped her off, they would sail out into deeper water and cast their nets over the side for makkrel. Life aboard the boat did not differ that much from life aboard the ships she had sailed on, but she guessed it would be different once they began their work. It seemed a hard life, the men aboard rough and ready, but the camaraderie between them suggested they cared about each other, and each knew what he would be required to do to make the trip successful.

The next day, the city of Karnstein appeared off the dock'ard bow, and Orlikksin guided the fishboat into the dock. They wished her well and slapped their huge hands on her back as she clambered onto the dock.

She turned and watched them head out to sea. It had been a short voyage, but she had enjoyed it. There had been an openness and honesty about the five men, and despite their roughness, she had enjoyed their company. "Catch lots of fish." She whispered the words to her crew-mates as the little boat became a smudge on the horizon, then she turned to face the city and whispered to herself. "Now for Gaish."

CHAPTER 13
YILMAY

Karnstein spread out before Yilmay. A small city the size of Ort, flanked on each side by high hills. Beyond the docks, the city seemed flat. The buildings she could see stood two or three storeys high and all seemed to be wooden. They all had red roofs as far as she could tell, some trait of the city, she guessed.

Corelle had little coin left and wanted to find Gaish as soon as she could, so she could not tarry in Karnstein. She hoped the Qagrue would not come, but if they did, the Steinlund folk might resist them. It seemed a brash but friendly land, and despite the anger she had felt in the Dockmaster's Offices in Juustein, she had warmed to the men on the boat and wanted their hard but simple life to continue uninterrupted.

As she walked north from the docks, she stopped three people to ask directions before she found somebody who thought they knew where Gaish's house might be situated. It would take her the best part of a day to ride there, and far longer to walk, he said. He gave her some rough directions and advised her to confirm them in villages and towns she would pass through. She could not decide

whether to set off at once and hope she could find a place to spend the night or wait for morning. The midday approached, and based on the man's directions, she felt sure she could not reach Gaish's house before darkness.

She stopped a man to ask about horse rental, and he directed her to a stable where he thought she could rent one. It seemed wise to enquire about the cost before she made her decision, but in the end, the decision became simple. The next day would be some sort of holiday, and the stable would not be open. She could not afford to wait two nights, either in terms of time or coin, so she asked how much a horse would be to rent for four or five days. She would prefer to spend some time with Gaish now she had come so far to visit him. To her dismay, she did not have enough coin to rent a horse, so she asked if she might find a less expensive stable.

The stable owner said she would not find a better price anywhere in Karnstein, then seemed to take pity on her. He took all her coin and urged her to take care of the horse. She rode north and hoped Gaish would lend her some coin, or she might be stuck forever in Steinlund. Once she recovered more, she could work her passage, at the least.

The little horse plodded out of the city and along the road northward, and Yilmay's thoughts turned to the night-time. A friendly farmer might allow her to sleep in his barn. She had thought her days of such bleak accommodations lay behind her, but she must entertain it once more.

In the first village she came to, she asked about Gaish's house, but nobody there could help her, so she rode on, hungry and unhappy. As the sun sank below the hills to the west, the day turned chilly, and she pulled her cloak tighter about her and urged the little horse to ride on. As darkness fell, she spotted a farmhouse ahead with a large wooden barn to one side of it. She did not wish to ride in the dark in a land she did not know. If she fell or took a wrong turn...

She reined the horse to a halt. "What do you think, horse?" It snickered, and she sighed. "I speak four languages, and you know none of them. That is inconvenient, know." She turned the horse into the farm lane and rode toward the house. Somebody must have seen her in the lane, because when she reached the house, a man and woman already stood in the yard, and the man held up a hand. Yilmay hoped the hand indicated a friendly welcome rather than a suggestion she should turn around or prepare to die. She gave them both a cheery wave and stopped her horse a few paces from them. "Good day to you."

The woman answered. "And to you. What can we do for you?"

"I wonder if you can help me find a friend." She had decided on a whim to pretend she needed nothing more than help with the precise location of Gaish's house, then if they had any idea and said she could not reach it tonight, she could throw themselves on their mercy. They might find it in their hearts to let her spend the night in their barn.

"Where does he live?" This time the man had spoken

She took Gaish's battered letter out of her pack. A waft of fish odour assailed her nostrils, and she imagined she must smell no better than the fishboat she had left earlier. She held the letter out toward the couple, and the man stepped forward to take it from her. He scanned it for a moment, then gave a low whistle.

The woman stared at him, a mixture of concern and curiosity. "What is it?"

The man looked up at her. "You have a long way to go, know. You cannot reach this place tonight. I am sorry, you are not where you thought yourself."

Corelle made a great show of distress. She hung her head and wiped a hand across her eyes in a dramatic manner. The horse lowered its head in an admirable show of solidarity with her evident disappointment.

The man looked at her, sympathy in his eyes. "So. You could

sleep in the barn if you like. It would be dangerous to ride at night. I would be unforgiven if some bad thing befell you."

Corelle frowned at the unusual word, "unforgiven," but raised her head, a slow measured reaction to his words, an act of relief even Deineike would have been hard pressed to better. "I would not wish to impose."

"It is no trouble, know."

"You say?" Yilmay's heart sank at the woman's unwelcome intervention. "She must sleep in the house, not in the barn."

Guilt overwhelmed Yilmay. "I cannot sleep in your house. I have been aboard a fishboat for the last three days. I stink."

"You do. I can smell you." The woman smiled. "We can give you a bath and wash your clothes. You will smell better then."

"You are too kind." Yilmay no longer needed to act, for their kindness shocked her.

From the house, a child's voice rang out. "Who is it, Mother?"

Yilmay raised her voice so they would all hear her. "I am Yilmay."

The man took a step toward her. "So. Let me put your horse in the barn, and my wife will take you inside for that bath. I am Farlichtah."

"And I am Errbuldot." The woman introduced herself. "Let us get you inside and out of those clothes." She smiled and held out a hand, and Yilmay climbed down from the horse to follow Errbuldot into the house.

Two children stood and stared at her as she entered, and one pinched the bridge of her nose. "She smells of makkrel." Their mother chased them away and led Yilmay up the stairs and into a tub room. Yilmay ran up and down the stairs to refill pails from the pump outside the door until the tub had sufficient hot water for her, then Errbuldot left her to soak. She luxuriated in the hot water, unable to remember the last time she had bathed.

Errbuldot had taken Corelle's clothes, so she dug in her pack and found clean trousers and a tunic. They did not smell as bad, but the taint of fish still clung to them. A wooden plug at the bottom of the tub could be pulled up to allow the dirty water to drain away. She wiped down the inside of the tub with a drying cloth, then went down the stairs.

Farlichtah had returned to the house, and he took her into their scullery. A large fire blazed in the corner, and Yilmay welcomed the warmth after the chill of the evening. He introduced the two children, both girls. "This is Errfardot, and this is Storfardot." Errfardot might have been six years, and Storfardot four years. There seemed to be some structure to the names of the children compared to their parents. They seemed not to choose such random names here as in Dur.

"What do you do? Are you a farmer too?" Errfardot seemed curious about the stranger in their home.

Yilmay could not tell the children she killed people for coin. "I am a mariner."

"So. I have heard of you, I think. And your friend, now I think on it." Farlichtah looked thoughtful.

It shocked Yilmay the story had spread so far that even on this remote farm, they had heard of the voyage. "You say?"

He laughed. "You learn our language well. At the market six passes ago, somebody said a ship had been all the way around the land, and we lived on some sort of ball. You sailed on that ship, but it sank, and few survived. Do I have the right of it?"

"That you do. We proved that Ictharelian is a globe, and our lands no more than a small part of it."

"Where are you from?" Errbuldot stirred a pot that hung over the fire.

"Dur. I am Durfolk."

"Why did your ship sink?" Errfardot had a child's curiosity, unafraid to ask difficult questions.

Yilmay smiled. "An enormous fish jumped out of the water."

She imitated the jump with her hands. "It landed on the ship and threw us all into the sea. The ship sank, and some friends pulled me from the water. We floated on a piece of wood to the shore. That is how we survived."

Both girls stared at her wide-eyed, their mouths open. When she glanced at the parents, they both mirrored their daughters' expressions. "How big?" Storfardot's high pitched whisper of amazement matched her shocked eyes.

"The fish?" The child nodded, her eyes wide with excitement. "Enormous. As big as your house, my guess."

Errbuldot, still by the fire, gasped. "You say?"

"That I do. We call them giants, and they swim not far off the southern coast of Steinlund at times. I have never seen a bigger animal in all my life."

Another night of tales from her voyage rushed past as they dined on a broth of makkrel. Errbuldot told the girls they must go to bed, and they complained. "We have let you stay up too late as it is. You have heard the stories now. Off to bed with you." Their father laughed even as he ordered them off to their beds.

"They are lovely girls." The girls ran up to their room after each of them had hugged Yilmay and wished her a good night.

"At times." Errbuldot laughed. They neither said "yes" or "that they are" in Steinlund. Rather, they made a statement about whatever had been said or asked, "You say?" Gaish had never said, "You say," but he had never said, "Know," either. She set the thought loose; Gaish had sailed with mariners who spoke many languages and had lost some of his Steinlund speech, nothing more. "They are good girls. We have no son, so they will need to learn how to run the farm for when we die, know."

"We might yet have a son." Farlichtah had a twinkle in his eye, and they all laughed.

As she lay in clean bedding, Yilmay again hoped the simple, joyous lives of these people would not be destroyed by the uncouth, violent Qagrue. She had loathed them for their invasion of Dur, and her animosity toward them had increased every day since she had learned of their plans.

Errbuldot gave Yilmay some food in the morning, and they directed her to Gaish's village. They wished her well, and the children needed another short tale and a hug before she rode off. All four stood in the yard and waved until she turned into the lane and lost sight of them behind a hedge. They had been more than kind, but she pointed her horse north and rode on toward the reason she had come here.

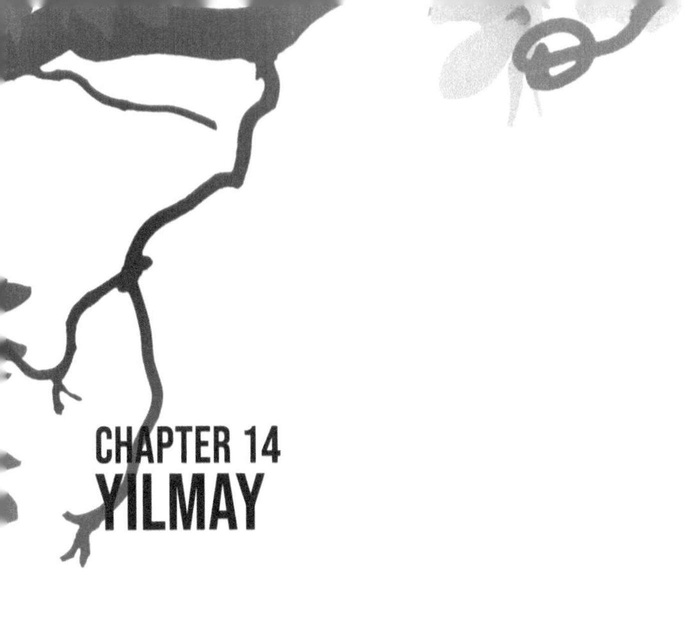

The midday had passed before Yilmay reached Targistvi, the village Gaish had mentioned in his letter. She asked for more directions, and an elderly woman directed her north of the village where she said Gaishkantah lived in a house on a large parcel of land. Rakulaj must have paid him a bigger sum than he had given Yilmay. Gaish deserved it. He had almost died, and but for him she would have met her ruin without any doubt. The little horse carried her along the road until she saw the entrance to a lane that resembled the one the woman had described. She rode down it and soon saw a house, two storey and made of wood with the usual red roof. She had not expected such a large house, with a small, well-tended lawn in front of it and two barns a little way off.

Yilmay reined the horse to a halt outside the house, climbed from the saddle, and rubbed her behind. She had not ridden for some time—years, she guessed. The saddle had hurt more than she had anticipated. Nobody came out to meet her, so she stepped up to the large double doors and rapped on them with her knuckles.

Yilmay waited ten heartbeats or so, then footsteps approached the opposite side of the door. She stood straight, ready to greet Gaish, but when the door opened, a strange man stood there. He stood at least two spans taller than her, slender and with short dark hair. He had bright grey eyes and thin lips. He smiled at her but said nothing, so Yilmay broke the silence. "Is this the home of Gaish?"

"Gaishkantah?"

"My apologies. I called him Gaish. His name took too much time to say." Yilmay gave him a smile she hoped would make the comment seem politer than it had sounded.

He raised and lowered his head once, as though to indicate he had understood. "He told me of somebody who called him Gaish once, some time ago."

"Yilmay. That is my name."

"So. That is the name he mentioned. He will be excited… I apologise. Where are my manners? I am Takishtah." He held out a hand. As she took it, Yilmay noticed the nails on his long narrow fingers had been shaped with care. He wore simple clothes, but of good making, and tailored to perfection. He seemed to take great pains over his appearance. She could only guess how dreadful she must look in comparison. "Come in, come in. I will bring Gaishkantah. We had been in the garden." He waved a hand in dismissal of his own small talk. "You do not care about that, I am sorry. Please, take a seat, and I will bring him. He will be so excited."

Yilmay sat in an armed chair in the large parlour. The walls had been hung with nautical items: the wheel from a ship, a large drawing of a three master in rough seas, even an oar from a rowboat. On one wall, the word "Home" had been spelled out with sticks, grey as though washed up from the sea, although that seemed unlikely; the nearest sea lay a day's ride away. Deineike would have been smitten with the house, and Yilmay felt a pang of sadness at the thought.

Feet pounded toward her from somewhere in the house, and

Gaish appeared. He wore trousers and a tunic of linen, and he slid to a halt on the wooden floor as he saw her. He raised both hands and steepled them at his mouth as he blinked several times in rapid succession. Yilmay smiled at him. "Hello Gaish." She rose from the chair.

He screamed, ran forward, swept her into an embrace, and twirled her around twice. Takishtah had followed him into the parlour, and he stood with a hand over his mouth and tears in his eyes as he watched them. Gaish held her at arm's length and studied her face. "Let me look at you. You still wear your hair short."

She smiled. "That I do."

"It is so good to see you again. I have thought of you often. Have I not, Takishtah?" He turned to the taller man.

"You talk of little else." Takishtah laughed as he wiped at his eyes.

"You have met Takishtah? Of course you have. He answered the door. He is the love of my life."

Yilmay had guessed as much but had not wished to misspeak and cause them embarrassment. "You have a beautiful home. Rakulaj must have rewarded you well."

"The house belongs to Takishtah. I am merely a guest." Gaish had a twinkle in his eye.

"Did Rakulaj give you nothing then?"

Gaish shook his head. "Did he reward you? He gave me a few coins and free passage to Steinlund."

Yilmay found it strange that for all they had endured, the only thing that had accrued to them had been the fame she did not care for, and a small amount of coin. Rakulaj had spent the coin to finance the voyage, but he had recouped his coin through the indemnifier, as he had explained in Arkkyd. After all else, they had been no more than crew. Doubtless Rakulaj made large sums of coin from the voyage, while their lives had almost been lost, and they made nothing but their wages, which had all sunk with the ship, although he had insisted she take the coin he offered her as wages, if nothing else.

"Let us not talk of coin." Yilmay swept the thought away. "I wish to hear how you met Takishtah and what your plans are."

"And I wish to hear all about you and Vamma." Gaish laughed and clapped his hands. "So. Takishtah, let us bring out a cask of good wine. My old friend has come to visit, and we will be perfect hosts."

Takishtah smiled at her. "I will stable your horse. Gaish can show you to a room where you can freshen up, and we will open that wine."

Gaish took her upstairs and made a bedroom available to her. It had a room with a tub and vanity stand off it, and she unpacked her meagre belongings. Thanks to Raolos, she knew what "freshen up" meant, and she splashed water on her face. The water did refresh her, and she sweetened her breath before she changed her clothes. Although Errbuldot had washed her clothes the previous night, they had become covered in dust from the road and still smelled of fish.

She stood at the window, which overlooked the rear garden. A few flowers brightened their otherwise empty beds, and more would doubtless appear as spring progressed. The sun shone and the temperature felt warm to Yilmay, but she felt sure sunshine and warmth alone did not drive the cycle by which flowers came and went. She suspected she saw at least one vegetable plot planted here and there among the flowerbeds. Beyond the garden, the hills that had flanked the road flowed down toward the house, and a wooden frame had been built a short distance from the house. A rope of some kind stretched from the frame to another, further away and higher up the hill. She wondered at the device and vowed to ask Gaish about it.

When she returned to the parlour, she found Gaish and

Takishtah at a table laden with goblets, a bottle of wine, and a platter of bread, meats, cheeses, and vegetables. She took a seat next to Gaish, and they began the tales that would bring them from Malkartas to today.

Gaish insisted Yilmay tell her own story first, and the two men sympathised with all her loss, although she left out much of the tale. She did not mention the deaths of the Guild members, and she altered the tale to exclude most mentions of her liaisons with the Qagrue in a bid to lessen the impact of the news she had travelled here to deliver, which she saved for later in the day.

Gaish had returned to Steinlund after he left Malkartas. He had travelled to visit his parents, who lived in a city north of Targistvi. While in the city, he had met Takishtah in a tavern, and they had struck up a relationship almost as soon as they met. Takishtah ran a merchant house and had been in the city on business. He travelled around the land from time to time, but his business had grown many times over in the ten years he had operated it, and he employed people who did much of the work these days. He specialised in silks and other exotic cloths from the south he shipped in through Juustein. He had been interested in the story of Yilmay's shop and said one day he would be honoured if she would make him something, which she agreed to do.

Yilmay asked why most men in Steinlund had "tah" at the end of their names, but not all. She had wondered about Orlikksin and his name while she had been aboard his fishboat. It turned they both meant the same thing: "son." What went before was the name of the man's father, which perplexed Yilmay. All men would be called the same thing as their fathers from now until the sun went out, she imagined. The difference between "tah" and "sin" derived from a time long ago, when the eastern folk used "tah" to differentiate themselves from their western cousins, who preferred "sin." It amazed her to learn all Steinlund men had a unique name that went before their ancestral name to identify them apart, but they only used the first name on formal documents.

Darkness fell, and two casks of wine had been emptied. Yilmay felt light-headed from the wine; she had not drunk this much in some time. Before she became too inebriated, she guessed she should reveal the reason for her visit. The two men paid her rapt attention as she told them what she had heard and what the arrival of the Qagrue had brought about in Dur. She urged them to leave Steinlund and head north or south before the Qagrue arrived, but Takishtah would not abandon his business. They probed her for more information, and she admitted ordinary citizens did not appear to have been killed, although Dur's leadership had been overthrown. The Qagrue had spread, and their own businesses had taken over those owned by Durfolk before they had arrived.

Takishtah saw opportunities for increased business, and Yilmay became frustrated with him. "Do you not care they will take over your land and change it to reflect their own culture, their own way of life?"

"We live a day from the nearest city and docks, and four days' ride from the next closest city. I do not think they will come here, know. Our little village has nothing they will value, I am certain." Takishtah seemed sure of himself.

She turned to Gaish. "I cannot believe you wish this. Do you want your own leaders overthrown and replaced by these people?"

He shook his head. "I do not, but what can we do about it? You said they have been in Dur for four years, or close to it, yet you ran your shop there. Can it be so terrible?"

She could not believe they were so relaxed about the news their land might soon be invaded by another people who would take control of Steinlund and turn it into an outpost of their people. "Most Durfolk despise them and wish them to leave."

Takishtah leaned forward and fixed her with an earnest stare. "And they might. In five years, or ten, who knows what the globe will look like? You two discovered lands almost nobody dared dream of. It is impossible to resist the tide of change your voyage will unleash. This may be a part of that. I do not think it wise to close our minds to any possibility, know."

Yilmay finished the wine in her goblet. Their casual acceptance of this as a necessary part of some greater change, and that she had played a part in the creation of it, infuriated her, but she could not be certain the wine did not influence her mood. As a guest in their house, she must also respect her hosts. She should have gone to their leaders in Juustein first.

She had left Ulmella to travel here and warn them, but they appeared unconcerned. Speculation on whether she and Ulmella had any future together would be a waste of time, but Yilmay had cast any chance of that into the wind, and all for naught, it seemed. The Qagrue would arrive and take control of a land as unprepared as Dur had been. What did she care, after all else? Why had she been concerned with the fate of a land she owed no allegiance to?

She raised her goblet, and Gaish filled it from a third cask. "It is good to see you again, Gaish. I am happy I have met you, Takishtah. I wish you both well, and I hope the Qagrue do no injury to you."

Gaish touched his goblet to hers, and they drank more. Yilmay asked about the wooden frame in the garden, and the men exchanged a conspiratorial glance. "We will show you in the morning. You will be amazed."

Gaish's cryptic words only intrigued her more. "Then tell me. I must know."

"Patience. You will learn tomorrow." Takishtah gave her a wicked smile that infuriated her, but she could pry no more information from them.

Yilmay had become inebriated, and the prospect of another morning where she could scarce rise from the bed did not appeal. "I have drunk enough, I think. If I am to learn about this thing tomorrow, then I must be at my best. I will bid you goodnight. Gaish, I thank you again. You saved my life."

He blew her a kiss, and she swayed as she rose from the table. She weaved her way to the stairs but missed the first step and landed on the palms of her outstretched hands on the staircase. "Oh dear." Yilmay giggled as the men laughed and asked if she had hurt herself. She reassured them she had not, navigated the terrors of the stairs, and fell into the bed. Sleep closed in on her and the Qagrue were forgotten for the night.

The next morning, she felt the effects of the previous night's wine more than she had anticipated. She must have drunk more than she believed at the time. She crawled from the bed and splashed cold water onto her face as she tried to drive the throb from her head and the pain from her eyes. It occurred to her she had not suffered from headaches or loss of memory since the trappaneesh—it might have worked, after all else. Her present woes came from nothing but last night's wine.

She slithered down the stairs, her legs unsteady. Gaish sat at the table, and he looked no better than she felt. "You also?" Yilmay clung to the post at the bottom of the rail.

"Shut up."

He pointed to the chair next to him, and she reached the chair without a fall, then collapsed into it. "Where is Takishtah?"

"He is in the garden, as bright as a silver scripulum, curse him."

"Scripulum? Is this a coin of Steinlund?"

"It is a silver coin. It is worth eight bronze siliqua, and eight scripulum are worth one gold solidi."

The currency baffled her. No doubt it would make more sense if she felt better. "Does the wine not affect him as much as us?"

He gave a short laugh. "It does not affect him at all. I hate him." He looked sideways at her, and Yilmay could see he did not hate Takishtah.

She laid a hand on his arm. "I am glad you are happy."

"How long will you stay?"

"A few days, or until I wear out my welcome. After that, I have a task I must accomplish." She did not wish to reveal too much information about that task.

"That sounds ominous. We are happy to have you here, nonetheless."

"Hello you two. You have risen at last." Takishtah breezed into the room with some flowers in his hand. "Shall I make us breakfast?"

"Is it fried makkrel?" Yilmay felt nauseous at the thought.

Takishtah made a face of displeasure. "It is not. Bread, fruit, and cheese is breakfast in this house. Fried makkrel indeed." He grumbled to himself as he turned and went off to prepare the food.

Yilmay tried to smile, but her face ached, and she thought it might have been more of a grimace. "So. This device in the garden. You promised to tell me this morning."

"I told you we would show you, not tell you. Curb your impatience."

"I hate you." She groaned, and they both laughed so loud, Takishtah poked his head around the door. He joined in the laughter, even though he could have no idea what he laughed at.

CHAPTER 15
YILMAY

After breakfast, Gaish suggested Yilmay change into some rough clothes, as she might get dirty from the morning's activities. Takishtah ran up the stairs while Gaish and Yilmay followed at a slower pace. Yilmay pulled on the clothes she had worn on the boat and the ride to the house. As she wondered what the device did, her excitement grew and almost drove away her self-pity about the after-effects of the wine.

Downstairs again, the men had also changed into clothes more suited to work than the better garments they had worn since she arrived. Once in the garden, Gaish took her hand and pulled her up the slight hill that led away from their garden toward the range of hills beyond. A short length of rope hung from the long one that trailed between the two wooden frames, one at the top of the hill, the other at the bottom. A sturdy branch had been attached to the shorter rope to form an inverted "T" at its lowest point, and a metal ring had been tied to the top through which the longer rope passed. The short rope and the branch could thus slide down the longer rope until it reached the frame at the bottom of the hill.

Takishtah opened a small trunk, took out a long, thin string, and

tied it around the shorter length of rope as Yilmay watched in confusion. Gaish had Yilmay place one leg either side of the rope that hung down, with the branch behind her knees, then instructed her to hold tight to the rope as he pulled the branch higher, up to her behind. Takishtah pushed her in the small of her back, and she stumbled forward. As her feet left the floor and the branch hurtled down the hill with her attached to it, she screamed in alarm and battled to retain her balance on the branch at the top of her thighs behind her.

The branch tore down the hill, and Yilmay clung with all her strength to the rope that dangled from above her. Despite her initial fear, excitement coursed through her as she rushed toward the lower frame, more than anything she had ever experienced outside of a bed, and she screamed with terrified pleasure again. The frame drew nearer, and she panicked, sure she would crash into it. At that moment, her feet contacted the ground, so she slowed herself by dragging her boots along the ground and came to a halt close to the frame. As the branch nudged her knees, she turned to face the men, raised both hands into the air, then let out a scream of delight that might have been heard in Karnstein.

She expected them to pull her back up with the thin string that had trailed out behind her, unseen, but they yelled for her to get off the branch. They used the rope to pull the branch back up the hill as she plodded up toward them. Takishtah whistled past her as he rode the branch down the hill, and when she reached the higher frame, Gaish had almost pulled the branch back. He leapt onto it and flew down the hill as Takishtah made his way back. Yilmay tugged the empty branch back up the hill and set off again.

They played on the device for hours. Yilmay could not resist the thrill of the flight down the hill and recalled a time in Ort when she had asked Deineike if they would ever fly with the birds. Deineike had doubted it, but she would have relished the joy of flight had she been here to enjoy it.

The men tired of the game, but Yilmay's excitement had not wavered in the least. She continued to tear down the hill and plod back up even when the men kissed and touched one another, and she had to pull the branch up the hill with her each time she returned for another flight. At last, as the sun sank lower in the sky, they persuaded her to return to the house and prepare for dinner. She had become filthy, but the agony of last night's wine had been long forgotten. Her face still ached, but that owed more to her huge smiles and screams of delight than the wine. The knees of her trousers were caked in mud from the many times she had fallen, and grass stains covered her tunic. Sweat ran from her, and her breath panted in and out of her lungs as she trudged up the hill for the last time. She rode the device down, then waited at the bottom while the men pulled it back, secured it, and returned the slender line they used to pull it back up the hill in the trunk.

Yilmay stood breathless at the bottom of the hill as the two men came down. "What do you call this wonderful device?"

Takishtah shrugged. "We have not named it. Gaish had the idea, something to do with a slide down a rope aboard a ship, if I remember aright."

"I will call it a ropebird then, since I felt like a bird as I flew down the hill." The smile stayed on Yilmay's face all night, even as she fell asleep, her filthy clothes in the tub to soak the dirt from them and mud still trapped beneath her fingernails.

Three days passed, and they took frequent walks in the area around the house. Takishtah knew a great deal about the local animals and plants, and they fascinated Yilmay. Some of the Steinlund animals did not resemble anything she had seen before, and she enjoyed Takishtah's descriptions of their lives. She flew on the ropebird every day, whether the men came with her or not. Despite the fun and the pleasant company, she needed to either persuade them of the risk of the Qagrue or leave for Argoya.

Their position on the prospect of invasion did not change, and she gave up. At dinner on the third night, Yilmay said she would leave early in the morning and try to find a way to sail to Argoya. When they learned she had no coin, they insisted they give her some. She resisted the offer, but in such dire financial straits, she weakened and accepted with some reluctance. Without coin she would get nowhere, and although it hurt her to take help from them, Takishtah seemed to have a lot of coin, and she doubted he would miss the pouch he gave her any more than Raolos had when he had given her coin.

She promised she would repay them, and he waved off her concerns. The next morning, she set out as the sun rose, food and water in her pack from the men. A tearful farewell left her melancholy as the horse walked along the road south, through the village and on toward Karnstein. She passed the farm of Farlichtah and his family but saw no sign of any of them. It had almost turned dark when she arrived in Karnstein, and she found an inn for the night after she had returned the horse to the stable and given the owner extra coin, conscious she had not paid sufficient when she had set off.

Part of her motivation for the day she had picked to leave the house had been to seek passage back to Juustein on the supply ship, and when she enquired at the Dockmaster's Offices, he confirmed it should arrive that day or the next. He told her few other ships came to the dock other than fishboats, although Corkannae ships sometimes called in. She reasoned a trip to Corkannae would not help her. It lay further from Argoya than Karnstein.

Yilmay sat on the dock through the morning but saw no sign of the ship. She found a small shop where she bought some bread she could nibble at through the day. The supply ship did not arrive, but if she stayed in the inn again, she might miss the ship if it arrived after dark and slipped away again before the morning. Worried, she went back to the Dockmaster, who assured her the ship would not leave until at least the midmorning no matter when it arrived. It would carry goods and passengers back to Juustein, and it never left before the midmorning.

Consoled, she stayed at the same inn, and when she returned to the docks in the morning a ship stood at the dockside. The master confirmed it as the supply ship, and when she enquired about passage to Juustein, the fare sounded reasonable, two silver scripulum. She paid the coin and went below. The passenger accommodation turned out to be one large communal room with bunks all around the outside. The ship provided no trunk to hold her pack and nothing but basic meals, but the low cost justified the austerity. The ship left Karnstein close to the midday and arrived in Juustein in the early hours of the third night. The winds had been against the ship the entire journey, and the sea had been rough. The floor of the common cabin became covered in vomit as many of the passengers fetched up. Around forty passengers had sailed west, and most of those she spoke to had left Karnstein in search of work in the larger city.

What work they might find once the Qagrue arrived, she did not know, but by then she hoped to be far from Steinlund. As the ship carried her west, she decided against a visit to the Duke of Steinlund, or his equivalent. In truth, she begrudged her time and anxiety for the land after Gaish and Takishtah had been so unconcerned. It had been a wonderful visit, but if they had no fear of the Qagrue, so be it. She would leave them to their fates.

Yilmay walked down the ramp onto the darkened Juustein docks, surprised by how busy they still seemed despite the late hour. Two three-masted ships stood at the dock. One came from Qanti, but to her delight, she saw Rakulaj's sigil on the other. Vyrrmod would take her out of her way, but from there she could reach Malkartas, where she hoped to catch a ship to Argoya. Her fame earned her a comfortable cabin on Rakulaj's ship, and she settled in for a long voyage.

She passed the first day seated at the bow in the hope she would see blue giants, but none appeared. The next morning when she woke, a heavy spring rain had set in, and she spent the morning in the common room. The master invited her to take some lunch with him and pressed her for some tales from her journey. The lustre of fame had long since worn off for Yilmay, and the constant repetition of the tales wore her down. She longed to be someone unknown. She could become Corelle again, but that name had also been well known among Rakulaj's masters.

The rain persisted for three days before it released the ship from its miserable embrace, and the sun returned to smile on the ship and its damp crew below. Steam rose from the wet deck as she walked to the bow to resume her watch for giants. They must be in the deepest part of the Torr Sea by now, but she saw none. The ship might have sailed too far south already. Indeed, she saw none at all on the voyage, and six days later the skyline of Arkkyd rose from the horizon before the bow of the ship.

Yilmay clutched her pack as she waited for the ramp to be secured in place. As she walked down onto the dock and felt the familiar unsteadiness in her legs, she considered her choices. While she longed to seek out a ship bound for Malkartas without delay, she thought Rakulaj might be offended if she made no attempt to visit him while she passed through Arkkyd. With any luck, he would not be in the city, and she could leave with no regret and little delay. The value of the free travel made it well worthwhile to remain in his favour.

When she enquired at his office, the clerk felt certain he would be delighted to see her. Despite her disappointment at the outcome, she decided to take a room at an inn and visit Rakulaj later in the day. In the morning she would seek passage to Malkartas, then on to Argoya. She had not thought much about Krage while she had been with Gaish and Takishtah, but now she had embarked on her mission to kill him, he often came to her mind. Much of her time on the voyage had been spent in thought about where he might be. He may have stayed in Argoya. In such an enormous city, he might believe himself all but impossible to locate if anybody came in search of him. He might even believe nobody would travel there bent on his ruin, after all else.

Of course, he might have left the city. Beyond Argoya, Yilmay had no idea how the land looked and did not even know the name of the land Argoya lay within. If other cities existed, equal in size to Argoya, she might spend ten lifetimes and never find him. She must roll the dice and try. If she died in the process, then so be it. *"What is scribed, must be,"* she told herself.

That night, a servant admitted her to Rakulaj's house, and Rakulaj greeted her with his customary warmth and thanked her for the visit. He introduced her to his wife, but his children had already been packed off to bed. He had ordered his staff to prepare a meal, and he begged Yilmay to take some wine with them. He listened with interest to all that had turned since they had last met, and he seemed disappointed the Qagrue planned to invade Steinlund, more so when she told him Gaish had refused to leave before they arrived.

He pried from her the fact she had arrived in Vyrrmod almost coinless, and he told her she could ask the master of any of his ships for coin at any time, and they would provide it. Yilmay felt reluctant to accept such an offer, though she thanked him. When she said she had a room in an inn for the night and did not plan to remain in Arkkyd for long, he insisted she stay at a house he owned where nobody lived for now. He would not take no for an answer and promised to send one of this staff to the inn tomorrow to take her to the house. She could stay there as long as she wished.

He gushed about a new design for a larger, faster ship he had agreed to finance. The ship would have four masts, would carry far more cargo, and would have greater speed than any current ship. He planned to commence trade with some of the lands discovered on The Ictharelian's voyage, as well as a further voyage to discover more of the globe.

Throughout the meal, Yilmay sensed something lay hidden in him. He seemed to listen to her with one ear even as his other ear waited for an appropriate moment to raise some matter that ate at him. She waited for him to approach the issue, and at length he seemed to come to a decision. His wife excused herself, and Rakulaj turned to face Yilmay. "Now you are here, there is a delicate matter I would like to discuss with you." She raised her eyebrows in an indication he should begin. "There are things here in the south of the Torr Sea I imagine you know little or nothing of. I do not believe these things have reached Dur yet, but I am certain they will. I made a mistake and became embroiled in them. I wish I had not done so, but now I cannot extricate myself."

He paused, and wiped at his mouth with a napkin, although he had eaten nothing for some time. "I agreed to carry an item that comes from the south. Opium—have you heard of it?"

CHAPTER 16
YILMAY

Opium. Not two passes ago, she had never encountered it. Now it made a second appearance in her life. "That I have. The healer who cut the hole in my head used it. It is a herb that helps to lessen pain."

"Its usage has expanded beyond this purpose, I fear. It induces joy in people, and a sense of great relaxation. People also use it as relief from their mundane lives and problems, and its use has spread in this part of the globe. It is sad, but once it takes hold of a person, they find it nigh on impossible to break its hold on them, and it can lead them to other problems. Its use is not yet widespread, I do not believe, but it soon will be."

"People are free to make their own choices, I imagine. How does this cause you problems? Do you use it?"

He shook his head in vehement denial. "No, no. I will not use it. I have seen how it takes hold of people. I cannot abide the thought I could allow this thing to destroy my life. It is grown to the south and brought here to be sold. Somebody approached me and asked if I would carry some to Vyrrmod in one of my ships, and I agreed.

I did not realise at the time it had such capacity to damage those who used it."

"You made a mistake, as you say. Do not carry it any more." Yilmay suspected more lay behind his words, but she grew impatient and wished Rakulaj would either abandon the topic or reach his point.

He gave a brief frown. "The situation has become more complicated, I fear. They wish to bring more of this opium here and insist I carry it. I have told them I wish to have no more to do with it, but they have threatened to reveal I have carried it for them. I fear this news could damage my business."

Yilmay could not see why, and she said so. Rakulaj said as it had spread, people had become concerned about the damage they saw it wreak on friends and family, and this had created a stigma to the opium. The Superintendent of Vyrrmod had stated his Administration would stamp out its use in the land.

"Then there is no problem, is there? The Upholders will track down those who bring the opium into the land and close down their operation." She could not help but see a similarity between the operation Rakulaj had described and Styrrach's scheme. The items Styrrach made his coin on did not create the social outrage opium appeared to have created, but the clandestine operation bore a sinister familiarity.

"Again, the situation is not that simple." Rakulaj squirmed in his chair. It seemed his involvement in this scheme brought him great anxiety. "I suspect a member of the Administration may be involved in the operation. He may have seen a way to earn coin from it at the start. The usage spreads, and the Upholders make little to no progress in their attempts to bring to book those involved in its importation."

"Which would include you, I imagine." How had he allowed himself to become so involved in this operation? He had always seemed so careful in his business affairs.

"It would, I am afraid. I wish to refuse to carry it, but if I do, word may get out I have done so in the past. If my customers prefer one of my competitors out of fear I am in some way implicated in the import of this plant, it could destroy all I have worked to build."

Rakulaj had made a terrible mistake when he had agreed to carry the wretched stuff at all and could not now disentangle himself, although he longed to. It must be a terrible dilemma, but Yilmay saw no way she could do anything about it and wondered why he had told her at all. "And?" His lengthy silence concerned her, and she did not think she wanted to hear what he saw as her involvement.

"I wish to ask a favour of you, but now it comes to it, I fear to."

Yilmay's sense of dread increased. He wished to be free of the arrangement, and she imagined he wanted her to kill somebody as part of his escape. Such work would be no better than the killings she had carried out for Styrrach, and she feared to hear him ask. "Then do not ask it."

"I must." He looked down at his hands in his lap. "I beg you to help me out of this mess. They threaten to expose me. If you could discover who they are, and if one of them does indeed serve in the Administration, I could use that information to counter their threats with threats of my own."

Had she misjudged his motive? He had requested something less than her initial concerns. "How would I bring this about? Why am I suited to it rather than one who already works for you?"

He loosed a low, grim chuckle. "I can tell you the name of the person who delivers the messages to me, for I have learned it. From him, you might obtain information and names that would provide me the escape I seek. I think you would be more… persuasive than any who work for me."

His intent had not been lost on her. He meant she might be seen as more of a threat than a clerk who worked in his business. She wished she did not have such a reputation but could not argue she deserved it. "I have urgent business in Argoya." Yilmay did not want this complication that might take days or even longer to resolve and would delay her.

"This evil destroys lives, Corelle of Dur. Please help me. I do not wish to be involved."

Why had he referred to her as Corelle? "I call myself Yilmay again. I am sorry Rakulaj, I do not have time to help you." She felt terrible she must let him down, but other matters called her.

"Most of the opium comes from Qagrue. That is where they have me send my ships to collect it."

He had played a high hand, or so he hoped. Yilmay reasoned he guessed she would act out of hatred for the Qagrue, who had invaded her own land, killed those she cared for, and now threatened Gaish's land. He had the right of it, to a point. She despised the Qagrue, but Rakulaj dealt with and enriched them, and she lost some respect for him at that moment. "Why do you work for those people? They are monsters."

"I do not work for them, I work for Vyrrmod folk. They choose to deal with the Qagrue, and they now have me hooked like a fish on a line. I cannot risk all I have worked for over this sickness that threatens to consume the people of my land."

"This is a problem you have made for yourself. I cannot help you. I plan to leave tomorrow."

"Please Yilmay, I beg you. I fear these people, and I fear they will do more to me than destroy my business. In Dur, you approached me with a proposition you claimed would restore fairness to the trade between our lands. I aided you then, and I have aided you since. I told you where you could find Glailam, and at that time I warned you I might need to make a call on the debt you felt you owed me. I regret I must point out these things, but I have no other option. Do not turn aside now when I need your help, please."

Anger stirred within Yilmay. She saw little difference between him and the people who threatened him. Both used underhanded methods to achieve their own ends. Rakulaj's attempt to use her guilt irritated her, and she stared at him for long moments as she controlled her fury. "How do these people contact you? You mentioned a messenger. Tell me about this man."

"You will help me?"

"Tell me about the messages."

"He delivers letters to my office at the docks. They tell me when I should arrive in Qagrue. I send a ship, and it returns with a cargo. What happens to it after it is unloaded from my ship, I do not know."

"That is precious little to go on. I cannot sit in your office day after day in the hope that somebody who delivers letters looks suspicious."

"Nilukap. That is his name. He lives on Rose Street in the poor part of the city."

"How do you know this?" Suspicion gnawed at Yilmay. The more the story grew, the worse it reeked of deception.

"A friend saw him leave my office one day and asked me later how I knew him. He described him as 'disreputable.' He said he had some unpleasant experience with this Nilukap when he employed him to perform some work for him."

Much about the story did not ring true with her, and she became more guarded. "There is no proof he is the one who brings the letters. He may have been there on an unrelated task, a courier for somebody else."

"That would be possible, but I asked one of my office clerks to follow him the next time he brought letters in. I regret to say he spotted my clerk and threatened him. The clerk said this took place on Rose Street. He is the messenger for the people who have me ship the opium."

The entire story sounded absurd. Rakulaj expected her to believe he had sent a clerk to follow this man when earlier he had said his own employees would not be suited to the task he wanted her to perform. That a friend would see this man leave Rakulaj's office, recognise him, and remember to mention it to Rakulaj seemed so inconceivable, it lay almost beyond belief. Yilmay had no time for coincidences, and when they piled on top of one another, as Rakulaj asked her to accept in his story, her instincts told her trouble lay at the heart of the tale. Rakulaj hid some aspect of the story, and that made her even more cautious. "Describe this Nilukap." She needed time to consider the situation further.

She had never doubted anything Rakulaj had told her until now. His information, and the help of his contact, had brought her to Glailam, and she had extracted her revenge on the former Bailiff. He had helped her many times, but this story made her anxious. Much had not been said, and the unspoken elements could mean her ruin.

Once Rakulaj had given her the description, she agreed to remain in Arkkyd for two days while she looked into the affair but made no promise beyond that. Rakulaj gushed his thanks, but he looked afraid. He might have become involved in something that placed him in personal danger. For all he had helped Yilmay in the past, she felt no responsibility for his safety if his own schemes placed him at risk. She felt certain he had lied to her tonight and had damaged their friendship in the process. She could not deny the debt he had mentioned, and she seethed at the injustice of the entire situation.

She wondered at the change that had come over him. He had once suggested he would withhold his help from her so he would not become entangled in any criminal act. That upright stance had now vanished like a mist of breath on a bitter cold morning, taken by the winds of greed, she imagined; greed at the coin he had been offered the first time he carried the opium. The change she saw in him had not been for the better, and it had led him to involve Yilmay in something she would rather not have become a part of, but she felt she could not refuse to repay the debt he had mentioned.

Yilmay would learn what she could, settle the debt, then board a ship and continue her quest for Krage. In the meantime, she accepted his offer of a house. She did not know how long she must make her coin last, and she would be reluctant to ask any of his masters for more. The house would preserve what little she had. She headed back to the inn, troubled and irritated.

The next morning, as promised, one of Rakulaj's staff arrived at the inn and showed her to the house. It lay some way from the docks, but the lengthy walk in the warm morning sun cheered her somewhat after the dark conversation of the previous night. The house stood in a small square known as The Plaza, a word Yilmay had never heard before. It stood two storeys high and had three bedrooms, two parlours, and a pantry with a large fireplace. It had a privy on each floor and a tub upstairs. Though it would be superior accommodation compared to the inn, Yilmay hoped she would not be there long. She would try to find this Nilukap and learn what she could, but she could not put her heart into the task. Rakulaj had not been honest with her, and she felt used. The man also gave her a pouch of coin she accepted as payment for the work Rakulaj wished her to do, although a small part of her reviled herself as she took it.

She asked the man who had brought her to the house for directions to Rose Street and set off without further delay to investigate the area. Rose Street lay in a poor quarter of the city, full of rundown houses and a few shops that sold basic food and supplies. Enquiries in the shops yielded no information on where Nilukap lived. Either the shopkeepers did not know him, or they would not betray him to a stranger who spoke Vyrrmod with a foreign accent. Yilmay wandered the street, little evidence of wealth visible. The few children she saw wore torn or patched clothes of poor making, and the adults wore similar clothes along with a beaten down attitude that suggested few opportunities ever accrued to them. They seemed resigned to a life of poverty where they must scratch wherever they could for a few coins to feed themselves.

CHAPTER 17
YILMAY

The poor quarters in Dur's cities seemed happier and more hopeful than this area, and Yilmay felt empathy for these people whose fates had been written by those richer than them, who looked down on them and kept them contained in these barren neighbourhoods. She sat on a wall next to a young girl with a dirty face, and clothes to match. The girl wore no shoes, her feet as black as night. Her dress was a poor fit, and in truth it looked as though it had been handed down to her from an older girl, such as a sister or neighbour. Her pitiful, thin face and frame suggested she did not get enough food, and her brown hair lay unkempt and ragged down her back.

The girl eyed her, suspicious, and Yilmay smiled at her. "My name is Yilmay."

"Are you an Upholder?"

"That I am not. Why would you think so?"

"You are not from around here." The girl looked up at Yilmay with hopeless, empty, defeated eyes.

"That I am not. I am here in search of a friend. I wonder if you

know him. His name is Nilukap." Fear leapt to the girl's eyes at the mention of the name. "What is wrong?"

The girl stood and seemed ready to run away, but Yilmay reached into her pocket and produced a small coin. "Here, take this and buy something to eat." She smiled at the girl, who stared at the coin as though she feared to trust it, that it might be snatched away from her as soon as she reached for it. Yilmay moved it closer to her. "Take it."

The girl's hand shot out and grabbed the coin from Yilmay's fingers before she took two steps backward. "He will kill you." An animal smile sprang to the girl's lips.

"Not if I kill him first."

The girl hesitated. Her body seemed ready to make a run for it, but something held her back, as though she had been tethered to a post that prevented her from any attempt to run. "You cannot kill him. He has a knife." Yilmay never took her eyes from the girl's as she reached into her boot. Once the fan had cleared the top of her boot, she snapped the blade open. She watched as the girl slid her eyes to her ankle, took in the fan, then stared again into Yilmay's. Yilmay closed the blade back into the guard and let the fan slide back into her boot. "He has killed others, better than you."

Yilmay guessed the girl's natural curiosity had triumphed over her fear, and she laughed a sardonic laugh before she delivered a soft reply, full of menace. "There are none better than me." The girl seemed about to respond but flicked her eyes to the opposite side of the street, and fear filled them again. As if the tether had been cut, she turned and ran, and her bare feet slapped on the hard street surface. She skidded around a corner and Yilmay lost sight of her.

Although she wanted to see what had scared the child off, Yilmay made no move to look at whatever the girl had seen. She guessed it had been a person, but Yilmay reasoned they would watch her now the girl had run off, and Yilmay wished to pique that person's interest. If she turned, they might hurry away, anxious not to be observed.

Footsteps crossed the street, but Yilmay kept her gaze focused on the corner the girl had disappeared around. To her surprise, the girl's face peered round the corner at street level, a smile on her lips. "What business do you have with the child?" A stern, low-pitched woman's voice snarled the question.

Yilmay slipped her fan from her boot, laid it in her lap, covered by her left hand, then turned her head, slow and unconcerned. The other woman wore a tattered dress and a short garment like a tunic, but open at the front. Her hair hung untidy around her harsh, round face, and she had a short, stocky frame. No friendliness shone from her eyes, and one or two people on the other side of the street stopped to watch. Yilmay could not let anybody believe the woman intimidated her. "That is my business, and none of yours."

The woman seemed surprised by the answer. "She is my niece, and I care for her when her mam is at work."

"Mam" must be some local word for mother. "You could feed her, if you do care for her as you claim."

The woman bristled and raised herself to her full height. Over her shoulder, others came out of houses to watch. "Who are you, to think you can come into my street and talk to me like this? I should knock you off that wall."

Yilmay gave a short, scornful laugh. "How would you do that? Long before you could strike, I would slit your throat from ear to ear." She moved a hand on her thigh, and the woman glanced down at the movement. Yilmay opened her fan, and the blade protruded from beneath her hand. The woman gulped. "I seek Nilukap. My guess is you are afraid of him, but you should be more afraid of me."

"Why do you seek Nilukap?"

"He owes me an explanation. A friend of mine has received harsh treatment. I want to give Nilukap the chance to persuade me it turned by accident and come up with some recompense that might spare his life." The woman's eyes widened. "Might."

"Do you peddle that filth also?" The question threw Yilmay, and it took all her Guild training not to betray her surprise. She guessed the woman referred to the opium. If Nilukap only delivered messages, why would he sell it? She cursed at herself; she had not thought it through. Distribution of the opium brought great wealth to some, but even at this low level, Nilukap must have access to it and sold it to enrich himself. She remained silent. "That girl will not be corrupted by your vile drinks."

The opium these people sold must come in a drink, mixed with water or some other liquid, like the herby drink the healer had given to her. The full horror of the impact of the sale of the opium occurred to her at last, that children like the girl might come by it. Their fates were already written to be miserable; the opium would only hasten their demise into the abject horror of an empty life and an early death. Yilmay did not wish the skinny girl to be destroyed by it. "That I do not. I come to end his trade in it. I know he lives on this street, but I do not know which house."

"He would kill me if I told you." For the first time since she had approached Yilmay, she looked afraid, as the girl had.

"That would be quite an achievement from where I plan to send him." Yilmay kept her voice low and calm.

The woman seemed to consider the words for a time. "How many years are you?"

Another question Yilmay had not expected, and this time she could not beat away the small frown that creased her forehead. "Twenty-eight." She had not quite lost count, but her true age now seemed more difficult to calculate.

"You are two years too many, and if I catch you with that filth around my niece, you will see no more years, knife or no." The woman walked off, and as Yilmay turned to watch her go, the girl whipped her head back from the corner.

The woman had implied Nilukap lived in number twenty-six, but she could not walk straight to the man's door now, or everybody who watched would know the woman had told her which house. Yilmay did not want to endanger the woman or, more important, the girl, so she stood, checked the house numbers, then set off in the opposite direction away from number twenty-six without a backward glance. She turned onto the first side street she came to, then the next, and walked until she judged she had passed the block where number twenty-six Rose Street would be, and another street further. She sat on a wall again until she guessed half of an hour had passed since she had talked with the woman, then turned the next two corners into Rose Street again.

The crowd that had watched her interaction with the woman had gone, and number twenty-six stood across the road from her. She had misjudged a little, but had arrived at her destination, nonetheless. Nilukap lived in a run-down two-storey house that resembled all the others in the street. Paint peeled from the door and the window frames, and an upstairs window had been broken at some point and never replaced. The terrace of houses it stood in had no walls or hedges, and their doors opened onto the street. The hour had progressed well past the midday, and she wondered whether he would be home at this time of day.

Yilmay saw only one way to learn the answer to the question, so she crossed the road and rapped on the door to Nilukap's house, loud, insistent. She waited, patient and watchful, and soon movement came from within. "Who is there?" A man's voice, mayhap Nilukap

"I bear a message from Rakulaj." Yilmay had not anticipated he might question her and had no better answer to hand.

After a short silence, the man spoke again. "Who is Rakulaj?"

He may have bluffed, but in truth he might not have been told any names, although Rakulaj's name would be painted on his office somewhere, she felt sure. "The ships. None will be available for three passes."

She heard a soft curse. "Why does he tell me this?"

"Who else should he tell?" Her message had been delivered, but she now realised she had not played a high hand. He might do no more than agree to pass the message along and not open the door.

"Is there nothing more?" She had been right, and she now needed to find a way to persuade him to open the door.

Stumped for anything else, she rolled the dice. "Do you have any to spare? I have none, and I crave it." She gambled on the information from the woman, that Nilukap sold the opium, and she hoped he would open the door, fooled by her request.

Another silence ensued, then she heard a bolt slide back inside, then another. It would not have been easy to gain access to the house had her bluff failed. "Come in." As she stepped into the house, he peered up and down the street. "I have some left, but until the next delivery, little remains. Rakulaj's news comes at an unwelcome time." He closed the door and beckoned for her to follow him.

The house stank, every wall smeared with dirt. Yilmay imagined it had not been cleaned for years, if ever. The man's clothes looked as though he had worn them for some passes, and his greasy hair hung down to his shoulder. They crossed a parlour with a few unmatched pieces of filthy furniture in it, and he stopped in the small rear scullery. "You will pay the same as everybody. No discount for Rakulaj's lackeys."

Yilmay bent to her boot, came up with the fan, sprang the blade, and pressed it to his throat. His eyes widened and he opened his mouth, but she clapped a hand over it. "Do not cry for help, or I will kill you. Who do you inform when the ships are unavailable?"

She took her hand away from his mouth. His breath stank. "If I tell you, they will kill me." He shook with fear.

"If you do not, I will kill you." She kept her tone casual, as though bored.

"I fear them more than you. You may give me a quick death. They will not."

Yilmay clapped a hand over his mouth again, reached down to plunge her blade into his leg, and he squirmed and tried to scream. "Who do you pass the information to?" His eyes wide with fear and pain, he shook his head. She reached down again and jabbed a finger into the wound her fan had inflicted, pressed it into his leg and twisted it around as he bucked and writhed in an attempt to break free of the torture. "Who?" She stared into his eyes. He nodded as tears of pain ran down his face.

She removed her hand, the fan back at his throat. "Ofturra." He gasped in pain as he reached down to his leg and pressed a hand against the wound. "He owns a tally house at the dock. I tell him after I have delivered the letters to Rakulaj. He takes the crates from the ships. What he does then, I do not know. It is not wise to ask questions. The less I know, the happier I feel."

She considered the response. "How do you know when to deliver the letters to Rakulaj?"

"I check at a courier's office each day. The letters are left there, and I take them to Rakulaj's office, then I go to Ofturra's tally house. That is all I do. I swear it."

The levels of secrecy impressed her. Even Styrrach had less security in his schemes. "You sell the opium. How do you come by it?"

"There is a seller. He buys it after it leaves Ofturra's tally house somehow, and he gives me some to sell in this street and two others. I keep some of the coin, the rest goes to him."

"His name?"

"Do you wish me killed?" His tears intensified, he moaned in pain, and he shook his head.

"It matters little to me." She could not decide how important the man who bought it might be. Once it had arrived, someone would buy it, and even if she killed them all, others would doubtless step up to take their place. She must try to find the names of all concerned at a higher level, information Rakulaj could take to the Superintendent, or whatever he had called the man. That should end the process, for a time at the least. If enough coin could be made, somebody would take up the opium imports again, she felt sure.

"What of me?" Nilukap whimpered as he spoke. "Are you my ruin?"

"That I am." She turned him away from her and swiped her blade left to right across his throat. His blood gushed out onto the floor, and he crumpled to the ground.

Yilmay stepped across his body and searched the few cupboards in the scullery. She soon found the opium in a small cask, poured it into the blood that pooled around him, and walked out of the house. She turned to shout a goodbye, then pulled the door closed behind her, walked up the side street from which she had approached the house, walked for some distance, then crossed the street and turned back toward Rose Street. Across from her, the girl stopped and stared at her.

Yilmay had heard the light footsteps behind her as the girl had tried to follow her. She smiled at the girl and beckoned to her. "Tell your aunt she need not fear Nilukap anymore." She gave the girl another coin.

Cautious, she made her way back to The Plaza and into number three, Rakulaj's house. She felt sure she had not been followed, but she ran up the stairs and watched from the front bedroom window for a time. Convinced nobody had pursued her, she reflected on the day's events. She would watch the tally house and see what routine this Ofturra kept. If she could find a way to speak to him alone, he might be persuaded to betray those above him in the organisation.

That could wait until tomorrow. Yilmay heated water over the fire in the tub room, then soaked in the tub. She had killed again. Vamma had left her because of the violence that dogged her, and she had not shaken that violence from her. As she had killed Nilukap, Yilmay had seen the face of the girl from the street in her mind, a child born into a future of despair, then sold fake dreams that would doubtless lead to her death. A fruitless life made worthless by others.

She decided to find a local tavern and enjoy a goblet of wine. With luck, it would not be one Rakulaj owned, lest he appear to learn what she had discovered. On a nearby corner, she found one that seemed clean and well-presented, the patrons better dressed than those in most taverns in Dur. The inn's name, The Weary Traveller, seemed suited to her, so she found a corner table where she could watch the door and ordered a goblet of red wine. The wine had a fruity flavour and bright ruby red colour, and she enjoyed it enough to order two more. Darkness had fallen, and she settled her bill and left. She walked home by a circuitous route and fell into a troubled sleep.

Deineike stood before her, hands on hips. "You killed again."

"I had no choice. I protected the girl."

"This girl?" Arella's voice cut through the air, and when Yilmay turned, Arella held the severed girl's head. Blood dripped from her neck, and the two coins Yilmay had given her had been pressed into her eye sockets.

"You killed her?" Yilmay stared at the girl's head, horrified.

Deineike replied. "You killed her. She loved you, and you killed her."

"That I did not." Tears ran from Yilmay's eyes as she protested her innocence. Rakulaj appeared behind Arella and ran her through with a sword, a vast two-handed weapon with a blade as long as Yilmay's height. Yilmay screamed as Arella dropped the girl's head and fell forward, and the sword waved from side to side above her body.

Deineike spoke again, her voice as soft as a breath of wind against a cheek. "I love you." Rakulaj produced a dagger and slit her throat.

"They loved you. You killed them all." Rakulaj unfastened his trousers, and his manhood had Styrrach's face at its tip.

Styrrach's face whispered, "I love you," and Rakulaj slashed his own manhood off with the dagger. Styrrach lay on the floor, gazed up at Yilmay. Silent, he mouthed the words, "I love you."

CHAPTER 18
YILMAY

Yilmay sprang up in the bed. Sweat dripped from her face onto the bedclothes. When she wiped at her forehead, her hand came away drenched. Outside, the sun poked its head over the horizon as another day began.

She splashed cold water over her face, wiped her body with a cloth soaked in the same water, then dressed and went out in search of a shop where she could find some food to take back to the house. She found a bread shop and bought a loaf, nibbled at it as she returned to the house. Once she had eaten half the loaf, she stepped outside, locked the door behind her, and walked toward the docks. The time had come to watch Ofturra's tally house and learn what she could of his movements.

It did not prove difficult to locate, and it might have been the largest on the docks. Vast double doors stood open already even at this early hour, and dockworkers came and went in a constant stream. She found a convenient bench where she watched the tally house for more than an hour. Six ships stood at the dock, all three-masters, Rakulaj's sigil on two of them, the Vyrrmod sigil on another that appeared to be owned by a different operator. Of the

others, one had come from Malkartas and two from Corkannae. It would be ideal to walk up the ramp onto the Malkartas ship and sail away. From there she could take passage to Argoya and resume her search for Krage.

It saddened her she had more work to do here first. A carriage pulled up outside the tally house, and the driver leapt down to open the door. A man in clothes of good making stepped out, a peculiar black hat on his head. The man spoke to the carriage driver before he entered the building. Doubtless, Ofturra had arrived for his day's work.

Two men in dark blue tunics passed her. Their tunics bore the sigil of Vyrrmod on a patch. Upholders. If she fell afoul of them, they might recall two unsolved murders from several years ago, but they paid her no attention other than a cursory glance, and they moved along the docks. If they returned and saw her still on the bench, they may become suspicious, so she needed a new spot to observe the tally house.

She scanned the docks and saw several benches, none of which would provide such a clear view of the building, so she stayed put. In time, she grew anxious in case the Upholders returned, so she rose and walked to the edge of the docks, then turned to watch the tally house for a time. It seemed unlikely she could stand there all day without any unwanted attention, but as she pondered the dilemma, she glanced down the dock and had an idea. One of Rakulaj's ships had tied up close by, and she might have a good view from the aft deck.

She ignored the quizzical looks of the dockworkers who unloaded the ship as she ran up the ramp and skipped up the steps to the aft deck. An officer stood watch near the wheel, but he had been distracted by a mariner, and she ran past him to the aft of the ship. From there, she had a good view of the tally house, so she sat cross-legged on the deck. Some time later, she heard voices behind her, and footsteps approached her.

A man's voice spoke. "Excuse me."

Yilmay turned and saw the officer next to her, his face a blank parch. "How may I help you?"

He seemed taken aback by the question, as though he had not anticipated it. He spluttered as he replied. "This is our ship, and I ask again how I can help you."

"You cannot. I wish to sit here until you sail, nothing more."

"We will not depart until after dark." Yilmay turned back to face the tally house. A perfect outcome. "You, however, may not remain aboard any longer. I will summon a mariner to escort you from the ship." He had recovered his composure, it seemed.

"That you will not, unless you no longer wish to work for Raku-laj." She did not take her gaze from the tally house.

"Excuse me?"

"That I will. I am sure you have much to do."

He gave a small cough. "Madam—"

"You may call me Yilmay, or Corelle if that suits you better."

A long silence followed. "Of course. I will send a mariner with some water."

"My thanks, but that will not be necessary. Your crew must have enough to do without they attend to my few needs." She turned to smile up at him.

He went back to the wheel, where two mariners had watched the exchange. He spoke to them, and they stared at her wide-eyed. Yilmay returned her attention to the tally house. The bright sun shone in a cloudless sky, and the warm weather made her vigil easy to tolerate. Ofturra did not leave the tally house throughout the day, and the sun had almost reached the western horizon. The crew and dockhands had loaded a new cargo, and the mariners worked to rig the ship for sea.

Her vigil could not continue much longer aboard the ship, but at that moment Ofturra emerged and walked away with another man. As Yilmay leapt up and ran for the ramp, she shouted her thanks to the master, who had appeared to take station by the wheel some time earlier. The crew and dockhands stared at her in curiosity as she set off after Ofturra, who walked up a road away from the docks. He and his companion entered a tavern, and she paused to consider what she should do.

She imagined the same carriage would take him home, but whether he sent for it or met it at some pre-arranged time she did not know. Either way, it seemed unlikely she could catch him alone and unawares, somewhere she could ask him difficult questions. Unless she could join him in the carriage, of course, but he would never invite her...

She had used the ploy before, and it would be no hardship. If she had time before the carriage arrived, she could attempt to persuade him she might be interested in a dalliance and hope he would take her to his home. If his wife waited at home, the plan would fail, of course, and he would know her if he saw her again. A difficult decision, and she cursed, caught between doubt and uncertainty.

If she blustered in without sufficient intelligence, things might turn awry. That had never been her way, and she decided not to risk her chances of a successful outcome. Better to wait for the men to come out and attempt to follow the carriage. It might be difficult to keep up, but she may learn where he lived and could watch the house to learn more of his movements. The dalliance plan need not be abandoned, but for it to have a higher chance of success, she would persuade Rakulaj to buy her some more seductive clothes than the everyday trousers and tunic she wore. She settled in the shadows of a shop doorway across from the tavern.

The carriage arrived an hour or so later as darkness fell. It passed her, and she ran up the street to the corner where it had appeared. When she glanced back, the carriage had turned to wait outside the tavern. Likely, it followed a set routine. Routines could bring people undone, and Yilmay did not understand why people did the same thing over and over until they became predictable. The carriage arrived at an appointed time each day, she guessed, and spirited him away to his home.

Sure enough, Ofturra and the other man came out and climbed into the carriage. She had not noticed the other man this morning, and she wondered who he might be. He carried himself in a way that suggested he might be a guard, but if so, why had he not been in the carriage this morning?

It mattered little. The carriage drew near, and she ran down the street it turned into. Though she tried to stay ahead of it, it soon passed her. She increased her pace, but soon fell behind. Her lungs burned and her legs ached, and she could not follow the carriage much longer, but it slowed to turn into another street, and when she reached the corner of that street, the carriage had come to a halt outside a large house surrounded by ornate gardens. The man lived no more than four streets from his tally house. Why did he use a carriage to travel such a short distance? It made no sense to her.

Both men entered the house, and the carriage pulled around the side and vanished from sight. Lanterns blazed in many of the windows. The man did not knock on the door, but strode straight into the house, so a servant must have opened the door. They must have expected him at this hour. Routine.

Yilmay watched until well after dark, then approached the entrance. The carriage drive had no gate, so she slipped into the gardens and crept closer to the house. A figure passed a ground floor window, and she stopped, motionless. If they glanced out of the window, she did not want them to see her by accident.

Around one side of the house, she saw Ofturra through a window. He had a goblet in his hand, and he spoke with another man, doubtless the one who had ridden with him in the carriage. What if they were lovers? If so, her plan to seduce her way into the house would fail, and she would need a new idea.

A woman entered the room and spoke to Ofturra. The woman's

clothes suggested she might be a servant, and Ofturra smiled and followed her out of Yilmay's sight. The other man remained in the room and gazed out of the window. Still as night, Yilmay waited for him to turn away so she could creep further along and try to catch another glimpse of Ofturra. She did not dare chance the slightest movement until he looked away. Though the darkness surrounded her, and he gazed out from a lighted room, he might detect any movement.

At last, the man turned and left the room through a different door from the one Ofturra and the woman had used. Yilmay released a long, slow breath of air she had held in her lungs while the man had gazed into the garden, then drew in another as she moved, stealthy as a cat, further along the side of the house. She saw Ofturra through the next window. He sat at a table and raised a fork laden with food to his mouth at regular intervals. Nobody shared the table with him. Either he had no wife, or she ate at a different time.

Yilmay watched him eat for a while, but nobody joined him. He dabbed at his mouth often with a napkin, and she soon grew bored with his meal and made her way out of the garden, into the street, and back toward The Plaza. She would roll the dice on the seduction ploy, and if that failed, she would watch him until an opportunity presented itself. If the other man had been his guard, he would pose a complication, but she felt confident he would not bring her undone.

As she neared her house, she decided to call into The Weary Traveller for a goblet of wine. It had been a long day of inaction, and she would be glad of the relaxation for a time. She watched in amusement as a couple of patrons, the worse for drink, became embroiled in an argument about something and almost came to blows. The innkeep intervened and calmed the situation down, and one of the men left the tavern with one last hateful glance at his adversary.

Yilmay considered a second goblet of the wine but felt she should preserve her coin lest she have more urgent need of it later. She returned to the house, pumped water into a pitcher, then poured some into a cup. A door caught her eye she had overlooked before, but when she opened it, it only led outside to the rear of the house.

Tired, she carried the pitcher and cup up to the bedroom and lay in bed to reflect on the two days that had passed. She had learned little, and the layers of protection the operation had in place might mean she would learn little more. The desire to leave and head to Argoya consumed her, but she had promised to help, and she would keep her word up to the point she could achieve nothing more. In truth, she felt she owed it to the little girl on Rose Street more than Rakulaj.

The next day, she called into Rakulaj's office, but he had not come into work that day. She asked for some coin, and the clerk asked how much. Rakulaj must have passed the word she worked for him, but she did not know how much she would need, so she told him what she wanted to buy. He gave her some coins, and she thanked him. As she reached the door, she turned to him and asked him to tell Rakulaj that if he wanted company or updates, she might be at The Weary Traveller if he did not find her at the house.

She studied the Vyrrmod coins once she had moved some way from the docks. He had given her ten terks, the large silver coins that represented ten gilks. A gilk had been worth more than a groat from her recollection of her time in Arkkyd with Pettra. Ten terks would convert to around twelve regals. Insufficient for a ballgown of her making, but adequate for something that should present her in a more favourable light to Ofturra. It irritated her to buy clothes rather than make them herself, and she could recall only two occasions when she had ever done so; when she had travelled to Taro's farm, and when she had allowed Vamma to buy her some clothes in Tanasttra.

If she had time, she could have bought cloth and made something more spectacular. She frowned at the negative thought. In Ort, she had made three dresses and a wescoat for four in three days, so without doubt she could create something in the few hours that remained until she left for the tavern. When she told herself it could not be done, her resolve stiffened. A nearby garment shop sold dresses of reasonable making. One seemed suitable, only seven terks and with a low front that would accentuate her ample breasts, but a long skirt that would hide her boots. She had no shoes, and no desire to spend coin on a pair.

She agonised over the purchase of the dress. In the end, she spent so long in the debate, she left herself insufficient time to find and purchase material and complete the making. She bought the dress, even though it needed some adjustment. The adjustments would be easy enough for her skills, and the dress would be a perfect fit.

She finished the alterations at the house in The Plaza and gazed at herself in a reflecting glass. She looked good and felt certain Ofturra would desire a dalliance with her if his tastes ran to women. "I would lie with myself." She laughed at the jest until she saw the stubbly hair on top of her head, and the ugly scar where the healer had cut her. She tied a kerchief about her head, then thought it did not suit the overall appearance she desired. To hide her head, she needed a shawl, or even a hat.

Yilmay could not recall a time when she had ever worn a hat. *"I could always borrow one of the failed pies from the Duke's men."* She sniggered at the memory of the hats. Time had moved on more than she had guessed, and she pulled her boots on and left the house, her coin pouch in a small pocket she had sewn into the skirt.

She found a hat shop near The Plaza, but the prices were outrageous. Closer to the docks, she found another with more reasonable prices, and for fifteen gilks she found a hat that would suit. It resembled a hood, with a ribbon that tied under her chin. Even at fifteen gilks, she thought it an exorbitant price for something so unpleasant, but the pale green colour matched the dress well enough, and she could not present herself to Ofturra with stubble on her scalp and the ugly wound.

She entered the tavern, her breaths controlled, no evidence of nerves visible to any who glanced at her. Let the festival begin.

CHAPTER 19
YILMAY

Yilmay took a seat near the counter and ordered a goblet of wine. She had cut it fine, and Ofturra and his companion entered the tavern soon after. As she had guessed, the drink in the tavern formed part of his routine. They ordered wine, stood close together in the tavernroom, and talked in hushed tones.

Yilmay had hoped they might sit, and the fact they did not indicated they might not stay in the tavern for long. With little time to lose, she plumped her breasts to show more of her cleavage and rose from the seat. She moved toward the two men, who did not appear to notice her. What if they had no interest in women? Yilmay pushed the thought from her mind. She would deal with that complication if it arose and would not wish it into existence.

Close to Ofturra, she pretended to stumble and sloshed some of her wine on his companion. She gushed apologies as she wiped at the wine with her hand, and he seemed annoyed. Ofturra made some comment about accidents, and she turned to face him as though she had not noticed him until that moment, then tilted her head to one side and gave him a coy smile.

"Oh my." She held out her hand. "I am Vamma." She could not

risk her own name. Fame brought free rooms in inns and free travel on ships, but it also had less useful implications.

He surprised her when he took her hand, raised it to his mouth, and brushed her fingers with his lips. "Ofturra, and do not worry about my companion's tunic. I am sure the wine will wash out, and I can quite see how you might have lost your balance." He made no effort to disguise the way he made eyes at her breasts, and the look and the comment made her nauseous.

The act must continue, so she batted her eyelashes as she had seen Deineike do in Raolos's Offices. "But my goblet is now empty."

She pouted and sounded pathetic to her own ears, but he took her goblet from her. "Allow me to remedy that." He called the innkeep over to order another round of drinks for each of them.

"The time—" Ofturra interrupted his companion with an aggressive wave, and he did not complete the sentence.

It had proved so easy to hook him, Yilmay feared he might be wise to her ploy and toyed with her before his companion slid a blade between her ribs. She gave the companion a warm smile, keen to keep him on her side lest he object with more vehemence to Ofturra's fascination with her, or rather with her breasts. Even on the tips of her toes, she barely came up to the man's jaw, and she whispered in a seductive tone. "I apologise if I delay you." He glowered at her.

The innkeep returned with their drinks, and Ofturra clinked his goblet against hers. She noticed he did not clink his companion's goblet, but her attentions must focus on her mark, since she felt certain the other mistrusted or disliked her.

Yilmay spoke to Ofturra again. "Do you live close by?"

"I live four streets from here."

In truth, it had surprised her he lived so close to the docks. Although he lived in a large house, it had not been built in the best quarter of the city. "So close. From the cut of your clothes, I would have expected you to live somewhere more fashionable."

"I have not always been wealthy." Had a note of self-importance crept into his voice? "I grew up in this area and have great fondness for it, so I bought land and built myself a rather large house. It is close to my work."

She laid a hand on his arm. "What work do you do? Something important, I am sure."

If Ofturra heard the cluck of disapproval from his companion, he ignored it. "I own a large tally house. The largest, in truth."

Yilmay raised a hand to her mouth in mock surprise. "The largest? I imagine many things about you are large." She glanced down at his groin, then gave him a suggestive smile. It sickened her, but she must ensure he invited her for a dalliance.

Yilmay drained her goblet and gave him an unambiguous look. He needed to know that for the price of a goblet or two of wine, she would be his. "Another drink?" He had fallen for her ploy.

His companion reached over and removed the hand she had again placed on Ofturra's arm as he made the offer. "We must leave. The hour is late, and the meal will be ready." His clipped words conveyed every morsel of his irritation.

Yilmay pouted at Ofturra. "Oh. It is for the best, no doubt. Another goblet and I feel I would quite lose control of myself." A lustful look crossed Ofturra's face.

His companion leaned close to her and hissed into her ear. "How much do you charge? I will pay you extra to leave now."

Yilmay pulled an indignant look to her face. "How dare you? Do you take me for a common courtesan? Never have I been so insulted. Never."

The companion held her gaze. Yilmay believed he had killed in his life. Something about the way he held himself suggested he would not hesitate to plunge a dagger into her here and now. She wondered if he saw the same in her. "Ruptrak, how can you speak to a woman thus?" Ofturra had a note of anger in his voice. "Please apologise at once."

Ruptrak's eyes held no apology even as his lips uttered one. It might be best he did not suspect her any further, so she looked down as she wiped at her eye with the back of a hand. "Think nothing of it. I over-reacted. I apologise."

Ofturra broke the awkward silence. "Vamma, my companion has the right of it, we must leave. My meal will be ready soon." She looked up at him, disappointment on her face, her breasts thrust out toward him. The moment had come. How would he play it? "Would you care to join me?"

She fought down a whoop of elation, and instead tried to look thoughtful. "Where do you take this meal?"

"At my house."

She rubbed her chin as though deep in thought and judged it prudent to pretend some reluctance, as though some sense of decorum gave her pause. A courtesan would have accepted without hesitation, but she had declared herself not a courtesan, if not quite a woman of virtue.

He spoke again. "I mean no discourtesy." Her act had been good enough to convince him she felt reluctant, it seemed.

"None is taken, I am sure," She fluttered her eyelashes again. "I would be delighted." She thought it best not to push her luck lest the invitation be withdrawn or Ruptrak intervene again.

Ofturra downed the rest of his wine and offered her his arm. She slipped her own through it, no longer bewildered by the gesture. He led her to the door and left Ruptrak to settle the bill. He helped her up into the carriage, which waited outside as she had guessed it would. Once Ruptrak climbed up into the carriage and took a seat opposite Yilmay and Ofturra, the driver urged the horse forward.

CHAPTER 20
YILMAY

They followed the same route the carriage had taken the previous night. Routine. Nobody spoke until they reached the house, but Yilmay linked her arm through Ofturra's again as they lurched along the street. When they pulled up outside the door of the house, another man stepped forward and pulled the door open, dressed in similar clothes to Ruptrak, an additional guard, no doubt. Two guards might pose a problem, but she would deal with that issue if it arose. Never panic. No complication is irredeemable.

The inside of the house suggested great wealth, greater even than Raolos's, and Yilmay guessed the tally house alone did not provide all Ofturra's wealth. The opium must make him a vast sum. A servant offered to take her hat, but she declined. The woman scowled at her, and Yilmay guessed she had breached some convention or other, but the alternative seemed less acceptable.

Ofturra asked the servant to show his guest into the parlour, and she followed as the three men stood in the hallway. The servant asked if she would like a drink, and she asked for a cup of water. It

would not do to become inebriated, and she had already had three goblets of wine.

She had made it into the house, and now she must secure an invitation to his bedroom, a task that should not prove difficult. Alone in the room, she plumped her breasts again, then gazed around. The furniture all appeared to be made from a wood similar to Ortwood, the chairs upholstered with deep crimson velvet offset with gold braid. A cupboard against one wall held a vast collection of journals, and another seemed to be full of artefacts she guessed would be worth a Duke's fortune.

Ofturra came into the room, and a servant appeared with a goblet of wine. He took it from her, raised it toward Yilmay, and she favoured him with a seductive smile. He must not lose interest. "What a beautiful house." She gazed around in obvious wonder.

"How nice of you to say so." She suspected his apparent modesty might be false, that he revelled in his wealth. "You do not wish any wine?" He nodded at her cup.

"That I do not." She cursed herself—she had revealed herself as a foreigner. Vyrrmod folk used "yes" and "no." He might not notice, or he might have already guessed from her accent. "I spoke the truth earlier. I fear the wine has gone to my head."

He nodded and favoured her with a vulgar smile. "You are not from Vyrrmod?" He sounded casual, but Yilmay must be on her guard. She had slipped up.

"Dur. Zhanghar, if you know it."

"I do not."

"It is a tiny city compared to Arkkyd." "Tiny" flattered Arkkyd, but she wished to stoke the fires of his pride and keep him content.

A woman appeared and informed Ofturra dinner awaited. Mayhap he had sent some word to the staff for an extra dinner to be served, and they had prepared sufficient quantities to accommodate the instruction. She hoped all the staff did not share the same food as Ofturra, and one of them would not go without on her account.

Servants brought in a meal of meat and vegetables. Yilmay did not recognise the flavour of the meat, and when she asked him, Ofturra called it veal, which he said came from a young milk cow, or cow as he called it. She had never eaten such lean meat, and although she enjoyed it, she felt guilty she ate a young animal, killed before it had a chance for life.

Yilmay accepted another goblet of wine as they ate, and Ofturra drank two more at the table. Afterward, he invited her to sit with him in the parlour. They made some small talk, but he made no attempt to touch or seduce her. He sat in an armed chair, so she rose and sat on one of the arms. He made no move, so she ran her fingers through his luscious dark hair. She guessed him to be around fifty years, but his hair did not have a hint of grey in it. "Your hair is so thick." She affected a sultry tone to her voice.

"What colour is your hair? Why do you not remove your hat?"

"My hair is brown, but I had an accident. A tree branch fell on me, and I had the wound closed. When they did so, they cut my hair off. I miss my long hair, and I am mortified by both my short hair and the wound."

He laid a hand on her thigh. "I am sorry. I understand how people can be cruel and judge others by their appearance alone."

Yilmay needed to increase his desire, so she leaned down and kissed the top of his head. "Thank you."

She left her face close to his head. He turned to look up at her, and at last reached up to pull her mouth down toward his. He pulled her onto his lap, and she did not resist. She suffered his kisses and the rough scrape of his end-of-day stubble against her cheek. He did not appear to have much experience, and he did not thrust his tongue into her mouth, but she moved hers around inside his mouth and moaned as though consumed by desire. He fumbled at her breasts and squeezed them, crude, as though he tested a fruit for ripeness. Did he know nothing of how to please a woman? It appeared not.

"Is your wife not at home?" The final potential complication.

"I have never married." His raspy voice hinted her moment had come.

"Then let us go upstairs." She nuzzled his ear with her nose. He did not move, so she licked the inside of his ear, and his breath grew heavier. She ignored the vile taste of his skin and pulled him from the chair. "I must have you." She sighed with longing, and at last he led her out to the hall and up the stairs.

His bedroom made the one in Pettra's house appear small. From one wall to the other must have been at least five of her lengths, and an enormous bed dominated it. Yilmay pushed him down onto the bed on his back and straddled him. She bent forward to kiss him, then rubbed her breasts over his face before she purred, "Let me take my boots off."

She sat beside him and reached down to take her fan out of her boot. "Boots?" It seemed he only then realised she had said boots, not shoes.

"Boots." Her lips curled into a snarl as she lay beside him and pressed the opened blade against the underside of his chin.

"What are you about, you fool?" No fear in the hissed words; nothing but anger consumed him, it seemed.

"I met your friend Nilukap a day or two ago, and he referred me to you." He tried to push himself up to his elbows, but she grabbed at his engorged manhood and squeezed his stones. He lowered himself back to the bed. "Do not call out, if you want to live. Tell me who is in charge of the opium enterprise."

Through clenched teeth, he spat out, "You will never leave here alive, you stupid woman." Her blade flashed to his cheek and nicked him, and he gave a startled cry as blood trickled from the cut.

"We will see who remains alive once I have my information. Tell me who is above you."

"You have no idea who we are, and how powerful we are. The Upholders cannot even touch us, so why would we be afraid of you?"

"Why can the Upholders do nothing against you?"

"Because of…" He fell silent. He had almost given her a name, mayhap the Administration contact Rakulaj had hinted at. "My men will cut you to pieces and I will feed you to my dog." Rage dripped from his words.

"I may die, but you will not feed me to your dog, for you will die first. The quieter you are, the better your chances of survival." Yilmay tore the idiotic hat from her head, wadded it up, pushed it into his mouth. His eyes raked over her scalp, disgusted. She held her hand over his mouth and moved her blade to his manhood. "Do you wish me to remove it?"

Eyes wide with fear, he shook his head from side to side. She cut the buttons from his trousers and pulled them open, then pushed the tip of her blade into his stomach near his manhood. He squirmed and groaned. "Do you still not wish to tell me what I want to know?" Although he shook his head, Yilmay had confused herself with the question and could not tell whether he would or would not tell her.

She pulled the hat from his mouth, soaked with his spit, and wiped it on his tunic. He gasped as she tugged it loose. "I do not know who is above me. Nilukap comes to my tally house when a delivery is due. Men I do not know carry the crates into the tally house, and others come to collect them. I know nothing more than that."

"Who pays you?" He must have lied. He had almost slipped up and mentioned a name earlier.

"A courier brings a pouch after the crates have gone. I know nothing of who organises it. Even if I did, they would kill me if I told you. They will kill you—I hope you realise this. Who do you work for? If you tell me, I can argue for some mercy for you."

A mistake. "Argue with whom?"

"Curse you." He spat at her. "I would die before I would tell you anything. You are already as good as dead."

A knock came at the door. "Have you retired for the night?"

"Help." Ofturra cried out, and the cat was out of the sack.

Yilmay slashed at his manhood with her blade as she jumped from the bed. The door opened, and Ruptrak ran into the room. He stopped short when he saw the blood that gushed from his employer's crotch. Ofturra screamed, clutched at his manhood, and came up with it in his hand, severed almost halfway down its length.

Yilmay pushed herself forward and drove her blade into Ruptrak's neck while he remained distracted, then flicked it to one side and opened his throat. He fell to the floor, and she heard footsteps on the stairs. Ofturra's screams grew weaker, but he had drawn attention. From the shouts that rang out, multiple people rushed up the stairs to his aid. Yilmay ran to a window and looked out. Nothing lay between the window and the ground. If she planned to jump from the window to escape, she would fall two storeys. Could she survive such a long fall?

Feet approached the door, and Yilmay had no time to weigh her choices. The night had turned awry, and she must escape or die. She pulled the window open, clambered onto the sill, and, with no time to lower herself from the the small ledge outside the window, leapt outward. The fall seemed to last forever. Her legs crashed into the soft earth of a garden bed. The impact jarred up her legs and into her spine, and she collapsed forward, hands outstretched to break her fall.

Her hands hit the ground, and her fan flew from her grip. Her face smashed into the earth, followed by her body, the air pushed from her lungs in a noisy, undignified grunt. She lay motionless for a moment, then her survival instinct drove her to drag herself up from the ground. She shook her head, gulped in a vast draft of air, then retrieved her fan and thrust it into her boot. Nobody had been foolish enough to jump from the window after her, but doubtless they would rush down the stairs and be here in heartbeats. Unable to determine which side of the house she had jumped from, she set off toward a fence ahead of her. Every step sent waves of pain through her body. With a cry of agony, she limped on, her eyes on the fence. It stood almost the same height as her, and she pulled herself up it despite the pain.

Voices drew near, and with one last effort she swung her legs over the top of the fence and tumbled down the other side. She landed with a splash in water and sank into its cold depths, unprepared. With no time to draw in a breath, it seemed she had met her ruin, but some impulse drove her to kick her legs, and she swam, the desire to live driving her arms and legs to push her toward the life-giving air above her. With a gasp, she broke the surface and swam onward as fast as her battered body would allow. She drew short, shallow breaths, each more painful than the last. Shouts of frustration came from the fence. Nobody followed her over it, either because they could not swim, or did not wish to. Her hands touched solid ground, and she pulled herself out of the water. She had no idea what water she had fallen into, but she lay on her back and gazed up at the lights of the night sky as she tried to suck air into her lungs and ignore the agony that coursed through her body.

It would not do to lie here and wait for them to find her. They would cut her into the pieces that had been promised. She dragged herself to her feet and stumbled toward the dark shadow of a building ahead of her, step after insufferable step. She reached the building and turned to lean on it, but her legs gave out, and she slid to the ground. Tears begged for release, but she had no time to sit and wallow in her pity. She must flee at whatever sluggish pace she could sustain, and she gritted her teeth as she pulled herself to her feet again and moved around the side of the building. A light shone ahead of her, and she made for it.

The light shone from a tavern, and the sounds of rowdy patrons escaped from the windows and door, music in the background. A minstrel must entertain the crowd, but Yilmay stepped out onto the street and passed the tavern. As she walked, she cast about for some building or landmark she might recognise.

How she found her way back to the house, she did not know with any certainty. By fortune, she had walked toward the correct area of the city, and at some point she recognised The Weary Traveller, where she had enjoyed a goblet of wine the last two nights. From there, she could navigate to the house. By the time she opened the door, her legs threatened to give out beneath her, and she slithered to the floor, raised her knees to her chest and her hands to her face, and surrendered to the sobs that poured out of her.

She collapsed onto her side and lay there in tears until she fell asleep. When she woke, she still lay against the door, and daylight shone through the parlour window. She had learned nothing, but she had survived, more by luck than skill. The tears gushed from her eyes again.

CHAPTER 21
BESANONI

Besanoni considered his time in Vyrrmod might be done. He had grown bored of the land, and no request for his specialised skills had come his way in the last three passes; none that interested him, at the least. He had rejected those he had received as either beneath him or not worth the meagre coin on offer.

The two men before him now, however, laid out a suggestion that intrigued him, and he gave serious consideration to the proposed task. The one who had introduced himself, Torrekult, had spoken the most. The other had not introduced himself and spoke only from time to time to correct the other over some point. Besanoni guessed the mysterious man ran the organisation but did not wish to soil his hands in the sordid details of the work they asked Besanoni to perform on their behalf.

Torrekult had outlined a juicy problem, and Besanoni's skills were ideal to resolve it. They imported opium from the south, it seemed. Besanoni had no opinion on that. He did not use it, but he knew it had gained popularity, and if these two had the appropriate contacts, they might reap vast rewards if the use of the herb took

off even more. Their operation had seemed smooth and perfect, but as ever, it had been a touch too perfect. A complication had arisen, and Besanoni did not think he could resist the true intrigue of it.

They could still ship the opium north, but their distribution in Arkkyd had suffered complications. Somebody had slashed the throat of the courier who delivered messages and arranged the ships and the storage of the opium until their customers arrived to collect it. They distributed it to six other cities as well as Arkkyd, but now the owner of the tally house where they stored it had also been killed, along with one of his guards.

At that point, Besanoni had leaned forward, enthralled. The tally house owner's manhood had been slashed from him, and he had bled to death in his own bed. Far more delightful though, the killer had been a woman. They had met in a tavern, and he took her home in the belief she would enter into a dalliance with him. He had fed her, taken her up to his bedroom, and she had killed him and his guard before she leapt from a second storey window and dived into a large pond to make her escape. Such a delicious tale enthralled him so much, he might seek her out and kill her for nothing, as long as she first told him how she had brought the thing about. It had been much more than bold; it had been impertinent, and he admired her art. After all else, it would almost be a pity to kill such an inventive and talented killer, but when Torrekult had told him how much they would pay him, he accepted.

The woman drank at a tavern, it turned, and they asked him to kill her after she left the tavern. It seemed some nerves had been frayed by the secretive murderess with such deadly talent. Yilmay, her name, and an attractive woman by all accounts. She had utilised her looks to great effect to use herself as the bait in the trap for the tally house owner. More, he had already heard the name. Her fame as a member of the voyage around the globe preceded her prowess at the art of death. His admiration for her grew.

He would lay a trap of his own, similar to hers, he decided. The payment arrangements finalised, the two men left, and Besanoni worked on his plan. Her talent deserved recognition, so he would use her own body and looks against her, as she had used them to her advantage so well. The idea excited him, and he longed to implement the plan as soon as he could.

A mental image of her with the man's member clutched in her hand as she dived from the window came into his mind, and he smiled. He spoke aloud. "Well done, Yilmay. Well done indeed."

CHAPTER 22
YILMAY

Yilmay lay in the tub. The hot water soothed some of the aches from her body but did nothing to salve the disappointment and frustration at the way the night had progressed. She knew nothing more about the operation and had wandered too close to her ruin for comfort.

Bruises on her knees, feet, arms, and hands told the tale of the moment she had crashed into the ground. Her face had been cut, her knees bled from several gashes, and at some point she had cut her left forearm, a half span gash that would leave another scar behind. She could not recall how she had cut the arm. The fence may have slashed her, or it might have been a result of the fall. She had washed all the cuts with diligent care, but although they no longer bled, she had struggled to walk by the time she had reached the safety of the house. Both her legs ached, and more so when she tried to walk. Her nose might be broken, and in truth, she could not understand why she had not broken more bones. Mayhap she had, and some permanent disfigurement would result. She had no healer to go to and did not want to go to Rakulaj for more help lest the opium organisation watched him.

They would kill her on sight if they could get their hands on her. Whether Ofturra lived or not, she had done him terrible injury and killed his guard as well as Nilukap. They must be furious, and if Ofturra lived, his line had been torn. His manhood would never recover, and she believed he would have bled to death.

She should abandon the whole thing and leave for Argoya. She had run out of ideas, and the organisation would now be even more careful than before. It might be impossible to learn any more. While she might have disrupted the operation for a time, she doubted she had destroyed it. They would recover, and Rakulaj would remain embroiled in the scheme. In truth, it did not seem such a burden to carry a cargo and enjoy a share of the spoils. He had grown nervous, nothing more. In Styrrach's organisation, they had not tolerated any weak strand in the rope. Rakulaj had been lucky. If he kept quiet, they would not know it had been him who had asked her to intervene, and as long as he continued to make his ships available, he should be in no danger.

The water had grown cold, and she hauled herself out of the tub with a wince as her weight reminded her how much her legs and ankles ached. She gave herself a token wipe with a cloth and collapsed onto the bed. For two days she had bathed and cleaned her wounds and had not left the house. All her bread had gone, and she needed to venture out and buy some food before she died of hunger.

She dressed and tied a kerchief around her head, checked her fan sat in her boot, pulled them both onto her feet with a groan of pain, then snatched up the pouch of coin and dropped it into her trouser pocket before she hobbled down the stairs. The dress she had bought lay in a heap at the bottom of the stairs, cast from her the morning after her escape. She had not picked it up. Dried earth and blood stains covered it. She opened the door and looked out into the twilight, surprised by how late it had become as she lay in the tub.

She hobbled down the road. Now she moved a little more, she found the aches did not trouble her as much. To describe herself as fast would be inaccurate, but she moved well in the circumstances. She bought two plain cakes from the baker's shop and ate them as she stood outside in the street and looked around. The Plaza had been built in a better quarter, and Yilmay gazed at Arkkyd's skyline. It no longer held any appeal. Time to move on. Rakulaj had asked for her help, and she had tried but failed.

A goblet of wine would be welcome, so she headed for The Weary Traveller. The innkeep greeted her with a warm smile and mentioned he had not seen her for a night or two. She felt comforted somebody had missed her, at the least. He brought her a goblet of wine and she settled down to watch the patrons. It had been a warm day, and the tavern windows stood open. A cool breeze blew in through them and over the settle where she had seated herself. She felt comfortable and ordered a second goblet, more from laziness than need. It felt good to watch the patrons come and go, enjoy the cool evening breeze, and sip at a pleasant goblet of wine.

Three men came into the tavernroom and stood inside the door as they scoured the patrons, and Yilmay felt uneasy as soon as she saw them. Something about them did not sit right with her, like the three people in Argoya. They wore clothes that did not fit the quarter and had a shiftiness about them that aroused her suspicions. One of them stood almost a span over any other man in the tavernroom, and he paused as his eyes settled on her. He said something to his colleagues, and they glanced over, then headed for a table.

The innkeep brought them each a tankard of ale, and they sipped at it. They spoke little to one another and glanced over at her too often. She decided to leave, but as she picked up her goblet to drain it, the tall one rose and approached her. He had a round, red face and lanky brown hair that fell past his shoulders. "You are on your own."

Yilmay nodded, and her eyes danced to his companions. They had not moved, but they watched. She recalled The Parmen Inn, where a similar encounter with Hiw had led to disastrous consequences. These men had not been sent by the Guild, at the least, and they might be nothing more than three men who took an ale on their way home after a day's work. She suspected more lay behind them, nonetheless. They may have been sent by the opium organisation to capture or kill her.

"May I join you?" The man pressed on once he had realised she would not reply.

"I am about to leave." Yilmay drained the wine from her goblet.

"That would be a great shame, since you are the only woman here, and I would like to get to know you better." He smiled, but the smile had no warmth.

"That would not be possible. You do not know me at all, so how you could improve your knowledge of me, I cannot fathom." The others had not moved, and his forehead creased. She guessed he tried to unravel her words to find some sense in them.

"My name is—"

"Of no interest to me. Good day." She stood.

He looked hurt, but she did not care. The three of them concerned her. At her best, she might kill three inexperienced, intoxicated men who pestered her for a dalliance. These three had consumed little ale since they had entered, and looked as though they had some experience in violence. Meantime, Yilmay was far from her best in her present condition. She had always prided herself on her calculations of the likelihood of a good outcome, and her heart told her a brawl with these three here today would turn awry for her. She must leave and hope they did not follow her.

The tall man reached out as though to hold her so she could not leave, but she swatted his arm away, gave him a venomous stare, then walked out of the tavern without a backward glance. She had not paid the innkeep, but she would return tomorrow and give him the coin. To her disappointment, she heard their footsteps behind her as she set off up the street. Worse, at the next corner another man leaned against a wall. He did not glance her way, but she had never been a great believer in coincidence, and his presence there increased her anxiety.

An alleyway lay ahead, and she decided to turn into it and run off. She would not be capable of much speed, and the men would catch her with ease. On the other hand, if they had no interest in her, it would take her away from them. It would soon be dark, and if she got a good enough start down the alleyway, she might lose them in the streets beyond or find a house to run into.

Indecision had no place in any plan, so as soon as she reached the alleyway, she turned and ran. Thanks to her injuries, she felt no faster when she ran than when she had walked, and she would not even make it to the next street if they pursued her.

They did. They closed on her, and a hand pulled at the back of her tunic. He tugged at her, and she tried to slip out of the tunic and leave him with it in his hand. That opportunity disappeared when a hand grabbed at her shoulder and pulled her backward. She fell back into him, and they both went down, but she twisted and swung a punch at him. It failed to connect, and she landed on top of him. As she landed, she drove her shoulder into his sternum, and he rewarded her with an "oof" as her body drove the breath from his. The other two had arrived, and she scrambled for her fan.

With a yell of defiance, she dragged herself to her feet and swung her fan in an arc. She caught one of the men in the stomach and heaved her blade across his body as he let out a yelp. Blood sprayed from him and drenched them all, and he grasped at the wound with both hands, as so many victims of her deadly work seemed to do. He staggered backward and fell to his knees. One down, two to go.

Wrong. Behind the one who stood, uncertain, before her, the fourth man turned into the alleyway and made for them. Her ruin had come at last, but she would take as many of them with her as she could.

The man on the floor kicked at the backs of her knees and she fell forward, landing on already painful, bruised kneecaps. The one who still stood aimed a punch at her. It caught her in the shoulder and knocked her sideways. She swung her blade at him and slashed his thigh open. He screamed in pain, but the one on the floor kicked at her and struck her in the hand. Her fan flew from her grasp and skittered across the alleyway. A lucky blow, but it altered the balance in their favour.

The one with the cut thigh fell to one knee, and fury blazed in his eyes. The fourth had almost reached them, and she had no more than a few heartbeats to live. She punched down at the one who had kicked her fan away and caught him in the stomach. Once more she drove the air from his body, but now the fourth had arrived.

To her surprise, he swung a blow at the man on one knee and knocked him sideways. The victim lay motionless on the ground, and the fourth man dragged the one on the floor away from her. She scampered over to her fan and came up with it in front of her as the other turned to face her. He panted from exertion.

Nervous energy rushed through Yilmay, and she shook with anger. "Stand aside. I will kill them all."

"That would be unwise. The Upholders will be here soon, I am certain." He pointed back toward the street, where three figures stared down the darkened alleyway toward her. "We must run, or we will be arrested."

"There is no 'we.' Look to yourself." She set off at what passed for a run and wished the attack had taken place while she had been capable of greater speed. Her right knee throbbed in agony, the damage from the fall at Ofturra's house compounded by the hard fall in the alleyway. She had added to her collection of cuts and bruises also. Three streets away, she stopped and turned. She saw no Upholders, but to her irritation, the man from the alleyway had followed her. "Why do you follow me?" She still held the fan in her hand. It dripped blood, and she hoped she had killed the one whose stomach she had slashed.

"I want to make sure you are safe." He placed his hands on his knees as he gasped for breath.

"My thanks. I am fine. My thanks for the help also."

"Think nothing of it. I suspect you had the better of them even without me." He gave a short laugh. "I could not stand by and watch a woman attacked, nonetheless. Why did they chase you?"

She could not risk the truth since she had no idea who he might be, this helpful stranger who by chance had been on hand to help her. "A dalliance, my guess. One I did not wish."

He extended a hand toward her. "My name is Besanoni."

She switched the fan to her other hand and took his. "Yilmay."

"*The* Yilmay? The one who proved Ictharelian is a globe?"

Her fame wore her down. She felt like an old pair of work trousers, tired and threadbare. "I did not prove it. Everybody aboard that ship proved it, and many of them paid the ultimate price for that proof."

"Nonetheless, it is an honour to meet you, and to have played some small part in your survival after that cowardly attack."

She mulled his name. It did not sound like a Vyrrmod name, and she said as much.

"I am from Corkannae, in truth. And I return the favour, for Yilmay is not a Vyrrmod name either, regardless of the fact you sailed on that ship from here."

"Dur."

"Excuse me for this question, but why do you carry a weapon? It does not seem ladylike."

"I do not know this word." Another person who used words

she did not understand. "If it means gentle and reserved, then I am not ladylike. Far from it. Trouble has always travelled with me."

"That hurts me to hear. We all deserve a little peace in this life, but you seem not to have enjoyed as much as you are owed."

She snorted. "I am owed no peace." She stopped herself. Danger lay in any casual mention of her past, and she did not trust this Besanoni. His easy charm would not distract her from her own safety.

He gave her a curious look. "You are harsh on yourself. Come, allow me to escort you to your home. I will sleep better if I know you are safe."

"My thanks, but I need no escort. I will be fine." Yilmay did not want him to learn where she lived. She could not be certain he had not been a part of some scheme to find and kill her.

"You may well be, but my conscience will not. Is it such a hardship to endure my company for a little longer?"

"That is not the point—"

He interrupted her. "Your knee has been injured. Allow me some concern it might not bear you until you can arrange attention to it. If you fall, you might suffer more hurt. Please?"

She sighed. It seemed he would not be easy to dissuade. "Very well. I will tolerate you until we reach my street."

He inclined his head toward her, and she looked around as she tried to fathom where they had ended up. Once she had worked out where they were, they set off for The Plaza. Besanoni filled the walk with idle chatter about Corkannae and his adventures since he had left. He had sailed south to Qanti to seek his fortune as a young man, he said. He had not found Qanti to his taste; too hot, and with little opportunity to amass coin as they had been involved in a war with Qagrue, and it had cost them a great deal. He had made his way north through the land toward Vyrrmod. His tales involved a great many references to the beauty of the women in this town or the loveliness of those in that village, and she suspected he fancied himself quite the ladies' man.

He had travelled northward through Vyrrmod until he found himself in Arkkyd. He had found frequent work but had not accrued the fortune he had set out to achieve. He laughed. "Not yet, at the least." He seemed to have an irrepressible faith in his capacity to find the fortune at some point, although Yilmay thought his aimless journeys would be unlikely to yield it. None had accrued to her, and unlike him she had great skill at a valuable trade, at the least. Whenever she pressed him on why he had moved on so often, he gave a laugh and tapped the side of his nose in what she took to imply some dark secret he could not mention. She suspected husbands of his dalliances might have loomed large in many of his decisions to journey on.

His tale might have been no more than half told if Yilmay could have walked at her usual pace, but the fresh injury to her knee slowed her even more, and on two occasions she thought it might give way as she clutched at him until she felt she could continue. In truth, his insistence he walk her home had proved useful.

She would not let him see which house she lived in, so she stopped at the entrance to The Plaza, thanked him for his company and his assistance.

"You must see a healer in the morning about your knee."

His concern seemed genuine enough, and the knee did send spasms of pain through her body. "I am a visitor to the city. I do not know of any healers here." She also had limited coin, but she might persuade Rakulaj to help her with a healer, since her injuries had been incurred on his behalf.

"I know of one. I could take you there tomorrow. His rooms are not far from here."

"How convenient." She again became guarded. Another fortunate fragment of the tale of the night that saw him sweep into her life and render assistance, though she had never met him before.

He appeared to pick up on her caution. "You do not trust me, and you are wise not to. When I say he is not far, I had forgotten your limited mobility. For me it would not be far, but in your present state you might find it an arduous journey."

"Where are his rooms?" She hid her reaction to a spasm of pain that drove up her thigh from the knee.

"On Highguard Street, three or four streets from here."

Rakulaj's offices at the docks lay more than four streets away, and he might send her to the same healer. The longer walk would tax her strength, whereas this other healer would be a simpler journey. On the other hand, she could not bring herself to trust Besanoni or his apparent concerned generosity, and she did not wish to become indebted to him for his acts of kindness. The knee might well require attention, however, and she did not want to risk permanent damage if she did nothing about it. How could she decide?

"You hesitate." He showed no hint of disappointment. "You are cautious. Come, you need to get into your home and clean and bandage that knee. I will wait for you here two hours after the sunrise tomorrow. If you appear, we will go to the healer together. If you do not, I will leave and wish you well."

She could find no fault with his proposal, and the knee did hurt. "My thanks. I may see you tomorrow." She smiled at him, and he turned and walked away without a backward glance.

Once he had turned a corner and vanished from sight, Yilmay hobbled toward the house. She cast multiple glances behind as she sought to convince herself he did not lie somewhere where he could watch her and learn which house she entered.

CHAPTER 23
BESANONI

As Besanoni walked away from The Plaza, he reflected on the events of the last hour or so. He had entered the alleyway after the three men and expected to see Yilmay dead on the ground. To his surprise, one of the men knelt on the floor as blood poured from his stomach, another lay on the floor, and blood ran down the leg of the third. The men were nothing to him, hired hands whose sole job had been to flush her from the tavern in panic as the three of them pretended they wanted a dalliance with her.

His orders had been to kill Yilmay, but as he ran toward the fight, certain she would kill his men if he did not intervene, a sense of curiosity overcame him, and he laid out one of the men and pulled the other away. He persuaded her not to kill them all, and as she ran off, he decided to follow her. The stroll back to the house had revealed a complex woman, and she intrigued him. He decided he needed to know her better before he killed her. He tried to convince her to visit the healer with him the next day.

Besanoni could not say he found her attractive, but something in her demanded to be understood, and she had proved resourceful and difficult to kill. He did not want to die at her hand, but he resolved to learn more about her. He admired her skill; she had let him talk about how he had arrived in Arkkyd but had not offered a morsel of information in return.

The line, "I am owed no peace," intrigued him more than anything else she had said. A story lay behind those five words that promised intrigue, and he smiled as he turned the corner, determined to hear the story before she died. She would have watched him until he passed from view, so he did not turn to check. He would have been disappointed had she not been there, and he did not need to see her to know he would not go to his bed disappointed tonight.

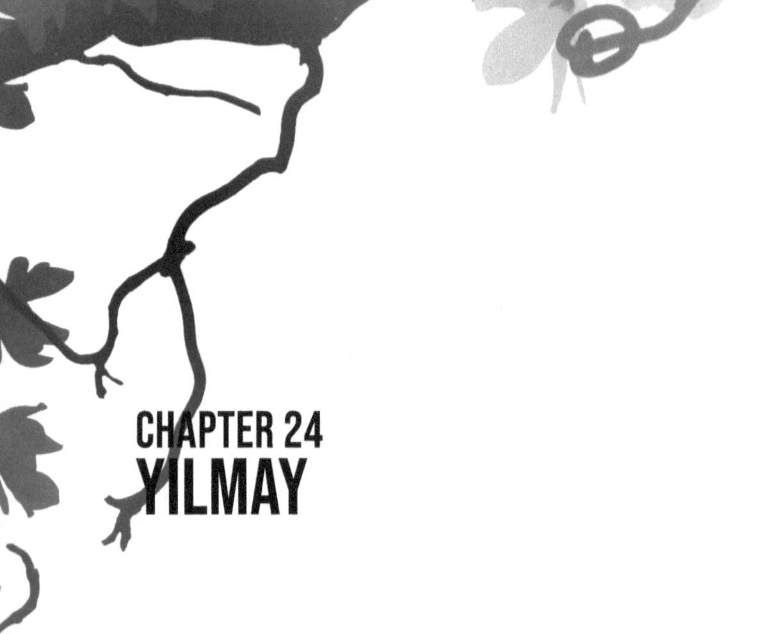

CHAPTER 24
YILMAY

Inside the house and with the door locked, Yilmay felt foolish for her display of distrust as Besanoni had done no more than attempt to help her, but she could not shake her concerns. The coincidences added up to one conclusion, and it worried her. The men had entered the tavern in search of her, and nothing could convince her they had not. They had been bent on the attack, and it had nothing to do with a dalliance. Besanoni's intervention had come at a fortunate time, as her fan had been lost to her at that moment. With it, she believed she might have fought off the three men. Without it, the outcome would not have been so assured, and his assistance had turned the brawl in her favour.

She could not overlook the coincidences, nonetheless. How did he come to be on that exact corner at that exact time? Why did he decide to approach the alleyway and involve himself in affairs that were none of his concern? The healer he knew, though he had lived in Arkkyd for a short part of his life. One coincidence might be genuine. Two stretched belief. Three coincidences in one encounter, in her experience, meant no coincidence at all.

Yilmay dragged herself to the scullery and took Besanoni's

advice. She drew some water from the pump, drank a cup and used the rest to clean the dirt from her knee. A deep cut still oozed blood, but she thought the pain deeper than the cut, and reasoned some bone or sinew might have been damaged or knocked askew. The knee would not flex without pain, and Deineike's experiences with her own arm and leg suggested the lack of flexibility indicated some serious damage.

She could find no bandages, so she cut clean strips of cloth from the ruined dress to bind the fresh cuts on her legs and arms, then cleaned her blade, lost in her thoughts about the extra risk Besanoni had introduced into her life. Arkkyd had lost its lustre, and she determined to leave as soon as she could, while she still lived.

He must work for the opium people. She could draw no other conclusion, but why had he helped her? He could have joined the assault, the four of them united to leave her dead on the ground in the alleyway. They may have told him to learn how much she had learned, and who she had shared that information with, before they acted. They might want to know who had sent her, so they could include that person in their justice.

Besanoni had killed before. She could tell from his demeanour, the way he moved, how easy it had been for him to disable the man in the alleyway. It followed he had been sent to kill her, but he had not. Yet. It puzzled her, and more so that he seemed determined to help her.

Weariness clouded her thoughts, and she called it a night. She crawled up the stairs and winced in agony at each step. Tomorrow she would visit this healer and hope he could bring some relief. What Besanoni's arrival in her life meant, she would decide under the morning's sun. Exhausted, she collapsed onto the bed in her clothes and fell asleep almost at once.

The morning brought a clearer head after a good night of sleep, but her knee ached no less than it had the night before. She navigated the stairs with difficulty. The sun had already risen before she had woken. As ever, this made the time of day difficult to discern. So little progress had been made in her lifetime. Somewhere, somebody turned a glass every hour as the sand ran out, she imagined. For the rest of the globe, it fell to guesses and wishes to even know how far into the day they had progressed.

When would somebody create a more accurate way to measure the passage of time? It must come, but instead people dedicated themselves to the creation of faster ships or the abuse of the bounty the globe provided, such as opium. They fought and invaded each other's lands rather than work together to educate people like Deineike how many years she was, and to provide a way for her to know it throughout her life. All people should know how to read and scribe. Instead, every man, woman, and child who did not had been left to scratch an existence the best way they could while others grew wealthy on the sweat of their labour. People had no freedom to love whomever they wished because other people despised them for it and wished them dead. It made no sense, and it cast Yilmay into a dark mood as she closed the door behind her and limped to the end of The Plaza to await Besanoni.

She wanted to be early so he would not see which of the houses she lived in, but felt ashamed of herself, nonetheless. Had she not bemoaned the unfairness and madness of the nature of people a few moments ago? Now her own mistrust drove her decisions, and she thought herself no better than those her mind had chastised.

Rather than place more weight on her knee, she sat on the ground. No bench had been put at the entrance to The Plaza, but the ground had served her many times in her life and would again. When at last Besanoni appeared around the corner, he gave her a cheery wave and walked toward her. She wondered again why he did not fulfil his gest. A night of sleep had not convinced her he did not intend to be her ruin.

He helped her up from the ground, and his assistance might have made the difference between a visit to the healer and a day seated on the ground, for she would have struggled to rise alone. "You have bandaged your cuts, I see."

"That I have. You are late." With luck, the accusation would deflect him from the fact she had been there before he arrived. She did not want him to know she had guessed his purpose.

"Am I?" He glanced up toward the sun.

"Who knows? Why do we have no accurate way to guess the hour?"

"You are a thinker, my guess. I have never considered that, yet now I wonder about it."

Deineike had been the thinker, not Yilmay. Deineike's mind had picked at everything, desperate to know why rather than what, how rather than why. Yilmay missed Deineike. So many years had passed, but the hole inside her created by her lover's death had not been filled, and she doubted it ever would be. "Let us be off. I am as slow as an explanation from the Duke, and I would not wish the healer to have left before I arrive."

"The Duke?" They set off side by side.

"We have a Duke in Dur. Or rather, we did, before the Qagrue came. If ever a man spoke more ponderous, pompous words than the Duke, I would run as fast as the wind before he could open his mouth." She laughed as she recalled the Duke's interminable speeches.

"As fast as the wind? I doubt you could run as fast as a cart with no horse at the moment."

She bristled as he teased her. "You could not catch me if my legs functioned as they should." She had stretched the truth.

"I would try, make no mistake."

The comment lay between them, and while Yilmay did not know what he had meant, her anxiety increased. She had not intended to hold out any hint she had any sexual interest in him. He might have meant he would pursue her so he could kill her, and that thought concerned her as much as the former.

After a lengthy silence, he asked why she wore the kerchief on her head. She explained the story about the giant and the mast, and he seemed fascinated by it. The tale took them to the healer's door. Besanoni opened it and gestured for her to precede him.

To enter a strange building ahead of somebody determined to kill one might be the last action one would take. Hesitant, Yilmay grasped the inner edge of the door so her arm lay across Besanoni and took a step into the hallway beyond. If he made his move, her arm might impede his strike so she could fight back. He closed the door behind her, and she wondered when he would decide to strike.

They entered a parlour where a woman sat at a desk. "I do not need to ask who the patient is." The woman laughed as she looked up, then invited them to sit in one of the five wooden chairs spread around the room and said she would tell Alkaltis they wished to see him.

Yilmay whispered to Besanoni, "Alkaltis is the healer?" He nodded.

The woman returned to the room and sat at the desk again. She scribed at some parch and did not look up until an elderly man entered the room. The man handed her a small piece of parch. "How much does it say?"

"Nothing." The woman smiled, and the man looked perplexed. "There is nothing to pay." She smiled again.

The man turned and walked from the room with a shake of his head, and the woman looked at Yilmay and Besanoni. Once the door closed behind the man, she explained. "Alkaltis will not charge those of limited means. He does not think it fair. They do not ask to become ill."

The words resonated in part with Yilmay's earlier thoughts, and she admired the position. At that, another man, tall and slender with neat grey hair, appeared at the door to the room and beckoned to her. "Come through." Yilmay struggled to her feet. Besanoni half rose, but the tall man said he would help her, and he took her elbow and guided her from the room down the hallway into another room, smaller than the first.

When Yilmay said her knee gave her the most pain, he asked her to remove her trousers while he investigated. He knelt, studied the knee, and prodded and felt it despite Yilmay's stifled cries of pain. At length, he stood with a sigh. "Can you bend the knee?" She gave him a demonstration of the limited mobility of her leg.

He mumbled something she did not hear, and he sat at a desk. He scribed something on some parch, then turned to her. "I cannot feel any break in the kneecap or the bones that connect to the knee. You say you fell and landed on the knee, so I suspect you have damaged the tissue that connects your thighbone to your shinbone. We call them ligaments, but you do not need to worry about that. Cold, rest, and bandages should heal it up over time. It may be some time before it heals. Many passes, even. That depends on how careful you are with it. If you use a staff to walk with and keep your weight off it, it will heal faster than if you continue to walk around as normal and throw yourself to the ground. I can give you some herbs for the pain, but I do not recommend we send you to a chirurgeon unless it refuses to mend. Questions?" She had not anticipated he might ask her if she had any questions, and she had none. "Good." He turned to the desk again and scribed something on his parch. "Take this to Hurtalli in the parlour and she will give you the herbs."

"My thanks." He helped her to her feet.

Yilmay limped back to the parlour and handed the parch to the woman, who opened a cupboard against one wall of the room and took out two jars. She pulled some herbs from each and placed them on a piece of parch she folded around them. "Here are your herbs. Mix them both into some water morning and evening until they are all gone. Not too much at a time. Try to make them last. They will help the pain."

"My thanks. What is the cost?"

"Nothing"

Yilmay pulled the pouch from her pocket and placed a terk on the desk. "I would like to pay if that is acceptable. If that is too much, it will help with the elderly man's treatment."

Hurtalli bobbed her head in acknowledgement of the gesture. "That is kind of you."

They left the building, and Yilmay gave Besanoni a brief explanation of the report from Alkaltis. He nodded once. "I am relieved it is nothing more serious. I knew somebody once who shattered their kneecap. That injury took a long time to recover from and needed a chirurgeon's intervention."

"Nothing so serious for me, I am happy to say. My thanks for your help."

"Will you use a staff as he suggested?"

Memories of Deineike as she hobbled around on her staff flooded Yilmay's mind. "That I will not, unless my knee shows no sign of improvement."

He drew in a short breath. "I hunger. Have you eaten today?" Yilmay admitted she had not. "Then I know of a tavern that serves a spicy broth that will fill both our bellies if you will accompany me."

She stared at him, again uncertain why he acted as he did. A meal would be welcome, although the thought of spicy food held limited appeal. His eyes bored into her own, and she thought he looked not unlike a small boy who pleads for a favour from its parents. He might feed her now and kill her an hour later, but she had once heard a phrase about the closeness of those who wished you harm, although she could not recall it now. "Let us go."

CHAPTER 25
YILMAY

Besanoni wandered along beside Yilmay as he guided her to the tavern he had in mind. It stood some way from the healer's rooms, closer to the docks, and the walk proved difficult. By the time they reached the tavern, she longed for a break and collapsed onto a settle with a long, grateful sigh. Besanoni fussed around her until it drove her to distraction, and she snapped at him, told him to order her a goblet of red wine. He called the innkeep over and ordered two bowls of the broth, a tankard of ale and a goblet of wine.

Yilmay decided to come clean on her financial situation. "I should tell you I am low on coin."

"I would not have guessed, after you volunteered to pay for your own care as well as that of another when no payment had been expected."

"I said I am low on coin, not on morals. That old man could not afford his care, and the healer made the same judgement about me. I used his services, so it is appropriate I pay for them."

He studied her face for five or six heartbeats. "That is a fair view of things."

Such a strange response, Yilmay thought. It had been correct rather than fair. Had he used the wrong word? The wine came, and she took a sip, surprised again at the quality. She had not yet found a wine in Vyrrmod she did not like, and she wondered whether they had access to wines that could not be bought in Dur. She did not know how wine came to be but imagined it to be the juice from some fruit or other.

"You seem troubled." Besanoni's words interrupted her thoughts.

"Do I?"

"What is it you say? That you do." A smile danced on his lips to tease her.

Troubled. The word seemed inadequate to describe all that had turned in her life, but too severe to represent her thoughts on the quality of Vyrrmod wine. She sighed. "Where would I start?"

"That sounds ominous."

"Do not expect me to pour out all my woeful problems to you. I am a private person."

"I see this." Their conversation paused when the server brought two bowls to their table along with bread, spoons, and napkins. Steam rose from the bowls, along with a spicy smell that made Yilmay's mouth water.

She dipped her bread into the broth and nibbled at it. It tasted pleasant, and the spice seemed to be more heat than flavour. She had been concerned it would be heavy with cloves, which she did not care for, but her earlier anxiety had been unnecessary. The broth had a spicy heat that lingered on her tongue and in her throat, and she gasped, her tongue out of her mouth. Besanoni laughed and dipped his spoon into his broth.

They ate in silence for a time, the wine a perfect complement for the broth. Her goblet stood empty before she had finished the bowl of food, but she did not ask for another. The midday had not long passed, and she did not want to become inebriated before darkness even arrived.

As they approached the bottoms of their bowls, Besanoni returned to the earlier conversation. "How could somebody so famous have so many troubles?"

"I fail to see how fame guarantees happiness." She became cautious again as he probed her private information.

"That is a valid point. I tried to address an inconsistency in you. You have accomplished so much and seen the entirety of the globe. It seems unusual you suffer with such concerns as you appear to. You seem... lost."

She pushed her bowl away and studied him. His tunic and trousers gave little away, light brown and of poor making. They could be found on almost any man in the poor quarter. He stood less than a span taller than her, with thick blond hair that hung to the collar of his tunic. His blue eyes never settled on anything for more than a few moments, a sure sign his profession involved surreptitious activity. She imagined women who found men appealing would be attracted to him and might not notice the dagger she had spotted at his belt. "How long have you been in Arkkyd?"

The question seemed to take him by surprise, and he leaned back as his eyes widened, then recovered his composure. "Three years, give or take."

Yilmay imagined the words, "give or take," implied a rough guess. "You must have been young when you left Corkannae for Qanti."

"Indeed, little more than a boy, still wet behind the ears."

Another curious phrase she did not understand. "What does that mean?"

He huffed. "It means I knew almost nothing of life outside my own family."

A frown creased Yilmay's brow, and she pondered the words. "I do not understand the connection. I knew somebody once who would have spent the best part of the day in conversation until she had unpicked the reason for such an odd phrase." The innkeep came to the table, and they ordered another drink each. As he picked up the empty bowls, Yilmay asked him, "Are you wet behind the ears?"

A look of surprise crossed his face. "No, madam. I am long in the tooth, rather."

Yilmay threw her head back. "I have no idea what that means either."

They all laughed, and the innkeep explained. "It means I am old. You can tell the age of a horse from its teeth, so they say. The longer the teeth appear, the older the horse."

"I did not know that." Besanoni rubbed his chin.

"Do you know why people"—Yilmay shot Besanoni a glance—"use the phrase 'wet behind the ears?'"

"I believe it refers to the birth of a cow's young. The mother cleans the birth fluid from the new-born animal and cleans behind its ears last. That is how I understand it, at the least."

"How do you know so much about animals, an innkeep in a city?" Besanoni seemed engrossed in the animal tales.

The innkeep laughed. "I will bring your drinks." He left without any answer.

Besanoni stared after him and rubbed his chin again. "Curious."

The conversation about the phrases and their explanation had distracted Besanoni, it seemed. Yilmay guessed a question designed to unmask his true intent might catch him unawares. "Have you ever heard of opium?"

He snapped his head around. "Opium?"

"Opium." She did not want him to avoid a trip that might reveal his motives.

"I have never heard of this."

He seemed guarded. If she had the right of it, and he had been sent to kill her, he must know her background and might expect his eyes to betray him to her. If he thought she suspected why he had been in the alleyway last night, he might strike. She wanted the game to last longer, and to discover the name of whoever had ordered Besanoni to kill her. "It is a herb. It has been used by chirurgeons and other healers in the south for some time to help relieve pain. Its use has spread, and people now use it for their own pleasure, as some will drink too much wine or ale."

"Is this connected to the wet ears or the long teeth in some way?"

She laughed at the humour of the question. "That it is not. The people who bring the opium into the land grow rich on the misery of those who use it and find they cannot stop. It is unfair." She would use his sense of her fairness. "Even the Administration of this land is involved, I hear."

He seemed reflective. "That would be unusual, if it harms their people."

"A few days ago, I encountered a man who sold it." She studied his face for any sign he knew the story, any small thing that might trip him, but he controlled his reactions well. The innkeep brought their drinks over, and they thanked him. "He supplied it in the poor quarter, among the city's poorest and most desperate people." Nothing. He did not react. "Even to children, I hear."

"To children?" If the thought horrified him, he did not show it.

He had weathered the initial surprise of the question, and she doubted she could get any further with the topic for now. She wanted to keep him surprised, uncertain, so she switched course again. "Did you send those three men to kill me last night?"

Once more he controlled his emotions. Either she had misread his intentions or he had great skill as an actor. Yilmay's frustration grew—he gave no indication of guilt or prior knowledge of the issues she had raised. "Why would I have sent them to kill you?" He wore a look of confusion.

Yilmay could not read his inscrutable face over the rim of her goblet, and she sipped her wine. The confusion could be genuine or false, but his face had shown the appropriate emotion each time she had asked questions that ought to have tripped most men. He had not convinced her, however, and her opinion had not changed. If anything, his superb act had made her more wary of him. If he struck, he might do so with no sign that would alert her. "Do you wish me dead?"

He glanced down at the table and shook his head. When his eyes came up to meet hers, they spoke only of sorrow, of regret. "That is a strange question. Why would I wish you dead? I barely know you."

Wearied by the act, Yilmay decided to leave. "You should keep it that way." Vitriol crept into her voice as she drained her goblet. If he wished to kill her, let him act. He would not find her an easy mark.

As she stood, he reached out and placed a hand on her arm and resisted her efforts to shrug it off. "What does that mean?" He looked so hurt, Yilmay wondered for a heartbeat whether she had misread him, but she knew deep within she had not.

Still ready to leave, she glowered at him. "Why are you here?"

"I told you, I needed to eat. Hunger is not a crime in Dur, is it?"

When Yilmay had been a small girl, the woman who owned a shop across the road from their home had taken a dog for a pet. Yilmay thought it cruel to keep a dog as a pet, and she distrusted the animal, but Saboti, its new owner, cared for it with relentless devotion. She took it for walks every day and fussed over it without end. When she had first brought it home, it had been young, and Yilmay thought it nothing more than a ball of fur on legs that yapped at shadows and could never keep still. Its features lay hidden under the mass of fur that covered its face. Its eyes peered out like two small dark holes in a skein of wool. When Yilmay met Saboti a few days after the dog had first appeared, she thought she saw a hopeless misery in those two dark eyes, an animal forced to endure a tragic form of human life rather than the creature it had been birthed to be.

Besanoni's face reminded her of the dog. He wore hurt and pain on his face, as though every misunderstood person in the land had been folded into this one man at this one moment. "I do not mean why are you in this tavern." Yilmay sat again. "I mean why are you here with me? Why did you help me today? What brought you to that alleyway last night?"

"I live nearby." Another coincidence. They stacked up so high, they would tower above Mount Belram. "As I returned home, I noticed the three men follow you into the alleyway. I have already told you I could not stand by and watch them injure or kill you. Why are you so suspicious?"

He had not been on his way home. He had leaned on the wall before she ran into the alleyway. People who returned to their home did not lean on walls unless they had become exhausted and needed to rest. Besanoni could not be tricked into the revelations she sought, but she would not abandon the quest to learn a name from him to help her understand more of the puzzle. "As you say, I am sure they intended to kill me. I believe that gives me permission to be suspicious. The Upholders also seek me, I am sure."

"Why?"

She had gone too far with the mention of the Upholders. Either she could pass the remark off with the excuse they would seek her over the brawl in the alleyway or tell him to mind his business. She could then leave Arkkyd, leave Rakulaj to his ensnarement in the opium business. It did not concern her, after all else. Other matters far to the north were more important, and leaving seemed an inviting proposition in that moment.

CHAPTER 26
YILMAY

As she considered the prospect, the dirty face of the girl near Ofturra's house came back to Yilmay. That girl had little enough to look forward to and would be easy to seduce with a herb that promised some respite from the hostile streets she had been raised on. The opportunity to learn something from Besanoni could not be spurned yet. Yilmay might not learn anything that could help the girl, but she must not give up without the effort she believed the girl deserved. Deineike would not approve. At the thought of her lover, Yilmay smiled. "I killed someone. A guard." That would be sufficient information, and would match what he already knew if those who had sent him to kill her had told him the full story.

"You have killed someone?" The dog's face disappeared, replaced by surprise.

He had over acted, she felt. He must know she had killed someone, but even if he had not, he had seen her defend herself in the alleyway. "Come now. Do not look so shocked. You cannot tell me you have never killed. I have spent enough time in the company of killers to recognise one."

He gave a defeated laugh. "You are right. I have killed men before." Men, not one man, she noted. "I have to eat, and coin is coin, after all else."

Yilmay sat in silence for a moment and digested his side of the conversation. He said nothing, and she felt uncomfortable with the quiet. "I knew somebody from your land." Klordia had been from Corkannae, Yilmay seemed to recall. The information had been offered when they had tried to obtain an appointment to see Raolos many years earlier. "She came from Gzart, I believe."

The sip of ale Besanoni had taken at that moment shot from his mouth. Most of it found its way back into the tankard, but some splashed on the table. He wiped his chin, and his laughter drew a glance from the innkeep. "You mean Gzark." He spluttered and coughed. The mistake had not been funny enough to justify his reaction in Yilmay's opinion, but she felt the burn of embarrassment in her cheeks. "I apologise. I have embarrassed you. Gzark is the city you mean. It is a horrible place. Nobody good comes from Gzark."

Yilmay could not disagree with his assertion based on the one person from Gzark she knew. The animosity that remained in her heart for Klordia after all that had turned in the unfortunate woman's life surprised her. She shoved back inside herself the desire to tell him how unpleasant her relationship with Klordia had been. "How do you know this?"

"I am from there." He laughed as he confessed to his lack of character, and Yilmay frowned at his offhand attitude. "What is the name of your friend? She might be my sister. Horrible woman." He took another sip of ale.

Another coincidence. How many more would he produce from his sleeve before he realised how far he had stretched credibility? "Her name is Klordia."

The stare of disbelief he gave her lasted so long it became almost comical. "Klordia? She *is* my sister." The announcement shocked Yilmay, but her shock gave way to further mistrust as he delivered yet another coincidence. It had become ridiculous now, but at that moment he laughed again. "I jest, I jest." He extended a hand toward her in what she took to be some gesture of reassurance. "I have never heard of her." He laughed again. "Your face." His grin mocked her.

She had fallen for his jest, which had been well played and had earned the laughter she gave it. Sadness soon washed over her, however, and guilt she had laughed at Klordia's expense. "She is dead."

Merriment turned to sympathy as fast as the blink of an eye. "Klordia is dead? I am sorry to hear this."

"Why? You did not know her." Other people's sympathy made Yilmay uncomfortable, as though it might in some way excuse her part in whatever had befallen the unfortunate whose death came after Yilmay had touched their life.

"I am sorry for you, not her. It hurts to lose a friend. I have lost many."

"*Nowhere near as many as me,*" Yilmay thought. "I took vengeance, but not enough. I am to blame for her death. I still have lives to take in payment of that debt."

"It seems you are in the vengeance business."

With a shake of her head, she replied. "If I am, then it is a terrible business." The unpleasant turn of the conversation had left her despondent, and she stood again, ready to leave. She intended to return to the house and decide whether to pursue this peculiar wisp of a plan or abandon it and leave for Argoya.

"Do you like the water?" Besanoni's question stopped her in her tracks.

"The water?"

"The sea, rivers, lakes. The water."

For most of the time they had been in the tavern, Yilmay had tried to trip him with her questions, and he had endured them all without any hint of who had sent him or what he planned. As she had been about to leave, he had caught her unawares with a question unrelated to the things they had talked about. "I used to be a mariner. You know this."

With a small nod, he continued. "I have access to a small boat. We could take it out onto the water. A small cove not far to the west of the city is so beautiful, it might even restore the hope of somebody as broken as you."

An isolated cove with nobody around—the perfect place to kill someone. A dagger in the ribs while the scenery distracted them, the body unlikely to be discovered for some time, if ever. On the other hand, that death need not be hers, and if he planned to act, she might beat him to it and kill him. She might learn more information also, but in truth the thought of the little boat on the water, the sails filled with wind, the cares of her life rocked away for a time by the swell; these things appealed to her the most. "Why not? I have no other plans."

They chatted as they walked to the docks, her knee still painful. He asked whether she had ever been married, and she wondered about an appropriate response. In the end, she settled for the truth. A total stranger, and one of the few times in her life she had ever admitted she preferred women to men, another strange twist along the path she had taken.

"That must be a difficult life to live. Nothing about you is simple, Yilmay."

Had Deineike not said something similar once, in Torric or Vjort? "That it is not." They walked on in silence until they turned into the wide street that led to the docks. "You are not offended or horrified by this news?" Curiosity about his reaction had eaten at her since she had made the admission, and she could resist it no longer.

"It is none of my concern. I like you, and I would be delighted to lie with you. You might realise the joys you miss." He laughed, and she aimed a playful swipe at his arm. "Who you choose to lie with is of no consequence to me, and I make it a habit to live in such a way that if a thing does not affect my life, I pay it no mind."

An opportunity had presented itself to return to the subject of the opium. "What of this herb, opium? It does not affect you, but I cannot see how you can ignore it and say you do not care."

The time stretched on, and he made no reply, so she pressed him again. "You ask a difficult question. I do not know how I feel about the opium. I do not use it, and I do not judge a man on how he makes his coin. I have done things that brought me no pride." A few paces later, he pointed out the boat they could use to reach the cove, and Yilmay forgot about the opium as she looked over the boat.

It had one mast and a hull not much longer than Besanoni was tall. Some people might doubt the small boat would be suited to the waves of the Torr Sea, but if they stayed close to the coast, Yilmay imagined the boat would be safe for the trip. It looked well-made and well maintained, and the light wind posed little threat, she thought. She stepped into the boat, and it rocked under her.

Besanoni clambered in with caution after her, one leg at a time and a hand on the dock at all times. He did not appear as comfortable as Yilmay on the water. As he struggled into the boat, she asked him whether he would sail it.

"Would you prefer to?" He did not look at her, his concentration devoted to his efforts to board.

He had given the answer she had hoped for. "I would enjoy that."

Besanoni sat on the wooden seat in the middle of the boat, but she asked him to move to the seat at the front of the boat and explained about balance and weight. He changed seats with care while Yilmay checked the rudder turned in both directions.

She hoisted the single sail, and they untied the ropes that held the boat at the docks. All the small boats were moored at the western end of the dock, well away from the cargo ships and fish-boats. The little vessel's sails picked up the wind, and Yilmay steered it away from the dock.

As she manoeuvred the boat out from the dock, Besanoni watched and praised her ability to handle the craft. As ever, she blushed at the compliment. In her opinion, the boat handled as well as any she had sailed, and with the wind against her, she lost herself in the joys of the manipulations of sail and rudder. The little craft tacked back and forth as they moved along the coastline. The boat responded to her every input on the tiller attached to the rudder, every adjustment to the sail. Despite the light wind, they made good speed, and Yilmay thought the little vessel might scamper at a decent speed with a following wind.

As the coastline slipped by on their dock'ard side, Besanoni relaxed, although even as he gazed around and smiled whenever he caught her eye, he kept one hand on the gunwale of the boat at all times. For her part, Yilmay abandoned herself to the pure joy of the sea, the wind on her face, the crack of the sail, and isolation from the cares of life on the land. The water slid past below them as they carved their way through it, and she guessed if she threw Besanoni overboard, she could sail the boat away and vanish from all her cares forever.

Her reverie came to a halt as he pointed to the shore and called out they had reached the cove. Yilmay turned the boat south toward the land. Besanoni had not lied; the sheltered cove took her breath away with its pure yellow sand and lush green surrounds. Nobody could be seen, and the only sounds came from the boat as it cut through the water, the wind in her ears, and a large white bird that circled overhead and called to them as though it begged for food.

As the boat grounded, Besanoni almost fell, and Yilmay stifled a laugh. She leapt out, heedless of the water that sloshed into her boots, and urged him to join her in the water so they could pull the boat up the sand. The tide must not snatch it and abandon them here.

A rope lay in the bottom of the boat, and she tied one end to the prow before she limped to a small tree near the waterline and made the boat fast to its bough. She took off her boots, slipped her fan into the waist of her trousers, and enjoyed the sand between her toes as she stood on the shoreline. The sun warmed both the sand and her face, and she felt at peace.

Besanoni took off his boots and walked toward her with an occasional hop that suggested he found the warmth of the sand uncomfortable. They wandered up and down along the water's edge at Yilmay's slow, difficult pace. They chatted for an hour before Besanoni wanted to sit and enjoy the tranquil environment. A bird stood on a rock nearby, and Yilmay did not recognise it. It had long, spindly legs, a long neck and a long bill. Its white feathers gleamed in the sun, and it spread its wings out as though it flew.

She pointed it out to Besanoni, and he called it an egret. "It has long legs so it can wade in the shallows and hunt for food."

"What does it eat?" Yilmay wanted to know more about the bird.

"Fish, reptiles, shellfish."

"Shellfish?" The word meant nothing to her.

"Sea creatures with shells."

A hand over her eyes to shield the sun from her vision, she gazed at him. He sat to her left, and he seemed relaxed and content. "How do you know so much about this bird?"

"I come here often. Whenever I can, in truth. Also, I was a fishman in Gzark."

She tried to remember how old he had told her he had been when he had left Corkannae. Young, she thought he had said. He had not seemed comfortable in the little boat either. The fishman story rang false with her. "Gzark lies on the sea, then?"

"It is on a lake. The lake is fed by a long wide river, the Reticca. It is rich in fish, and the lake is home to a great many of them. My father and I took his little fishboat out onto the lake most days and brought home a bounty we sold in the city. The coin kept all six of us."

"You have brothers and sisters?"

"I have a sister and two brothers, and my grandmother lived with us." He turned to her. "Why are you so interested in my life?"

She leaned to one side and nudged him with her shoulder. "Shut up." A silence settled on them, disturbed only by the waves as they broke on the sand. "Do you miss your family?"

He pursed his lips. "I cannot say I do. My grandmother died, and I never liked my brothers. They will be fine without me. I have made my choices, and regrets will not change them."

The sun sank lower in the sky, but before she could leave the cove, Yilmay must make one last attempt to learn something to help her decide what to do when she returned to Arkkyd. "You have not answered my question about how you feel about the opium trade."

With a sigh, he turned away and fiddled with the sand between his legs. "How did you learn of this thing?"

"Somebody asked me to look into it for them. Nothing more."

"Can they not help you? Do they know all you have learned?"

Something in the way he asked the last question aroused her suspicion again. Although she probed for information, she could not escape the sense he also sought to learn something from her. She decided to lie. "That they do. They know it all. Even the involvement of the Administration."

"Who is this friend? Are they not in a position to help you?" His eyes remained focused on the sand, and it seemed he now probed her, not the other way around.

"I would prefer not to say. There might be danger to them."

A piece of wood lay near his hand, nothing more than a twig, and he picked it up and drew swirls in the sand with it. Yilmay said nothing and waited for him to respond. "I want to help you." He had replied at last.

"Help me with what?"

"The opium, although I know little about it."

"Why?" Had he meant the words, or had he tried to deceive her? He might distract her before he drove his dagger into her, or he might attempt to find out all she knew and draw Rakulaj's name from her. Her mother had often said, "*Honey attracts the bees.*" She had meant that a kind disposition made people keener to help than tartness ever could. Yilmay did not believe bees would be attracted by honey, since her limited grasp of how bees lived led her to believe bees made honey rather than gather it.

He continued with his sand sketches. "The children, my guess. When you told me they sold it to children, it did not sit right with me. At first, I felt dismay you might have lied to me, but I now realise I cannot take that chance and allow children to be exposed to something that might destroy altogether their already slim chances. You said I should care, and you have the right of it. I should."

Every part of her wanted to believe him. Every part except her heart, and her heart told her his words had been insincere. She could not deny the fates written for her had left her jaded and disillusioned, incapable of trust when she suspected help or friendship disguised an ulterior motive. Nonetheless, Besanoni had admitted he had killed, and she felt certain he had been sent to kill her. His change of heart would be hard to believe even if she had fallen for his charm and they had lain together, but that prospect had been snatched from him. She continued to probe. "What would you do next?"

"I think I would try to find some information that would link the Administration to the ships that bring the opium to Vyrrmod."

Yilmay gazed out on the waves as they ran to and from the shore, but she did not reply. "How good a killer are you?"

Another question she had not expected. "Good enough, my guess. I am still alive, and many talented people have tried to bring my ruin to me."

From the corner of her eye, she saw him nod. "You are broken. Something about you…"

He fell silent, but the comment had intrigued her. "What?"

He dropped the twig, pulled a dagger from his belt, and her hand shot toward the waist of her trousers.

CHAPTER 27
YILMAY

Before Yilmay's hand reached her fan, Besanoni held up his other hand, reversed the dagger in his grip, and handed it to her, handle first. "I wish to tell you something."

Either she had fallen too deep into her own thoughts or she had become lost in his words, but he had beaten her. He had his dagger in his hand before she could reach her fan, and that made it almost certain he would have killed her had he wished. She twirled his dagger in her hand. It felt well balanced, but a little heavy for her taste. "Then tell it."

"You have guessed right, I think. I have been sent to kill you, and I believe I could do so."

No hint of weakness could be shown in this moment. He must believe her capable of his ruin. "If there is anything afterward, many men are gathered there who grumble to one another of how they believed they would be good enough."

He ignored her barb. "Those who sent me to kill you did not tell me about the opium. They told me you had interfered with their business and killed some of their colleagues."

"You did not wonder what business they might be involved in that would lead me to kill them?"

"I have already told you. That did not affect me, and I did not ask it because I did not care."

"Now we have that cleared up, what comes next?"

"Yilmay, I do not wish to kill you. I cannot get back to Arkkyd without you." They laughed at the jest made in fraught circumstances. "I believe you do not wish me to kill you either."

Yilmay stared off across the Torr Sea as she replied in a quiet voice he must have found difficult to hear over the waves as they broke on the sand. "Do not be so certain of that."

"This is why I do not wish to kill you, in part. I said I like you, and I meant it. I wish to help you."

"And how will you help me?"

The twig retrieved, he resumed the swirls in the sand. "I could tell you the name of the man who hired me."

The name of that man had brought her here in the first place. With luck, he would be the next step up in the organisation, but she must not appear too keen. "That will not help me. I need a link between him and the ships." Other questions had been evaded, but now the truth had been revealed, Yilmay wished to investigate the incredible string of coincidences. "Did you send those three men after me?"

His laughter skipped out to meet the wave that crashed onto the shore. "I did. I apologise."

No confirmation had been required. The truth did nothing more than give Yilmay the satisfaction she had guessed right. "They were terrible."

"I cannot deny it. Three thugs I hired in a tavern, nothing more. I had expected them to be better though. Had I not run toward you, I fear you would have killed them and left me no opportunity to save you."

A quiet laugh, little more than a breath of acknowledgement, formed in her throat. "Where is your other dagger?"

"In my boot. Where do you keep yours?"

"I carry only one. It is at my waist."

"That is… bold. It is fortunate I aided you after all else. Without your weapon, the fight might have turned awry for you."

"There is more than one way to milk a mutton."

He laughed. "It is '*milk a cow.*'"

"It is? Do not mind me. I am from Ryl." He could not be right, in truth. "We do not say 'cow.' I do not believe you are correct."

"What do you call them?"

"Milk cows."

"There is more than one way to milk a milk cow. You are right. It sounds ridiculous."

"Then I have misremembered it." She laughed. "I am prone to do so these days."

"What happens now?"

She needed a name. "I will hear the name of the one who sent you, but unless I can link him to the ships, I am no further forward."

"I could tell them I have killed you. They might believe you begged for your life and revealed the name of your friend. They would ask me to kill him, I am sure."

Most men seemed to believe women could not be important figures in life, and irritation twitched in Yilmay's breast. "Or her."

"My apologies. In truth, the longer they retain my services, the more we might learn. I would need your friend's name if we are to try that plan, and you seem reluctant to reveal it."

She had several options, and she tried to arrange them in her mind. "How much did they pay you to kill me?"

"Two hundred terks."

She whistled, amazed. "I am worth that much?"

"You are to them. Their operation brings much coin to them, I guess."

"You should kill me. That is a lot of coin."

He did not laugh at her jest. "You are already dead inside, I think."

Her nuisance value to them surprised her. Two hundred terks— an enormous sum. "What is the name of the one who hired you?"

"Torrekult."

Almost an entire day to obtain the name, but she had it at last, if he had told her the truth. "Is he in the Administration?"

"He is not. The Administration man attended the discussion, but he would not reveal his name."

She shook her head, disappointed. "He is the link to the ships; I am certain of it. I must find his name."

"Torrekult must know his name. They met me together."

"I must find a way to get this Torrekult to tell me the other's name." Yilmay had spoken out loud, but her words had been spoken to herself, in truth.

"Let me help."

A crucial moment had arrived. She had a name. It might be a false name, but she did not believe it would be. "The risks are too great. I am not yet convinced I can trust you, and if you turn on them, they will kill you if they learn of it."

"That may be true. They may try to kill me anyway if they find out I have failed them. They are not killers, however, while I am."

In her mind, Yilmay conceded his point. The people who became rich from the opium had been no threat, other than the guards Ofturra had surrounded himself with and now Besanoni, a hired killer from outside their organisation. "Let us pretend you are to tell them you have killed me. How do you contact Torrekult and collect your coin?"

"He owns a footwear business. Once you are dead, I am to go into the shop and ask for some cheese."

"Cheese?" Somewhere in the back of her mind, a doubt niggled at her about the truth of the story. The introduction of the cheese seemed farcical to her.

"Cheese. He will tell me he does not sell cheese, and I will leave. That night, a courier will come to my room with the coin."

The cheese story stretched her belief in the entire tale. Wilash had once mentioned a phrase his father had used, however, and she struggled to recall it. It went something like, "*If a thing seems impossible to believe, it might be true.*" She had misremembered it, but it still held a grain of wisdom. "That will not work. I need him, not his courier. How many people work in this shop?"

"Two or three, I think. I am not certain. I walked past the shop once, to check the task was genuine. I found the cheese story far-fetched and foolish."

"*As do I,*" Yilmay thought. "Three staff? How many pairs of shoes and boots does this man sell?" With an embarrassed laugh, Besanoni admitted he had not considered that aspect. "I need a way to lure him out in place of the courier." Torrekult would be the only one who could tell her the name of the man in the Administration.

"I could ask for opium rather than coin."

Yilmay laughed at the many comical ways the tale played out. "Which flavour cheese must you buy to obtain opium?"

"I will go into the shop and tell him I wish to speak to him about a different method of payment. I will insist he comes to my room that night and promise him the name of your friend. I am certain he will meet with me to learn that."

"It might work." She doubted it would.

"I would need the name, of course, but that is not urgent, unless you wish to tell me now." Yilmay said nothing. "Either way, may I have my dagger back?"

"That you may." Yilmay thrust it into the side of his throat up to the hilt, and the tip of the blade emerged from the other side. Blood poured from both wounds, and he reached up to the dagger with both hands as blood gurgled in his throat. She drew her lips back in a snarl as she watched the life fade from his eyes. He fell backward onto the sand, and his blood pooled around him, turned the sand into red mud. Her patience with the games they played had run out, and she did not believe his change of heart. She imagined he had realised he would not learn Rakulaj's name from her lips and asked for his dagger to kill her with.

She found the extra dagger in his boot, pulled it loose, and tucked it into the waistband of her trousers, then untied the rope from the tree and threw it into the bottom of the boat. The boat proved difficult to push back into the water alone as the tide had turned, the water further out than when they had arrived and the wet sand, which sucked her feet down into its embrace rather than give her a firm footing, refused to cooperate with her endeavours. She grunted with exertion as she pushed the boat until it floated, then jumped in and sailed back to Arkkyd with one backward glance at Besanoni's body as it lay on vermilion sand.

Torrekult. The name might have been invented, of course, but she thought Besanoni only had two objectives. If he could not prise Rakulaj's name from her, he would kill her. He had pushed too hard for the name for it to have been any different. He may have liked her, as he claimed, but for two hundred terks, he would have killed her. She had no doubt, and she felt no remorse. He had rolled ones.

She tied the boat up, more than a little sad she did not own it herself. She wondered if it belonged to this bootseller. It mattered little. If he existed, she would find him and learn what she could from him. The sun had almost disappeared below the western horizon, so Yilmay decided to head back to the house. If she asked around for Torrekult's shop, word of her search might come to his ears, and he might hide himself away for a time. Tomorrow would suffice for a thorough search, but for now she would check every shop on the way back to The Plaza.

Yilmay wound through the streets in her usual haphazard way, but despite an even more circuitous route tonight, she saw no sign of the shop. Once inside the house, she slumped into a chair and reflected on the day. Her search for the shop had yielded no result, and the random twists and turns she always took whenever she went anywhere meant tomorrow's more methodical search might cover areas she had already checked.

She had felt no remorse when she killed Besanoni, another in a long line of victims. Had she grown comfortable with who she had become? The thought frightened her, and she dismissed it. Enough contradictions already made up the fabric of her life. She had forgotten the word Deineike once used to describe two things that contradicted each other, but even if she could recall it, it would not apply to a life filled with so many contrasting elements. Darkness folded itself around her, but it brought no comfort as she once more rued the fates written for her.

"This will not do." She spoke out loud, then rose from the chair and hobbled to The Weary Traveller. If she had learned one thing over the years of her life, it was that she must not give her mind free rein to wander down paths of self-incrimination and self-hatred. If she did so, despair would dog her steps and twist her heart to wring every last tear of guilt and shame from it. A goblet of wine would help, and she enjoyed the simple pleasure of observation as people came and went through the tavernroom. Sometimes she amused herself and invented small stories about them; why they visited the tavern, or what important things might turn in their lives. The tales she created for them were always funnier or more reckless than their real lives might be, but that constituted the fun of the game.

She restricted herself to two goblets of wine and paid for them, along with the goblet owed from the night of the attack, from a pouch whose contents dwindled faster than she wished. The house felt dark and alone, and she longed for a soft, warm body to share it with. Deineike would have been her first choice, but anybody would have sufficed. The tavern had not improved her mood, and she took off her clothes and climbed into the bed.

Sleep brought no relief from the melancholy that had overtaken her. Beneath a blood red moon, she stood on a shoreline of vermilion sand as Deineike danced naked with Besanoni. Besanoni carried his manhood in his hand, and a red gash spilled blood where it ought to have been. He held it aloft, and Deineike pulled it into her mouth. As Yilmay watched in horror, Deineike devoured it, followed by Besanoni. A disturbance in the sand caught Yilmay's eye, and as she stared in disbelief, Pettra rose up from the red shore. Her wrists were bound behind her back, and she cried for Yilmay to beat her. Deineike snarled and grasped Pettra by the shoulders. "I love her, not you." Deineike screamed into Pettra's face, and Pettra cried frozen tears that clattered to the sand with a tinkle. Deineike regurgitated Besanoni's manhood and used it to slash Pettra's throat. As Raolos's first wife sank through the sand back to wherever she had come from, Deineike turned to face Yilmay with a maniacal laugh. "Jorinda. I alone love you."

To Yilmay's relief, she awoke from the dream. The sun had not yet risen, but Yilmay feared to sleep again. Dressed, she drank a cup of the herb drink and wandered out to the nearby bakery, where she bought bread and carried it with her toward the dock. Arkkyd's skyline sprawled before her in the soft red glow of the sun as it peeped over the horizon, and she despaired that she could find one shop in the vastness of the city.

She stopped, then turned and headed toward the better area where Rakulaj lived. If Torrekult employed two or three staff, his shop must sell a large number of pairs of shoes and boots. To search in the poor quarter for such a successful business might yield nothing, and she rolled the dice his shop would be in a more affluent part of Arkkyd.

The morning brought nothing but frustration and disappointment as she combed the streets with methodical attention, along one street, then back down the next. As she walked, she nibbled at the bread, uncomfortable with the inflexibility of her rigid search pattern. She doubted anybody would follow her, but without her customary deviations, sudden turns, and abrupt halts, she felt exposed. Nonetheless, she stuck to her method.

Two hours after the midday, she accepted she had set herself an almost impossible task. With only a tiny part of this district covered, she had seen no sign of Torrekult's shop. Her slow pace hindered the effort, but even had she been capable of greater speed it would take days on end to comb the entire city for a shop that might not even exist. She gritted her teeth against the pain from her knee but would not allow it to hinder her efforts to find Torrekult.

Ahead of her she saw some shops in a row, one of which sold shoes. A sign above the window suggested she had not found Torrekult, but she rolled the dice and entered anyway. A woman behind a small counter looked up and greeted her. Yilmay explained she wished to find Torrekult. To avoid embarrassment, she made up a story about her brother and claimed he had bought shoes from there that had come apart after a short time. He did not wish to complain, but she could not allow the matter to slide.

The woman gave a small smile as she listened to the tale, and when Yilmay asked if this shop belonged to Torrekult, the woman appeared horrified. "Oh my, not at all. His shop is three streets away." Once directions had been obtained, Yilmay thanked the woman and left. If she had continued for another hour, she might have found the shop anyway, but that hour had been saved at the least. Satisfied Torrekult did exist, she set off.

From across the street, the front of Torrekult's shop impressed Yilmay. It occupied the space two or three houses might have taken up, with windows along the entire front. Shoes and boots stood on shelves and boxes in ambitious displays behind the windows.

Inside, two men and a woman stood together near a long

counter. The woman could be discounted, but which of the men, if either, would be Torrekult, Yilmay could not determine unless she entered. Besanoni might have chosen the name because he had walked past the shop in truth, given the childish nature of the cheese story.

The longer Yilmay waited, the higher the chance a customer would enter, so she strode across the street and pulled the door open to the jangle of a bell fastened above it. All three of those in the shop looked up as she entered, and she approached the nearest man.

"I have come for some cheese." The man's brow wrinkled, and he seemed confused. She turned to the other man, who stared at her open-mouthed. "Are you Torrekult?"

An initial hesitation suggested he meant to lie, but with his staff there, he seemed to think better of it. "I am. Who might you be?"

Yilmay wondered why he had not simply said "Yes," as Vyrrmod folk would normally do. "Besanoni sends his regards." She stared into his eyes.

Fear crossed his eyes, but he blinked it away. "Who?"

If she had not seen the fear, Yilmay might have wondered whether Besanoni had been a false name. "Next time you send somebody to kill me, find someone better." In the corner of her eye, the woman raised her hand to her mouth.

Torrekult bit at his lower lip for a moment, then seemed to gather himself. "You should leave Arkkyd while you still can."

"Believe me, I have many other things I wish to attend to, and I want to leave. First, I must tear down your operation." She gave him a wry smile. "Can I claim the two hundred terks?" When Yilmay glanced at the other two, they both seemed bewildered by the conversation. "Do you not know the true nature of your employer's interests? They extend far beyond footwear."

"Whoever you are, get out of my shop before I call the Upholders." Torrekult tried to recover his composure. "You are not welcome here."

"You should ask him." Yilmay ignored him, spoke to the other two. "I am certain you would be fascinated."

The woman started when Torrekult shouted, "Leave my shop."

If the Upholders came, they would take her into custody, and it might emerge she lay behind several deaths in the city. That would be disastrous, and she decided the message had been delivered. They would act against her again, she did not doubt it, so she left the shop, frustrated and angry. Although Torrekult had been found, she had made no further progress. Should she wait until he left the shop and follow him, to kill him or try to learn more, at the least? He might follow through on his threat to summon the Upholders, so for now she decided to return to the house rather than risk an encounter with them.

Every street added to her despondency. As a favour to Rakulaj, and against her better judgement, Yilmay had investigated the opium organisation. Four bodies later, she knew little more than when she had begun, and she wondered what Rakulaj had expected her to do. Three days had been wasted, and while three days made only a small difference to her life, those days had ended any prospect of future peace for her in Vyrrmod, and all for naught.

Frustration turned to resentment. *"Curse you, Rakulaj,"* she thought. *"You involved me in something I wish I had never heard of."* The visit to the shop had done no more than notify Torrekult and his cohorts she had killed Besanoni. They would send more killers after her, and in time they would succeed. The hour had grown too late to do much more, but tomorrow she resolved to leave a message at Rakulaj's offices she had found nothing but the name of a bootseller. The message delivered, she would find a ship to carry her to Malkartas. This pointless chase would end tomorrow. Tonight, survival would be her main aim. The morning would come, and Yilmay would be gone.

CHAPTER 28
TORREKULT

After the woman left, Torrekult told his staff she had been a madwoman, and he would report her to the Upholders at once. They nodded as though they agreed with him, but their expressions suggested they had understood nothing of what had turned.

The bell jangled as he pulled the door open and scurried out into the street. After two paces, he stopped. What if she intended to flush him out of the shop and kill him? She had killed three already, four if she had also killed Besanoni. She had been right about one thing—they should have found a better assassin to dispose of her.

He checked up and down the street and decided she had not waited for him, so he scurried off toward the Administration Offices. Despite the protestations of an aide, he demanded an immediate appointment with Dalkarjat and intimidated the aide with all manner of threats about the future prospects of their continued employment. When the timid aide showed him into Dalkarjat's office, the Commerce Administrator sat behind his large desk with his chubby fingers splayed on the wooden surface. His round face showed concern, but Torrekult thought abject fear would be more appropriate.

Dalkarjat raised an eyebrow. "Something is awry?"

Torrekult sank into a chair. "Yes, something is awry." He drew in a deep breath. "She came to my shop. That woman, Yilmay. She asked for cheese." Dalkarjat frowned but did not interrupt. "She has killed Besanoni. There can be no other explanation. He gave away all we had discussed before she slew him. What manner of monster has set herself against us?"

"Calm yourself, old friend."

"Easy for him to say," Torrekult thought. It had not been he who had faced her threats in the shop.

Dalkarjat's smile did nothing to reassure Torrekult as the Administrator continued. "We will take care of her."

Torrekult tapped a foot on the floor to match the rhythm of his heart, which pounded in his breast. "How? We offered that idiot a vast sum and she bested him. She killed Ofturra in his bed, and one of his guards. She cut off Ofturra's... She is not some frail, useless old crone. She terrified me." Instinct drove him to place both hands over his groin, as though Yilmay might appear at any moment and slice off his own manhood.

"Calm yourself." The Administrator repeated the two words least likely to calm anybody down. "Tonight, we will have her killed. She lives at number three in The Plaza, and there she will meet her ruin."

"Who will kill her? If Besanoni could not do it, who? He came with excellent recommendations, but he was nowhere near good enough. Where will we find better?" Dalkarjat did not reply straight away, and Torrekult grew nervous. "We cannot use Upholders for this task. The risk of exposure is too great."

Dalkarjat held up his hand, likely to calm Torrekult, but it infuriated him instead. It seemed the Administrator patronised him. "We must use the Upholders. I will speak to Jefhalis in the Magisterial division as soon as you leave. His Upholders will go to The Plaza, and things will go… wrong. She will be killed. A tragedy."

Torrekult frowned as he tried to unravel Dalkarjat's intentions. "Why would he send his Upholders to capture her?"

"I understand she is sought in connection with two murders."

"No." Torrekult lowered his voice to a frightened whisper. "You cannot implicate her in the murder of Ofturra and his guard without great risk our connections will be exposed. Houses in The Plaza are owned by upright citizens who would not lie if they saw these events take place. It is too dangerous. It is reckless."

"Relax. I will not involve Ofturra or his useless guard. Jefhalis's Upholders have sought her for many years. She is a prime suspect in the deaths of a Dur woman and an Arkkyd citizen in the city many years ago. She went by the name 'Corelle' in those days."

"Why would the Upholders kill her without any process? Our law does not permit it."

Dalkarjat's evil smile chilled Torrekult. "Jefhalis's Senior Sergeant will be on duty tonight, and he will persuade Jefhalis he should lead the force that apprehends her. I know this because the Senior Sergeant is my brother by law. I played a large part in his successful appointment to his current role."

For some reason, Dalkarjat's confidence did nothing to settle Torrekult's unease. "Too much coin is involved for any mistakes."

"There will be no mistakes. The sun will still rise tomorrow, and we will still be rich. We will find someone to take over Ofturra's tally house, and that person will find another courier. Soon the opium will once more flow through the city and the coins through our fingers. Do not fret. This Yilmay is a thorn I will pluck from our skin tonight."

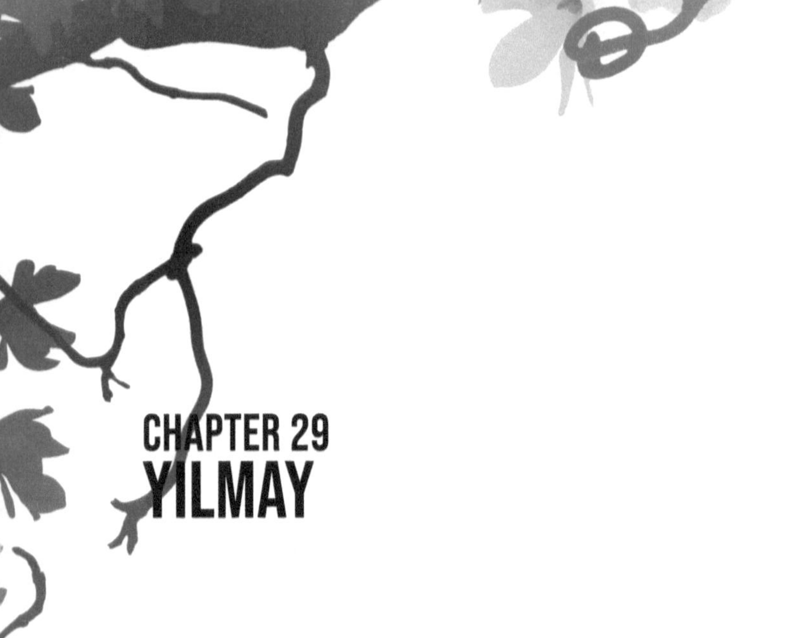

CHAPTER 29
YILMAY

Yilmay opened the back door of the house and stepped out into the chill of the evening. The day had been cooler than previous days, and the breeze that sprang up as she had made her way back to The Plaza turned it colder as it blew into her face. Behind the house lay a small garden, and beyond that a wooded hill rose toward the horizon. What lay beyond the hill, Yilmay did not know, but it mattered little.

The trees on the hill sprouted thick foliage and grew to three storeys or higher. They had been planted close together as saplings, and now they formed a dense, dark canopy within which people who wished to hide would be undetectable. Yilmay did not recognise the trees, but they would suit her purpose. To her left, the trees extended beyond the two houses at the entrance to The Plaza, and beyond them another road whose name she had never noticed ran perpendicular to the square.

Yilmay walked into the gloom beneath the trees and stumbled often on the fallen foliage that littered the floor of the wood. She searched for a tree with low branches, so she could haul herself up into the cover of the canopy. It must also give her a view of her

house. A lantern shone in the parlour and another in her bedroom. She imagined Torrekult and his organisation would try to kill her tonight. If not, they might try tomorrow night, but they would be disappointed; she would have left Arkkyd by then.

It took close to an hour for her to find the perfect tree, simple to climb and with an uninterrupted view of the house from the higher branches. Thick foliage would hide her from sight, but as she peered through the leaves, she had excellent visibility of The Plaza. To keep a clear head, she had not drunk any of the herbs from the healer, and she winced with pain when she knocked her knee on the trunk of the tree as she manoeuvred into a comfortable position.

Once comfortable, she snapped off a few small branches to improve her view and settled down for a lengthy wait. That wait proved to be lengthy indeed, and she fell asleep beneath the lights of the night sky at one point. No cloud covered the sky, and had it not been for the threat to her life, it would have been a beautiful night, protected by the trees, quiet, and a pleasant temperature hidden away where the cold wind could not find her.

The hours dragged by, and she wondered whether they might not come for her tonight after all else. The prospect of her bed for the rest of the night appealed, and she prepared to climb down in the darkness. Movement caught her eye, and she froze. Men in the dark blue tunic of the Upholders moved into The Plaza. Eight of them—the number seemed excessive for one woman, but by now, no doubt, she had earned something of a reputation.

Why Upholders? Only one explanation made sense. Torrekult had spoken to his colleague in the Administration, and since their assassin had failed, they had sent Upholders. At the house, the Upholders huddled together as one of them whispered some instructions, it seemed. Three of them separated from the others and came around to the back of the house. The one who had spoken to the others approached the house and knocked on the door. When he received no answer, he knocked again, louder, and shouted, "Upholders. Open the door."

Lanterns sprang alight in some of the other houses. Upholders peered through the house's windows as the man knocked at the door once more, then turned to one of the others. He ordered the man to kick down the door, and the crack as the wood splintered under repeated attacks from the sole of his boot carried across the night to Yilmay's tree. The Upholders entered the house and could be seen at times as they passed various windows.

They stayed inside for some time, and Yilmay imagined they discussed their disappointment and what they would do. She had dropped her pack a few trees away from the one she sat in, and she had arranged the house to give the impression she had left. That had been her intention at the least, and she hoped it had worked.

The Upholders came out at last and walked away, defeat evident in their slumped shoulders. The door of one of the other houses opened, and a man shouted to the Upholders to enquire what they were about.

"We seek a murderer. A woman. We heard she stayed here, but she seems to have fled."

"She has been there for a few days. We have seen her, but not today. Who has she murdered?"

"The murders were some years ago now. A woman and a man. Let us know if you see her."

"I will do. Goodnight to you." The man went back inside his house and the Upholders trudged away, the shuffle of their feet on the hard-packed dirt of the street a solemn song of disappointment and failure.

Yilmay almost fell out of the tree at the mention of the deaths of Pettra and the stallholder. She had thought the investigation would have been closed by now—it had been almost five years since they had died. How could these Upholders have known she had killed the man? She had not killed Pettra, but accepted it might have appeared as though she had.

There could be only one explanation for the arrival of the Upholders tonight in connection with such an old crime, and Yilmay did not want to admit it to herself. It could not be, and yet it must be. The Upholders had gone straight to number three. They had not enquired beforehand at other houses in The Plaza. Yilmay had not given the house number to Besanoni, and he had not seen her enter or leave the house. She had not mentioned the deaths of Pettra or the stallholder, but the Upholders possessed all those pieces of information.

Her head in her hands, she sat in the tree for almost half of an hour and strove in desperation for an alternative explanation, one that would not devastate her as much as the horrible thoughts that urged her to accept them as truth. Bereft, she looked up to the sky, and a tear trickled down her cheek. Betrayal had become a familiar travel companion, but never betrayal by someone she thought of as a good friend.

Rakulaj had sold her, as Styrrach had all those years ago, the betrayal that had set in motion all that had turned since. Rakulaj, whose friendship she had valued so much, had told Torrekult and his organisation everything they needed, and they had sent the Upholders to take her into custody, never to be seen again.

A sense of remorse edged into her mind. If Rakulaj had already told Torrekult and his friends about her, why had Besanoni pestered her for the name? They did not need it, and that might suggest his offer of help had been sincere. She had not needed to kill him. She shook her head, violent side-to-side movements to dispel the feeling of misery. He had pestered her for the name, so he felt he needed it. Rakulaj would not admit to those he feared he had been the one to hire Yilmay, so it made sense they would need the name of the person who had set Yilmay against them. She had made the correct decision, after all else.

Why? Why had Rakulaj asked for her help if he intended to have her killed? What wrong had she done to him that would lead him to such behaviour? There could be only one way to learn the answer to that question, so she clambered down from the tree, retrieved her pack, and set off.

After the initial dinner, she had not returned to Rakulaj's house. She had dealt with him through his office. It had seemed important to maintain a distance between his family and the sordid business she had undertaken for him, but he had broken a bond of trust, and she arrived at his house in a rage. That would not do for the work ahead, so she slowed her breaths and focused her mind on the task ahead. She must suppress the furious anger that burned in her as she walked. A calm and clear mind were needed to end the life of someone she had called friend for so long.

CHAPTER 30
YILMAY

The back door to the house had a simple lock, and she defeated it with ease, then crept into the house without a sound. In the quiet darkness, she waited for her eyes to adjust to the deeper black of the interior, where no moonlight penetrated. The door had opened into the house's scullery, and two doors led off it. The staircase had been near the front door, on the opposite side of the house, so she ignored the door to her left and pulled open the one ahead of her. Silence hissed in her ears as she listened for any indication somebody upstairs might have heard a noise and risen from their bed to investigate.

Satisfied, she walked down the hallway until she saw the staircase to her left. She climbed the stairs with caution and kept to the wall, where any noise from a loose tread on the stairs would be less likely. At the top of the stairs, she paused and listened again. Many doors opened off the landing, and it reminded her of Raolos's home. She pressed an ear to the first doorway but heard nothing, and likewise at the second door, but at the third door she heard a light snore. Children might snore, of course, but this snore did not sound as though a child made it.

The dice must be rolled, and if they came up ones, Yilmay might be undone. The door handle did not squeak as she turned it with small motions, and as soon as the door opened wide enough, she slid into the room.

The size of the room convinced her she had found Rakulaj's bedroom. Two shadowy forms lay ahead of her in a large bed. The snores came from the figure to her right, and she crept forward on the thick carpet until she looked down on Rakulaj. A table stood beside the bed, the shadowy form of a lantern on it. Her silent fingers soon located a flint.

Before she struck it to the lantern, she slipped her fan out of her boot. As light sprang to life in the room, Rakulaj stirred. His eyes half-opened, and he glanced up at her. For a heartbeat, it seemed he had not registered who loomed over him, then he sprang up in the bed.

"Corelle?" He sounded sleepy and confused.

If he had hoped his wife would not wake, the woman dashed that hope at once. "What… Who are you?" She sat up and rubbed at her eyes.

"Your wife should go to your children." Yilmay kept her voice quiet and calm, and although the woman protested, Rakulaj hushed her and told her to go to the children's rooms, take them downstairs. His explanation they had business to discuss did not appease her concerns, but at length she allowed herself to be shooed from the room. "Why?" Once his wife had gone, Yilmay fired the question at Rakulaj.

"Why what?" Bleary-eyed from sleep, he might be confused, or he might have stalled for time.

"Why did you betray me? Why did you ask me to investigate these people even as you planned to bring my ruin?"

"I do not know what you mean." He spluttered, nervous, his face pale.

With a glance at the bedroom door, Yilmay continued. "Unless I miss my guess, your wife has taken the children to a neighbour's house, where someone will send for the Upholders. When they arrive, they will either find you alive or dead. It matters little to me which. Why?"

With a sigh, Rakulaj lay back in the bed. "You talk of things you know nothing of."

"You think so? At least four are now dead, one of them an assassin sent to kill me. I learned one name too many, and tonight, the Upholders came to The Plaza in search of me. They mentioned Pettra and the man who hurt her. There is but one way they could have known which house their alleged killer slept in. You told them."

"I told you the truth. I did not… I do not wish to be involved, but I have a wife, two children, and a business. These people are dangerous. What if they harmed my family? I became afraid, and I told them I had learned some information about you. What else should I have done?" Tears rolled from his eyes.

"You did what you had to do. You sold me to protect your family."

"There is coin in that drawer." He pointed to a cupboard. "Take it, take it all, but spare me, I beg you."

The fan in her hand felt heavier than all the burdens laid on her throughout the years since she had joined the Guild. Rakulaj had a wife and children. If she killed him now, there would be nobody to care and provide for them. "I cannot fight you, Torrekult, and however many others are involved. I cannot fight the Upholders of a large city. I came here to kill you, though you have helped me many times." He gasped and closed his eyes. "You are a husband and a father, and your children and your wife have bought your life tonight. Hold them close, for you owe them a great debt, the greatest debt of all."

The soft carpet felt like spring grass beneath her boots as she walked out of the room and down the stairs once she had taken the heavy pouch of coin from the drawer. Outside the back door, she slid the fan back into her boot and set off for the poor part of the city. It would not be easy to take ship, she reasoned. When the Upholders had not found her at The Plaza, they would have ordered the docks watched in an attempt to apprehend her there. Even if they had not, they would do so as soon as they learned she had been to Rakulaj's house.

There would be another way to leave, but it involved risks. They would watch the main docks but might not patrol the western end where the little boat lay. She might manage to take the boat and sail to Jaiselnia. If she kept close to the coast, she thought the boat would be seaworthy enough for the trip. Once safe in Jaiselnia, she could find a ship to Malkartas.

Her assessment had been correct, although it surprised her how many Upholders wandered the docks with lanterns. The light from them all shone so bright, it took all her skill to hug such shadows as she could find until she reached the boat. The ropes untied, she pushed the craft away from the pier. She did not run up the sail at first, but once she had drifted out with the current to where she felt safe, she hauled it up and pointed the boat west. Shouts from the dock indicated the boat had been seen, but she had a head start on them, and even if they took another boat from the dock, she felt confident she could outsail them.

The wind blew in her favour, and she made good time with no sign of any pursuers astern. She hugged the coastline and could not resist a peek at the cove. She took the boat in as close as she dared, and Besanoni still lay on the sand in the moonlight. His body had moved, and she guessed animals had moved it as they tore at his flesh for their supper.

Late the next day, she saw a house close to the shore and she brought the boat into land. She had not left Vyrrmod, but the owners were happy to sell her some food and water. Yilmay sailed on for three days until she saw a town or city ahead. Her exhaustion made the buildings swirl and flicker against the blue sky behind them. She had slept little for three days, and her eyelids felt so heavy, she struggled to keep them from closing. She did not sail to the docks but tied the boat to a tree on the shoreline and walked to the outskirts of the town. Jaiselnia, at last. No longer a fugitive from justice, she took a room at an inn and caught up on sleep.

Her rage at Rakulaj ate at her, and she regretted she had not killed him. He had used her, although he had not been the first to do so. He had used her, then betrayed her, and it rankled. She could never return to Vyrrmod in her life, all thanks to his faithlessness. The anger would blaze within her for a time, then fizzle out to a dull resentment. Experience had taught her that much.

She bought passage on a small, rundown ship to the largest city on the Jaiselnia coast, Leikilst. From there, she took passage to Tanasttra in Malkartas. There, she must await a ship bound for Argoya. She would need to spend every day at the docks until she found one. A nearby inn, The Bird And Fish, offered rooms that did not stretch her pouch of coin, and as she did not know how long she would need to stay, cost seemed important even though Rakulaj's pouch contained a substantial sum.

Her leg healed well, and she took a long walk around the city. She ventured to the part of the city where Wilash's smith stood and called in to visit him, but his smith had been closed for a time, and the sign on the door gave no indication of when he might be back. Raolos's trading house still functioned, but she did not recognise the name of the new operator.

The Rzankir appeared two days later. Yilmay would have sailed on any ship headed to Argoya, but the Rzankir would be perfect, since she already knew the master. In truth, she had expected to wait longer for a ship to make the long journey north, and the fact The Rzankir arrived so soon cheered her more than she had words to describe. As with her last visit, she felt out of place in Tanasttra for reasons she could not explain to herself. A bench near the

Rzankir's berth offered Yilmay a chance to sit and watch as the crew unloaded the ship.

A large amount of cargo came ashore, while more dockhands brought another to the dock alongside the ship, ready to be loaded aboard once the holds had been emptied. She paid little attention to the men who scurried up and down the ramp as she wondered whether she could recall all the tasks she might be called on to perform if Adjtish Schteyen, the master, would hire her on as crew. If he would not, she must wait for another ship. He did not carry passengers.

Once the goods had been offloaded from the hold, the ramp emptied for a time before the mariners loaded the new cargo, so Yilmay walked up onto the ship and climbed the steps to the aft deck. Adjtish Schteyen stood at the wheel, his head bowed over parch charts that guided the ship on its long journey. At the sound of her feet, he glanced up and gave her a smile.

"The globe woman." He had spoken in Kuirbekian. It surprised her he had remembered her at all, but he had also recalled she spoke Kuirbekian.

Certain his recollection of her would be a favourable sign, she asked whether he had any spare crew positions for the return journey to Argoya. He had an almost full crew, but he agreed to take her on in a junior role. The position mattered little to her. She would not be required to pay for passage, which would make the journey easier on her coin, and her thanks were genuine. The Rzankir would not sail until the next day. The tide would be high at one hour after the sunrise, and she could join the crew then.

Her last night on dry land for some time, she reflected as she walked back to the inn. Once she had told the innkeep she would depart the next day and settled for her room, she ate a meal and drank some wine in the tavernroom before she went to bed. Sleep seemed elusive, and she blamed her mixed emotions of excitement and trepidation. At last, she would sail to Argoya and continue her search for Krage and the vengeance she owed him, and that excited her. Before they arrived, she must work on the Rzankir for two tendays, which made her anxious. Once more, the image of the giant as it crashed to the deck of The Ictharelian and cast her into the air ran amok through her mind. Although she told herself such an event could not happen to the same person twice, she felt certain she could never again be comfortable aboard a ship for any length of time.

She did not know what hour she fell asleep, but she had left the shutter open on purpose, and the sun woke her. Once she had dressed, she grabbed her pack and ran to the docks. The Rzankir had all but made ready to leave, and she ran up the ramp and reported to Adjtish Schteyen. He called an officer and introduced her as a junior mariner for the return journey.

The officer took her to the common area and showed her to a cabin with ten bunks. He pointed out a trunk she could store her belongings in for the duration of the voyage, told her to stow her pack, then find him at the bow, where there would be some ropes to coil before they set sail.

The cabin felt much the same as cabins on previous voyages, and she felt at home at once. As she dropped her pack into the trunk, she heard voices. One of the voices sounded familiar, and she glanced up as three mariners entered the cabin. One of them stopped in his tracks and glared at her.

She straightened and returned his stare before she spoke.

"Hello, Wilke."

CHAPTER 31
YILMAY

Yilmay stood straight and stared into hate-filled eyes. The silence lasted some time, and the two mariners who had entered with Wilke both glanced from her to Wilke and back as though they sought answers for the long, uncomfortable silence.

"You." Wilke broke the quiet. "What brings you aboard this vessel?"

"I could ask you the same question, since this is not my first service aboard the Rzankir."

Wilke flicked his eyes to each of his companions in turn as though he needed confirmation of what he had heard. "You are no mariner."

One of his colleagues disavowed him of that belief. "Yes she is, and a good one. I remember her from a previous journey."

Yilmay nodded to the man, whose face seemed familiar. "I am more than a mere mariner. I sailed on The Ictharelian and proved we live on a globe."

Disbelief in his eyes, Wilke glowered at her. "In truth, that is of no consequence. You and I have some unfinished business."

"That we do." Yilmay's fan sat in her boot, and to pull it out would take valuable heartbeats. If she went for it now, and Wilke guessed her intent, he might attack her. He was a big man, and if he connected with a powerful blow, he might knock her to the ground. What the other two mariners would do in that situation could only be determined if she became embroiled in a fight with Wilke.

One of them spoke, uncertain. "Now then. I see there is something between you, but master Adjtish will not stand for any brawls aboard the ship."

"He will stand for this one." Wilke's voice sounded like the low growl of the wild beast that had almost killed Yilmay in Tryngelk, and he folded the sleeves of his tunic up his arms, ready to fight, it appeared.

Corelle did not take her eyes from Wilke, but in the periphery of her vision, one of the men turned and ran from the cabin.

"Do you want to follow this course?" Yilmay did not want to fight Wilke and risk that Adjtish might throw her off his crew. "It cannot end any way but in your death."

He loosed a dismissive laugh. "I think not. Justice is owed for three lives taken, thanks to you."

Yilmay recalled Wilke had once said something similar in Ort or somewhere as she had looked for a ship to sail on with Deineike. "Three lives you say? How do you reckon me answerable for three deaths when I did not kill anybody from your ship?"

"The master and two mariners, one of them my friend, Fybjarra, he whom you accused of murder."

"Your friend killed the mother of the woman I loved. These others, I know nothing of. Why do you believe me involved in their deaths?"

"That he did not. He denied it. After you left, two men came to the ship and demanded the master. They killed him on the deck, then picked two of the crew out and killed them also."

"While you stood by and did nothing?" The tale surprised her, and she could not make sense of it.

Wilke bowed his head. "That I did, curse me. I did not wish to be the fourth." His head snapped up. "The blood is on your hands. If you did not send those men, then why did I hear them mention your name? Corelle, that is your name, correct?"

Corelle? They had asked for her by name? "Styrrach." She breathed the word aloud.

"What turns here?" Adjtish Schteyen's voice cut through the tense atmosphere in the cabin. "I will have no brawls among my crews. If you have scores to settle with one another, I will put you both off here where you may settle them as we sail for Argoya."

"There are no scores, master." Yilmay's eyes never left Wilke's.

"Then shake hands and be about your duties." The master's gruff voice left no doubt he would make good on his threat.

Without hesitation, Yilmay extended her hand toward Wilke. His response took a heartbeat longer, but he took her hand and shook it. Yilmay pushed past him and headed for the door. "Master." She nodded as she passed Adjtish Schteyen.

Yilmay walked out onto the deck and headed for the bow to find the officer again. He had her coil some ropes as the ship made ready to sail, then sent her up into the nest as they sailed north through the stretch of water between eastern Malkartas and western Dur known as The Neck. She scanned the horizon and both sides of the ship for hazards, the encounter with Wilke uppermost in her mind.

A sorry turn to find herself on the same ship as him, and she would need to keep her wits about her and her fan at hand. Adjtish Schteyen had made it clear he would stand for no nonsense, but his eyes could not be everywhere on the ship at all times. Yilmay imagined Styrrach had ordered the deaths of the three men aboard The Friendship in payment for the fact the master had carried her, Deineike, Wilash, and

Klordia to Ort against his orders. Although the death of the one Wilke had called Fybjarra had doubtless been sheer fortune, the deaths of the other two weighed heavy on her. They would not have been killed had it not been for her, and it disappointed her to learn of even more deaths she had brought about, by accident or design.

By the end of her watch, they had sailed well north of Tanasttra, although the ship had not yet cleared The Neck. She climbed down the rope ladder to the deck and wondered how safe she would be in her cot that night if Wilke slept in the same cabin. In the common room, she ate some food and spent some time in idle conversation with some of the other mariners, several of whom recognised her from her voyage south from Argoya. Word of the disagreement had spread, as had the news that Wilke had called her Corelle rather than Yilmay. It might be time for hard decisions about her name and about whether to attack Wilke if an opportunity presented itself. Adjtish Schteyen's reaction if she killed Wilke concerned her, nonetheless.

She went to the bow to relieve herself before she turned in, but from the deck she saw somebody already squatted there. The mariners relieved themselves through a hole in the hull at the bow. They called it the head. She waited at a polite distance, then realised who crouched at the head. Wilke.

Yilmay stepped forward. Wilke had turned to pull up the tow rag, the piece of cloth on a length of rope that trailed in the water. The mariners used it to clean themselves after they had used the head. With his trousers around his ankles and his attention on the tow rag, Yilmay pulled her fan from her boot, stood beside him, and whispered his name

He turned toward her in horror, caught in a compromised position. "Curse you." He clenched his teeth.

"Fear not, I am not your ruin. I come to offer you a compromise. Let us hold off on our disagreement until we reach Argoya. Once we have left the ship, we will revisit it. I have no wish to kill you aboard the ship and be hanged from the yardarm."

His grim laugh drifted off in the wind, and he returned to his task with the tow rag. "So be it. I will see you in Argoya." He pulled up his trousers and walked off. When she felt sure he had left, Yilmay lowered her own trousers and relieved herself into the hole. The Rzankir had no board or seat at its head, so mariners had to squat to relieve themselves. Men, of course, could stand to pass water, but Yilmay could not.

The next few days passed without event. Wilke and Yilmay shared the same cabin, but they stayed apart and never spoke to one another. Yilmay decided to return to her birth name once they arrived in Argoya. On her watches, she spent a great deal of time in the nest or on her hands and knees on the deck with a cloth and a pail of water. The deck must be cleaned almost every day to keep the boards clean and splinter-free, since many mariners worked in bare feet much of the time.

Five days into the voyage, the ship sailed in deep seas. Yilmay climbed the net to the nest to take her watch. Ahead, the sky had turned as black as night, and a storm approached. The master had ordered the ship made storm ready; all hatches closed, all doors secured, the sails shortened ready to heave to if the storm came straight for them. In such deep sea, the nearest land would be too far away to run for, so they must ride out the storm. As it came close, the ship would heave to. The wheelman had already lashed himself to the wheel so he could control the drift of the ship in the swell, and Yilmay roped herself into the nest. She would not stay in the nest once the storm hit, but she must keep an eye on it and warn the crew as it came closer.

White bolts of fire crackled between the sky and the sea in the black depth of the storm, and Yilmay watched, entranced. What made the fire? Yilmay did not know; she had never seen its like before, and her heart pounded a drumbeat of dread in her breast.

She feared to sail into such a powerful storm. Although she had sailed in rough seas, the angry monster that boiled in the sky beyond the ship's bow resembled nothing she had seen before, and when she raised a hand before her face, it shook with terror.

Ahead of the storm, the wind whipped the sea into large waves with foamy white heads. The white flecks of water floated on the air, and even high up in the nest, they hit Yilmay in the face. The waves had grown large and dangerous, and she felt it best to leave the nest and head for a cabin. She had been thrown from a nest once in her life already, and she had no desire to repeat the experience. As she climbed from the basket and descended the net, the ship rolled from side to side and pitched up one side of the wave and down the other, and it required concentration and all her strength to descend the net.

The deck lay no more than her own height below her when movement caught her eye. The wheelman may have loosened his ropes, or one may have broken, but he seemed to be in a fight to re-attach the ropes around himself, and as she stared in horror, a large wave broke over the bow. It smashed over her and all but knocked her from the net, but she clung on with all her might. When it passed, the wheelman had gone.

Yilmay rushed down the net and staggered toward the stern of the ship. She could not see the man anywhere, and the wheel spun from side to side as the sea pushed the rudder in one direction, then another. Her balance failed her several times, and she sprawled on the deck, picked herself up again and struggled on toward the aft deck. She pulled the door to the common area open and screamed, "Man overboard."

Anxious faces appeared before her as the mariners crowded round and yelled questions at her. The master pushed through the crowd. "Who is overboard?"

"Wheelman." She panted, exhausted by the effort of the walk along a deck that tried to heave her off the ship.

"We must have a wheelman." Adjtish Schteyen chose four men to go out and lash one of them to the wheel before the others retreated to safety.

"We must bring him back." Yilmay fought for breath to speak as she struggled to draw air into her lungs.

The master stared at her as though she had lost her mind. "He has gone down to Helchik's treasure. He is beyond our help."

He made to turn away, but she grabbed at his arm. "We cannot abandon him in these seas. He will drown."

"So it is." He wheeled to face her again. "We cannot put a rowboat into these seas. It will founder, and all aboard it will follow him down to the treasure."

She stared at him, defiant. "Then I will go alone. I will not leave him out there."

CHAPTER 32
YILMAY

Adjtish Schteyen's eyes blazed with fury, and he yelled at her, his face red with anger. "Belay that, mariner. That is an order. He is gone."

"I will go with her." A voice came from the rear of the crowd, and Wilke pushed himself forward.

"None of you will go. Do I not make myself clear?" Adjtish's spittle shot from his mouth and landed on Yilmay's face.

Two others protested; they could not leave their crew-mate behind, and despite a furious argument in which Adjtish Schteyen threatened to sail away and leave them, they prevailed. The ship could not sail in the storm, and the man might well be close to the ship. They lowered a rowboat from the leeward side, and the four of them set off. The master ordered them to keep the ship's lanterns in sight, but that proved impossible as the little boat rode down into the troughs between the enormous waves before it struggled up the face of the next, then rushed down the far side.

They did not find him, and some time later, the cold, the wet, and the despair drove them to abandon the search and return to the ship. The lanterns could not be seen, and it took them some time to

find the Rzankir again. Mariners threw ropes down and the four in the rowboat made them fast so the mariners could haul the little boat up to its stowage on the deck. Yilmay and the other three fell many times as the wind and waves whipped the little boat about as though it were no more than a piece of parch, but at last they lay on the ship's deck, and hands helped them to their feet and into the common area.

The master appeared. "Did you see any sign of him?"

Yilmay hung her head, dejected. Blood dripped from a cut on the back of her hand, received in one fall or another, she guessed. "Nothing."

His anger seemed to burn out, and concern replaced it on his face. "You tried, and few would have done. Away to your cabin, dry yourselves, get yourselves warm."

The four threw their soaked clothes from themselves and dried themselves with cloths. Yilmay's hair had grown, and it hung past her ears in wet, shapeless strands as she rubbed it with a cloth. She pulled dry clothes from her trunk and dressed, then wrapped her blanket around herself and sat miserable on her cot. Cold penetrated to her bones and onward to her innards, and her shivers threatened to shake the vessel apart, more violent than the storm.

Wilke appeared before her, a blanket in his hand. "Here, take another. Warm yourself."

She took the blanket with gratitude and pulled it around her. "My thanks." Her teeth chattered and threatened to cut her tongue in half as she spoke.

"You are hurt." He pointed to her forehead even as she glanced at the back of her hand.

She raised her uninjured hand to her head, and it came away bloodied. "It is nothing. A scratch."

"You have sand, for a woman. Few would have insisted they wished to venture out into those seas in a tiny boat to look for a man almost certain to have gone down to the treasure."

Yilmay looked up at him, surprised and embarrassed by the compliment. "You came also. You should tell yourself the same tale. You did well. For a man."

He laughed. "I may have misjudged you. Why did you want to search for him? I cannot even recall his name."

"Nor can I, but I have been there. I have been in the water, and it frightened me. It still does, whenever I think about it. It is a cold, lonely way to die. I hoped I could save him."

"The giant that sank your ship, is that what you mean?"

She smiled, a mixture of despair and resignation. "You have heard the tale?"

"I believe every mariner in the Torr Sea has."

"So I am famous, is that it?"

With a laugh, he told her she looked tired and should sleep, and she agreed with him. She lay back, closed her eyes, and did not open them again until Wilke shook her awake.

"Rouse yourself, woman. It is time to send Lzastish Relluhen down to the treasure."

"Who?"

"The man who went overboard last night. I learned his name."

"He has gone to the treasure already, then. Let me sleep."

"Up, and now. On deck, and bring a coin."

He left, and she dragged herself out of the cot. If he had played a jest on her, she would kill him, there would be no question about it. If he roused her and told her to bring her coin to the deck for nothing more than a game of cards or dice, she would slit his throat and take the consequences.

The entire crew had gathered near the main mast, all with sombre looks on their faces. Wilke cried out as she approached them. "She is here."

The master faced the waters, calm now the storm had passed. "We say farewell to Lzastish Relluhen. Take these coins with you Lzastish, and down to the treasure with you. Add these to

Helchik's hoard." Every mariner pulled a coin from his pocket and cast it into the sea, so Yilmay copied the gesture.

As she made her way back to the common room in search of some food, one of the other mariners explained how the ceremony took place whenever a crew member died at sea. One of the many superstitions among mariners, Yilmay reasoned, but she thought the gesture sweet, and it warmed her inside.

In the common room, she ate some cheese and wondered when her next watch would begin. The storm had passed, but it had so disoriented her with the loss of Lzastish Relluhen and the long, exhausted sleep, she had lost track of time. One of the mariners who had worked on her watch each day since they had left Malkartas sat at the next table, and she asked him when they would be on watch again.

"Four hours, give or take a few sexags."

Yilmay wrinkled her nose at the unusual word. "Sexags?"

"The parts of an hour." He laughed at her bemusement. "Do you people of Dur not reckon the passage of time?"

"That we do." Had she sounded more defensive than she had intended? "We have eleven passes each year of twenty-six days, each divided into twenty hours."

He nodded, in agreement, she guessed. "And...?"

With a shrug, Yilmay answered. "Nothing. Moments and heartbeats." He frowned, and she elaborated. "I can guess an hour, more or less. Less than that, there is no measure but moments and heartbeats. A moment is twenty heartbeats."

"Why twenty?" Every mariner in the cabin listened to the conversation.

She laughed, bashful. "I cannot keep track of them beyond twenty with any accuracy." She felt her cheeks flame with the red of embarrassment.

"But nobody has any way to measure an hour?" She shook her head. "We measure sixty sexags in each hour."

The explanation did not make complete sense. "How do you know how long a sexag is?"

His face a blank, he stared at her for a moment, then the entire room burst out in spontaneous laughter. "I do not know." Tears of laughter ran down his face. She joined in the laughter, and an officer peered around the door and asked what had amused them so much. Somebody made a clumsy attempt at an explanation, which only made everybody laugh the more.

The weather turned perfect, the wind kind and the seas gentle for the rest of the voyage, and the days blurred together as the ship cut through the water toward Argoya. Try as she might, Yilmay could not grasp the concept of the sexags, and she abandoned the effort. Aside from the strange concept, the word itself embarrassed her as it resembled the word for physical intimacy.

One or two days out from Argoya, she sat at the bow while she had some spare time between watches. To her surprise, Wilke arrived and sat beside her. They had spoken little since the night of the storm as they each busied themselves with their work and those mariners they had formed the closest friendships with. Although she had not spoken to him, she had spent time with him in her mind. The dilemma of the agreed brawl wore at her. She did not doubt she could best him, but when he lay dead at her feet, what then? Would the authorities drag her to the nearest tree and hang her? She felt sure they would, but until she had killed Krage, she must not die. Vengeance first, death afterward.

"We are close to Argoya." Wilke did not look at her, his eyes fixed on the horizon.

"That we are."

"When we left Malkartas, we vowed to resolve our differences at the end of the voyage."

"That we did." They sat in silence for a time as the ship ploughed on through the sea. "I travel to Argoya in search of some-body, and I intend to kill that person." He drew in a short, sharp breath but did not interrupt. "If I kill you before I have killed him, they will hang me. I feel no sadness at the prospect of my death, but I would prefer to fulfil my task before I am hanged. If not, he will escape without any payment for the many wrongs he has done to me."

"This tale is not what I expected."

She gave a soft laugh. "I apologise. The man I seek is called Krage. You may know the name. He declared himself Duke when he led the Qagrue to Dur."

He spat on the deck. "I know the name."

"He did more than bring the Qagrue to Dur. He is responsible, direct or indirect, for the deaths of some people I cared for. He forced himself on a woman I loved and gave her a child. Both she and the child are now dead. He arranged for the murder of the Senior Tally Master, Klordia. When he brought the Qagrue to Dur, he or his companions hanged the Portreeve of Ort, Ibie, a friend of mine, and another friend lost his life in the fight to keep the Qagrue out of Ryl."

He tutted. "I see why you seek him, but how can you kill such a violent man?"

"I can do it, and I intend to. Afterward I will find you, and you can kill me in vengeance for your friend, although he murdered the mother of Deineike."

"He denied what you accused him of."

She shook her head and shrugged. "He admitted it to me. He claimed to have been in his cups on the night in question. No matter, he is dead now, and you shall have your vengeance."

"I see." He fell quiet, and Yilmay sat with the wind in her hair, at peace with her decision.

She had no idea how to find Krage, of course, but would deal with that once she had arrived in Argoya. She did not glance at Wilke as she spoke. "What will you do once you reach Argoya?"

"I know how to do one thing. I am a mariner and have always

been a mariner. I will sail further, I think. I left The Friendship when I heard of the new lands discovered by your voyage. I will explore more of them until I can work no more." He paused. "What of you? Do you have a trade?"

She nodded. "I have two trades. I am a garment maker, and an excellent one, if you can believe it. My making has been worn by Portreeves and their wives."

"I am impressed." He laughed. "You must make me a wescoat fit for a Portreeve. What is your other trade?"

Her other trade could not have been more different from the one she had learned as a young child in her father's shop. "Death."

After some time, he spoke again, quietly. "There is a chance I could not best you, in truth. I have brawled often, but I have never killed."

"Do not worry. I promise when I find you, I will have completed my vengeance, and you may kill me with no fear."

"I do not care for this reputation. Killer of a ferocious woman who stands no higher than my shoulders, and I killed her with a pillow over her face while she encouraged me to finish her. I do not think any will fear me afterward."

With a laugh, she realised she could not dispute his words. "That they will not."

"I could help you seek this Krage. Some help might be useful to you."

"My thanks, but I do not think you are cut out for the killer's life. I have always worked alone, and if I fail to kill Krage, he will kill me. I do not want to babywatch you and risk the distraction that would bring."

Wilke pushed at her and laughed. "I wish you luck with your search for Krage. He is owed all you wish for him, for his betrayal of our land. Once he lies dead at your feet, do not seek me. Return to making and abandon this deadly trade. Find joy."

"I have known it little enough."

"You might find it here."

Could she find joy once Krage had been killed? It might be possible. Yilmay had been wrong about Wilke. He had protected his friend, in truth, nothing more. She regretted much in her life, and her reaction to him aboard The Friendship could now be added to that list. The arguments with Deineike about who had killed her mother had misted her mind, but she could not hide behind that excuse. "That I might. I hope you find some."

He stood and stretched. The sun had begun its descent of the sky to the west, and her watch would start soon. "Take care." He moved off and left her alone at the bow.

CHAPTER 33
CORELLE

Corelle, as she called herself once more, stood on the docks of Argoya and gazed around, astonished by the frantic activity of the docks. The Rzankir had docked the previous day at twilight and the crew had worked for over two hours to unload all the cargo from Malkartas. They had been paid, and the custom in Argoya had been the same as everywhere she had ever sailed to. They had all gone to a tavern and become intoxicated. Of course, somebody said something about someone and somehow, as sometimes turned, the tavern erupted into a vast brawl. As a result, a horrible purple bruise on one of her eyes and cuts on her lip and one cheek accompanied Corelle's headache and bilious stomach. Nothing had changed; she had joined in and been pummelled to the floor. No doubt she could have killed any one of them, but she had not mastered the skills of the unarmed brawl and came out of it as poor as ever. All good fun, and she thought Wilke might have been the one who had cut her lip, in truth.

When she woke in the cabin, the smell of stale bodies, stale drink, and stale blood almost made her fetch up, a story that would serve as an excuse if her stomach decided to empty itself this morning. She had one plan, and no idea how to achieve it. Krage must be found and killed, then she would consider her next plan, if she survived the first one.

Krage must have arrived by ship, so she resolved to begin her enquiries with the larger businesses that offered cabins aboard their ships. There must be a great many ways to sail to and from such a vast city, but she hoped Krage's wealth might mean he would favour ships with luxurious cabins.

The Rzankir belonged to a business owned by a woman, although Corelle could no longer remember her name. Her tally house, or goods house, Corelle seemed to recall, had been toward one end of the dock, she thought, so she set off without hesitation to make enquiries there. Memories of her previous visit to the office flooded back to her, none of them good. She had struggled to make herself understood in Kuirbekian, the only language both Corelle and one of the women behind the counter had any grasp of. Corelle could still speak no words of the language of this city beyond a few phrases she had picked up aboard the ship. Most of the mariners had spoken to her in Malkartasian, which resembled Kuirbekian so much, they had made themselves understood most of the time.

The words emblazoned on the front of the goods house still bewildered her, but she recognised the enormous building. The language barrier would be a problem in her search for Krage unless she could master the language of Feshtersov. Aboard the ship, she had learned Argoya lay in the south of the land of Feshtersov, although they called it a nation rather than a land. The language would wait. She would search for Krage and learn to speak more of the Feshtersov language as she went along.

She pushed open the office door and studied the faces of the three women behind the counter. One of them seemed familiar, but she might not have been the woman who spoke Kuirbekian. The women looked up, and Corelle asked if any of them spoke Kuirbekian. One of them nodded and asked how she could help, not the woman whose face Corelle had thought she recognised.

"A friend of mine arrived in Argoya some time ago and I need to find him." The woman nodded and smiled, and Corelle waited. "Can you help me?"

"Where is your friend?"

"I do not know. That is why I am here."

The woman frowned. "I not understand. You wish me to help find a friend, but you not know where is?"

"That I… yes. He will have arrived on one of your ships." Not true, she imagined, but not inconceivable.

"He is mariner?" The frown remained.

"That he is not, he will have been a passenger."

"Then no."

"You will not help me?"

She shook her head, and her horsetail swished around behind her. "I cannot help. No passengers on the ship."

Corelle puzzled on her words. Did she mean the business owner did not carry passengers on any of her ships? "You have no passengers on your ships?"

The woman laughed, and Corelle realised this must be the same woman she had tried to talk to when she came here with Gaish. "I have no ships."

Corelle waved an arm around the office. "This business has no passengers on its ships?"

"Yes. Ckazatch Otohen has no passenger ships."

Corelle drew in a breath to clarify the answer, but she had run out of patience. She turned to leave, but a thought occurred to her. "Does anybody operate passenger ships here?"

"Yes. Passenger ships go with Poygartch Stalldehan."

"Where is her office?"

"His office. Along dock that way." The woman pointed back the way Corelle had come.

"My thanks." Corelle could summon no sincerity into the thanks as she left the office, even though the problem lay with her. She had come to a land where she could not speak the language and felt annoyed by a difficult conversation with someone who spoke a limited amount of a foreign language but made the effort to try.

She stopped various people along the dock to ask for the office of Poygartch Stalldehan and dismissed her idle consideration of the woman's language skills. Almost an hour later, she found the office she sought. Not as big as the building of… the last building she had been to, but large, nonetheless. Would she ever get the hang of their complex names? At the least, the names appeared simpler than the Qagrue names had been.

The wooden building did not seem to be a goods house, as the other had been, rather a large office with two extensive windows either side of the central door. An office did not need to be so big, but that did not matter. Corelle opened the door and entered the office. Three women and two men stood behind the long counter, and people stood in lines before each one on Corelle's side of the counter. Unsure how to proceed, she stood at one end of one of the lines and waited as the people in front of her shuffled forward to replace the person who left the counter. Soon, only one man remained between her and one of the staff. She had not understood a word she had heard except "*gyukh*," which she recalled meant "ship" from the few words she had picked up aboard the Rzankir.

A man smiled at her across the counter, and her turn had come. Corelle took a deep breath and went through her languages. He did not speak any of them, but one of the women looked over and replied in Steinlund. "You speak Steinlund? I am from there. I can help you. Please join my queue."

Corelle did not understand the word "queue," but after all else, she had already reached the counter, so she imagined the woman would help her once she finished with the man she had been busy with. She moved across beside the man, but the woman behind the counter pointed at the line of people who waited for her and repeated her instruction. "Please join my queue."

Protests sprang to Corelle's tongue, but she swallowed them on the deep, resigned breath she took instead. If she argued with the woman, she might not help her, and that would leave her with the man who could not speak any language she could understand. She trudged over to stand behind the last person in the line and waited all over again.

The line shuffled forward until at last the woman smiled at Corelle and spoke some words in her own language before it seemed she remembered, and she greeted her in Steinlund. "I seek a friend who arrived here a while ago on a ship from the Torr Sea."

"How did they arrive here?"

"On a ship."

The woman laughed, a soft tinkle that somehow carried scorn on its cheerful brow. "None of our ships travel to the Torr Sea. Which route did your friend take?"

Corelle wrinkled her brow in consternation. How could there be no passenger ships from the Torr Sea? She had already met at least three people from Steinlund here, and Krage had come here, if Denstal had told her the truth. "How else can they reach here? How did you get here?"

"From northern Steinlund, they could have sailed to Hielund, then on to here. That is how I arrived. Or they might have sailed on the cargo ships operated by Ckazatch Otohen and other owners. There are other routes from eastern Corkannae, but they would be compli—"

"How are all these routes available, but I know nothing of them?" Every word the woman had spoken had amazed Corelle further and further. "Passengers do not sail on the Rzankir."

The woman shrugged and gave Corelle a smile of condescension. "They do if they can afford it. Adjtish Schteyen will carry passengers if they reward him well enough."

Something else Corelle had not known. "Let us say he arrived from Steinlund through the land you mentioned."

"Hielund?"

"Indeed. Would you have a record of his arrival?"

She sucked on her lower lip, doubt in her eyes. "We might, but we cannot reveal that information."

Why could she not reveal it? That made no sense. "Why not?"

"Passenger information is private. We never say who is aboard our ships."

"What in the Five Cities makes it so secretive? Who would ever care?"

"You care."

The woman had the right of it, and Corelle sighed. "You will not tell me?"

"I cannot. The law will not let me. I am sorry."

CHAPTER 34
CORELLE

orelle turned and stomped out of the office. She had believed the Duke stuffy and caught up in the niceties of formal nonsense, but this land seemed ten times worse, with laws that would not even allow a person to learn if another person had been aboard a boat.

Corelle slumped onto a bench and watched the dockhands hurry back and forth with the goods the mariners brought off ships. She had been unreasonable in the office. It had not been the woman's fault, after all else. Her disappointment and frustration had got the better of her.

In Malkartas, foreign people who settled in the land must register themselves with the Council or whatever they had called themselves. It had been easy to find Raolos. Feshtersov might have a similar requirement. That would be her next move. The midday had come and gone as she had shuffled along lines of people in the pursuit of cats, as the expression went.

If she intended to ask the Portreeve, or whatever they called themselves here, she would have to find them. That should be easy enough, although the language would still confound her at every turn. She failed to find anybody who could understand her question, and more than an hour later, she found herself in a line of people who shuffled toward the Steinlund woman yet again.

"Welcome back." The woman gave her a half-hearted smile.

"I apologise for my rudeness earlier. I became frustrated, and I regret it now." The woman's smile seemed warmer after the apology. "Where would I find your government, or council, or whatever you call it here? Please."

At first, the woman seemed not to have understood the question, then she raised her head in comprehension. "The Parliament, you mean? Or the Sovran?"

"I do not know. I wish to see if they have any record of my friend's arrival. Whichever would be most helpful."

The woman nodded. "You need the Parliament. They deal with the civic issues."

Corelle had no idea what civic issues might be, but she could not allow herself to be distracted by words that tried to befuddle her. "Where is the Parliament?"

"They will not tell you any news of your friend I am afraid. They are bound by the same laws we are."

"I will take my chances." Corelle muttered, then forced a smile to her face.

"You will find them in Feshlist."

Corelle guessed Feshlist must be the name of some area of the city. "How do I get there?"

"Carriage. You would catch one behind the docks, on Sterrik Street."

"How far is Feshlist, then?" Corelle had little coin to waste on carriages when she could walk for no cost.

"Four days."

Corelle stared at her, unable to comprehend what she had heard. She had never seen a city as big as Argoya, but it could not extend so far, it took four days to cross it in a carriage? "Four days? It takes four days to reach a part of this city?"

The woman laughed, as though somebody had told her a jest Corelle had not heard. "Feshlist is not in Argoya. It is our capital city."

Corelle felt dizzy and placed a hand on the counter as the woman looked at her in sudden concern. A city this vast, yet not the capital? It defied belief. How enormous must Feshtersov be, after all else, if this vast city could be nothing more than a dock city? "My thanks. Serrk Street." Disconsolate, she prepared to head off.

The woman corrected her. "Sterrik Street."

"Sterrik." Corelle turned and left the office, then rushed back to the bench before her legs failed her and she fell on her face on the docks. It would be impossible to find Krage in a land so vast. She had not grasped the sheer size of the task ahead of her. It would have been difficult to find him in Alcmouth, but in this land, it would be all but impossible. She had embarked on the reckless pursuit of her vengeance, and she had been thwarted.

Nobody would have heard of Krage. There must be twenty people for every light of the night sky in Argoya alone, and who knew how many vast cities she would have to visit in search of him? She had precious little coin, and it might take her many lifetimes to track him down.

A tear dripped from her chin onto her trousers, and dejection crushed her down onto the bench. She had failed, and she had failed because she had set out with no plan, a leaf in a current carried where the water wills and with no more thought to its final destination than that it would arrive at some point.

Somebody stopped before her and said something she could not understand. She waved a hand, unable to look up to see who had spoken to her. The person's feet moved on, and Corelle decided to find an inn, take a room, and think of her next move. Melancholy cloaked her at the thought she may not find and kill Krage. Weary and despondent, she dragged herself away from the docks in search of an inexpensive inn.

Not far away, she found an inn that cost a few of the coins Adjtish Schteyen had given her as she left the ship, and she paid for one night in advance. The room on the third storey looked out toward a hill she thought might be the one where she had fought with the three young people, and she wondered whether they had all lived. Bored of the room after less than an hour, her thoughts miserable and full of self-reproach for her stupidity in the way she had come in search of Krage, she wandered down to the tavern-room, or whatever they called it here. She drank several goblets of wine, ate a meal, and stared with vacant eyes at three men who sat across the table from her one after the other and attempted to talk to her. She did not understand one word any of them said, and they all abandoned her in time.

The temptation to drink herself into another night of oblivion, as she had done so many times, nibbled at her, but she had little coin and no plan, and some part of her abandoned the idea and drove her up to her bed as the tavernroom became less busy.

In the darkness of the night, Ulmella returned to her. With pastries in her hands, she wandered along a row of chairs at a table and placed a pastry before each of the assembled guests. Deineike, Raolos, Wilke, and Denstal all grabbed at the pastries and crammed them whole into their mouths as Ulmella laughed behind them.

"Do not eat them." Corelle had warned them too late. Blood poured from all eight eyes and pooled on the table. Their flesh turned purple like Corelle's eye, and they fell forward with their faces in their own blood.

Ulmella laughed, and Corelle noticed Styrrach on the floor under the table with four long, pointed sticks. He pushed one up through the seat of each of the four chairs until the point emerged from the backs of the figures slumped on the table. Ulmella tugged on the stick that protruded from Wilke's back until his body toppled backward, and he lay on his back on the floor, pinned to his chair by the stick. Ulmella pulled her dress up and lowered her sex onto Wilke's face, and his body jerked as Ulmella panted with desire, her face red as her fists clenched, then unclenched, over and over until she screamed with release. As she screamed, a stream of murky, viscous liquid ejected from her mouth into a puddle on the floor, and Styrrach crawled from beneath the table to lap at it.

He looked up at Corelle, a sneer on his face, and Ulmella stood from Wilke's body. Her stomach expanded and grew bigger and bigger until it burst, and a large cake fell from her onto the floor before Corelle. Scribed on the cake in some form of sugar sweet were the words, "I Love You," and Wilke's dead eyes turned to her. "I love you." Ulmella screamed as he sighed the words.

"I love you." Their voices blended as they chanted the words over and over. "I love you."

Corelle's eyes snapped open, and she stared at the ceiling of the room. Light crept around the edge of the shutter, and another day had begun outside in the streets of Argoya. What would she do today? Had she already run out of options after one day? That could not be. She had been frustrated yesterday, nothing more. She would visit the wealthy quarter and make some enquiries there. Her luck might hold, and she might learn something of Krage's whereabouts.

She needed some fresh air and some food. A headache troubled her, but her stomach seemed settled. In truth, she had not drunk a great amount of wine; enough to help her forget her disappointment, no more. She pulled herself from the bed, picked up her pack, headed down the stairs and out into the street.

The sun had climbed above the rooftops and promised a warm day. She wandered further away from the docks in search of a pastry shop, but instead emerged into a crowded marketplace in a large square. She hoped she could find a pastry stall in the market, so she wandered up and down the lines of stalls in search of something with which to break her fast.

Ahead, she saw a stall that sold bread and pastries. An elderly woman stood at the stall and picked over the bread until she seemed satisfied. She held out a few coins, and the stallholder took them with a nod, none of the friendliness and compassion Corelle had seen Vamma display on her stall.

As the woman moved aside so Corelle could cast her eye over the baked goods on the stall, a commotion from behind distracted her. A small contingent of people passed, three men in green tunics armed with short swords, then a woman in an elaborate velvet cloak. Her long red hair flowed down her back like a second cloak. Behind her came three more men in the green tunics.

As the last of the men passed Corelle, the elderly woman moved another step, and the man crashed into her with his shoulder. The old woman spun backward and fell to the floor, and a gasp went up from the few people around the stall. The man walked on a step, then stopped and turned around. Corelle knelt to the old woman, who seemed fine other than a sense of confusion over what had turned. Corelle scanned her head but saw no blood, and she looked up at the man, who glared his defiance at her.

Corelle snarled at him. "You should apologise." The man frowned. Of course, he had not understood her. Two other people helped the elderly woman to her feet. When Corelle pointed to her, the man gave a short laugh, and her temper frayed. She stood, closed the distance between her and the man with two brisk steps, then balled his tunic in her fist and pointed to the woman again as she yelled at him. "Apologise."

CHAPTER 35
CORELLE

"What has turned here?" A woman had spoken in the language of Steinlund.

Corelle flicked her eyes from the man to the woman in the velvet cloak, who stood before her, hands on hips. The fire in her eyes burned as bright as the flames that danced in her red hair beneath the morning sun. Her full lips were pressed tight together and accentuated her high cheekbones. Beside her, one of the men wrapped his fingers around the grip of his sword, but the woman held up a long, slender finger toward him before she returned the hand to her hip.

"One of your men knocked this woman down." Corelle pointed to the elderly woman. "I want him to apologise." She had replied in Steinlund.

The woman's blue eyes glanced to the old woman, and the fire in them died away to leave clear blue water that sparkled as deep as Arella's before Corelle had closed them. "He will apologise, but he does not speak your language. You spoke Dur, did you not? I regret I do not speak your own language, so it is lucky you speak Steinlund."

"That I do." Corelle's anger cooled, and the woman's beauty and calm demeanour captivated her.

The woman nodded but said no more for ten heartbeats. At length, she turned to the man who had knocked the old woman over and said something to him Corelle could not understand. Though she spoke in a soft voice with no hint of anger or violence, the man looked downcast at her words, and when she fell silent, he went to the old woman, laid a hand on her shoulder, and spoke soft words Corelle did not catch and could not have understood had she done so.

The woman in the cloak returned her attention to Corelle. "I thank you for your concern for the older." The term "older" sounded unusual in Corelle's ears, and she imagined it had lost something in translation from Feshtersov to Steinlund. "I am Sovsdot Lorgallehna Orkbarat." The woman held out a hand toward Corelle, palm downward, as the Duke had done in Alcmouth many years ago. Nobody had explained the gesture to Corelle, although Raolos might have indicated she had been meant to kiss his hand. Did this woman expect the same?

Corelle thought it would demean them both for her to kiss the hand of a stranger, no matter how important she must be to have so many guards, so she reached her own hand out to shake the woman's. One of the guards shouted something, and the woman drew her hand backward a touch; almost imperceptible, but Corelle spotted it. She had committed some kind of cultural mistake, she reasoned, and she felt herself blush. "My apologies." She withdrew her hand. "I am Corelle."

The woman's laughter sounded like a crystal-clear waterfall on a spring morning. "I should be the one to apologise. You are unfamiliar with our land, our language, and our customs. I should have realised this. I have embarrassed you. This morning has been a disaster. One of my clumsy men has knocked one of our olders to the dust, and now I have embarrassed a guest in our nation whom duty would have me welcome."

Corelle found most of the words strange but did not want to cause offence again. "My thanks. Tell me, if you will, how you speak Steinlund so well."

Again, the woman laughed. "As Sovsdot, I am required to know many things and many languages." Whatever a Sovsdot might be, Corelle could not guess. "In truth, I love language, and we have many Steinlunders here in Argoya. The adventurous ones all seem to find their way here in time. I made it my business to learn the language. I cannot speak Dur, but I know Dur and Steinlund are neighbours, so I hoped you might speak Steinlund."

"How did you know I am from Dur?" It seemed a strange deduction for the woman to have made.

"I have heard the language, and while I cannot speak it, I recognised the dialect and some of your words. I did recognise the word 'apologise.' It sounds almost identical in Steinlund, as you must know."

Corelle could not fathom this woman with her dainty movement and flowery speech. Sovsdot, dialect, older; these words meant nothing to her, and so many of them in so short a time. "Many of your words are a mystery to me, I am afraid." Why had she said that? She felt like the girl of seventeen years in Orgel's shop all over again, nervous and inept in the company of this beautiful woman. "I am from Ryl." She cursed herself the instant she said it.

The woman's incessant laughter deepened Corelle's embarrassment every time it burst from her lips. "I am quite sure Ryl is a wonderful place. How long have you been in our nation?"

"We say 'land' in Dur, and I arrived here yesterday." A foolish admission. She should have said she had been here longer. Why? Because… Curse it, what in the Five Cities had this woman done to Corelle? No sensible thought or word would come to her, and she had no explanation for how childlike she had behaved since the woman's first words.

"Then I understand why you know so little of our ways." A thoughtful expression crossed the woman's face. "Allow me to compensate for Mikotah's clumsiness. You and this delightful older must join me for lunch at the Seat. I shall tell you some of our ways and help you learn a few words of our language, and I shall enjoy your company and some tales of Ryl, I hope. Shall we say tomorrow?"

The invitation caught Corelle unawares. She had no idea what the Seat meant but guessed it might be the woman's home. Who the woman might be, she could not guess, but from the way she spoke and the six guards, it would be reasonable to imagine she must be both important and rich. She might know something of Krage, and if she did, it would not pay to pass the opportunity by. If she knew nothing of Krage, Corelle would be out of pocket another night at the inn and nothing more. "Very well. How will we get there?"

"I will send a carriage for you both, have no fear."

Corelle had not meant to ask about transportation. Her question had been nothing more than a clumsy attempt to ask for directions. "That will not be necessary. For me, that is. I can walk. Although the old woman…" What a mess. Why did the woman not go away and allow the real Corelle to return to this body and this traitorous mouth that betrayed her every time it opened?

"Whereabouts is your home? Forgive me, I imagine you stay at an inn. Which one?"

Corelle grimaced. She could not remember the name of the inn. "I have no accommodation arranged for tonight."

The woman turned to a grey-haired guard and spoke some words to him. He nodded and replied, then turned to bark something at a younger guard. The younger one went to speak to the elderly woman, and as Corelle watched him, she realised a large crowd had gathered round. She had been so focused on the conversation, she had not noticed. Fortunate indeed Krage had not wandered by. He would have sent her wherever she travelled to afterward, and she would not even have been aware he was there.

The woman turned to Corelle again. "I suggest The Hillside Inn. It is splendid." She held out a hand toward the grey-haired guard, who dipped into a tunic pocket and came out with something he pressed into the palm of the woman's hand. The woman in turn passed it to Corelle, a small rectangular piece of metal, white in colour but with a stylised golden "L" embossed on its surface. "Show them this. I am certain your room will delight you. I shall reclaim the token tomorrow. I shall send the carriage at the midday. I look forward to lunch, Corelle of Ryl. Good day to you."

CHAPTER 36
CORELLE

Before Corelle could reply, the woman twirled on one foot, and she and her six guards set off toward whatever Corelle had interrupted. Or rather, her guard had interrupted. The crowd's silence gave way to raucous shouts, and they clapped their hands together in excitement. Some of them pounded Corelle on the back and spoke to her, although she understood nothing they said, and she nodded and smiled in response. The most common word she could pick out from the babble was "Sovsdot."

The old woman approached her and took both of her hands in her own, her dry, wrinkled skin like parch in Corelle's hands. The old woman nodded the entire time as she talked, her words no more than noise in Corelle's ears. Corelle smiled at her, pulled her hands away, and pushed her way through the crowd of appreciative friends she had made but could not understand. Everybody she passed touched her and spoke to her, and she grew concerned she might not be safe in the crowd.

She increased her pace and barged through the throng, which thinned the further she got from the pastry stand. In all the excite-

ment, she had not bought anything to eat, and her stomach growled with hunger. The streets were unrecognisable, as she had left the market in a different direction from when she had arrived. Once she had left the crowds behind, she slipped the token the woman had given her into a pocket and set out in search of some food.

On a corner of two wide streets, she saw a pastry and bread shop, but to her disappointment they did not sell the cream-filled pastries she had come to favour. A loaf of bread caught her eye. Embedded within it, she could see small round fruits of some kind, but her questions about it in all the languages she knew produced nothing but blank stares.

Though she knew nothing about it, she bought a loaf of the bread and found a small grassy square further along the street where she could sit and eat it. The fruits had a pleasant sweetness, and the bread had a spicy taste she liked. She ate the entire loaf in one go, though by the end she felt bloated and thought the decision unwise.

Her next task would be to seek out The Hillside Inn. She turned around and scanned the city skyline. Over the nearby roofs, she could see the top of the hill where she had fought with the three young people. Based on its name, the inn might be on one side or another of that hill, so she set off toward it. After half of an hour or so, she stood at the bottom of the hill and realised she must have been wrong to think the inn could be here.

Her memory of the area had been patchy, it seemed. Paths through a large area of green made up most of the hill, and she saw nothing but houses. They did not seem all that big or well-maintained, but the houses on the far side of the hill had been larger, or so she thought. She set off up the hill and climbed to the top with none of the breathless exhaustion she had experienced the last time she had been here.

At the top, she stood on the bench and gazed around. Her

memory had been correct to some extent, although she must have approached the hill from a different direction. The larger houses lay a quarter turn down the hill, not on the opposite side as they had that day. No sign of the fight remained. The wine cask she had discarded had gone. Memories of the fight danced through her mind. Had the two men she had injured survived? The fates could not be rewritten, so she shook the memories from her and headed down the hill toward the large houses. She should have asked the woman to scribe the name of the inn so she could show it to a local, at the least.

The homes in this part of the city suggested their owners must be wealthy, the houses large and with neat rear garden areas. An alleyway between two of the houses led Corelle to the street beyond, where she gazed around in hopelessness. Nothing that even resembled a shop could be seen, much less an inn. Even if she found it, she doubted she could afford this inn and would need to find one less expensive and return to meet the carriage at the midday tomorrow.

A man emerged from the door of one of the houses, dressed in trousers and a tunic of fine making. He set off down the street, and Corelle ran to catch him. She called to him, and he turned, a puzzled look on his face.

"The Hillside Inn?" she asked in Dur, then repeated it in Steinlund, Kuirbekian, and Vyrrmod. His expression did not change. He had not understood her, and she wracked her brain for a way to get her question across. She pointed to the hill behind the houses and steepled her fingers together in an impression of a hill, then pointed to her side. With her hands pressed together, she lowered her head onto them on one side and closed her eyes in what she hoped would be a decent impression of sleep.

The man stared at her for a heartbeat, and she began the process again, but at that moment, his mouth opened, his eyes widened, and he seemed to have grasped her meaning. He pointed down the street, then beckoned as though she should follow him. Corelle could see no point in any attempt at conversation, so she walked a pace behind him until they came to a corner. He pointed down the street and to the left. Corelle guessed he meant the inn lay down this street and to the left, so she thanked him as he continued on his way with a cheerful wave.

She wandered along the street until she reached another that led off to the left. It went a short distance before it reached the gates of another large house, so she ignored it. At the next corner, she looked left and almost collapsed to the floor in surprise.

Across from her stood a building so large, it might rival the Portreeve's Offices in Ryl. It had more windows than she thought she could count, and a large pair of double doors that stood open to the street. Two men in dark red trousers and tunics stood beneath a roof that protruded from the front of the building. The words scribed onto the gable of the roof made no sense to her, but she guessed they would say The Hillside Inn in the language of Feshtersov. As she could never afford to stay at such a grandiose inn, she hesitated, unsure what to do next. She had no idea where she might find a cheaper inn, but she would have to find her way back to the poorer part of the city, then walk all the way out here again tomorrow. The alternative would be not to turn up for the lunch at all, but the red-headed woman had captivated her, and she longed to meet her again.

It could not hurt to find out how much their least expensive room might cost, so Corelle plucked up all her courage and took the first step toward the inn's doorway. The two men turned their heads to watch her, and she imagined she looked a sorry sight to them in her travel-weary trousers and tunic, scuffed boots, a ragged pack across her shoulder, her untidy hair no more than a finger past her ears. She smiled at them as she drew near, and they bowed their heads and smiled in return. One of them spoke, a question in his tone, but she repeated the smile and walked through the open doors. Although she felt certain they watched her every step, she did not look back.

The doors opened into a vast lobby with a vaulted ceiling. The furniture looked lavish, made from some dark wood similar to Ortwood. Velvet curtains with braided cords stood at every window. Here and there, one or two people sat in armed chairs and spoke to one another in hushed tones. To one side of the lobby stood a long, dark wood counter, and behind it a man and woman, dressed in the same dark red as the men at the door, smiled at Corelle.

Corelle took a deep breath, summoned up the last reserves of her courage, and walked on unsteady legs to the counter. The woman smiled and said something, and Corelle dug in her pocket, pulled out the token, then laid her hand on the counter and opened her fist.

The man and woman both stared at the token on Corelle's palm, and the man raised his voice to say something. People in the red clothes appeared from everywhere and approached her. She feared they intended to take her into custody, and she dropped her pack and crouched as she reached for her boot. One of the men had come in from the door, and he picked up her pack. The man behind the counter had spoken throughout, and in some dark corner of her confusion, Corelle realised he had asked her if she spoke Vyrrmod.

"That I do." At last she had found somebody she could understand.

"Ah, delightful. Any guest of the Sovsdot is welcome here at The Side Of The Hill Inn." She guessed again something had been lost in the translation. "I regret the Sovran rooms are occupied already, but I trust our Parliament rooms will suffice. Jgorkal will show you to your rooms, and we will send the servitor to you to draw you a tub and attend to your needs. Do you have any questions?"

Corelle's head spun. What did it all mean? Who had this

woman been to command this much respect? How could Corelle afford rooms in this extravagant place? She doubted she could afford to sleep in a privy in this inn, but this man seemed determined to have her shown to fancy rooms where somebody would come and fill a tub for her, unless she had misunderstood. "How much do these rooms cost?"

"For a guest of the Sovsdot?" He laughed, and the others laughed with him even though they could not have known why. "There is no cost for such an honoured guest. It is our privilege to host you."

Corelle staggered to the nearest couch and collapsed full length onto it as the people in the red clothes fussed around her. She had never had a dream quite like this, and she did not intend to wake from it. Ever.

CHAPTER 37
CORELLE

The water in the enormous tub came up to Corelle's shoulders even if she sat upright. The foam from some substance the woman had poured into it rose around her as though she bathed in the clouds, and its aroma filled her nostrils, sweet and delicate like the scent Pettra had worn so often. Corelle could not recall the last time she had bathed, and she luxuriated in the experience. As the water cooled, the woman reappeared with a large golden pitcher and poured more hot water into the tub, and the steam from the water swirled and formed delicate twisted columns that reached to the ornate ceiling of the tub room.

Guilty at the time she had spent in the tub as she languished in the luxury of the hot water, Corelle climbed out after almost an hour. The woman appeared with cloths as soon as she stood and seemed determined to dry her, but Corelle shooed her away, unable to succumb to such decadence as a servant who would carry out so intimate a procedure. When she had dried herself, she dug in her pack for some clean clothes. If this Sovsdot whatever-her-name-had-been had sent her to such a high-quality inn, Corelle's clothes might be inadequate for lunch the next day, so she tipped her coins out onto the enormous bed in the bedroom and stared at them in abject misery. It seemed unlikely they would buy her an acceptable outfit, and she had no time to create one herself.

She walked into the parlour, an enormous room with several couches and armed chairs scattered around it. Beyond the furniture stood the dark wood door Jgorkal had shown her through when he brought her up the wide staircase to the top floor of the inn. She hoped the man behind the counter who spoke Vyrrmod could help her find an inexpensive tunic at the least, something better than the battered items she carried in her pack.

The same man still stood at the counter when she came down the stairs. He smiled at her and greeted her like a long-lost relative returned after years away. The story she had invented sounded implausible even to her, but it would serve better than a confession she would struggle to pay for a loaf and had no idea who had given her the token that had opened such luxurious doors to her. "My luggage is delayed, and I have need of clothes for a lunch with the Sovsdot tomorrow. My pouch is with my trunk and—"

"Madam, have no fear. I will have some dresses sent to your room as soon as your servitor tells us what size we should send for." He had interrupted her without a glimmer of doubt on his face and now offered to arrange for dresses to be sent to her even though he knew she could not pay for them. She might find some local maker who would desire the prestige of Corelle in one of their dresses, similar to the time the Portreeve's wife in Ryl had commandeered a dress of Corelle's own making.

She laughed inside at the foolish thought. "I thought some trousers and a suitable tunic would be appropriate."

He looked horrified. "For a lunch with the Sovsdot? Oh no, I do not think that will do at all. Is the lunch at the Seat?"

"That it is." Corelle gave him a glum nod.

He wore a look of such disdain, Corelle could almost taste the bitterness of whatever it had been about her clothing suggestion he abhorred. "Then, madam, trousers will not do. Leave it to me, please. Return to your room and I will send up some food. Would you like some wine with your meal?"

Corelle faced two choices. She could return to the room, grab her pack and try to find the abandoned house she and Gaish had once slept in, or she could remain here and be treated like a Duchess until tomorrow's lunch. "Red please." Wracked with guilt, she turned to trudge up the stairs to the enormous rooms.

Late the next morning, the knock at the door of the bedroom woke her. She felt terrible. She had drunk far too much of the wine and eaten too much rich food. The dresses had arrived, and, since Styrrach would no longer be enriched by her lavish choices, she had chosen a dark green taffeta gown with a lacy hem and a low-cut front. It had required some adjustment to fit her, but the woman who seemed to be the servitor had returned it within an hour, a perfect fit. Some well-made shoes had been found, and both the shoes and the dress had been stored in a large cupboard in the bedroom for the night.

Words she still could not understand came through the door. This must be a dream, she reminded herself, although as she rose from the pillow and her headache stabbed her in the skull, she wished she had chosen a less painful dream. "Come in." The door opened, the servitor peeped in, then smiled as she saw Corelle and came into the room. She had a tray in her hands that held a plate with some meats and cheeses alongside some bread. A cup and a pitcher completed the tray, and when she placed it on the bed, the pitcher held water. Corelle reached for the water and consumed a cup. It soothed her dry mouth but reminded her of the fragility of her stomach.

The servitor laughed and left her alone. Corelle propped herself on some of the vast collection of pillows scattered around the bed and picked at the bread and some of the cheese. She drank several cups of water and wondered how late she had slept. Other than the man behind the counter, she had yet to find anybody with whom she could make herself understood. She had told him the carriage would call for her at the midday, and after all the effort they had gone to, she could not imagine they would let her be late. Doubt ate at her. Had she told him about the carriage? What if she had not? She might have dreamt she had told him, after all else. How inexcusable would it be to accept all this lavish treatment, then not appear for the lunch?

In panic, she called out, and the servitor came into the bedroom. After some effort, Corelle managed to explain with gestures she wished to know how late it had become. The woman explained with a large arc she traced in the air before her Corelle guessed represented the sky. The servitor held an arm at a point less than halfway through the arc. Not the midday yet, thank the fates. To be certain, she would go down to the counter and ask the man to ensure she did not miss the carriage.

Her heart fluttered, and she reasoned she had grown anxious about another meeting with the Sovsdot. At the least, she must find out what Sovsdot meant. The servitor seemed satisfied Corelle did not need anything further from her, and she bustled out of the room. Corelle took another cup of water and some more bread, then dragged her reluctant body from the bed and dressed in her own clothes. She slithered down the stairs like the new-birthed milk cow she had once seen at Taro's farm, all uncontrollable legs and no balance. Unlike that little animal, Corelle at the least had a handrail to hold on to, or she felt certain she would have arrived at the bottom of the stairs face first, bloodied and battered.

"*Curse it.*" The man could not be seen. Two other men stood behind the counter, and they smiled as she approached them like a… She could not recall the name of the creature that resembled a snail without its shell, but she felt certain she must look no less revolting. "Is the man who speaks Vyrrmod here today?"

One of them smiled and called out. The man who understood

her came out of a door behind them to greet her like a long-lost friend again before she explained her situation. He gave a sympathetic laugh when she admitted she had been inebriated the night before and now felt awful.

He promised to have her ready by the time the carriage arrived, and she climbed the stairs again. Back in her rooms, she slumped face down on the bed and fell asleep. When the servitor woke her, Corelle jumped from the bed in panic. Had she slept beyond the midday? Why had they not woken her? The servitor pointed to the tub room, where Corelle found a tub of hot water and foam ready to crawl into. She closed her eyes as the water soothed and refreshed, but the servitor bullied her out again. Corelle had never dried herself with such soft cloths, and she luxuriated in them until she felt thoroughly dry, then used white paste to sweeten her breath.

With the help of the woman, Corelle pulled the gown on and slipped into the shoes. The woman fussed at her hair for some time, although her constant tuts of disappointment did little for Corelle's confidence. To complete the transformation, the woman applied some red powder to Corelle's cheeks, though it seemed ironic to Corelle to be preened and powdered like the women she had always disdained so much in her father's shop in Ryl.

After all else, when she gazed at herself in the reflecting glass, Corelle thought she looked attractive. The red powder highlighted her cheeks, curse it, and the dress suited her figure. Her rounded breasts protruded above the corset in a manner she felt was sensual but not too brazen, and she realised she had not brushed her hair for many passes. She doubted any two strands of it had regrown to the same length, but the servitor had done a decent enough job, given the poor material she had to work with. It looked clean and tidy, at the least.

Corelle's stomach had settled, but her head still ached as she descended the stairs. Her new friend stood behind the counter with the woman who had been with him yesterday, and other men and women in the red clothes of the inn stood nearby. They all clapped as she appeared, and she felt herself blush. She hoped the powder disguised her embarrassment.

"Beautiful, madam." The man had done so much for her, and she did not even know his name. She would rectify that oversight when she returned for her pack later, after the lunch.

One of the other men escorted her toward the door, but he stopped short and brought a chair for her to sit in. Almost as soon as she sat down, she heard the clip-clop of hooves, and a grand carriage, painted a dark red not unlike the clothes worn in the inn, appeared and swung around in the street before it came to rest close to the roof that protruded from the inn. A young boy jumped down from the rear and opened the door. The door man helped Corelle to her feet and escorted her to the carriage, where the other door man had placed a small step. She climbed in without difficulty, so unlike the awkward experience she and Deineike had gone through to board Raolos's cart the first time they had visited his home.

The young boy closed the door. Nobody but Corelle sat in the carriage, and she wondered whether a separate carriage had been sent for the elderly woman, or whether they would collect her on the way. Heavy curtains blocked the light and the view, and she tugged them back so she could see the city as they travelled. She did not recognise any of the streets they drove through, but she thought she could retrace the journey if necessary.

As the carriage trundled through the city streets, Corelle's thoughts danced back to Vyrrmod and the inn she had stayed in with Vamma when they left Malkartas. It had seemed so sumptuous at the time, and Vamma had made some jest about wanting to live in it for the rest of her life. The rooms there had been luxurious, but compared to the rooms in The Hillside Inn, they were ordinary, at best. Never in her life had she even imagined such rooms could exist, such attention could be lavished on a guest. Whoever the woman from the market turned out to be, her wealth must be impossible to imagine.

The carriage did not collect the old woman, and when Corelle first saw the Seat, she almost fell out onto the street. She had never in her life seen such an enormous building. At least twice the size of the Ducal Highhome, it loomed through her window as the carriage passed along a street parallel to the front of the building. A high black fence protected the entire frontage of the building, four storeys high and the length of… Corelle could find nothing to measure it by. In truth, the high fence appeared insignificant next to the splendour of the building behind it. The carriage took more heartbeats than Corelle could count to pass halfway along the front of the building, then did not turn into the two huge gates that stood at the midpoint. As the carriage drove on, Corelle wondered how many of the Feshtersov sexags it would take to walk the length of the Seat.

They had almost passed the Seat when the carriage swung across the street and toward a smaller gate held open by two men, swords at their belts. The carriage passed through the gate and beneath an arch in the far end of the building, built of deep red bricks. The builders must have exhausted the globe's supply of them in its creation. Beyond the arch lay a courtyard, and the carriage came to a halt. The young boy appeared and pulled the door open. An older man in the green tunic but with no sword appeared with a step he placed beneath the door so Corelle could step from the carriage with no risk to her dignity.

Once she had climbed out, the older man picked up the step, and Corelle hesitated, unsure what to do. Another man stepped forward from a door and bowed his head. He swept his arm toward the door, and Corelle guessed she should enter the build-ing. She followed him and he led her down a corridor. The carpet beneath her feet felt so plush, she imagined it could be no softer to walk over the top of a cloud in the sky. Raolos's carpets had been lush; this one required a word that might not yet have been invented to describe its softness. Although she knew nothing of the cost of carpet, she imagined it must have cost more coin than Corelle had found in Styrrach's chest to carpet this one corridor alone. A thought pushed into her mind. *"Who is this woman?"*

CHAPTER 38
CORELLE

The man ahead of Corelle paused at an open door and gestured for her to enter. Through the door, Corelle found herself in a dining room, though far larger than any dining room she had ever been in before. The table stretched out before her, and since the man had not entered with her, she felt compelled to pace out its length.

She had taken twelve paces and had almost reached the end, when a door opened behind her. When she turned her head, the Sovsdot walked through into the room dressed in a light brown silk dress of simple design but exquisite making that left Corelle breathless.

"Corelle of Ryl." The woman laughed as she spoke, her gentle voice like the patter of raindrops against a window. "Do you measure my table?"

"That I do." Corelle felt her cheeks flame again.

"In truth, I should have said 'my father's table,' for it is his, if everybody had their own."

Another bizarre expression that made no sense to Corelle. "Your

father must be successful indeed to own such a home as this, and such a vast table."

"Indeed. I am a poor host though, for I have not greeted you, nor offered you a drink. Welcome to the Seat and thank you for your attendance today."

"My thanks. And my thanks also for the rooms at the inn. They are… magnificent."

"Think not on it, please. Would you like a drink? Some wine?"

"I fear I drank rather more wine last night than I should. I ought not—"

"Nonsense." The woman laughed again, and her face lit up. "What is a meal with friends without wine?"

Corelle glanced at the table. Only two places had been set at one end. "Will the elderly woman join us?"

"Alas no. She felt an invitation to lunch with the Sovsdot would be far beyond her station. Do not worry, I have arranged for her to receive a substantial reward for her unfortunate tumble in the dust."

"That is most kind of you, Sovsdot. You did not knock her over, after all else."

"I am responsible for the actions of my men. They are loyal to a fault and sometimes take their duties more seriously than necessary. But please, call me Lorgallehna. Sovsdot is too formal, and we are friends."

The name sounded unusual but comfortable, if a trifle long. The term "friends," however, stretched the depth of their relationship by a wide mark. They had exchanged a few words, every one of Corelle's clumsy and childish, and this woman's life differed from Corelle's by such a margin, they could never become close, but Lorgallehna had already said it twice today. "Very well, Lorgallehna it is."

Lorgallehna crossed the room to stand before Corelle, then offered her arm in the gesture Corelle now understood. She linked arms with the red-headed woman and allowed herself to be led to the far end of the table. A woman in a green dress appeared and held a chair out for Lorgallehna to sit at the head of the table. The woman then held Corelle's chair, and she sat. The woman picked up Lorgallehna's napkin, which she draped over the woman's lap before she repeated the exercise with Corelle. She turned to Lorgallehna. "Red or white, Eminence?"

Lorgallehna cast a mischievous glance at Corelle. "Why not both, Yerinbulla?" The woman hesitated. "What is it, Yerinbulla?"

"It is but lunch time, Eminence."

As Corelle strove to understand how the servant could speak perfect Steinlund, Lorgallehna turned to her. "We are grown women, are we not, Corelle of Ryl?"

Corelle held both hands up. "Please do not involve me in this debate. Yerinbulla has the right of it. It is lunch time."

"Both, Yerinbulla. My friend jests." Lorgallehna gave another of those laughs, and the woman bowed her head and left the room.

"I do not know this word, 'Eminence.'" Corelle spoke in a quiet voice, a whisper almost, anxious Yerinbulla did not hear her.

"All will be revealed." A twinkle flashed in Lorgallehna's eyes. "But first, tell me all about Corelle of Ryl. I shall hear your tale. Why have you come to Feshtersov?"

Corelle had not been ready for the question, and could not deliver a truthful answer for fear of the consequences. Lorgallehna's blue eyes pierced her, and she reached for a quick answer. "I came here once before. It is vast, and it has occupied my thoughts since that day. I vowed to return and explore it more than I had time for on my last visit." The story sounded plausible, and Corelle felt proud of the deflection.

A young girl brought a silver tray into the room. It shone so bright, the sun through the window reflected from it and cast a point of light onto the ceiling that moved in step with the girl. She placed it on a low cupboard at the side of the room and ladled some broth from a bowl set on it into two smaller bowls. She brought the bowls one at a time to the table and set them down before first Lorgallehna, then Corelle, before she retired from the room.

The steam that rose from the bowl suggested the broth would be too hot to eat for a few moments, and Lorgallehna seemed to have no wish to abandon her questions. "What brought you here the first time?"

"I had become shipwrecked and passed through Argoya on my way home." At the least, that question could be answered with the truth.

"Shipwrecked? Your ship sank? Where had it been bound?"

"I sailed aboard The Ictharelian, the ship that sailed around the globe."

Lorgallehna's eyes widened. "You were aboard that ship? That must have been quite an experience. What did you do aboard the ship?"

"I am a mariner."

Lorgallehna laughed, then seemed to realise Corelle had meant the words. Her laugh froze on her face. "You are serious. You are a mariner. I have never met a woman mariner before. Incredible."

Corelle could not detect any sarcasm in her voice, and the Sovsdot's face suggested amazement at the concept. "If I am honest, the experience terrified me. When I sail on large ships these days, I am anxious, never as comfortable as I used to be, even though I have worked passage on several ships since that day."

"What drove you to become a mariner?" Lorgallehna picked up a spoon, took a small amount of the broth in it, then blew on it before she sipped at it.

Another question that must be handled with care. "I had lost somebody I loved, and I wanted to escape my sadness."

Lorgallehna reached across the corner of the table to lay a hand on Corelle's arm. "That must have been awful. I cannot imagine how dreadful that must be. Did you?"

"Did I what?"

A small flutter of the redhead's eyelashes suggested the question had offended Lorgallehna's sense of good manners, but she did not dwell on it. "Did you escape your sadness?"

The sigh that whispered across Corelle's lips had been involuntary. "That I did not. Worse, I found further sadness." As she weaved the fabric of the tale with streaks of truth, Corelle feared she would trip herself in the complexity of the story. She took a sip of the broth. It tasted delicious, although it had no meat in it, and precious few tubers.

"This conversation is too sad. It is your turn. You may ask me a question." Yerinbulla reappeared with two pitchers. She placed them both on the low cupboard. "White with the broth please, Yerinbulla." Lorgallehna's eyes never left Corelle's.

Once the woman had placed two shiny silver goblets on the table and filled them with wine, she left. "What does Eminence mean?"

Lorgallehna took another sip of the broth, then set her spoon on a plate to one side. "It is a title given to any member of the Sovran's family. My father is the Sovran of Feshtersov."

Corelle stared her incomprehension at Lorgallehna. She had never heard this word "Sovran" either, and to unravel the story might take many lunchtimes if every question left her in need of more information so she could understand the answer. "Is a Sovran an important person in your land then?"

Lorgallehna laughed. "You might say so. I cannot tease you any longer. He is the ruler of our nation. There is no man higher than the Sovran. He is the Supreme Eminence of Feshtersov."

Corelle stared at Lorgallehna, who leaned over and pushed a gentle finger under Corelle's chin to close her mouth. "He is the Duke?"

"If that is what you call it in Dur, then yes, I imagine he is. We call it Sovran."

"You are his daughter? Small wonder the inn treated me so well. You will be the Sovran one day." Corelle could not imagine how a simple garment maker's daughter from Ryl sat at a table and ate lunch with a woman who would one day rule a land as vast as Feshtersov appeared to be.

"Well, I hope not. My brother is older, and he will become Sovran when my father dies, unless something happens to him. To my brother, I mean." She smiled. Her smile reminded Corelle of Deineike's, full of warmth and friendliness, and it made her comfortable despite the fact Lorgallehna might be the daughter of the most powerful man in the land, and Corelle had come to her land to commit murder. "It is my turn now. I wish to know about this love that tore you apart so much, unless it is too painful to tell."

It would be. How could she explain Deineike to this woman, whose own life must be so different from anything Corelle or Deineike could ever have dreamt of? How could she admit to Lorgallehna that the lost love she grieved for to this day had been a woman? Better safe than sorry. "It is too painful." Lorgallehna's face fell. "I will allow you another question in its place." Corelle coaxed an easy smile to her face.

The tales went on, the wine disappeared, and the food came and went. Rich hog, vegetables and tubers cooked to perfection, exquisite small sweets, which Corelle ate most of. Lorgallehna laughed and waved at the plate on the small cupboard as she instructed the young girl to dish them all up into Corelle's bowl.

A third pitcher of wine arrived along with a grumpy frown from Yerinbulla. Corelle told Lorgallehna all about Dur, and how the Qagrue had come to take over, though she left out everything about the Guild and her time in Vyrrmod. Lorgallehna said the Sovsdot represented the Sovran from time to time in her father's stead, at functions and balls he did not wish to attend, and she must attend banquets, large and lavish meals at which important people from Feshtersov and beyond spent the evening with the Sovran's family.

"How long will you stay in Feshtersov?" Lorgallehna's voice slurred. One elbow rested on the table and her hand supported her chin.

"Until I find Krage."

Lorgallehna raised her goblet but paused before her mouth. "Krage?"

That had been a mistake. Curse the wine and Lorgallehna's easy company. "Old friend. He owes me coin." That had been a good story, and not far from the truth. He did indeed owe a debt, although it would be paid in blood.

Lorgallehna sipped at the wine and held the goblet in mid-air. She stared at Corelle over the rim of the goblet, and to her surprise, Corelle thought she detected a suggestion of something in the bright blue eyes fixed on her. Corelle shook her head. It could not be. This important woman with her life of wealth and power could not be interested in a dalliance with a woman. Corelle felt it would be viewed in a poor light in the circles in which Lorgallehna moved. "How much coin?"

"A hundred groats." Corelle's words turned to mud in her throat. Had the room become warmer in the last few moments? It must be the wine that made her sweat.

Lorgallehna's tongue poked through her lips and moved from side to side, unhurried, as though she licked her lips from some habit. "Do you ride?"

"Ride?"

"Yes. Ride on horses. Do you?" Lorgallehna took another sip of her wine and replaced the goblet on the table.

Her eyes did not leave Corelle's, and it seemed they drew Corelle toward them. Some form of trickery, Corelle imagined, a parlour trick the Sovsdot had known since she had been a little girl. "I am a poor rider." Someone had stolen her voice, but the thief had been kind enough to leave behind a substitute, a tragic, thin, cracked, unreliable thing that could, at the least, squeak out her pathetic words.

"We shall have to remedy that."

As Corelle struggled to unravel the reply, whatever trickery had bemused and befuddled her broke. Lorgallehna's chin slipped off the palm of her hand and she started, surprise on her face. Corelle could not contain her laughter, and after a heartbeat Lorgallehna joined in. Her laughter tinkled like a clear blue stream and ran toward Corelle barefoot through warm summer sunshine. When Corelle shook her head, the vision disappeared. She had drunk more than enough of the wine, it seemed.

Lorgallehna turned to look out of the window. "I wonder what the hour is." She turned back to Corelle. "Tomorrow morning at the sunrise. Wear suitable clothes for a ride. Do not be late." She reached out and closed Corelle's mouth once more with a finger beneath her chin. "Do not be late." She gripped Corelle's jaw and moved her head from side to side in an enforced shake of the head. "I will not be late, Lorgallehna." She pouted and mimicked a child's voice.

The pitiful excuse for a voice replied on Corelle's behalf. "I will not be late."

Lorgallehna released her jaw and leaned back in her chair. "I am inebriated. You have led me astray." Her eyes smouldered, and Corelle again thought she saw the invitation she believed she had noticed earlier.

At that moment, Yerinbulla came through the door. "Do you need anything, Eminence?"

"Please make the carriage ready to take Corelle of Ryl back to her inn."

"My thanks for lunch." Corelle thought her voice sounded less woeful, and she hoped the trickery Lorgallehna had laid upon her might have ended.

"I am glad you came. I mean it." Lorgallehna emphasised each word of her next sentence. "Do not be late."

"I will not." Corelle laughed, although she felt sure she would be unless the servitor helped her, as she also felt intoxicated.

Lorgallehna picked up the third cask she had requested Yerinbulla to leave on the table earlier. She held it over Corelle's goblet and tipped it. A trickle of wine ran into the goblet, and Lorgallehna's lips pouted again, this time in an expression of sadness. "All gone."

"I am sorry. I hope you have plenty more in case you have a blanket."

"A blanket? I have misheard, I think." Lorgallehna laughed again.

"You said you go to them with your father."

The intensity of the Sovdot's laughter increased, and Corelle smiled. "Banquet, not blanket."

Corelle stifled a sigh. Another woman who corrected her when she misspoke. She smiled again. It might be enjoyable, after all else.

Lorgallehna reached out and laid her hand on Corelle's. "I think we will be friends, you and I." Consternation knitted her brow. "You and me. Which is it?"

Corelle's sardonic laugh echoed in the large room. "You ask me, who does not know a blanket from a banquet?" They both giggled like small children.

Yerinbulla reappeared. If she noticed Lorgallehna's hand on Corelle's, she gave no indication she did. "The carriage is ready, Eminence."

Lorgallehna stood, unsteady, and Corelle followed her as she walked from the room and down the corridor. The soft twilight outside surprised Corelle. Lunch in this land took longer than she had been used to. The same young lad held the carriage door open, and Lorgallehna held her hand out toward Corelle. Inebriated, Corelle risked a response and lowered her head to place a tender kiss on the back of Lorgallehna's delicate hand. The Sovsdot leaned forward to whisper in her ear. "You are not meant to kiss the hand itself." She pulled back and gave Corelle a wicked smile. "I enjoyed it. The lunch, I mean, of course." She turned and re-entered the building. Corelle guessed some custom of the land dictated she did not remain as her guests left, but the comment that she had enjoyed it, which Corelle took to mean the kiss rather than the lunch, sent a tingle to her sex. Unless she had meant the lunch. No matter which she meant, Corelle believed it had been the kiss, and as the door closed, she sprawled on the bench seat, more inebriated than she had realised.

The red-clothed men at the inn door greeted her as though she might be the Sovsdot herself, as did the man who spoke Vyrrmod. She arranged to be woken before the sunrise so she could keep her promise not to be late for whatever Lorgallehna had planned for tomorrow.

She made it up the stairs with the assistance of the handrail and staggered into her bedroom. The servitor entered the room as Corelle kicked the shoes from her feet with an intoxicated giggle, and with the woman's assistance, she took the dress off and fell into the bed.

Once the servitor withdrew, Corelle lay on her bed and stared at the ceiling as it spun above her. She had drunk too much, but more than the wine had intoxicated her. Lorgallehna's face, her hair, the delicate hands, all swam between Corelle's eyes and the ceiling, which refused to keep still. With a contented sigh, she fell asleep, and the Sovsdot filled her dreams all night.

CHAPTER 39
CORELLE

"**G**o away. The sun has not yet risen." Corelle squinted at the lantern light that threatened to blind her. Her head pounded, and she needed water so she could peel her tongue from the roof of her mouth.

The servitor stood over her, a stern expression on her face. Corelle rolled over and buried her face in the pillow. Did the wretched woman never sleep? Why must she interpret everything in such a harsh way? When Corelle had said, "By the sunrise," she had not meant the middle of the night.

Lorgallehna's face swam into Corelle's mind, and the tinkle of the Sovsdot's laughter rang through her head. The laughter only made Corelle's head hurt more, but with a supreme effort, she slid from the bed onto the floor and sat with her back against the bed. "If she feels like I do, she will not come, after all else." The servitor helped her to feet. "What is your name? I have not asked, and I apologise."

The woman said something, but Corelle could not understand it. Had Lorgallehna not said she would help Corelle learn the language? She had not done so, and Corelle still did not know the

woman's name. Once Corelle had pulled on her trousers and a tunic, the servitor pulled open the shutters. Outside, the sky showed a hint of the sunrise that would arrive soon enough. She had left it to the last heartbeat, and she had assured Lorgallehna she would not be late.

She could not find her boots, and when the servitor retrieved them from a cupboard, Corelle froze. The woman could not have failed to notice the fan, and sure enough it still rested in the harness Corelle had sewed into the boot to hold it. What had turned? She had slept all night but did not even know where her fan had been, and she had all but forgotten her sole task here had been to kill Krage. Now she headed off before the sun had even been lit to ride horses with a strange woman who could have Corelle hanged if she broke some convention she knew nothing of.

"Curse it." Angry, she left the rooms and made her way downstairs. As soon as she turned toward the open doors, she stopped and lowered her head in dismay. The carriage stood outside already, the young boy at the door. *"I will not be late."* She had promised it, and yet Lorgallehna had arrived before Corelle had been ready.

One of the door men helped her onto the step and she pulled herself into the carriage. Lorgallehna sat on one of the seats, so Corelle sat on the other, and as soon as the boy closed the door, she collapsed sideways with a groan.

"You are late." Lorgallehna looked stern, reproachful.

"Kill me. The sun has not yet risen. I must go back to sleep."

"I am early, in truth. You see how anxious I am to see you? I, the Sovsdot, arrive early to an appointment with a commoner. Are you all right?"

"That I am not."

"You must learn to handle your wine. I am as sprightly as a young kitten, ready to chase the dreams of the day and cavort in the light of the sun, once it shakes off its sloth and arrives."

"I hate you." Corelle opened one eye to look at Lorgallehna. She wore a tunic of excellent making, red with golden flowers embroidered on it, and black trousers. Her red hair had been scraped back into a horsetail and she did, indeed, appear to be none the worse for the excesses of the previous day. Corelle closed the eye. "I hate you."

The carriage moved off, and the steady sound of the horses' hooves combined with the side-to-side motion of the carriage lulled Corelle into sleep. When she woke, she felt no better, and she opened one eye again. Although the curtains remained closed, sunlight peeped around the edges. Lorgallehna sat across from her, her arms folded, and her head reclined against the seat back. "Good morning."

"Do you never sleep? Do none of your folk ever sleep?"

With a laugh, Lorgallehna replied, "Of course we do." She smiled at Corelle. "Poor Corelle of Ryl, you suffer. I promise not to torment you again today."

"Where do you take me?"

"Where would you like me..."

The question faded away, and Corelle opened her other eye. Lorgallehna's cheeks reddened, and it seemed she might have been about to make a comment her father, the ruler of this huge land, might have thought inappropriate. Corelle had embarrassed the Sovsdot, and pangs of guilt mingled with Corelle's excitement that she appeared not to have misread the woman's eyes yesterday. She decided to change the subject somewhat. "You promised to help me learn your language."

"I do not think I promised, but I did offer. I shall help you. What do you wish to learn?"

Corelle fought down her desire to say she wanted to learn what Lorgallehna's body would respond to. "How would I ask where you take me?"

"*Agriash ti ick legghe?*"

The words sounded so strange to Corelle, she wondered whether she could learn the language, but she had learned three others, and it seemed she might have some ability to pick them up if she had enough time. "*Ackriash ti eek legay.*"

Lorgallehna laughed. "Close, but it is '*agriash*,' not '*ackriash*.' '*Legghe*' is the word for… remove, I think, in Steinlund, but the two letters in the middle must be said from the back of your mouth, so." She demonstrated the sound, which sounded like a hiss more than the hard 'g' Corelle had used.

Corelle practiced the sound a few times as Lorgallehna encouraged her. "*Agriash ti eek legghe*?" She felt pleased; she had mastered the phrase with ease.

Lorgallehna clapped her hands together. "Good. You are a quick learner. It is '*ick*' though, not '*eek*.' '*Ick*' means me, and '*ti*' means you. So you asked me 'Where you me remove' in truth. That is how we structure such questions."

Corelle blushed at the praise, then returned to the question she had asked. "Where *do* you take me?"

"To our house outside Argoya. The Retreat."

"The Seat and the Retreat? What odd names."

"The Seat is the seat of the Sovran. That house belongs to Feshtersov, and the Sovran and their family live there. That is how it has always been. The Retreat is my father's own home. We call it the Retreat because it is a way for us to escape the pressure of the city."

"Your father must possess a great amount of coin."

"I imagine he does, but he performs an important role. He works hard."

"You do not, it seems to me. You have time for lengthy lunches and trips to the country."

"You are right, I do have long periods when I am free to do whatever I desire, but I do not shirk my responsibilities. When I am called upon, I do as much as is required of me to the best of my ability. These few days happen to be a quiet period." She smiled. "How do you feel?"

"Terrible." Corelle's head still ached, but she felt better than she had when the servitor had woken her. "How far is the Retreat?"

"It is about four hours from the city. We will be there soon."

Corelle could not make the time add up. "How long did I sleep?"

"A long time. You must have been exhausted."

Corelle pulled one of the curtains open. The city had given way to flat agricultural land, similar to the Eastlands. The carriage trundled along a narrow road, and the scenery outside the window changed little. With a slight bump, the carriage swung off the road and onto a narrow track, stony and dusty. The ride became far less comfortable.

"Here we are." Lorgallehna sounded distracted as the carriage rattled down the track, and as it curved, the house came into view. Compared to the Seat, it did not seem big, but compared to any other building Corelle had ever seen, she thought it immense. Built from red brick, it rose three storeys into the countryside with countless windows and a high chimney stack at each end.

The carriage pulled to a halt to one side of the house, and the lad pulled the door open a few heartbeats later. A green-sleeved arm appeared in the door and Lorgallehna leaned on it for assistance to climb from the carriage. Nobody offered Corelle any help, so she climbed out by herself.

Four horses stood behind the carriage, men in green tunics on each. Corelle had not noticed them in the darkness at the inn, but she had been in no state to notice much, in truth. Lorgallehna must need guards everywhere she went. If only they had known her greatest threat rode in the carriage with her, and also her best chance to survive if the carriage had been attacked.

The large building the carriage had stopped in front of turned out to be the stable. Corelle followed Lorgallehna into the building and stood by while the Sovsdot chose two horses. Men leapt to pick tack off the wall and prepare the horses. "Do others do everything for you?"

Lorgallehna looked hurt, and Corelle regretted the question. "I am the Sovsdot. I can do these things, but my father employs others to do them. Shall I dismiss them and do everything myself? I do not think their families would be happy with you." She tossed her head in temper, and the red horsetail of her hair whipped around.

"My apologies for my rudeness."

Lorgallehna smiled. "Do not worry. Come. I intend to improve your abilities on horseback." She pulled herself up onto one of the horses and waved away the step the young lad from the carriage offered her. Corelle mounted her own horse with far less grace and dignity, and it skittered about the stable as though it sensed it would win any competition between them.

The grey-haired man Corelle had noticed at the market stepped forward. "Eminence, the men are ready to ride with you." Through the large door at the opposite end, Corelle saw the four men who had ridden behind the carriage. The grey-haired man must have ridden in the driver's box of the carriage.

"I do not need them here, Rodrik." Lorgallehna laughed and waved a hand at him. "We are safe enough."

"Eminence, please." Despite Rodrik's pleas, Lorgallehna seemed adamant. "Let them at the least ride some way behind where they can keep you within sight. You know your father's orders."

She sighed. "Very well, but a respectable distance please. Our friend is a poor rider, and I intend to improve that. She needs no embarrassment when your men snigger at her."

"I am not that bad." Nobody appeared to hear Corelle's objection.

Rodrik nodded. "Eminence."

Corelle rode out of the stable behind Lorgallehna, and they headed down a path that led away from the house, but soon turned off onto what Corelle believed must be pasture. The grass had a brownish tint to it, and she wondered whether the land suffered from a lack of rain.

As they rode, Lorgallehna said little, and at one point, Corelle glanced behind her. The four men rode some way back. Corelle did not think she could stand Lorgallehna's life, for all her wealth. To always be referred to as Eminence by people who lived to serve her, to be allowed to do nothing for herself, and to be accompanied everywhere by armed men; this seemed like no kind of life to Corelle.

"Let us trot." Lorgallehna clucked her tongue and dug her heels into her horse's flank. Corelle followed, but once the horse's pace rose beyond a walk, she grew less comfortable, and gripped the reins tight. Lorgallehna's horsewomanship, if such a word existed, amazed Corelle. The Sovsdot seemed so at home atop her horse, they almost complemented one another. She appeared to have ridden a great deal throughout her life.

They rode for over an hour, and hunger gnawed at Corelle's stomach. She had eaten nothing all day and regretted she had not arranged for some bread or some such at the inn. Lorgallehna turned her horse toward a lake at the bottom of a slope, and they rode in silence to the edge of the water, where Lorgallehna reined her horse to a stop near a tall tree whose leafy branches spread out wide enough to offer good shade from the warmth of the sun.

"This is my favourite spot to sit and think, and forget who I am for a time. Please join me." Lorgallehna dismounted, and Corelle joined her. Her first lesson from the Sovsdot had not improved her ability to get down from a horse, and she almost fell. One foot would not come out of its stirrup, and Lorgallehna had to help her. Embarrassment burned in Corelle's cheeks, and Lorgallehna's laughter did little to help.

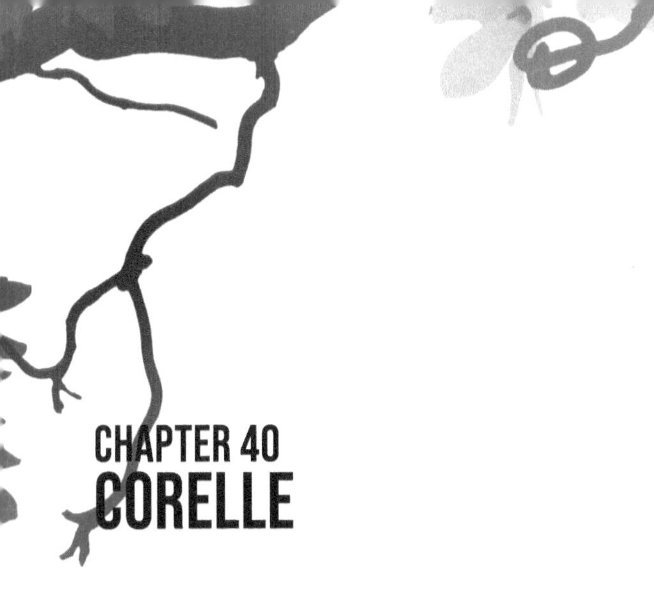

CHAPTER 40
CORELLE

Once the horses were tethered, the women sat together with their backs against the trunk of the tree and chatted about everything and nothing. Lorgallehna asked for some stories of Corelle's mariner life, and although she wearied of the tales, Corelle obliged her with some of those she thought would entertain the Sovsdot, who hung on every word.

In return, Lorgallehna talked of some of the drudgery of her life, and touched on some of the things Corelle felt she could not have endured. Even though her duty demanded much from her, she loved to escape into the country on a horse or wander the city streets. Anonymity could not be provided, as her father required guards to accompany her everywhere.

At that, they both glanced up the hill, where the four guards sat on the ground, their horses close by.

"You became a mariner because you had lost someone you loved. Your husband, I imagine?"

Corelle picked up a twig and scraped the ground with it while she considered her response. "I have never been married." The red-

headed woman made no reply, and Corelle glanced sideways at her. "You are a beautiful woman. Are you not married?"

Lorgallehna's unexpected sigh of misery surprised Corelle. "My family want me to marry. My father, in particular, wishes me to marry well. The son of some important businessman or even a high ranking member of a noble family from another nation. *Est ick nessen barite.* I do not desire this." She pulled a face of disdain.

Corelle frowned. "Why do you not wish it?"

Lorgallehna picked up a small stone and threw it toward the water. "Men are clumsy brutes."

"Brutes?" Not for the first time in her life, Corelle wondered how she would learn another language when she seemed unable to speak the ones she knew already.

"Violent. Unpleasant. Not gentle like..." She fell silent, and Corelle did not know what to say. Lorgallehna's usual sunny disposition seemed to have evaporated into melancholy in such a short time. The red-headed woman looked at her with a squint as the sun tracked down the sky and shone beneath the canopy of leaves above them. "Do you not agree?"

"I..." Such a complex question, Corelle thought. How best to answer it? "Some, but not all. I have known some men I loved, and some I did not care for at all. They are not all 'brutes,' as you call them."

"The ones I know are." A miserable mumble that made Corelle uncomfortable.

"Then you have had an unfortunate life." Rodrik had not seemed the type of man Lorgallehna described, and he seemed to spend a great deal of time with her. Corelle wondered what had given her such a tainted view of men. "In truth, I know them either as friends or enemies. I have not lain with one." She took a deep breath. "I lie with women." She left Taro out of the confession, as she could see no easy way to explain that relationship.

"I see." A lengthy silence followed. "Before you became a mariner, the love you lost. A woman?"

"That she was."

"You did not wish to marry her?"

Corelle gave an ironic laugh. "That I did, but women cannot marry in Dur. It is viewed as deviant for two women to lie together."

"That is sad. It is not so in Feshtersov."

"Women can marry here?"

"I confess I do not know, but I see no reason why not. If one person wishes to marry another, it is their business alone. I do not think the Parliament would have any opinion on it."

"The Parliament?" The woman in the office had mentioned it, but Corelle had learned no more about it.

"My father makes the rules, or the laws if you will, with his advisors. It is the Parliament's job to administer them, as well as collect the taxes, build new roads and so on. They do all the civic work. I doubt they could interpret any law to suggest women could not be married to each other." The revelation amazed Corelle. Feshtersov appeared far more advanced in its views than Dur. Or rather, than Dur had been, since now it would be bound by the Qagrue's views on such matters. Lorgallehna sighed. "I imagine we should head back. We need to reach the city before dark."

"That we should." Now it came to it, Corelle longed to sit beneath the tree with this woman for all the hours that remained to her. She turned to the Sovsdot, whose cheeks had turned bright red. "What is wrong?"

"These things we have talked of. They interest me more than the prospect of a marriage to some man I know next to nothing about."

Corelle felt if she rolled the dice now, she might be hanged before the morning. There had been many hints that Lorgallehna found her attractive and wished to pursue some form of dalliance, but it would be deadly to misread all she believed and dive into deep waters where she might drown. She settled for the old expression, "*It is better to be cautious than to be witless.*" She stretched her legs out before her. "Then marry the businessman's daughter instead."

Lorgallehna laughed, and her mood seemed to brighten. "You are funny. Thank you for your attention to my foolish talk. We should return to the house." She stood and untethered their horses. Corelle took the reins the Sovsdot held out to her. Up the hill, the men roused themselves and mounted their horses. They waited as Lorgallehna and Corelle rode up the hill past them.

"Eminence." One of the men nodded as the women passed, and Lorgallehna smiled at him.

They spoke little on the ride back to the house. In the carriage, Lorgallehna spent some time talking about her family. She claimed red hair and blue eyes were an unusual combination, although many members of her family had been granted this rare characteristic, something to do with bloodlines and parentage. Corelle dozed off at one point and felt guilty when she woke, but Lorgallehna made no fuss. Darkness had almost descended as the carriage pulled up outside The Hillside Inn. As the door opened, Corelle half rose, but Lorgallehna leaned toward the door and spoke to the young lad. "A moment please." She pulled the door shut. Corelle sat again, and Lorgallehna leaned forward to place a hand on each of Corelle's thighs. Their lips met, and Lorgallehna's tongue explored Corelle's mouth, gentle and uncertain, like somebody who searched for a lantern in a darkened room.

Corelle's heart pummelled her ribs so hard, she feared it would burst from her breast. She longed to pull the Sovsdot from the carriage and take her to her rooms for a night of ecstasy, but the risks were too great. Lorgallehna pulled away, and Corelle whispered. "I do not wish your father to hunt me down and kill me. Is this wise?"

The sadness from earlier appeared on Lorgallehna's face again. "You are right, I imagine."

"Good night."

"*Lurten dani'sket.*"

On her way into the inn, as the carriage and the four guards moved away down the street, Corelle stopped at the counter and asked for the name of the servitor.

"Her name is Herryat."

"My thanks. *Lurten dani'sket,*" Corelle said, unsure whether she had pronounced the words correctly.

The man smiled. "*Lurten dani'sket.*"

Corelle climbed the stairs and lay on the bed. The servitor came in with a question on her face, but Corelle waved her away. "*Lurten dani'sket Herryat.*"

With a smile, Herryat replied. "*Lurten dani'sket, paril jo Sovsdot.*"

As Herryat pulled the door closed, Corelle vowed to ask Lorgallehna what the phrase had meant. She undressed, ate some fruit from a bowl on the table in the parlour and climbed into bed. For the second night in a row, Lorgallehna filled her dreams, and morning found Corelle refreshed but with an unfulfilled need between her legs.

After she had eaten some breads and meats Herryat brought up to her, she wandered the streets, determined to better acquaint herself with the city. As she walked, she thought back over the last three days. Krage had all but been forgotten, and whenever she had been in Lorgallehna's company, the Sovsdot had almost driven thoughts of Arella, Deineike, Pettra, and all that had turned in her life from her mind. She gazed at herself in a shop window. Her clothes, despite the quality of her making, had aged and looked weary. How had Lorgallehna described her when Corelle had collapsed into the carriage yesterday morning? Commoner? How could she, a commoner in her tattered clothes, present herself at the Seat and insist on an appointment with the Sovsdot? Ridiculous.

She must change her focus back to the task at hand and forget the red-headed woman who filled her dreams but with whom a relationship would be impossible.

She stopped to gaze into another window and noticed a man across the street, his back to her. He stared into the window of a garment shop, the window display full of gowns and dresses, women's clothes. Why would a man be so interested in such a window? She had relaxed too much and had taken no notice of her surroundings, nor had she used any of her Guild training in a bid to throw off or expose any who followed her. This man might seek nothing more than a dress to buy for his wife, but she would soon learn.

Corelle ambled further down the street, then patted at both of her trouser pockets before she pulled out her coin pouch, stared into it, then slammed it back into her pocket. She turned as though annoyed and saw the man again from the corner of her eye. He stared into a different shop window. Despite his obvious training in the arts of secrecy, she had exposed him. Nonetheless, the lack of caution irritated her. She had allowed herself to be followed and had not marked her pursuer soon enough.

Who followed her? Krage, mayhap, although how he knew she had arrived in Argoya she could not guess. The man might work for Lorgallehna's father, or even for her. Why would they follow her? It might be a coincidence, but Corelle had never trusted in coincidences. At the next corner, she turned down the street that crossed the one she had been on and entered the first shop she came to. She went straight to the back of the shop and watched the street. The man did not pass the window. Even if he had done so on the other side, it would have confirmed he followed her.

The shopkeeper spoke to her, but she had no words to form a response other than *"Lurten dani'sket."* The man appeared confused, but Corelle strode from the shop, turned to wander back where she had come from, and soon noticed her shadow. He stood across the street, one building back from the shop, but the instant he saw her, he turned and walked away at a brisk pace. He may have guessed she had marked him, or he wanted to find a vantage point from which he could pick her up again. She did not hurry after him, which would confirm she had noticed him. Her unfamiliarity with the city worked against her as she did not know of a place where she could spring a trap and ask him for answers.

It would not do to meander in random directions. The man would suspect she looked for a place to trap him and might abandon the pursuit. She came to a pastry shop and stopped to buy a small cake. She gazed around, casual but alert, but could no longer see the man. Had he abandoned the pursuit? That might be so, but had another taken over from him? For half of an hour, she wandered the streets, and at length, she came to the docks. How she had got there, she could not say, but she had not spotted anybody who followed her. An idea came to her, and she headed for the passenger ship office. Several lines of people had formed up inside, and she joined one of the lines. When her turn came up, she muttered, *"Lurten dani'sket,"* and left the office.

Nobody had left any of the lines before they reached the counter, and she had checked everybody who loitered outside the office while she had been inside. She felt sure nobody followed her now. Mayhap nobody had at all, and it had indeed been a coincidence. Cautious nonetheless, she pushed through the crowded docks and made her way back to the inn. She took several detours, and some of them proved necessary because she did not know with any certainty how to get back to The Hillside.

She sat in one of the chairs in the entrance lobby for some time but saw nothing out of the ordinary. While there, the man who spoke Vyrrmod approached her and handed her letters that had arrived earlier in the day, and she tucked them in the waistband of her trousers until she felt satisfied nobody suspicious had entered the inn.

Corelle went up to her room, uncomfortable but uncertain. Had she imagined the man had followed her? She pointed to the tub, and Herryat pumped water into it as Corelle tore the seal from the letters. The seal had caught her eye the moment the letters had been handed to her. It bore the same "L" symbol as the token Lorgallehna had given her and she had forgotten to return on either of the days she had spent time with the Sovsdot.

She read the letters. They had been scribed in Steinlund in a small, neat hand, Lorgallehna's, she imagined. Once she had read them, she read them again, then let them flutter to the floor. Lorgallehna had invited Corelle, Hero of Dur, to a banquet at the Seat in three days' time.

Corelle could not go to a banquet with all manner of important and wealthy folks in attendance. A commoner, Lorgallehna had described her as, and she felt certain commoners would be frowned on by such people.

Corelle did not know what a banquet entailed, but she thought it would be a lavish meal for which she would need a dress of the highest quality making. Her coin would not run to such a dress, and she could not impose on the inn again. She could not go. She could not *not* go, in truth. It might be her best chance to see Lorgallehna again, and she could not turn down that chance.

She saw one solution and no others. Corelle would have to make herself a dress fit for a Sovran's banquet, and only two days to make it. No time to bathe. She gathered up all her coin, asked at the counter where a materials shop could be found, and set out with no clear idea what she wanted to create. She knew her size; she would buy material sufficient to craft something, and she would be the best dressed woman at the banquet.

CHAPTER 41
LORGALLEHNA

As Corelle stepped out of the carriage, Lorgallehna wanted nothing more than to follow her into the inn and spend the night in her bed. Corelle's hesitance could only be because of Lorgallehna's position as the Sovran's daughter. She had admitted she lay with women, and nothing in her behaviour suggested she found Lorgallehna unattractive. Lorgallehna's position as Sovsdot would not allow her such simple pleasures, of course, and she must tread with care in this new friendship.

Once the carriage dropped her at the door of her suite in the Seat, she wandered into her bedroom, her servitor in attendance. She allowed the servitor to undress her, then sat on the stool before the reflecting glass as the servitor brushed the long red hair that framed her pretty face, with fine features and blue eyes. Lorgallehna lowered her eyes to take in her breasts and slender waist. "Zerxmine, am I attractive?"

"My pardon, Eminence?" Zerxmine's voice faltered in confusion.

"Am I attractive? Do people like me?"

"The people love you, Eminence."

Lorgallehna took the woman's wrist in her hand, held the hair brush away from her head, and turned in her chair. "But would they lie with me?"

Zerxmine's eyes widened. "Eminence, has somebody pressed themselves upon you?"

"Nobody has, do not worry. Would a woman lie with me?"

The servitor's face reddened. "Eminence, if you command it, I will lie with you, though you must have no shortage of suitors."

Lorgallehna laughed and reached up to stroke the woman's cheek. "My apologies, Zerxmine, I have embarrassed you. I did not mean you, although any would be lucky to have your love. There is somebody I..." She paused, uncertain of whether she should continue.

Zerxmine smiled. "Eminence, all love you. If this person does not desire you, they have lost their mind."

"I know nothing of these things. The men my fath... the Sovran has paraded before me have all bored me. This woman excites me, but I do not know how to win her."

"Is she of noble blood?"

"That she is not. She is a commoner."

Lorgallehna gave a sardonic laugh. "The Sovran might see her as unworthy and may not approve, unless she owns a business or has some other renown."

Lorgallehna stared at her servitor, filled with a despondent sadness, then the word "renown" triggered an idea. "Zerxmine, thank you." She embraced the woman. "You have provided the perfect idea." Zerxmine seemed confused, but it did not matter. Lorgallehna would not abandon her desire for Corelle, not yet at the least.

CHAPTER 42
KRAGE

Krage sat at the desk in the large room in his house. Once he heard of the new lands beyond the Torr Sea, he had decided to leave Jaiselnia, where he had fled to from Dur, and establish a new life in one of these lands, far from the reminders of all the disasters that had turned in Dur since Styrrach had failed to shroud that wretched woman, Corelle. Those disasters had culminated in the Qagrue's coup against him, after he had devised the idea in the first place. It had been outrageous, and it burned at his insides.

At that time, only one of the new lands could be reached from the Torr Sea, so he had paid a vast sum to secure transport for him and his guards from Malkartas to Argoya. The enormous city suited him well, and no reminders of Dur or any of the other pathetic little lands around it disturbed his enjoyment of his new life. He had ample coin to enjoy the rest of his days in luxury, and he had bought a large house in a better part of the city.

All had seemed perfect until Ricrid knocked on the open door and Krage waved at him to enter the room that served as his office. "One of the men has returned from a visit to the upholsterer."

Krage had waited weeks for the cursed upholsterer to return his favourite chair. He had taken it away to change the fabric for a pattern more to Krage's tastes but had not yet returned it. Krage had bought the chair from the previous owner of the house and had never sat in a more comfortable chair in his life, but the gaudy pattern revolted him. Ricrid continued, a strange excitement in his movement, his words. "He saw something that will be of great interest to you. Corelle is in Argoya."

Krage dropped the scribing tool onto the desktop and stared up in disbelief at Ricrid. "Corelle? Here?"

"That she is. He saw her. He followed her for a time, but he believed she had marked him, and he slipped away."

Krage muttered. "She would mark him." The jade had proved countless times how accomplished she had become at her arts. She would have marked him, and had he not made the decision to abandon his pursuit of her, she might have killed him. "How has she come here? Curse her. Is there nowhere on this wretched globe I can be rid of her?"

"Argoya is enormous. She will never find you, even if she looks for you. It could be coincidence. When last we heard of her, she had become a mariner. It seems likely she has sailed here and will soon enough sail away again."

"She may not find me, but that does not mean I do not wish to find her." Krage drew his lips back into a snarl.

"I advise against any search for her. She remains dangerous, and we know nothing of why she has come here, or with whom. I will recruit more guards. We will be more vigilant and let her sail away to fates that need not involve you."

Corelle. What brought that jade here? She must have come in search of him; there could be no other reason. He could not take the risk; one night he might wake with her blade at his throat. He must act first. After all else, he knew of her presence in Argoya, but she did not know he had sailed here. Nobody did. Unless... "Nobody knows we are here, do they?"

"That they do not."

Had something crossed his eyes as he spoke? Krage could not afford delusions, but he could not afford betrayal either. Ricrid had been loyal for four years or more since they had first taken over Dur. Krage trusted him, but... Enough foolish thoughts. "Could she have learned of our voyage? As a mariner, she might have heard some word from a crew member aboard the ship from Malkartas."

"All things are possible until they are not. Will we delay our plans?"

"That we will not, although that is for me to decide." The plans he had worked on for the last two years could not be abandoned on account of one jade. It might not even have been Corelle, rather some woman who resembled her. "They are too advanced now. Within a pass, the proposal will be ready, and the Sovran will have it. If that oily wretch of an advisor has done all he promised, the Sovran will hold our plans and be well disposed toward them. I hope to get some sense of his progress at the banquet. If the job has not been done as promised..." He looked up at Ricrid, who nodded. No words had been needed.

"I will find more guards. More caution at this crucial time cannot be a mistake."

Rage and anxiety poured scorn into Krage's response. "If you feel you and your men are inadequate, then by all means hire more." He returned his attention to his work. Ricrid left the room, but the atmosphere did not leave with him. Worry, doubt, fear— Krage breathed them all in long into the day. Corelle had brought them into his house, curse her.

CHAPTER 43
CORELLE

Surrounded by red silk, Corelle sat on the floor of the parlour. She had searched many shops until she had found the material she wanted, as close to the colour of Lorgallehna's hair as she could get, and had spent most of her coin on the cloth, some thread and a new pair of scissors. She already had a making kit in her pack she felt confident would be adequate for the dress.

Parch lay scattered around her, abandoned designs for the most part, but at last she had created one she liked. Simple enough, but with a bodice she hoped would not scandalise the Sovran's guests. The neckline extended up to her collar bones, but she would leave a cut-out between her breasts, and include pleats on the breasts themselves. The design would accentuate her full breasts, but she hoped it would not be considered too bold. She wanted to appeal to Lorgallehna but not be ordered to leave the banquet because her dress revealed too much. A small gather at the rear of the skirt created a slight train that would trail behind her.

Satisfied with the design, she set about the making. She measured herself again, then measured the various lengths of cloth

she would need. By the time she had finished, Herryat had closed the shutters, lit the lanterns and urged her to go to bed at least three times. With a yawn, she decided to leave the work for the night. The light would be better in the morning, and she would be less tired and, therefore, less prone to a mistake with her scissors that could result in disaster.

For two full days, she laboured on the dress, with Herryat's help. The servitor had some skill at making and did some of the stitching, and they worked on two parts of the dress at the same time. They chatted little as they worked, but Herryat worked with Corelle to improve her knowledge of the local language.

The night before the banquet, Corelle devoted over an hour to clean her fan. It would not look out of place, and she felt sure other women must also carry them. Hers had seen work theirs would not be suited to, and it took hard labour to bring it back to its original shine and to ensure no traces of dried blood lingered where they could be seen.

The next morning Corelle tried the dress on for the first time. Herryat gushed and cooed at her appearance in the dress and insisted she should lend Corelle some shoes she owned that all but matched the colour of the dress. In truth, the shoes could have been a little smaller, but some parch pushed into the toes soon remedied that. Herryat spent over an hour with her hairbrush and some powders until she deemed Corelle looked suitable. With her cheeks powdered red, and further powder on her eyes and lips, Corelle thought she might now fit in with the high society women in Orgel's shop, and she hoped she might not look out of place at the banquet.

Nervous, she paced the lobby of the inn as the staff hovered nearby. Some of them seemed as caught up in the glamour of the occasion as Herryat. In time, the carriage arrived, and the door men helped her climb into it, the restrictive, tight skirt of her dress an impediment she had not considered. She had not created any sleeves on the dress, but because of the many scars on her arms, she had scraped together enough silk to fashion a shawl she draped around her shoulders.

This time, the carriage turned into the large double gates at the centre of the building. Other grand carriages stood ahead of hers, with others off to one side, and men in various ornamental clothes hovered nearby. The night would be more magnificent than any experience in Corelle's life, and her anxiety had grown so much, she felt she might fetch up. Sweat formed on her brow, her hands shook, and she pressed Wilash's fan to its most valuable use ever as she waved it before her in a futile effort to cool herself. At last, her carriage passed beneath the enormous arch at the front of the building, and she peeped from behind the curtain as it approached a sizeable group of people arrayed in fine clothes near a set of large double doors.

She spotted Lorgallehna among the crowd. The Sovsdot appeared to greet people as they descended from their carriages, then introduce them to a group of people who stood together on the steps before the guests entered the building.

Corelle's carriage lumbered forward once more then bounced to a halt. The door opened, and she stared into the face of the Sovsdot. Her red hair had been curled, and it floated around her face and down her body, which wore a cream dress of exquisite making, adorned with gold brocade. A gold chain around her neck held a large gem of clear blue that matched her eyes. She looked magnificent.

"Corelle." Lorgallehna smiled a warm greeting as Corelle stepped down from the carriage. The Sovsdot gripped each of Corelle's elbows and kissed her cheek, a far more familiar greeting than on the occasions she had extended her hand for Corelle to kiss. "I am so excited you came."

Corelle smiled. "Why did you call me 'Hero of Dur?'" Corelle fought to control her heart before it leapt from her chest. She longed to sweep the woman into her arms, kiss her, then drag her into the carriage and ravish her. Such urges must be resisted, or she would swing from the nearest tree, she did not doubt.

"You sailed aboard the ship that opened all our eyes to a greater knowledge of our globe. What title could better fit so intrepid a person?"

Corelle smiled, relieved the title related to her voyage aboard The Ictharelian and not because of the discovery of aspects of Corelle's past in Dur she would rather keep hidden for now. "But why did you invite me here?"

"You fascinate me." The red-headed woman lowered her voice. "I needed to find a reason to invite you, and your exploits on that voyage satisfied my father's aide. What a beautiful gown." Lorgallehna's eyes swept down Corelle's dress, lingered for a heart-beat on her breasts.

The design had had the desired effect, and Corelle smiled. "My thanks. I designed and made it myself."

"No." Eyes wide, the Sovsdot's surprise gratified Corelle. "You must make a dress for me, then, if you have this skill."

Corelle felt herself blush. "Eminence, I am not worthy of the honour. The gown you wear tonight is far beyond my skill." It must have cost half the coin in the land, Corelle imagined.

"Nonsense, yours takes my breath away." That had been the idea, of course. "I am amazed at your skill."

"In truth, I am out of practice."

Another carriage had pulled up, and Lorgallehna flicked her eyes to it. "Come." She turned to the people on the steps. "My brother, the Sovssun." The man extended a hand, and Corelle guessed it would be appropriate to kiss the air above it, as foolish as the gesture felt. "Representatives of our Parliament." Three men bowed to her, and she returned the gesture. "Please follow Georket. He will take you to the ballroom. I will join you later." The man Lorgallehna had gestured to bowed to Corelle. "Enjoy the blanket."

The corners of Lorgallehna's mouth twitched, and Corelle resisted the urge to poke out her tongue.

Georket led her along a plush red carpet into an enormous room full of people. He waved to a woman, who approached and said something Corelle could not understand. The woman held a tray before her, and Corelle guessed she had asked if Corelle would like a drink. *"Vint ru, talik."* Herryat had taught her the phrase that meant "Red wine, please," and she hoped she had said it right in her nervousness.

The woman bowed and moved off, as did Georket. Corelle stood where they had left her. She knew nobody, had no idea how to behave, and could not speak ten words of Feshtersov, in truth. It would be pointless to mingle in the crowd and would make it harder for the woman to find her with the wine.

Men and women in fine clothes filled the room, and the babble of conversation threatened to deafen her as she waited, nervous and uncomfortable. The woman returned with a high-quality goblet filled with red wine, and with a nod of thanks Corelle took it from the tray the woman held. The Sovran's wine tasted delicious, by far the best she had ever encountered, and she carried her goblet across the room toward a corner, where she stood alone and sipped at the wine. Lorgallehna entered the room and spoke to an older couple dressed in formal clothes of exceptional making. The woman wore a plain gold circlet in her hair and a beautiful rose coloured dress, elaborate and of faultless making. The man had a long thin sword at his hip, attached to his body by a complex series of straps, but none of the other guests appeared to be armed.

Georket rang a bell and spoke words Corelle did not understand. The guests followed the two older people, Lorgallehna, and her brother through another set of doors, and Corelle reasoned the time had come to eat the banquet. She lingered to the rear of the crowd, unsure how to proceed. In truth, she now regretted she had come at all. These were not her people. They had such social status, she could never hope to mingle and be accepted among them. She had no idea how to behave, and could not understand a word anybody said.

Georket appeared beside her and took her elbow in a gentle grip, steered her to a chair, and bowed as he left her. Everybody else stood behind chairs, so Corelle copied them. Her table sat at one edge of the large dining room. Three others filled the room, two parallel to hers and one perpendicular to the other three at which Lorgallehna and her family stood, as well as other men and women dressed in impressive finery. Once everybody at that table sat, the rest of the room followed suit. Corelle made herself comfortable in her chair and studied the table.

There might well have been even more cutlery at each place setting than at Raolos's house on the first night she had eaten there, and she recalled Raopul's instructions to start on the outside and work inward. The food had a strange spiciness Corelle could not quite persuade herself she enjoyed, and she found every course too rich for her taste. A platter of cold meats part way through the dinner appealed to her most, and a fishy broth that followed it. One of the courses involved some kind of shelled sea creature, and she struggled to spoon any of the meat out of it. She did not care for what little she got. A plate of small, sweet pastries appeared late in the evening, and she enjoyed one of the courses at last. As she ate them, she gazed at the table over from her own, and to her horror, she spotted a face she recognised from descriptions given to her by Wilash, Denstal, and others.

Krage.

CHAPTER 44
CORELLE

Krage. How could he be here? She remembered the day she thought she had been followed. Had they followed her ever since, and Krage had come here to kill her? That could not be the case, and it had been a foolish thought. Krage could not have entered without an invitation, and she did not imagine he could be armed, whereas she had her fan.

Deep in conversation with the man next to him, Krage did not notice Corelle for some time, but his eyes, like hers, scanned the room. At first, they passed her by, then snapped back to her. His face became a picture of surprise, but hatred soon replaced it. They stared at one another for some moments, then a voice from her right interrupted her. She glanced toward the sound, where the man with the long sword had stood to address the gathered diners, but she could not understand him.

He spoke for some time, and Corelle's eyes wandered between him, his daughter, and Krage. It seemed Krage spoke the language, as he laughed when others did and clapped his hands together at times, but his eyes often returned to Corelle.

How could she kill him in this room with a crowd of onlookers?

It could not be done. She could follow him as he left and waylay him outside where fewer eyes could see. He, however, would have guards who would await him outside the building, and they might strike her down before she could kill him.

The man with the sword stopped his speech and everybody rose to their feet and clapped their hands. Corelle followed their example, and people drifted away from the tables and out through the door by which they had all entered. Corelle had lost sight of Krage; he must have left the table already. She glanced around, lest he appear from behind her and slit her throat, but she could not see him. Lorgallehna sat at her table, deep in conversation with her brother, so Corelle rose and returned to the first room, where a band of minstrels played soft music in one corner.

She stood near the minstrels and saw Krage. He spoke to a tall, bald man, but snapped his eyes to her every few moments. Krage's height surprised Corelle, taller than most Guild members she had encountered. He had spotted her again before she had seen him, but he seemed unprepared to act against her. The bald man led Krage away through a smaller door to one side of the room, and Corelle turned her attention to the minstrels.

One of them had a fine voice, a young man whose high, clear tone suited their music to perfection. Corelle could make out nothing of what he sang about, but the melodies and his voice enchanted her, and she tapped her foot in time to the tuneful music while others paired off and danced.

"Do you like the music?" Corelle did not turn as the voice whispered in her ear, but a tender hand rested on her hip and warm breath teased at her neck.

She touched the hand. "I cannot understand what he sings about."

Lorgallehna listened for a time, then translated.

"I stand at the gates of your cities of dust.

I look to the east as the sun turns to rust in my eyes.
I listen to your voice in the clear light of dawn.
I watch as your lips turn the night into morning and lies.
You gave me all I desired."

Corelle could not fathom the meaning of the words, but she thought they spoke of betrayal, or love turned awry.

"Walk with me in the garden." The Sovsdot's warm breath in Corelle's ear aroused her.

Corelle followed her toward a set of double doors and through them into the night air. "A beautiful night." She followed Lorgallehna down some steps into a garden bathed in the light of many lanterns. Flowers grew everywhere in well tended rows and smaller recesses beside the paths. Corelle did not recognise any of them, but they made a colourful sight and gave off a sweet, heady aroma.

"Did you enjoy the food?"

Time for the lies Corelle had become so well versed in. "That I did. The sweet pastries were as delicious as any I have eaten."

"I try not to eat too many of those." The red-headed woman laughed. "They go straight to my hips."

"Then you have eaten the right amount, for you have beautiful hips." Corelle grimaced at her words, a poor, contrived compliment.

"I thank you. Let us visit the maze."

"Maze? I do not know this word."

"It is a puzzle of sorts. There is but one way out, and many false turns. It will be fun."

It sounded far from fun to Corelle. Frivolous at best, but she imagined frivolous might pass for fun among people with more coin than spare time. The maze turned out to be a high, twisting hedge that could neither be seen through nor over, and the deeper into it they went, the more lost she became. Despite her Guild training, Corelle doubted she could retrace her steps, and she hoped Lorgallehna knew the secret to their escape, or they might both die in the maze.

They had turned back from multiple false turns that led only to another section of hedge that barred their passage when they saw a bench. Lorgallehna sat and urged Corelle to sit next to her. "Have you enjoyed the night?"

"That I have not. No sooner did I arrive than some lout teased me about my recollection of the word 'banquet.'"

"Such cruelty. Identify the offender, and I will have them thrown into the sea."

"She is unmistakeable. She has hair as red as the warmest flame and blue eyes as bright as the deepest ocean." Corelle bit her tongue. Had she overstepped a boundary? Despite her flowery words, she could not believe Lorgallehna had brought her into the maze to talk, and the memory of the Sovsdot's soft lips on her own made her sex tingle.

"Is she pretty?"

"Her beauty would take your breath away."

A brief silence ensued, then Lorgallehna leaned toward Corelle and kissed her. Corelle's heart leapt as the red-headed woman's tongue probed inside her mouth, apprehensive at first, then Lorgallehna raised a hand to the back of Corelle's head and held her tight as their tongues interlocked in passion. A hand slid up to one of Corelle's breasts and teased at her nipple through her dress, and Lorgallehna gave a small moan of desire as Corelle slid her hands around the Sovsdot's waist and pulled her closer.

Lorgallehna pulled away. "You desire me." Lust lent a husk to her voice.

"That I do."

"You are no longer afraid?"

It would be wrong to say the repercussions of such a relationship did not weigh on Corelle's mind. "That I am, a little. I cannot deny it."

"We cannot lie together here. I will be missed soon if I have not been already. I have some houses. You could stay at one of them."

"That I could not. You have already done more for me than I have any right to expect at the inn."

"If you stay at the house, it will cost me less, and I can come and see you there."

Less? "You pay for the room at the inn?"

"Of course I do. The inn is a business, like any other. I pay your bill."

Corelle pushed away from her. "I am not a banquet for your pity to gorge itself at."

"It has naught to do with pity. When I saw you at the market, I wanted to reward you for your kindness, but now—"

"You are a Sovsdot, and must be discreet, so I must skulk in your house and be available when you desire a dalliance. Is that it?"

"No. That is not how it is at all. I want you, and I do not want you to leave. Why must you react with such vitriol?"

Corelle could not answer the question. Her reaction had been foolish. Lorgallehna did not need to do anything for her, yet she had been nothing but kind since the incident at the market. With the little coin she had left, Corelle could not stay in Argoya on her own, and now she knew Krage remained in the city, she could not leave. "My apologies. I have had a little too much rich food and good wine. I should not have been rude."

"You will stay at the house?"

"That I will."

"Good. I will come to the inn for you tomorrow. I must return."

"If we can find our way out of the maze." Corelle gazed around, concerned.

"I have played in this maze since a small girl. I could find my way out with my eyes closed. I toyed with you to see if you could find your way out."

Lorgallehna took Corelle's hand and led her through the twists of the maze until they emerged onto a path, the Seat visible again. The minstrels' music drifted across the garden on the still night air. Lorgallehna's lips brushed Corelle's, then they walked side by side toward the building, hands no longer entwined.

As they re-entered the ballroom, Corelle saw Krage at the door with the bald man. They shook hands, and Krage turned and left the room. She wondered whether she could catch up with him and find some way to kill him, but Lorgallehna insisted she introduce Corelle to her parents.

Only as they approached the Sovsdot's parents did it occur to Corelle she would meet not only Lorgallehna's parents, but the Sovran of the entire land of Feshtersov. Lorgallehna spoke as they approached the man with the long sword, then to the woman beside him. Lorgallehna acted as translator between her parents and Corelle, a slow, painful process, but necessary.

"Ah, the hero who sailed around the globe." The Sovsdot's mother held out her hand, and Corelle followed the ridiculous kiss-the-air routine.

The Sovran glowered at her but did not extend his hand. Instead, he spoke, gruff-voiced. "You must have some tales to tell."

"That I do. I would be happy to share some of them with you at some future time, if you wish." Corelle smiled at him, but he did not return the favour.

Lorgallehna's mother stepped into the awkward conversation. "What brings you to Argoya?"

"I seek an old friend whom I believe to be here."

"A friend from Dur?"

"That he is not." Another lie. She did not wish to reveal the full story. "He is from Vyrrmod."

"I trust you will find him." The older woman turned to her daughter. "How do you know Corelle, dear?"

"We met in the market. Did I not tell you the story? The day Mikotah knocked the older down."

"Oh, yes. I believe I recall something about it."

The Sovran seemed out of patience with the exchange. "Quite. Forgive us." He glanced at his wife, and they moved off.

Corelle heaved a sigh of relief. The Sovran had said almost nothing to her and acted as though he disapproved she had attended his lavish banquet, and the translation had been awkward. No doubt Lorgallehna had added sugar to more bitter words when she had translated. "He hated me."

"He did not. He is the Sovran. He meets dozens of people every day. He is like that with everybody. He must mingle and exchange pleasantries with everybody here, many of whom he cannot stand."

Lorgallehna wandered off to talk to other people in the room as Corelle watched, unable to tear her eyes from the beautiful redhead. She talked with everybody with total ease, an occasional touch on the hand or the arm as though they had all been the best of friends through all their lives. The woman had been born into this life, and she excelled at it. She laughed at every jest, teased some of the older men, nodded earnest agreement with others, but they all smiled as she moved on to the next guest.

Most of the guests had gone, and women with trays had brought Corelle at least three more goblets of red wine. She sat in a chair near the minstrels, who seemed about to end their performance. Lorgallehna appeared before her, the same smile on her lips as with the other guests, but in her blue eyes, Corelle saw something she hoped had been reserved for her alone.

"Time to leave, I think." Corelle gazed up at the Sovsdot, consumed with desire.

"The banquet is ending, it is true."

"The blanket goes on in my rooms." Corelle gave her a suggestive smile.

"Soon enough." An expressive smile sprang to Lorgallehna's lips in response. "I will escort you to your carriage, and I will come to the inn mid-morning tomorrow."

"I look forward to it." Any who overheard them would not catch the undertones of sexual tension in the brief conversation, but each word, each syllable, aroused Corelle's passion, and she felt its heat in her cheeks.

They walked out to the carriage area, to any eye two women who walked and made idle conversation together. Lorgallehna offered to help Corelle into her carriage and took her hand to aid her up to her seat. She gave the hand a small squeeze as she bade Corelle goodnight, and soon the carriage trundled its way back to the inn.

Corelle hoped the relationship with Lorgallehna would develop further once she moved into the house, but the banquet had brought other news. She now knew for certain Krage lived somewhere in Argoya, and she must dedicate every available hour to her attempts to find him.

What joy Lorgallehna might bring her could not yet be guessed, but Krage would not bring her any joy until he lay dead at her feet, and she would bend herself to that task at the first opportunity. She told the man in the inn, whose name she had still not learned, she would leave in the morning and climbed the stairs. Herryat appeared and helped her out of the dress, and Corelle crawled into the bed. The pressure of the creation of the dress and the awkwardness of the banquet had exhausted her. She soon fell asleep. Nightmares of dead bodies carved into multiple pieces and strewn around the maze plagued her all night despite the wine she had consumed, and she woke late, tired and angry. "Where are you?" She spoke to Krage, though she had no idea where he might be. "I will find you, and I will kill you."

She climbed from the bed, dressed, and went down to the lobby to await Lorgallehna and whatever fates were written.

CHAPTER 45
CORELLE

Lorgallehna's house had two bedrooms, a privy and a tub room upstairs, with a large parlour and a pleasant scullery downstairs. To the rear, an enclosed grassy area offered seclusion from other houses. It felt comfortable from the moment Corelle entered it, and when Lorgallehna pushed her down onto a couch, fell on top of her, and kissed her, she thought she might be content here for a time.

Time moved on, as it always did, relentless and tireless, and Lorgallehna visited the house every two days or so. Despite Corelle's desire, Lorgallehna did not yet seem ready to take the final step and lie with her. They kissed and touched each other's bodies, but each time Corelle's hand strayed between the red-headed woman's legs, Lorgallehna pulled it away. She often said something like, "Not yet," or words to that effect. Corelle could not decide whether she lacked the courage to take the final step or teased her, but it frustrated her.

Every day, she explored the city, not in search of familiarisation, but in a bid to find some information on Krage. She asked

Lorgallehna about him, but she had not noticed him, and Corelle did not want to push the matter too far at this stage. When Lorgallehna said she had duties at the Retreat and would be away from the city for a few days, Corelle took advantage of the extra time alone to increase her search activity but made no progress. Krage seemed to have disappeared, and she found no trace of him.

Corelle scribed to Gaish and told him all that had turned in Argoya. She thought he would enjoy the story of Lorgallehna, and she gave him the address of the house and asked him how life under the Qagrue had turned. She closed the letter with love to both men.

Four days later, Lorgallehna returned and came to the house before Corelle had risen one morning, removed her dress, and slid into the bed. This time, she did not pull Corelle's hand away, which found the Sovsdot's sex wet and receptive. They fulfilled each other for almost two hours, and afterward they lay together in the bed. Lorgallehna's voluminous red hair cascaded around Corelle, and the other woman lay on her side with an arm draped across Corelle. When Corelle turned to kiss her, she saw something more in those blue eyes, something she dreaded. Lorgallehna drew ever closer to the three words Corelle would be thrilled to hear but feared to, nonetheless.

Lorgallehna had brought some food from the Seat, so they went downstairs and ate breads, cakes, cheese, and fruit in the parlour while Corelle revealed more of her background. Lorgallehna did not seem afraid when she learned Corelle had killed. The Sovsdot commanded an army, it turned, although Corelle needed an explanation of "army," five thousand men, armed and ready to fight, although Corelle could not grasp how many that might be, nor could she imagine why the land needed so many fighters.

Lorgallehna laughed. "That is only my army. My brother and my father have their own armies. We have had several wars in my lifetime. We enjoyed a peaceful relationship with a nation to the north, Ishter. They had no Sovran, and we often traded with them. Their Parliament had some disagreement with ours about trade terms, and an incident occurred on the border where their army, for some reason, attacked a unit of my brother's army and killed them." Lorgallehna paused, sadness in her eyes. "My father declared war on them without hesitation. Do you understand war?" The word Corelle had not understood in Ryl reappeared, and she shook her head. "It is hideous. The armies of two or more lands fight each other over whatever slight has occurred until one crushes the other, or a deadlock is reached."

She sighed. "In this case, we annihilated them. My father burned down their Parliament and killed all the Ters, the members of their Parliament. The name Ishter tells you a Parliament rules the nation. Feshtersov tells you a Parliament and a Sovran rule. That is how it is in this part of the globe. We destroyed Ishter's armies and claimed their land for our own. My brother's army serves there, and he spends much of his time there."

She took Corelle's hand and gazed at it before she continued. "Our nation has grown to the size it is today through many such wars. That is the only one I have fought in, however."

Corelle smiled, then the full import of Lorgallehna's words sank in. "What? You fought?"

"Yes, of course. I am the Sovsdot, I cannot send my army into battle unless I am prepared to fight with them."

Corelle sat upright. "How did you fight?"

"With a sword, of course. How else does one fight?"

"You fought men, with a sword?" The tale could scarce be believed.

"Do you think me unable to fight, to wield a sword? You have killed, I have killed. These are our paths."

Corelle shook her head, bewildered. "You seem so dainty and prim, yet you can wield a sword."

"Prim? I act it when I need to. I fancy I could best you with a sword. And Corelle, please do not say 'what.' It sounds so rude. Please say 'my pardon.'"

"My apologies. I did not enjoy the refined childhood you did, Eminence." Lorgallehna aimed a playful swipe at her, which missed. "I do not doubt you could best me with a sword, but you would be dead before it cleared your belt."

"Scabbard."

"Wha… my pardon?" Corelle laughed as she corrected herself.

"I do not keep my sword pushed through my belt like some cutthroat. I wear a scabbard, a leather sheath it sits in. Regardless, how would you kill me before I drew my sword?"

"With a dagger. Faster, every bit as deadly, but lighter and easier to wield in close quarters."

"I will take you to the barracks. Rodrik will show you how efficient a sword can be. If you are nice to him, he might teach you how to wield one. You may even aspire to become my equal." She smiled. "You are more than my equal in the art of love, I confess it. I desire more lessons." She slid her arms around Corelle's neck and nibbled at an ear.

Lorgallehna dozed after they had sated each other again, and Deineike's dark hair, her blue eyes, her smile, stole into Corelle's mind. To her horror, she realised she had not thought much about her former lover since she had met Lorgallehna. Guilt stabbed at her, and she closed her eyes with a sad sigh. There had been three women who had been more than a one-night dalliance since Deineike: Vamma, Ulmella, and now Lorgallehna. Only the red-headed woman had driven Deineike from her thoughts, or had it been time that did so? How could she know? She sighed again.

A tenday later, as she had promised, Lorgallehna took Corelle to the east of the city to her army's barracks, a large area, fenced off. The Sovsdot explained the barracks' layout; buildings to house the soldiers surrounded large, flat patches of ground where they trained. Other buildings stored weapons and other items of war.

The barracks seemed almost as big as Yerrsun, and once again the sheer size of this land, or nation as she should call it, amazed Corelle.

As they drove out in the carriage, Lorgallehna told Corelle any woman could join an army and fight alongside the men. "Women are not second-class citizens here. If I had been born before my brother, I would become Sovran when my father dies. We can own businesses; we can do anything we want."

It seemed so reasonable as Lorgallehna described it, yet in Dur such things had been unthinkable. Raolos had done his best to change the land when he had appointed Klordia as his Senior Tally Master, but Raolos had died, and the Qagrue now ruled Dur.

Rodrik travelled on the carriage, in the driver's box, as ever. He appeared dedicated to Lorgallehna, and it comforted Corelle that when she could not be with the Sovsdot, Rodrik and her guards would protect her. At the barracks, he sent one of the guards to bring a sword for Corelle, and he returned with a short weapon that made Corelle's blade seem tiny by comparison. It felt heavy in her hand, and they showed her how to swing it, where to aim and how to score blows that would disable her opponent. She humoured them and followed their guidance, but the sword weighed too much, and she doubted she could ever wield one.

Lorgallehna acted as translator again. Corelle had picked up some Feshtersov, but still insufficient to hold a conversation alone. She battled two of the Sovsdot's guards, and they beat her with ease. As she fought the second one, she lost her balance and fell on her face in the dust. They all laughed, even Lorgallehna. Corelle picked up a small twig from the ground and held it pressed to her side, determined to show them how useless the swords would be against a trained assassin.

"Well done." She laughed as a distraction. "You could never stop me though, if I decided to kill your Sovsdot."

Their own laughter increased. "We are six, and trained fighters.

Her Eminence can also wield a sword as well as any man. We could cut you down long before you could reach her."

Corelle nodded. "You are six, and you might kill me. Not before I could kill Lorgallehna, I wager."

Their laughter died, and their hands moved toward the swords in their scabbards. "You are unarmed." Rodrik sounded wary.

Her sword lay in the dust where she had dropped it. "Am I? What about..." As they hung on her words, she sprang into action and swiped her twig across Rodrik's throat and that of the man next to him before either of them could react. She stepped behind Lorgallehna, who stared at her stupefied, and pressed the twig to her throat. "Two of you dead, your Sovsdot dead, and not a sword clear of a scabbard yet." She laughed, pleased with herself.

"With a twig?" Rodrik did not sound as amused as Corelle. "You jest."

Corelle dropped the twig, bent to her boot and produced her fan. "Not with a twig. With this." She popped the blade from the guard.

Rodrik stared at her, and such anger simmered in his eyes, Corelle wondered if the display had been a mistake. She did not wish to make an enemy of the grey-haired man, nor of the other guards, so she snapped the blade closed and slid it back into her boot.

"Well done, Corelle. You are a hero of Dur after all else." Lorgallehna gave a laugh, and the atmosphere relaxed, but Rodrik still did not seem pleased.

The training over, the two women climbed back into the carriage as the four guards mounted their horses. Rodrik and another of the guards rode on the carriage. As they trundled back toward the house, Corelle whispered to Lorgallehna. "Did I go too far?"

"You embarrassed Rodrik, I think, when you killed him first.

You are right though; you could have killed me. You made it look so easy. That will make him uncomfortable about you, since he sees only threats and complications. Do not worry on it. I shall talk to him later. All will be well. All must be well."

"Why must all be well?"

Lorgallehna took Corelle's face in her hand and stared into her eyes. "Because I love you."

The words struck a chill in Corelle's heart, but Lorgallehna would not release her grip, and she could not look away. "I cannot say the same." She said the words, but her heart told her that, while she did not love Lorgallehna now, it might not be long before she did. "I do not love you, but I could not stand to be apart from you."

Lorgallehna released her face and sighed. "Then we must tell my father."

The thought petrified Corelle. "Is that wise? He may not take it well."

"I am the Sovsdot. My father must know everything that turns in my life, which includes the person I love. He will continue to search for a match for me otherwise."

"I doubt your love for me will bring that search to an end." Corelle realised she might end up as no more than a dalliance outside Lorgallehna's marriage bed. She did not relish the idea.

"Corelle, *ickt gghil*, the moment he learns we are joined, he will cease his search. I have chosen, and I have chosen you."

Corelle frowned at the unfamiliar word '*gghil*.' She had learned '*ickt*' meant my, but she had not encountered this new word before. "*Ghhil*?"

"It means 'love.' *Ickt gghil*. My love."

The carriage stopped outside the house, and Lorgallehna asked the driver to wait as she went inside the house with Corelle. Corelle feared for Lorgallehna to tell her father of their relationship. "I ask you to delay before we tell your father, please." She feared his reaction, but she also felt they did not yet know each other well enough for such a course of action.

"Why? What are you afraid of?"

Time for another lie. "I am not afraid. I would like to learn more of your language. It is tiresome when you must translate all the time." Lorgallehna laughed. "What amuses you?" The Sovsdot's infectious laughter threatened to sweep Corelle along with it.

"He speaks many languages, as do all my family. I believe he even speaks a little Dur."

The revelation made sense, as he doubtless met emissaries from many different lands, but now the banquet confused Corelle even more. "Then why did he not speak to me in a language I understood at the banquet? Your mother also."

"My love, you are a commoner. He is a Sovran. Had you been a noblewoman, he would have spoken your language as a mark of respect and been insulted if you could not speak any of ours. You have not earned his respect."

"I had the right of it on the night. He hates me. No doubt he will have me hanged the moment you tell him you love me."

"We do not hang people in Feshtersov. We behead those who deserve death for their crimes."

It seemed brutal to Corelle to behead somebody. In many ways, Feshtersov seemed progressive compared to Dur, yet some aspects of their lives seemed crude and violent. "I still wish to learn the language more. I must earn his respect, it seems, if I am to continue to persuade his daughter to come to my bed."

"Very well. You have twelve days to learn our language."

"Twelve days? Why twelve days?" There could be no reason to hurry. Corelle would not mind if the Sovran never learned of his daughter's love for her, although the time Lorgallehna spent at the house while her guards waited outside might already have given rise to rumours.

"In twelve days, it will be my birthing day celebration. I will be thirty years old. The family will gather at the Retreat for the cele-bration. That is when we will tell my father."

Corelle blinked in confusion. "Birthing day?"

"Do you not celebrate your birthing day in Dur, then? What a strange nation it must be."

"Most people do not know when they were born, me among them. I believe I am twenty-nine years. I do not know for certain. Few have any idea."

"How odd. I know when I was birthed. The learned men keep records of every event that pertains to the Sovran's family, but all Feshtersov folk know their birthing day. I think." She looked doubtful.

"Can all your people read and scribe?"

"Scribe? Oh, you mean write. I do not believe so. Many do, but not all, I would guess."

"Then it is doubtful they can count far, and they may have no idea of when they were born, or how many years they are."

Lorgallehna's bottom lip protruded, and her brows knit. She used the expression whenever she gave any matter serious thought. "You may be right." She laughed. "Scribed." Her eyes twinkled and she pulled Corelle close and kissed her. "Twelve days." She pulled the door open and left Corelle to watch the carriage disappear up the street. Her mood had turned sour, and she could not determine whether Lorgallehna's departure had brought on the despondency, or the prospect of the Sovsdot's announcement to her entire family in twelve short days, and the certainty the family would not take the news well. It might be both, in truth.

A memory flitted through her mind, a memory of a time gone by in Argoya, when she had felt she could not live in such a vast city, yet she now intended to. She pushed the thought aside. Why dwell on it? Corelle had broken so many vows, another would not matter, added to a pile that was sure to grow even higher the longer she lived.

She closed the door and went inside. Twelve days to learn an entire language. It could not be done. Her grasp of the language so far might amount to thirty words. The celebration would be a disaster, and she would doubtless lose her head before it ended. The thought did nothing to brighten her mood, and she spent an unhappy evening until she went to bed.

CHAPTER 46
KRAGE

Krage's men had found no trace of Corelle since the banquet, and Krage had not learned why she had been invited. Had he been able to kill her on the night, he would have done so. He could not let her affect his plans, and he believed she must have come to Argoya in pursuit of him.

"Why, after so long?" Krage had lost count of the number of times he had asked his Senior Aide the question.

"I know not, but we cannot allow her to derail our plans." Ricrid always said the same, curse him. "Two years we have worked on this, and we are so close. We must remain focused on one objective. Do not become distracted by Corelle. Our men search for her, and if we cannot find her, it seems doubtful she can find us."

Krage chewed at his lower lip in consternation. Ricrid had the right of it. Krage could not allow her to become a thorn in his thumb now with his grand plan so near to fruition. For two years, he had nourished his relationship with one of the Sovran's senior advisors even as he and Ricrid worked on their plan. His plan, in truth, although Ricrid had been helpful. With the Sovran's support

and help, Krage could bring it to fruition, but the time must be right, and the proposal must be perfect. Soon, the Sovran's daughter would celebrate her thirtieth year, and Krage had been assured the Sovran would be in as good a mood as ever.

With luck, the Sovran's joy at the event would make him more receptive to Krage's proposal, which would be presented to him after the happy occasion. If he agreed, all would be restored in Krage's life. Corelle could not have guessed Krage's plans, and her appearance in Argoya must be nothing more than an unfortunate coincidence. He must not overlook it but must also not give it more consideration than it deserved while he completed his scheme and remade himself the person he had been born to become.

Krage turned his attention to Ricrid again. "You may have the right of it. Keep up the search. Find her. Kill her if you can. In the meantime, the plan continues." A shiver of excitement ran through his body, and he permitted himself a small smile. It did not pay to celebrate early, but he felt confident the work they had done would yield the reward he desired. He would make everything right, and some people would pay a terrible price once he did so. He waved a dismissive hand at Ricrid, a trick he had picked up from his old friend, Styrrach.

CHAPTER 47
CORELLE

Twelve days had been nowhere near long enough, and despite a valiant effort, with hours of help and encouragement from Lorgallehna, Corelle had made inadequate progress. She felt unprepared for the complex conversation that would take place at a family event. Lorgallehna assured her her family would understand and would accommodate her with explanations of words she did not know.

In her endeavours to learn more of the language, Corelle had neglected to make herself a dress for the celebration and suggested she could wear the dress from the banquet again. Lorgallehna had been horrified at the thought and insisted she buy one. They chose a simple crimson dress with little adornment but of fine making. Sleeves that draped to Corelle's elbows hid all but one of her scars, and a modest scooped neckline would be demure enough for the occasion. Lorgallehna loaned her a gold chain and hung a ruby amulet from it. It hung outside the neckline of the dress and would match well, they decided.

The day had come, and the carriage arrived outside the house. The night would be spent at the Retreat, and Corelle picked up her pack in which she had placed the dress, a change of clothes, and her vanity kit. She had abandoned her attempts to calm her nerves not long after she had woken, resigned to a day of anxiety that would end with her head separated from her body after all had been confessed to the Sovran.

Corelle locked the house behind her and climbed into the carriage. Lorgallehna kissed her and asked whether she had forgotten the dress. When Corelle explained, the Sovsdot's blue eyes flashed, and she pulled the dress from the pack and draped it along the opposite seat. Her own clothes had gone on ahead, it turned, in a carriage that carried nothing but clothes. Corelle guessed Lorgallehna must have even more clothes than Pettra.

Corelle spoke little on the drive, consumed with nerves. When they did speak, they used Feshtersov as much as they could so Corelle could practice. By the time the carriage turned into the long drive that swept down to the enormous house, Corelle's heart pounded so fast, she feared Krage would hear it and track her down, drawn by the noise it made.

To her disappointment, a servitor showed her to her room, and she realised she and Lorgallehna would sleep apart. The red-headed woman suggested they take the horses down to the lake for an hour once they had settled, and Corelle agreed, pleased to be out of the house, away from any risk she might encounter the Sovran or any of his family for a while longer.

They met up at the stable and chose two horses, four soldiers a respectable distance behind them. Corelle had spent some time in thought about the prospect that everywhere she went with Lorgallehna, soldiers would follow them. Rodrik had seemed aloof since the day at the training ground, but the others seemed to have forgotten the incident and treated her the same as ever; they ignored her.

The two women sat under the same tree and discussed how the event would run later. It all sounded too pompous for Corelle, but when your lover was the third most important person in the entire land, such formal events could not be avoided. The sun hid behind cloud, and Lorgallehna told her the winter that would arrive in a pass or two would be colder than Dur. The spring and summer had been drier and warmer than usual, and the crops had suffered as a result.

Across the lake, a horse appeared, and its rider galloped around the edge of the water toward them. Corelle reached for her boot, but Lorgallehna laid a hand on her arm and nodded her head toward the guards. All four had drawn their swords and moved close to the Sovsdot, their eyes fixed on the rider. Corelle gazed around in case the rider had been sent as a distraction but saw nothing to alarm her.

As the rider came closer, he reined to a walk. A tall man with short red hair, a long grey cloak wrapped around his body against the chill in the air, walked his horse toward them and leaned forward to pat the horse on its neck. Lorgallehna leapt to her feet and ran toward the horse. "Jaddemal. How delightful to see you."

The man climbed from his horse, and the soldiers sheathed their swords. "Happy birthing day, cousin." The man swept the Sovsdot into his arms and twirled her around as she wrapped her arms around his neck. "I rode out to the old *yarech* and thought it must be you under your favourite tree. You look fabulous, as ever." He kissed her cheek and seemed to notice Corelle for the first time. "And who is this?"

"Corelle, come and meet my favourite cousin, Jaddemal Orkbarat, the older son of my father's brother."

Corelle stood and approached the man. She expected him to offer his hand for the peculiar kiss, but he bowed his head instead. "Corelle. My pleasure. You are friends with my cousin?"

"That I am." Corelle replied in Feshtersov and had understood much of the conversation, but once Lorgallehna spoke Steinlund, so did Jaddemal. She had not known the word *"yarech"* but thought it mattered little.

Jaddemal stared at her for a moment, then raised his eyebrows and took Lorgallehna's hand. He handed the reins of his horse to a soldier and led his cousin over to the tree. The three sat under the canopy of the tree and chatted about the night's festivities. Jaddemal did not ask Corelle where she came from, but his exuberant personality soon won her over, and she laughed at his less than respectful discussions about some members of the family.

"If the Sovran has a brother, why would he not become the Sovran when your father dies?" Corelle had uncovered another mystery in the line of the Sovran.

Jaddemal answered her question. "The Sovran's title would have passed to my father had the Sovran died childless. Once Lorgallehna's brother popped out of their mother, he became the next in line. That is how it is."

Corelle reasoned the line of the old Duke of Dur would have been little different before Krage and the Qagrue came along to turn everything the wrong way up. "I see." Her thoughts had gone from the Sovran to her own land and its enemies.

As the sun peeped out beneath the layer of cloud, Jaddemal sighed. "I imagine we should return to the house and prepare for the night's fun."

They rode side by side, the four soldiers a respectful distance behind them, and stabled the horses before they entered the house. Jaddemal made Lorgallehna promise him a dance, then attempted to obtain a similar promise from Corelle, but she declined, afraid she could not dance anywhere near well enough to match the standards she felt sure the family would display. He seemed disappointed but ran up the stairs two at a time and left the women in the lobby.

"I must get ready now, as must you. Do not be afraid, *ickt gghil.* It will go well, I know it. How could they not love you as I do?"

Lorgallehna kissed Corelle on the tip of her nose and skipped up the stairs.

Corelle sat on her bed and wondered why Lorgallehna said, *"ickt gghil,"* rather than "my love." She might use it as an endearment between the two of them, or she disliked the way it translated. Something more for Corelle to investigate at some point. She sighed and tried to control her hands, which shook like leaves in a storm.

CHAPTER 48
CORELLE

A young woman came in and offered to help Corelle ready herself, and she agreed, since she had little skill with the powders that must be applied to her face to fit into such high company as the Sovran of Feshtersov. The woman made Corelle look as though she belonged, but she had become so nervous, she thought she might fetch up. The woman left, and Corelle sat on the bed again. How could she face the night? Her lover planned to tell the most powerful man in the land that rather than marry the son of an important noble from another land, she wished to spend her life with a garment maker's daughter from Dur who had killed so many people, she had lost count, among them three women who had loved her.

Corelle had not mentioned her fear to Lorgallehna, that any woman who said those three words condemned themselves to an early death. As far as Corelle knew, Vamma had been the only one to survive, but she could not be certain the stallholder still lived. Corelle thought back over her time in Ort, then Steinlund, Vyrrmod, and now Feshtersov, and decided Vamma must have

given birth to the baby she conceived while married to Raolos. She hoped the birth had been uncomplicated, and mother and child would live long lives.

A knock at the door startled her, and the young woman reappeared to say all the others had assembled, and Corelle should join them. In truth, she did not want to go, but now she had arrived at the Retreat, she had little choice. With a nervous sigh, she stood and followed the woman down the wide staircase. Her mouth had become drier than any morning after too much wine, and her legs threatened to give way with every step. The final insult, to enter the room and fall face first to the floor under their contemptuous gaze. She had been calmer when she killed, but her trusted methods failed her now. She could not control her heart rate or her nerves. The voices of the family rose to meet her from a room to her left, and her stomach churned. How could they not have already guessed why Corelle had been invited to the celebration? She did not belong to the family, and the rumours must have spread far and wide by now.

The voices grew louder, the young woman opened a door, and Corelle entered a large parlour. Twenty people or more stood or sat in the room, most with goblets in their hands or nearby. Corelle recognised the Sovran and his wife, then Lorgallehna turned her head and smiled before she said something to the older woman she had been in conversation with. The Sovsdot crossed the room and greeted Corelle with a kiss on the cheek. "You look spectacular." Her hot breath in Corelle's ear seemed even more seductive in such exalted company.

In truth, Corelle thought herself plain and underdressed compared to the finery on display in the room; spectacular dresses, enormous pieces of jewellery, hair that must have taken all day to create, men in fine tunics and wescoats, and the Sovran with his ridiculous long sword strapped loose at his hip. Lorgallehna looked the best of all in a beautiful tan silk dress with dark brown contrast piping at the shoulder and cuffs. A dark brown sash around her waist accentuated her perfect figure. "Compared to you, I look ordinary. Let us leave and head up to my room." Corelle reasoned she would make the last, desperate attempt to escape the evening.

Lorgallehna fiddled with the ruby around Corelle's neck. "You tempt me, I cannot deny." She wore a mischievous grin that spread to her eyes.

"When will you tell everybody?" The thought boiled Corelle's stomach again, and she exhaled a heavy, nervous breath.

"We will tell father alone first. I do not want to place him in a difficult position. Later though. Come and meet some people."

She took Corelle's arm and led her toward her brother. "Corelle, this is my big brother, Sovssun Oriamel Orkbarat." Oriamel looked a lot like Lorgallehna to Corelle's eye, the same red hair and fine, high cheekbones. His blue eyes sparkled with some mischief he kept to himself. He stood close to two spans above Corelle, and he bowed his head toward her.

Corelle returned the gesture. "Eminence. A pleasure to meet you."

"You trained her well, Lorga." He gave his sister an affectionate smile. "I am pleased at last to meet the woman who has kept my little sister away from the Seat for two passes or more." The twinkle in his eyes reminded Corelle of Lorgallehna's own. "I hear you will talk to father later. In the meantime, you can trust me. Your secret is safe." He laughed again, and Corelle decided she liked him. Corelle could not guess what manner of men had given Lorgallehna such a low opinion of men in general. Not her brother, she imagined. He did not seem like a brute at all. "My wife is somewhere. Near the wine casks, no doubt." He smiled and bowed his head again as Lorgallehna pulled Corelle off in a different direction.

Corelle whispered, her throat so dry, she feared the words

would become stuck. "I would like a goblet of wine to steady my nerves." Lorgallehna gestured to a woman, who brought two goblets on a bright silver tray to them. The clear white wine in the goblet seemed to sparkle, and when Corelle sipped at it, it did indeed contain bubbles that burst in her mouth. It had a dry, yeasty taste, and Corelle thought she liked it more than the red wine she had always drunk.

Lorgallehna introduced her to everybody; uncles, aunts, cousins, Oriamel's wife, and the names ran away from Corelle's memory as soon as Lorgallehna piled each new one on the others. She had another goblet of the wine, a bell rang, and the Sovran and his wife led the guests through to a dining room whose table glistened with cutlery, plates, cups, and goblets as grand as those at the banquet. How these people stayed as thin as they did, Corelle could not guess, if they ate and drank like this every night.

Lorgallehna sat alongside her father, her mother on the Sovran's other side, Oriamel next to his mother. The others sat on either side of the enormous table, and to her relief, Corelle found she had been seated next to Jaddemal. He talked and jested with her throughout the meal and explained what each course involved. Corelle had gone through the courses at the Seat without any idea what she had eaten, and as Jaddemal described some of tonight's courses, she wished at times she had remained ignorant of what she placed in her mouth. The tongue of a young milk cow tasted familiar, but she struggled to eat it once Jaddemal had told her what lay on her plate.

Lorgallehna smiled at her often but talked to those nearest to her. At the end, the servers brought in a large cake with some small candles on them. Jaddemal explained that tradition required the person whom all these fine people celebrated to blow out all the candles in one try, and Lorgallehna almost succeeded. She sucked in a large draft of air and blew at the candles with her cheeks puffed out and her lips pursed, but at the last, one candle sputtered and would not be extinguished. With a second swift puff of air, Lorgallehna blew it out and everybody clapped their hands and cried, "Happy birthing day," as Lorgallehna beamed around the table and dabbed at her eyes with her napkin.

Thanks to Jaddemal and the wine, Corelle had enjoyed the night far more than she had expected to, and when everybody returned to the parlour, and a small band of minstrels struck up a tune, the Sovran bowed low to his daughter, took her in his arms, and they danced around the room while everybody else stood and watched, many with kerchiefs to their eyes.

Soon, almost everybody danced, and Corelle thought every man danced with Lorgallehna. Corelle declined several invitations, unable to follow the complicated steps involved in the dances the family showed off on the makeshift dance floor. Jaddemal tried his luck again, and Corelle confided in him she had no idea how to dance like the others.

That turned out to be a mistake, as he insisted he be allowed to teach her, and with great reluctance, she allowed it, her clumsy attempts to follow his instructions almost disastrous on more than one occasion as they almost fell. At one point they danced close to Lorgallehna, who laughed aloud as she passed them.

At the end of the dance, Jaddemal bowed and thanked her, but she guessed it had been a trial for him to lead such an incompetent dancer around the floor. Corelle slumped into a chair, but as she considered another glass of the wine, Lorgallehna loomed over her, her hand extended, no smile on her face. "It is time." She pulled Corelle up from the chair.

The anxiety returned, and Corelle's stomach threatened to flip and send the entire meal out of her mouth onto the dance floor. She had known Lorgallehna for little more than two passes, and it seemed ridiculous they must tell the Sovran anything of their relationship. Although Lorgallehna had been adamant, and Corelle had never questioned it, it made little sense. Why did they rush to mention anything after so short a time? Lorgallehna's explanations about the search for a suitable match and the expectations of the family and the people of Feshtersov seemed foolish at this point, but the Sovsdot pulled her through a door and into a room that seemed like an office.

The Sovran stood near a large desk of dark wood. Rows of journals filled every wall, and a lantern on the desk provided the only light. Lorgallehna closed the door and turned to her father. Corelle shrank back, cowed by the enormity of all this man represented in a way she had not felt when she had met the Duke of Dur. Before her stood Antones Orkbarat, Sovran of Feshtersov, and she felt faint with fear.

Lorgallehna drew in a deep breath. "Father—"

He held up a hand to interrupt her. "I can guess what you are about to say, Daughter. I ask you now to think hard before you speak again. Thirty years ago, your mother birthed you, and you have brought me pleasure and pride in equal measure every day since. What I guess you will ask me tonight, I ask you to take a moment to consider. If it is what you desire above all else, then proceed. But take a moment, please."

Lorgallehna took a long deep breath and looked at Corelle. For a heartbeat, Corelle thought the Sovran's words might have changed her mind, but she extended a hand, and Corelle took it in her own. "Father, this is Corelle, and I love her. We ask your blessing."

He sighed and studied Corelle for a time. "You are from Dur, is that correct?"

"That it is, Eminence." Corelle's voice shook with the dread of this moment, and she guessed she sounded like a frightened child caught with forbidden foodstuff smeared across its face.

"Your people take no family name as I understand it. Corelle is the sum total of your name?"

"That it is."

He nodded, and Corelle worried her lack of a family name cast her in a poor light. "Do you love my daughter?"

Corelle had not anticipated the question, though it now seemed logical he would ask. "I… That is, I admire her, I care for her, and I could not abide the thought of a day without her."

He nodded thoughtfully. "But you do not love her, as she loves you."

Corelle stood upright and met his gaze with all the pride she could muster. "That I do not, and she knows it. The fates are written, and if it is my fate to love her, I would consider myself fortunate indeed to love and be loved by her." This had not gone as she had hoped, and she had floundered with her answers. They should have waited longer, after all else.

"Will you marry?"

Another question she had not expected. "In my land, we would not be permitted to marry. It has not occurred to me we might."

"For the Sovsdot to lie in the bed of a… of somebody she had not married would not be proper."

"Then yes, I imagine we will marry, if that is acceptable in your law."

He stared at her. "Our laws have nothing to say on the matter. If I permit you to marry, you may marry." He looked to Lorgallehna and smiled. "Lorga, you know I love you. Everybody loves you. The people respect me, but they do not love me, and they will not love your brother when he is Sovran. They love you as they loved your mother when first we married. I must think of them as much as I think of you in this matter." Lorgallehna did not reply, and he paced in front of the desk for a time. "This is my decision. For now, we will make no announcement, and you will not marry. When Corelle—" he flicked his eyes to her, then back to his daughter— "can say in honesty she loves you, then I will bless you to marry, and we will make the announcement." He turned his gaze on

Corelle. "Do nothing to make my daughter unhappy, young woman. Feshtersov can be quick to anger, and our anger is fierce."

"Eminence." Corelle gave him a respectful nod.

"I have seen what a terrible dancer you are. You even made Jaddemal look clumsy, and he is the finest dancer in the nation. Nonetheless, go and dance with my daughter, and talk with me again when all I have decreed is in place."

CHAPTER 49
CORELLE

Two days after they returned from the Retreat, Corelle went back to her unsuccessful search for Krage, and she continued to devote all her spare time to it for most of another pass. She returned often to the street where she had seen the man who had followed her, while at other times she wandered the streets of the wealthier districts of the city and made enquiries, but all without luck. The fact Krage had been at the banquet suggested to Corelle he still had great wealth, so she did not spend any time in the poorer parts of Argoya.

Lorgallehna had been busy with some important nobles who visited from another land, and they had seen little of one another for several days. They had arranged for her to slip away late after a family dinner she must attend and come to the house. She arrived so late, Corelle had fallen asleep, and the key in the lock of the door woke her. The dainty step on the stairs confirmed Lorgallehna had arrived, and soon enough the Sovsdot slid into bed beside her, her lips on Corelle's in search of a passionate kiss. Corelle teased at the red-headed woman's nipples until they stood proud and erect, and

Lorgallehna's breaths deepened and quickened as her hand dived between Corelle's legs in search of her nub.

She soon brought Corelle to her first peak, and Corelle pushed her over onto her back and ran her tongue down the slim stomach of her lover, across her bush and into the warm damp opening of her sex. Lorgallehna gasped with desire as Corelle's tongue flicked at her, the taste of her in her mouth, the smell of her in her nose. As her excitement grew, Lorgallehna balled her fists in Corelle's hair and cried aloud, her pelvis raised from the bed as she urged Corelle's tongue to delve deeper inside her.

Afterward, they lay entwined together on the bed, the top bedsheet and blanket thrown to the floor. Lorgallehna planted small, delicate kisses on Corelle's arm as they recovered from their lovemaking. Lorgallehna broke the silence. "Dur came up at dinner tonight."

"It did? Why?"

"It seems one of father's senior advisors persuaded him to consider a petition from a wealthy man. The man's name is Egrak, it seems. He claims to be the rightful Duke of Dur and asked father to send an army to Dur to restore him to his place. Southerners invaded, appar—"

Corelle sat upright in the bed. "Krage." She whispered, almost afraid to say the name out loud.

"His name is Egrak. I am sure you told me you travelled here in search of your friend, Krage. This is not him."

"He is not the rightful Duke. He hanged the Duke when he brought the Qagrue to our land and took control of it for himself. The Qagrue threw him down, betrayed him."

"It cannot be this man. You must be mistaken." Lorgallehna looked doubtful.

"I saw him at the banquet. I wondered why he attended, but it must have been part of some plot to persuade your father to back him in his bid to throw the Qagrue out of Dur and take it for himself again."

"Would that be so bad?"

Lorgallehna had no knowledge of how Dur had been before the Qagrue, before Krage. Krage had no more right to declare himself Duke of Dur than Corelle did to declare herself Sovran of Feshtersov. "He has no right to the Duchy. He murdered our Duke. He is a ruthless killer, and he owes me a debt."

"I remember you said this at our first lunch." She smiled. "That day—"

"He does not owe me coin. He owes me his life." Corelle's anger churned inside her like the storm that had taken Lzastish, the wheelman on the Rzankir. Since the Qagrue healer had cut open her head, she had not experienced the previous rages, but one returned now with renewed fury.

"His life? Corelle, you must be wrong about this man."

"That I am not. His name, Egrak, which is 'Krage' backward."

Lorgallehna made her thoughtful face. "No, it is 'Karge' backward, but I will concede it has the same letters as Krage. What did you mean when you said he owes you his life?"

Corelle's anger had got the better of her tongue, and she had said things she had not intended to. She would not lie to Lorgallehna, but she must be careful with the truth. "He forced himself on someone I cared about and made her with child. In a difficult spot, she decided she could no longer face life with that man's child inside her."

"She took her own life?"

Lorgallehna's horrified whisper echoed around Corelle's mind. "She gave up her life, left with no other choice."

"Gave up her life? Did she take her own life, or did somebody kill her?" Confusion and concern showed on Lorgallehna's face.

How could Corelle explain that night unless she told the entire story? If she confessed she had killed Arella, Lorgallehna might walk out and leave her, and who could blame her? "She sacrificed herself to another."

Lorgallehna wiped at her eyes, all the pleasure and excitement of earlier in the night stolen from the room, replaced by misery, anger, and questions that could not be answered. "What of her killer?"

She could use Pilos to deflect from the truth, but if the real tale emerged later, Lorgallehna's sense of betrayal may not stand the test as Deineike's had done. Better to tell the truth now than risk it might emerge later. Corelle could not make that decision. She might lose Lorgallehna, the woman she... "Lorgallehna, I love you."

Tears spilled from the redhead's eyes, but they did not seem to be from happiness at that moment. "You say this now? What prompts it now? What is the truth of this tale?"

"Curse you, Krage." With a sigh, Corelle continued. "She gave her life to save mine. I would have died, but Arella chose to die in my place."

"Is this why you became a mariner?"

"That it is not. That is another tale. I had been betrayed. I took vengeance on the one who betrayed me, and Arella died also, caught up in a web of evil neither of us knew anything of at that time."

Lorgallehna lay motionless and stared at the ceiling. "I understand your anger at this man, but you cannot kill him. If you kill him here, you will be beheaded. He has committed no crime in Feshtersov he deserves punishment for."

Corelle wracked her brain for a solution. "In Vyrrmod, they have a custom that allows a person to challenge another to a fight to the death. If the cause is just, and the custom is adhered to, there is no punishment."

"What a peculiar tradition. We have no such custom here."

"I must find a way." Corelle's anger would not allow her to

stand by while Krage returned to Dur and reinstalled himself as Duke, and she did nothing to thwart him.

"Corelle, my love. There is no way for you to kill this man here. I cannot see you beheaded for the crime of his death. I could not stand it."

"Will your father grant him the aid he seeks?"

Lorgallehna sucked air across her teeth. "It is unlikely, I think. We have not had a war since we conquered Ishter, and peace is preferable to another war. We know nothing of Dur, and this man is not a citizen of our nation. Dur is so far south, and my father has no interest in it. I believe he would not have mentioned it to me but for you."

"Then how can I have vengeance for Arella and her unborn child?"

"You cannot. I am sorry."

Corelle pounded the palms of her hands on the bed. Krage sat in a parlour somewhere in the city, with plots to reinstate himself as the Duke of Dur, and she could do nothing about it. Her frustration grew so great, she thought she might scream. "You could help me."

"I am the Sovsdot. I am not a murderer. I share your outrage, and I love you, but I cannot become involved in this. I urge you to let it go from yourself. I now regret I mentioned it."

"What I feel is more than outrage." Tears ran from Corelle's eyes.

"I am sorry, *ickt gghil*."

"Tell me where he lives, at the least."

"I cannot do that, you know this."

Corelle turned to gaze down at her. "I thought you loved me?"

Lorgallehna blinked away fresh tears. "That is unfair. I do love you, and that is why I cannot tell you. I could not stand to watch you beheaded, your body cast into the sea."

Fury tore at Corelle, rage and frustration mixed in a volatile combination. She yearned to have Krage under her blade and could scarce control her voice. Screams rose to her throat, and she battled to fight them, repress them, keep her voice level. She clenched her fists. "I have sailed the seven seas of this globe, and I would be happy to turn them all vermilion with Krage's blood. Here he is within my grasp, but if I kill him, it will be my blood in the sea in place of his." The unfairness of the situation compounded her anger, added to her exasperation.

Lorgallehna took Corelle's hand and pried open her fist. "I love you." The Sovsdot spoke in a soft voice, meant to calm, doubtless.

"I have lived for little but vengeance for most of my adult life."

"Is that all you live for now?"

Corelle had not appreciated she had given the thought voice. "That it is not. I love you. You have given me a reason to live."

"Then let us spend some time at the Retreat, you and me alone. We can ride our horses, make love, and forget this man ever existed."

Corelle lay beside her and kissed her, a tender kiss she hoped conveyed her admiration and love for the Sovsdot. "I can never forget him. Nothing could drive him from my mind."

"I can think of something." Lorgallehna slid a hand between Corelle's legs.

CHAPTER 50
KRAGE

Krage received letters from the Sovran that denied his petition on the grounds Dur lay too far to the south for Feshtersov to have any interest in. The current era of peacetime would continue for as long as possible in the best interests of the nation's people. Four days later, he received even worse news.

Ricrid brought the latest disappointment. He had seen a proclamation posted on a tree nearby, and Krage had to leave the house to read it for himself. *"Sovran Antones Orkbarat announces that his only daughter, Sovsdot Lorgallehna Orkbarat, will marry her Consort, Corelle of Dur, in one pass at the Seat."* More information about the actual day had been scribed below, but Krage did not care about any of those details. His ire would have had him tear the proclamation from the tree and stamp on it, but two soldiers loitered nearby.

Now he could see why his petition had been denied. Corelle had whispered in the Sovran's ear and poisoned him against Krage. That cursed jade had meddled in his affairs again and had thwarted his plan. He stomped back into the house and collapsed onto a couch in the parlour.

Ricrid sat in an armed chair nearby. "A sorry turn."

Krage fumed on, his temper ready to break into a destructive rampage around the room in a heartbeat. Ricrid said nothing more, and Krage's anger fumed within him. "A sorry turn? That is all you have to say? She marries the Sovran's daughter. How in the Five Cities can a woman marry a woman? This land is as deviant as Corelle herself if they allow this."

"She has made herself easier to find, at the least."

He had the right of it, in part. Corelle would find it harder to hide herself from him now she had lured the Sovsdot into her web of unnatural behaviour. Bad enough she had killed his unborn child, destroyed the Guild, and fought him tooth and nail as he launched his scheme to become Duke of Dur. Now she had prevented his attempt to reinstate himself as Duke and had persuaded the Sovran of Feshtersov to approve of her deviancy and permit her to marry the Sovsdot. She would now be so powerful in this land, she could employ the Sovran's armies to hunt him down and kill him. He could not stay here.

While she would be easier to find, she would also find it easier to locate him. She threatened his life, and Krage intended to defend that at all costs. "We must leave Feshtersov as soon as possible."

Ricrid did not hide his surprise. "Leave? Where will we go? Corelle will follow you wherever you go. We must kill her."

"How will we kill her?" Krage made no attempt to conceal his rage. "She will be safe behind the guards and walls of the Seat, and we will never get close to her. If you have nothing useful to say, I suggest you say nothing."

Ricrid sat in silence for some time. "The Sovsdot often ventures out in the streets among the people. That is why they love her so much. Corelle might accompany her on one such excursion."

Krage sighed with frustration. "That she does, but she is always guarded. If we kill her guards to reach Corelle, we will lose our heads, and if we kill the Sovsdot at the same time, the crowd will tear us to pieces. We must leave, and we should not delay." Ricrid drew a breath to speak, but Krage glared at him. "We leave. Whether you will come or stay is yours to decide. I care not."

"When will you leave?"

"Within a tenday. I have some business interests I will need to finalise and retrieve coin from. Prepare yourself. If you wish to leave, that is." Krage stood and went to his office. He slammed the door, pounded his fists on his desk, and muttered aloud. "Curse you Corelle. I hate you." Then he pulled some journals onto the desk, opened one, and started the lengthy process that would inform him of what he needed to do to gather his coin together ready to depart.

CHAPTER 51
RICRID

Ricrid sat in the chair for some time after the office door slammed. He had served Krage for at least four years, and while he had been paid well, he had not been set up for life as Krage appeared to be. The same could be said of Sisnop, for whom he had worked in Torric. Rumour said Corelle had killed Sisnop in Ort. None of his fortune had come to Ricrid either, although he had killed many times on his former Guildmeister's orders. They all used him, used all the Guild members, and made themselves rich in the process.

Ricrid liked Argoya and did not want to leave. He had little personal time thanks to Krage's demands, but he had met a local woman, Queltia, and he had grown to enjoy her company as much as her body. He had served the Guild with loyalty, but if Krage intended to leave Argoya, then it was time Ricrid gave some thought to his own future. He had not been required to kill since they had fled Alcmouth, and he did not miss it. Death had gnawed at him throughout his years in the Guild, and it had eaten away some part of him he doubted could be replaced.

If Krage wished to leave, and Ricrid chose to stay, he might find work and settle down with Queltia. His skills lay in the protection of Krage these days, no longer called on to kill. He had been happy to help Krage at first and had looked forward to a return to Dur, but now Queltia had him doubtful. Since the Sovran had rejected Krage's proposal, the decision had no longer been required, until now. Rather than a triumphant return to Dur, and the prospect of his appointment as Bailiff, it seemed he must now leave Argoya tethered to Krage's coattails as the former Guildmeister sought a new home where he could hatch more plans to appease his frustration.

Ricrid would have been prepared to make the attempt on Corelle's life if Krage had ordered it. It might have cost him his life, but he still had some skill, and three of his men had come with him from Torric. At the least, they knew one end of a dagger from another, and the four of them might have struck her down. Krage, it seemed, had decided to abandon his intent to kill her, no doubt because he did not wish the fates to be reversed, and Corelle would kill Krage without any doubt. He had become slow, careless, and dependant on Ricrid and the others. His trousers had grown in size and his ego along with them.

The office door opened, and Krage appeared surprised to see Ricrid seated in the chair. "What are you about?"

"Nothing, as you can see."

"Do I pay you to do nothing? I thought I paid you to protect me."

Ricrid gave a small dismissive laugh. "Are you in danger, then?"

Krage narrowed his eyes and stared at his Senior Aide. "Bring water. I am thirsty. Then make sure the men do not relax as you do. If Corelle comes, we must be ready." He returned to the office and slammed the door. Again.

Ricrid sat on the couch for twenty heartbeats. His time in the Guild had made him cautious, reluctant to act on impulse, but a thought occurred to him at that moment that went against all his instincts. The idea was madness, but it excited him to think he might do something so irrational and unplanned. It would be the complete opposite of how he had lived for so many years. What better way to mark the end of one part of his life and the start of another?

He rose and went into the office. He did not slam the door, and Krage did not look up. "Place the pitcher on the table." Ricrid did not move, and in time Krage looked up at him. "Where is my water?"

The shock and surprise in his eyes as Ricrid's dagger plunged into the side of his throat seemed almost comical. His blood spurted out onto the desk and the carpet. The journal in front of him turned vermilion, and he fell forward onto his face with a wet thump. Ricrid retrieved his dagger and wiped its blade on the tunic of his dead ex-employer. Krage would take him for granted no longer.

Ricrid gave a sardonic laugh. "I can still kill." He went to the corner of the room and lifted the carpet, prised up the floorboard, and pulled out a box. Its weight surprised him. Only Krage had ever touched it before. Most of Krage's coin, Ricrid would never find, but he knew where some of it lay hidden, and it would be enough.

Ricrid tipped some of the coins onto the floor, then carried the half-empty box out to the parlour. He called one of the guards in from outside the house, told him to bring as many of the others as he could find within the hour, then went to the scullery and pumped some water into a pitcher. He filled a cup from the pitcher, carried it to the chair he had been seated in, and sat again.

Two hours later, the box had been emptied, the men all paid off and told Krage no longer required their services. Ricrid locked the door of the house and walked to Queltia's home. She could scribe; he could not. Queltia had a small house in a poorer part of town and worked as a cleaner in a local inn, where she worked hard all day, six days a week. While she could soon give up the arduous work, he would say nothing to her until his impromptu plan had all come together.

Today, she had a day off, and she scribed the note at his request. It read, *"Meet me at The Cloak And Staff tomorrow at the midday. Ricrid."* She asked him what the note meant, but he could not tell her yet, though he promised to do so in a day or two. He walked from Queltia's house to the Seat and approached one of the guards at the main gate. Three others watched him like birds of prey, hands on the hilts of their swords. He believed he could kill them all if he wanted, but today he would not take that risk. He handed the note to the guard and impressed on him it must reach Corelle of Dur, the Sovsdot's Consort, today, without fail. The man told him Corelle had not yet taken up residence at the Seat, so Ricrid insisted they send a messenger to her home without delay. He offered the guard some of Krage's coin, but the man would not accept it. The guard promised to do all he could to get the note to Corelle.

Ricrid walked back to Queltia's house with a spring in his step. He had chosen the tavern because it would be busy. Corelle would not come alone, that could be guaranteed. He did not want her men to strike him down before he could speak to her, and a tavernroom would provide more witnesses than Corelle would be comfortable with if she intended to kill him. He had not told her the address of the tavern. Somebody in the Seat would know, and Ricrid did not doubt she would be there if she received the note. He had done all he could today. Later, he might wonder about his actions and even regret them. For now, he foresaw only a positive outcome for him and Queltia. He should have done it many passes ago, but he had done it, at the least. He whistled as he walked, some song he had heard once in Torric but could no longer remember the words to.

CHAPTER 52
CORELLE

Corelle lowered the note and looked up at Rodrik. "Where is this inn?"

"Close to the market where you first met the Sovsdot, Eminence."

"Please, do not call me that. I am not part of the family, and I would rather you call me Corelle." Rodrik bowed his head. No doubt the stubborn old man would continue to call her Eminence despite her protests. "Why does he want to see me? What trickery does Krage plan?"

"I cannot answer that question, Eminence." Corelle's sigh did not interrupt him. "I advise you not to go."

Corelle understood Rodrik's concern. Krage planned an attempt on her life. Why else had his man sent the letter and requested the meeting? She did not know Ricrid, but Denstal had mentioned him in Ryl before Corelle had sent him wherever he travelled to afterward. He would try to kill her, but she might kill him instead. If he attacked her, she would be justified when she struck him down in her own defence, and Lorgallehna's father would have no excuse to cut off her head.

They had chosen a tavern, where there would be many patrons as witness to whatever turned. Krage might attempt some bargain for his life, but he would find Corelle in an unreceptive mood if he did so. She had made her decision. "I will attend."

It was Rodrik's turn to sigh. "Very well, Eminence. How many guards will you require?"

A good question. It would be dangerous to go alone, and in truth the more witnesses the better if the opportunity to kill Krage presented itself. If she took too many, he might have a change of heart about any attempt to kill her, and she might lose her chance. Quite a dilemma. "Four guards. Do not tell Lorgallehna, Rodrik. She will worry."

"If she asks—"

"Then tell her nothing. What if she wishes to accompany me? She could be in danger."

Rodrik nodded, a glum expression on his face. Corelle had played the best hand she could. The old man would not place Lorgallehna's life in danger and would keep quiet for the Sovsdot's sake.

Corelle struggled to sleep that night. Lorgallehna came to the house less since the announcement they were to be married, but tonight Corelle would have relished the Sovsdot's slender body in her arms. She lay awake, her mind filled with all that could go wrong the next day. Sleep came, but the sun soon chased it away. Corelle worked at her blade with a whetstone as she waited for the guards to arrive.

Rodrik came with them, and they brought an extra horse for her to ride. Corelle reasoned Rodrik had joined them out of respect for her, but she might have preferred a younger, more agile soldier. The sand fell, and no time could be wasted in argument, so they set off for the tavern and arrived early. With so many guards and horses, it seemed pointless to attempt any surveillance to see what awaited them. All five strolled into the tavernroom, and Corelle gazed around.

She saw Ricrid at once. Only one of the patrons could be from the Guild, slight, eyes that never stayed still, no drink before him at his table, which overlooked the entire tavernroom. Their eyes met, but neither acknowledged the other. Corelle continued her inspection of the tavernroom, as Ricrid must have guessed she would. To her surprise, she saw no other patron who looked as though they might be a Guild member. Either the others hid somewhere, or Ricrid intended to lure her to some quiet place and kill her there.

The innkeep looked her way, but she waved him off and strode across the tavernroom to stand at Ricrid's table. "I am here."

"I see this. You are not alone."

"You did not ask me to come alone. What is it you and that weasel wish with me?" Vamma's grandfather had explained what a weasel was; some kind of animal of low cunning, if she remembered it right.

Ricrid stood. "Come with me. Your men may come also."

He strode from the tavern, Corelle and the guards behind him. They collected their horses and led them through the streets behind Ricrid. He walked for some time, close to an hour, Corelle thought, and they found themselves in a far better part of town. "Could we not have met you somewhere closer to where you plan your move?" Ricrid neither replied nor turned to look at her.

At last, Ricrid stopped before a fine two-storey house made of pale blocks with a small, neat garden at the front. He stepped up to the door and used a key to unlock it. Corelle and her guards tied their horses to the gate and followed him inside, weapons drawn. Corelle smelled death the moment she entered, but she said nothing. "Krage is in his office." Ricrid pointed to a closed door. "He wishes to see you alone. I will stay with your men."

"Do not enter alone, Eminence." Rodrik laid an anxious hand on Corelle's forearm. "It may be a trap."

Corelle doubted there would be any trap. Something must have turned awry between Krage and Ricrid, if the smell meant what she believed it did. "It will be fine Rodrik. I will be but a moment, I think."

Joy. Disappointment. Relief. Resentment. All four emotions, and more, passed through her as she gazed on Krage's body. Joy that he lay dead but disappointment she had not killed him. Relief her vengeance need play on her mind no longer but resentment Ricrid had ended Krage's life and robbed her of her chance to do so. All the leaders of the Guild had been killed, and its reign ended.

Even in death, Krage remained taller than most Guild members, most of whom were short and slight. Despite Krage's height, his robust body seemed to have been overweight prior to his death. As she gazed on the pale, empty thing Krage had become, she pondered all that had turned to this point. With his death, the last of the Guild's leaders had gone wherever they travelled to afterward, the final vengeance for all those whom Corelle had loved and who had lost their lives as a result of Styrrach. Could that be enough? Could it ever be enough? Corelle had not stilled Krage's heart; another had done it in her stead, and the bitter taste of that lack of fulfilment threatened to bring bile to her throat.

All her adult life, she had sought revenge. She had dispensed it, even to Krage, in some indirect way. She had drifted through life at the dictates of vengeance, at the whim of others, at the commands of death itself. She could never forgive herself for all she had done, but what had that self-loathing brought her? More deaths, more friends who breathed no longer, more lovers dead in the shadow of her passing. Had it been worth it? What was left for her now?

Lorgallehna. She had known joy with the slender, red-headed woman, and she loved her, the only woman she had loved since Deineike's death. Could that love survive the tormented, empty shell Corelle had become? She doubted it, but she wanted it. She did not deserve happiness, but she craved it. There could be no future for them unless Corelle abandoned the guilt, the hatred of herself. It would be no simple task, but in truth, she wearied of the person her bitterness and anger had turned her into. The seventeen year old Corelle who had met Arella could never return, but the despicable twenty-nine year old Corelle need not remain for the rest of her days. Let this be an end of it. Krage was dead, and Corelle's rancour at herself must die with him, or she would be destroyed too.

She sighed. The old saying, *"The rest of your life begins now,"* came to mind, but it sounded wrong. No doubt she had mangled it, as had often been the case in recent times. However the phrase went, she promised herself she would try to put the past behind her and dwell on her anger no more. Well, once more. She loomed over Krage's corpse, whispered, "Good riddance," and spat on his head.

She closed the office door and stared at Ricrid. "Why?"

"Why not? They made themselves wealthy, and now my time has come. They shrouded you, and many others. I might have been the next one sold for all I know. All I ask is for you to enjoy your ceremony, enjoy wedded bliss, and trouble me no more. I have enough to get by, and this house. I too have a woman I would like the chance of some joy with. No ill blood sits between you and me. I have not wronged you."

His explanation made sense. One more question remained. "What of Raopul, the Bailiff's son?"

Ricrid nodded. "He lives. Krage ordered it otherwise and paid us a handsome sum for the deed. We found a sympathetic old woman in Alcmouth, gave her the coin and told her to take the boy somewhere safe. Beyond that, I know nothing."

"Why did you not obey Krage's command?"

"He was eleven years. Would you have obeyed?" Corelle said nothing. "Enough. Do we have a bargain?"

"What of Krage?"

"You may leave him to me. Such work is unsuited to the hands of the Consort of the Sovsdot."

Rodrik gave a polite cough. "Eminence, if this man has killed somebody, he must face justice."

Corelle turned to the older man. "He has not killed anybody. A mutual friend will hand over their business to him, nothing more."

Ricrid smiled at her as she walked from the house.

orelle had thought Lorgallehna's family large at the celebration of her birthing day, but no more than a small part of the family had been invited to that occasion, and many more streamed into the city in the days prior to the wedding. All the family houses were required to accommodate them, and Corelle had to move into rooms in the Seat, where she skulked around the corridors and tried to avoid everybody. If she had the misfortune to meet some distant relative of the Sovran, she faced an endless stream of questions about herself and the ceremony.

In truth, she knew little about the wedding itself except it would be an immense affair at the front archway of the Seat, with the people gathered in vast numbers to watch. In private moments, Corelle confessed to Lorgallehna she felt abject terror about the day, but in public she had to adopt what she referred to as her "Eminence face" even as she hated the term "Eminence" and pleaded with everybody not to call her anything but Corelle.

All her earlier doubt about how fast things had moved toward such a prestigious and irrevocable event as a wedding had come to a head once Lorgallehna had told her of the letters from Krage to

the Sovran. Despite her words to Lorgallehna's father on the Sovsdot's birthing day, Corelle had realised she did love the Sovsdot, and the relationship had brought some peace to her at last. She had endured few nightmares since the two had met, and she felt a level of contentment in Lorgallehna's company she had not felt since Deineike.

Despite the realisation, she still thought they had known each other for too short a time to commit to a marriage. It seemed so final, such a vast commitment until she learned of the letters from Krage to the Sovran. She had known for some time Krage lived in Argoya, of course, and had tried hard to find him. Once the announcement had been made, he would show himself, she reasoned. Despite a voice that nagged at her she had used Lorgallehna to pursue her own ends, she had agreed to the wedding, certain Krage would make some attempt to kill her before she could marry the Sovsdot. If he did so, she would be justified when she killed him. Instead, Ricrid had killed him in her stead, and while it irritated her she had not struck the fatal blow, Ricrid had, no doubt, thrown him into the sea, never to be seen again. It would serve as justice for all he had wrought, and she had promised herself not to dwell on the things that had stirred her rage and disgust at herself any longer.

Two days until the wedding, and she hid herself away in her rooms. The Seat had become so full of family and other important well-wishers, she had found it impossible to avoid them unless she stayed out of sight in her parlour throughout the day. She had seen next to nothing of Lorgallehna for days as the Sovsdot worked to finalise the details of the wedding. A knock at the door of her rooms surprised her, and she begged her servitor to answer it and say she had gone out. She hid in the bedroom with the door cracked open so she could listen.

Lorgallehna. Thank the fates. She ran to her lover's arms. "I have missed you so much." She nuzzled into the Sovsdot's neck.

"I have missed you also, but I have been busy with preparations. Even now, I am here on wedding duties, although it does my heart good to see you. I love you."

"Wedding duties? Can we not run away together and live in a small house somewhere where nobody knows us? All this fuss..." Corelle longed for a simpler life, and wondered whether she could cope with life as a member of the Sovran's family.

"That sounds wonderful, but no. I am sorry, but I am the Sovsdot, and the people expect a grand occasion if I am to marry my heart's desire."

With a sigh, Corelle stood up straight. "What must I do?"

"Rehearse. Tomorrow we must rehearse."

Corelle frowned. "Rehearse? What does this involve?"

Lorgallehna smiled, her eyes bright with happiness. "We must learn all we need to do on the day, and the best way to do that is to practice."

"Training?"

With a laugh, Lorgallehna aimed a swipe at Corelle's arm. "You could call it that. Rehearse. Tomorrow in my father's rooms one hour after the sunrise. Be there. Do not be late."

"I will not be late." Corelle had said the same to Lorgallehna once before, inebriated at their first lunch together. She had felt so terrible the following morning, she had almost been late, in truth.

The rehearsal involved a great deal of not much, in Corelle's opinion. She stood around and watched as Lorgallehna and her father practiced their entrance, then the Sovran said a great many words, and Corelle and Lorgallehna mumbled some more. They had each scribed vows to one another, but Lorgallehna said it would be bad luck to reveal anything of them at the rehearsal.

To her horror, Corelle had to learn how to wave. It would be necessary to wave to the crowds gathered to watch, it seemed, and it would not do to wave a casual hand, then rush inside in search of some wine to get her through the day.

As the hours ticked by, Corelle's entrance had to be rehearsed. It had been agreed Jaddemal would escort her onto the platform on which the ceremony would take place. Lorgallehna would then make her entrance, but Jaddemal arrived late. Corelle's rehearsal had been delayed until he came, but at long last he appeared, and the rehearsal could end.

Corelle returned to her rooms. She had been less than truthful when she had said her vows had been scribed. Although she had begun them many times, she could find no words, unused to such formalities. Her vow seemed simple enough at its heart; she would love Lorgallehna and take care of her. She would slit the throat of any who tried to harm the red-headed woman, although she doubted she could include that vow. The vows must be completed tonight before she could go to bed.

Her dress had been made for her by the finest garment maker in Argoya, it turned. It had involved many days of measurement, discussion and disagreement, until she tired of it and insisted on a white taffeta gown with a short train, fitted at the waist and with a low-cut neckline. Against her own judgement, she agreed to have some gems sewn onto the dress to accentuate it. She would carry a small bouquet of Feshtersov flowers she must, it seemed, throw to the crowd afterward. According to tradition, whoever caught it would be the next person to be married. The unnecessary pompousness of the entire day had wearied her long before the rehearsal, and she sat at a desk with some parch and tried to create something that would suit as her vows tomorrow.

She went to bed late, exhausted, but with her vows scribed. When her servitor came to wake her, she had endured a fitful sleep, but she hoped her nerves would carry her through the day. Her hands shook as she ate some breakfast, and her stomach suggested the food had been wasted, since she felt sure she would fetch up. The night of the banquet or Lorgallehna's birthing day were nothing compared to how anxious she felt today. By tonight, she would be married, and a part of the Sovran's family. Corelle, humble daughter of a garment maker from Ryl, clandestine killer, mariner, woman who had brought about the deaths of so many and had escaped her own death by the slightest margin countless times, married into the most powerful family in Feshtersov. How had it turned? Who knew?

The time had come to put the dress on and submit to the powders. With the aid of a second woman, her servitor helped her into the dress, arranged all the bits and pieces that hung from it, all quite unnecessary in Corelle's opinion, and they gazed at her in admiration. "You look beautiful, Eminence."

They sat her on a stool and primped and fussed at her hair, still barely to her shoulders. The servitor wanted to know what had turned to give her a small patch of skull where no hair grew, and Corelle told her a mast had fallen on her. "I see." The woman's face suggested she did not see at all. Few had, in truth.

They produced powders they applied in such vast amounts, Corelle all but lost sight of them in the cloud that rose from her face. She coughed in pretend affliction, and they waved their hands in her face with such vigour, she could not control her laughter, and they told her off and pretended to be hurt by her jest. After an age, they seemed satisfied, and they walked her to a reflecting glass.

Corelle had no idea who the woman in the sketch before her could be. Arrayed in a dress that had cost more than a ship, powdered, her brown hair piled in a cute bun atop her head, she saw a Corelle she had never seen before. She looked at her hands, and they were still the hands that had claimed so many lives, but they had been attached to a doll. "How long will the ceremony last?"

"An hour, more or less." Thank goodness. She could bear an hour in this outrageous costume, then she could cast it from her and lay in bed with Lorgallehna. "Then there is the reception tonight. That will last all night, I am certain. Such a wonderful day."

Reception? Must she wear this ridiculous gown all day? It would be unbearable. Lorgallehna had deceived her. No mention had been made of a reception, whatever that might be. Knuckles on the door disturbed her misery, and the servitor ran to answer it.

The hour had come. Corelle walked along the corridor beside Jaddemal, who wore a green tunic and cream trousers with a green stripe down the outside of each leg. At his hip he carried a sword in a scabbard. Corelle's arm looped through his, her hand laid palm downward on his forearm, which he held outstretched at his side.

He whispered to her as they approached the outer door. "Nervous?"

The noise outside deafened her, and they had not yet opened the door. The crowd must be immense. "I think I may fetch up."

He laughed. "You will be fine. You are about to become an Orkbarat. Our family motto is, 'We keep our breakfast to ourselves.'"

She looked at him, aghast, then saw the twitch at the corner of his mouth and grinned. "I hate you."

The door opened, and they walked out onto the platform. The crowd yelled and screamed. Corelle had never seen so many people in one place, and her legs became weak. She felt Jaddemal's arm lock to support her, and she flashed him a grateful look. They took their position, and Corelle scanned the crowd. Guards stood every-where, and a line had been created before the Seat with a long, ornate red rope. The gates to the street stood open, and the crowd extended beyond the fence into the street. Near the rope, as she flicked her eyes across the faces, something caught her attention, and when she looked again, Ricrid stood there, dressed in a good quality tunic and with a short, pretty woman at his side, her face rapt with joy as she watched the ceremony.

As an enormous roar rose from the crowd, Corelle knew

Lorgallehna had appeared. The people did love her, but so did Corelle, and she would be hers forever. It seemed like a dream.

Corelle could not resist a glance at Lorgallehna as she and her father took their positions. Her dress of brilliant white so resembled Corelle's own, it seemed some making subterfuge might have taken place. Lorgallehna gave her a quick smile, then her father stepped forward, and her brother stepped up to take his father's place at his sister's side.

To either side of the wedding party, rows of chairs housed the family, Lorgallehna's mother at the front along with her brother's wife and young child and other prominent members of the family. Those seated four rows back might have little value to the family, but they had seats on the platform, after all else.

The Sovran waited for the crowd to quiet. He showed no impatience at the time it took, although Corelle felt sure she would faint long before the cries and cheers died away. At last, he spoke. "I, Sovran Antones Orkbarat, welcome you all to the Seat." The crowd cheered. How easy it seemed to please them. "We welcome you today for the wedding of my daughter, Sovsdot Lorgallehna Orkbarat"—he paused as the cheers and screams broke out again—"to her Consort, Corelle of Dur." The applause and cheers might have been less rapturous than those for Lorgallehna, but they came, and Corelle glanced toward Ricrid, who cheered and clapped the loudest of them all, she thought. Their eyes met, and she smiled.

"The Sovsdot and her Consort stand here before you today ready to declare themselves bound for life. If there is any here present who claims they are unfit to exchange these vows, then speak now." A deathly hush fell on the crowd, and Corelle's heart pounded. What if Ricrid yelled out that she had killed countless men, slit their throats and left them in a pool of their own blood? She glanced at him again, and he raised a finger to his lips in a gesture of silence.

Corelle thought the Sovran let the silence go on longer than necessary, but at last he turned toward the women. At that, Jaddemal pulled his arm free of her hand and drew his sword. Lorgallehna's brother did the same, and in unison they shouted, "I wish to take her from you. Will you yield?" as they held their swords in battle readiness. After a pause, they both cried aloud, "I will yield," and sheathed their swords.

Jaddemal held out his arm again, and Corelle laid her hand on it. With a mischievous grin, he whispered, "We had to adapt that part somewhat."

The Sovran turned to the crowd once more. "Corelle of Ryl will now speak her vow."

Jaddemal whispered again. "Speak loud."

"I am Corelle of Ryl." Her voice sounded pitiful, and somebody in the crowd shouted, "Speak up." She cleared her throat and began again. "I am Corelle of Ryl." This time she shouted, and no more interruptions came. "I vow to love and care for this woman for as long as I live. If harm must befall us, I vow it will be mine to bear. She is mine, and I am hers, until I go wherever I travel to afterward." The crowd's ecstatic roars almost deafened Corelle. She had guessed a short vow would be to their preference, and it seemed she had not rolled ones.

As the cheers subsided, the Sovran addressed the crowd yet again. "Sovsdot Lorgallehna Orkbarat will now speak her vow."

Lorgallehna's voice rang out across the crowd, who fell silent and hung on every word. "I am Sovsdot Lorgallehna Orkbarat. This woman is one of you, a woman of the people. She is not of high breeding, but her heart is above mine, and above those of my family. It is pure, and her love is all I desire. She is like you. She is you. I love you, and I love our nation, but I love her more. I wish to take her from you. Will you yield?"

The stunned silence that fell on the crowd lasted a heartbeat, then as one they all screamed, "I will yield." Tears dripped from Corelle's eyes. Lorgallehna had played the highest hand Corelle had ever seen played. The crowd loved the Sovsdot, and now she had made them love Corelle also. She had made her one of their own, married into the most powerful line in the land, but one of their own, nonetheless. The crowd roared and stamped their feet, and the noise would not die down for so long, Corelle wondered if the reception might need to be cancelled.

Beside her, Jaddemal coughed and wiped at his eyes. Lorgallehna's mother cried without shame, and her father stared at the crowd and did not turn to face his daughter. Corelle guessed he feared he might cry also if he did so. After many moments, the noise subsided, and the Sovran spoke again. "I am Sovran Antones Orkbarat. Before you stand Sovsdot Lorgallehna Orkbarat and Consort Corelle Orkbarat." Corelle had not realised she would be given an extra name. She had used so many through her life, what difference could one more make?

The crowd again burst into ecstatic cheers and yells, and Lorgallehna turned to Corelle and kissed her, which provoked even more raucous celebration from the crowd. Arm in arm, they stepped forward off the platform and waved at the crowd until Corelle felt her arm would fall off. Lorgallehna went to one side of the crowd, turned her back, and threw her bouquet of flowers back over her head. A scream went up as somebody deep in the crowd caught it and held it aloft.

Corelle studied the woman next to Ricrid, then turned her back and threw her bouquet. She could only do her best, but when she turned again, it had been enough. The woman had caught the flowers and had wrapped her arms around Ricrid's neck as she jumped up and down with excitement. Corelle smiled at Ricrid, and she thought he mouthed, "I hate you." His smile said something different.

The reception wore on, too much rich food, vast quantities of wine, and so many people who came to congratulate the couple, Corelle felt as though her arm had been torn from her shoulder and her cheek worn through to her teeth by kisses. The Sovran danced with his daughter, then Corelle made his daughter endure a clumsy dance with her, and deep into the night, it had all ended, and their servitors helped them out of the dresses in Lorgallehna's apartments.

Alone, they stood face to face, naked, exhausted, and married, against all odds. It seemed like a dream. How could two women marry at all? Much less, how could Corelle of Ryl now be married to this beautiful woman, third most powerful in the land, or nation, as she must now learn to call it? It could not be. She would wake up soon in a small, smelly cabin aboard a ship somewhere in the middle of the seas. She stared into Lorgallehna's eyes. "I love you."

Lorgallehna smiled. "Then take me to our bed, wife."

THE END

ACKNOWLEDGMENTS

"Speak My Name"
  Performed by Adventures With Alice
  Written by Debbie Rollason
  © Hand Elephant Records 2009
  Lyrics reprinted by permission

Cover by Adrian DSGNS

Torr Sea map by Lara Mitchell

Dur map by André Barbeto

SPECIAL THANKS

Ailsa. The love of my life. Without you, none of this could have happened.

Jo & Rob, Wendy & Danny, Joseph. Thank you for your unfailing support.

Christopher Cross. Your music carried me through all the tedious edits. I never got permission to use Sailing. Song rights are a minefield of red tape involving multiple countries.

Rosie. Our beautiful little cat. I love you.

Everybody who reads my books. To come to the end of Corelle's tale seems unreal. I would have abandoned the project long ago but for you. Thank you, from the bottom of my heart.

ABOUT THE AUTHOR

HAYLEY PRICE has always been a storyteller. Throughout her life, she has told her story through songs as the principal songwriter in several bands, most recently Adventures With Alice, whose songs feature in many of her books.

A New Zealander, Hayley currently lives in Canberra, Australia, with her long-time partner and a grumpy, bossy cat called Rosie. She loves baseball and suffers eternal torture as a fan of the San Francisco Giants. Music has been a major part of her life, and outside of her own compositions, she is an enormous fan of Christopher Cross as well as Daryl Hall & John Oates and under-rated 80s UK prog-rock band Voyager, who once named her their #1 fan.

Hayley's first book, The Vermilion Ribbon, received an Honorary Mention in the 2024 The BookFest Award for LGBTQ Fantasy, a 2024 Indie BRAG Medallion, and was a finalist in the ABLE Golden Book Awards 2024. Her second book, The Vermilion Cross, won third place in the BookFest Awards for LGBTQ Fantasy.

LINKS

Here are some links I hope you will find useful.

My website: https://hayleyprice.net

Please leave a review for this book. Find a link at bio.site/ hayleyprice